M000189376

THE LUCKY TWO
By
Yvette Doolittle Herr

To Patty,
May God bless you with
rainbows and smiles.
Yvette D Herr

Copyright @ 2017 Yvette Doolittle Herr
TXu 2-055-059

All rights reserved. No part of this book may be reproduced, stored or transmitted by any means-whether auditory, graphic, mechanical, or electronic – without the written permission of the both the publisher and author, except in the case of brief excerpts used in critical articles and reviews. Unauthorized reproduction of any part of this work is illegal and punishable by law

Cover Design
By
Linda Nichols

ISBN -13: 978-0692908310
ISBN-10: 0692908315
All characters are entirely fictitious and based on the imagination of the author. Any resemblances to persons living, or dead, are purely coincidental and unintended.

Createspace Publishing 2017

Dedication:

To my husband and friend, Travis, who has given me love and a life filled with experiences I would never have dreamed could happen. To my sons Bryan and John, who have brought me great happiness. Without all of them this story would not be written.

Acknowledgements:

Forgiveness from the experts who work in the professional communities of commercial fishing, law enforcement, media services, and scientific weather forecasting is humbly requested for any, and all, inaccuracies. The descriptive narrative establishes action and scene, and is not intended to misrepresent the superb work, and public service, provided by the people who work in these professions.

Thank you to Travis' sister, Linda Nichols, for the cover artwork. With only a brief description she captured the big picture.

Thank you to my friends Linda Caron and Martha Spiva who read the very,very long first draft. Their excitement about the story encouraged me to finish the project.

Grateful appreciation is given to the Anderson family, and descendants, for their positive contributions to the heritage of the fishing industry, the inspiration for the story.

Holy Bible scriptures are taken from the New International Version, copyright 1984.

Prologue:

As all eyes opened to the light on the dawn of a new day, no one knew it would be a day very different for the humans and the cats who called the marina on Panama City Beach, Florida, their home.

The differences between one day and the next day are defined by the predictable and the unpredictable. Events are often unforeseen. Sometimes things happen so fast there's no time to think. Sometimes things happen so slowly that you don't know how to stop thinking.

Each day in the life of every human and animal is a series of events, or repetitions, with all days beginning like all others. Each day begins with a rising sun that spreads a soft, opaque, grey light that fades the faraway stars. The light of the sun brightens the day with each passing minute until the darkness is completely erased. Darkness, again, always follows the light. Without fail, the repetitions of the sun occur. There may be many choices, or few choices, on any given day. The actions taken to fill the space of a day make the events of each day a part of life's history. There are days that give reasons for happiness and hope. There are days that give reasons for sadness and despair. Decisions must be made, and owned, for each and every day. If living in fear of darkness, the light of a new day becomes a dream come true.

A loving heart survives anything and resists an invasion of darkness. It is all that is required to make home a happy place. Animals and humans, both, have a need for love and a happy home. It is not necessary to travel far to find perfect love or home. Love begins in the holder of the heart and, when shared, the light of the world only gets brighter with each new day.

You see. You hear. You touch. You smell. Love is the guide to happiness as we experience all of these senses

Giving and sharing these senses, two loving hearts will become a lucky two.

CHAPTER 1: KING'S CASTLE

Each day the Captain Anderson boat marina made the perfect, ideal home for King, one of many cats who lived there as permanent residents. King had lived there a long time, especially if looked at it in cat years. His home was a small eight by eight foot wooden storage shed, rarely unlocked and opened, filled with frayed boat ropes, empty gas cans, small cardboard boxes of miscellaneous boat supplies and very, very used discarded pieces of fishing lures, lines and tackle. The smell inside was a mixture of salty air, dead fish, gasoline and oil. It was an odor that would shrivel the nose hairs of any human if the door was opened on a hot, humid summer day.

"Haha!" he said happily on the day he discovered the small, ragged, rotted opening in the wooden wall of the shed. The hole was just wide enough for him to squeeze through. First his whiskers, then head, and then his entire body squeezed through the hole and on to the inside.

"This is just a purr..fect place for a cat like me!" He reacted to the pleasant thought and his round eyes closed into slits of contentment. His vocal cords vibrated as he calmly purred and sat on the rough concrete floor to enjoy his good luck. "I can curl up and sleep under a roof. Every morning I will start my day looking out of this hole and watch the beautiful boats leave to go out on their fishing trips. I won't even need an alarm clock to start my day."

King knew what an alarm clock was. His former owner, who had dropped him off at the marina when he was a teenage cat, had an alarm clock that made an annoying noise at the crack of dawn. The owner would use his foot to kick King off of the bed, grumble his way around the house, and then be off to work for the remainder of the day leaving King alone in the house. His owner usually returned from work in a very bad mood, worse than in the morning, and provided King with only dry food. This was if he remembered to put any food in the empty bowl at all.

Since the day he was dropped off at the marina, King discovered waking up in the morning could actually be a pleasurable experience. The early morning sound of boat engines rumbling under the surface of the water was a good sound. He associated the sound with the return of boats that would bring fish back to the docks later in the day. There was always an excellent chance he would eat well on any given day.

He learned to be very careful around people from his former owner, whom he did not miss. He was always grateful when a boat captain threw a fish in his direction. Finding food was never a problem at the marina, like it had been before he arrived there. Soon

1

he grew to be a large, stocky, muscular male cat, wise and happy. His short fur was glossy black and his eyes were a blue green aqua color, like the Gulf of Mexico.

In time King also learned the names and habits of the other cats who called the marina their home. People call it animal instinct, but King only thought of it as paying attention to the behavior of his own species. He came to know who was a lazy cat, scaredy-cat, fat cat, mean cat, kind cat, smarty cat, bossy cat, fussy cat, prissy cat, sassy cat, or just plain pussy cat. He quickly learned who would be his favorite pals to hang around with for fun. And the marina was a really fun, fun, fun place for cats to live.

"The sun is already beginning to drop below the top of the wooden fence!" King's firm furry chin was perched on his stretched out front paws. He had just opened his eyes from an afternoon nap. He peered through a small crack in the wall of the shed. "This is the purr..fect time to get up and get ready for the boats to arrive!"

His body shivered after he rose up, stood on all four paws and stretched his stiff leg muscles. He felt sluggish after the nap inside the warm shed he thought was as good as living in a castle.

It is difficult for animals to stay cool in the summer months in Florida. The animals who lived in air conditioning were the lucky ones. A nap during the day, out of the direct sunlight, was the only option for getting out of the heat. The concrete floor was a little cooler than on sand underneath some bushes. His fur didn't get as dirty, either.

"A good fish dinner is on my menu tonight!" he said confidently and squeezed his body out of the shed. "But, before I present myself in public I better clean myself up a little."

The dank, dark, smelly shed caused his body fur to stink. He sat on the sidewalk and groomed himself. "A cat has to spend a lot of time licking to clean his fur," King thought! He licked both forepaws vigorously extending his claws to get between each white translucent nail. Then he licked his right forepaw and rubbed it around the back of his ears, over his face and across his long black whiskers in the motion of a figure eight.

He was far more interested in the sounds and activities outside around him. There were familiar sounds of the automobile traffic from the nearby bridge and road, sailboat lines gently clanging on a boat mast, and the voices and conversations of workers and tourists nearby in the parking lot and along the sidewalks. He trained himself to be on guard for unfamiliar noises.

The marina covered a large area of property. Along with more than 50 deep-sea fishing boats, there were numerous sailboats, sightseeing boats, and a dinner cruise boat that carried 350 passengers. Built around the marina was an array of businesses, including a processing area for fish caught daily, two seafood markets, a souvenir shop, a small tackle shop, and three large restaurants, one which had over six hundred seats for customers.

There was plenty of activity around the marina for the cats to live large and go about their lives with no interference except from a few other pesky seagulls and pelicans who also liked to eat fish.

"Sniff, Sniff, oooooh!" The smells created by the restaurant kitchens and remains of food tossed in large dumpsters lingered in the air and traveled the summer winds into the two little dots of his flat fuzzy nose. "That's the smell of empty shrimp boxes, I just know it!" he purred excitedly at the thought. "Smith's dumpster is the place to be!"

Once more he stretched his two front paws out as far as possible in front of him, placed his long black skinny tail straight up high, and arched his back like the first drop of a roller coaster ride. Proudly he thought, "I think I look presentable enough to impress any other cat on the block!"

He turned his head side to side, looking and listening for any reason to not make a run for the restaurant. "No obstacles," he thought and began a rhythmic trot on his soft black paw pads down the sidewalk toward the dockside area of Smith's Restaurant. The hot humid air in the late afternoon sun slowed down his pace but fortunately the shed, King's castle, was not too far from his chosen destination.

He headed to his usual spot, a hedge of bushes planted close to the wall of the restaurant. Three other cats were already there, sitting in a soft dirt spot. They all casually turned their heads to look at King when he arrived. Then all eight eyes focused back to the boat that had just arrived at the dock. The boat captain was preparing to unload the catch of the day.

Twelve hours earlier, before the sun popped up in the sky, the boat had left the dock with a load of bait and a lonely boat captain eager, and ready, to experience the thrill of catching a lot of big fish. He spent the day fishing at a location in the Gulf of Mexico where he was often successful when he had chartered customers, but today, like many other days before, he was alone. He desperately needed money from the fish he sold to keep his business afloat. Now the tired boat captain was back at the marina to unload the fish the fish he caught.

"I'll give you a dollar fifty a pound for the beeliners," yelled a tall, barrel chested, large man in a white apron frock standing nearby. Big Joe, as he was known around the docks by everyone, was speaking to the captain of the boat with the name 'Lucky Two' painted on the stern.

The young, but weary looking, boat captain stood bent over the boat's storage cooler and continued to throw out the fish. He did not look up or act like he had heard the other man.

"No more, no less!" the large man said more loudly, making sure that he was heard above any other noise. He was the head chef in the kitchen at Smith's and knew, from experience, that he would get his best deal from the young boat captain.

3

"We-l-l-l" the young boat captain said slowly, thinking very carefully about what he wanted to really say. He brought his head up to face the large man. "I think one dollar and fifty cents a pound for the beeliner is not enough, but I'll take it if you also buy the grouper for four fifty a pound and the snapper for five dollars a pound."

Big Joe cupped his chin into the palm of his right hand and rubbed his beard stubble for a couple of seconds. He was clearly annoyed with the take all fish proposition. In a matter of minutes he said, "OK, but it better be all large snapper and grouper. I can't cut a good piece of filet off any fish less than four pounds. My customers won't like that!"

Clearly angered by Big Joe's comment the boat captain responded, "I understand what you want for your customers. Don't forget I have bills to pay for bait, gas, fees, maintenance, and insurance for MY customers. I don't try to cheat my customer so don't you think that I'm trying to cheat you or your customers!" He was younger, but didn't mind saying what he felt. "My fish are always the best. Isn't that what you tell me?"

Big Joe softened his tone. "No, no, I understand," he said trying to be friendly after agreeing to the deal. He waved his arm motioning another man, standing by the back door of Smith's, to come over. "You got your job and I got mine. We've all got to make a living and eat," the large man continued to talk as he waited for the employee to arrive. "I appreciate what you do," he said trying to express gratitude to the young captain.

The other Smith's employee, wearing a white T-shirt with the red and blue ink logo of Smith's Restaurant visible behind the front panel of the apron, jumped out of the doorway. He grabbed the handles of a yellow plastic wheelbarrow near the back door. When he reached the boat, he removed a square metal scale from the wheelbarrow. The scale would be used to weigh the fish.

The young boat captain continued to toss the fish onto the concrete while Big Joe assumed the job of placing them on the scale. The young boat captain kept a close watch and mentally tallied the measured weights while the chef's helper tossed the prime fish into the wheelbarrow.

After the fish had been weighed in each category the Smith's employee turned the wheelbarrow, full of fish, around and rolled it back to the kitchen where the fish would be filleted and cooked that evening for the customers soon to arrive.

"No fresher than this," Big Joe laughed and handed the young boat captain the slip of paper showing how many pounds of fish had been weighed. "Wait here and I'll get the money out to you."

"You're right on that!" the young boat captain replied speaking of the fish and the money. "I'll be waiting right here. Don't be long, either! I'm ready to call it a day."

"Aren't we all!" the chef snapped.

4

CHAPTER 2: LEAPING LIZZARDS AND SNAGGLE TOOTH

King flattened his ears and crouched in the bushes so he wouldn't be seen by the Smith's employee pushing the wheelbarrow. The men who worked in the kitchen were not at all friendly to any cats. They'd often cuss and yell scat at the cats louder than a cat could growl or hiss.

The kitchen workers were always chasing cats away from the back door and out of the garbage cans. They knew that it was cats who made a mess leaving fish bones and other scraps lying around the parking lot and sidewalks. Then the mess would have to be cleaned up by the employees who already had enough cleaning up to do in the kitchen. King knew this was true, but the cats shared guilt with others. The opossums and rats also visited the garbage cans.

One time a very bold cat named Snaggle Tooth jumped directly into the fish wheelbarrow as it was being pushed back to Smith's. He snatched a small Spanish mackerel and flew back out, escaping with the fish hanging out of his mouth. Snaggle Tooth ran first into the cover of bushes, then continued running along the side of the building, back paws scratching up dust in sandy spots, and finally dragged the fish under a fence to a safe area to eat it.

"Hey you, Snaggle Tooth Cat!" the worker screamed trying to stop him, but screaming wouldn't stop the cat. The nice fish was lost. Other people standing near the scene could only stop and laugh at the sight of a cat flying out of the wheelbarrow with the huge fish's head, one eye staring out of Snaggle Tooth's mouth, and the fish tail dragging on the ground as the cat raced away.

It was quite a feat for Snaggle Tooth. He was cheered on and treated like a celebrity by the other cats. Although he earned the reputation of a fish thief he was respected by many of the employees after that day.

That had not been the case before that day. Snaggle Tooth was ashamed of his name but learned to live with the nickname used by his feline friends and the people around the marina. Fishermen, restaurant employees, the fish cleaners and even the tourists who strolled around the sidewalks window shopping and looking at the day's catch would see him with his scarred face and exclaim, "Oh, my, that poor cat looks like a Snaggle Tooth!"

"ST, for short," King and all the other cats called him. The catchy sound of the nickname made ST feel good.

King remembered the day of the accident well. ST was only twelve weeks old on the day of the accident that scarred him for life and left him no other choice but to live with the name Snaggle Tooth. It was one of the hottest days in June, or maybe it was July. The setting sun glowed a fiery red above the horizon, casting a shadow from the tall masts of large boats. All of the cats felt lazy and bored while waiting for the darkness of evening to descend.

Snaggle Tooth was born with boldness in his blood. He was the feistiest kitten in the litter and had an enormous amount of energy. When he saw an opportunity for a bite to eat he wasn't going to miss out on it.

While his tiny body lay sprawled out panting on the soft sand in the scant shade under the bushes ST heard a noise, a faint rustle that only the perky ears of a cat could hear. He squinted to see better through the blinding rays of sunlight passing through a humid haze of thick air. He was not at all sure of what he heard, but knew it was small living creature. Bored and ready to do something, as most all curious fidgety kittens are, he ran in the direction of the noise without giving a second thought about it. King and the other cats stayed put and watched ST in lazy amusement.

ST's eyes picked up a small moving object and scooted at a fast pace behind it, though the weeds, litter and dust, under the bushes and out into the open parking lot next to Smith's. He soon discovered the black paved parking lot scorched his pink padded paws so he bounced and leapt, continuing to chase the moving object across another sidewalk and on through a narrow opening of a boarded gate that was part of a fence hiding a large metal trash dumpster for Smith's.

ST stopped at the opening on the side of the large metal container. His ears perked up to carefully listen for sounds. His tail switched quickly from side to side as he sat on the ground, watching and listening. He could hear scratching sounds as the small animal traveled into the depths of the garbage dumpster. He suddenly stood up on all four paws, wiggled the back end of his body and took a flying leap into the side opening of the garbage dumpster. It was nearly three feet from the ground but he had no difficulty jumping that high. He landed on a small, three-inch ledge, large enough for his four small paws which he kept neatly tucked in close to his body so they would fit.

He relied on his senses of sight and sound to seek the location of the small moving creature. The smells coming from the garbage can were confusing him and of no use on this hunt. "Was it a mouse?" he thought hopefully. "That would be so much better than a lizard or frog, but a lizard will do." His tiny tail switched again with excitement.

"Oh, I do hope, really, really do hope that it is not one of those pesky, nasty water bugs! This is not a place for a chase to find a water bug, which is not much good. No more good than a toy. I am not in the mood for playing with a toy in a garbage can!"

All these thoughts raced through ST's brain. Then without further thought he leapt on top of a stuffed black plastic garbage bag.

As soon as he landed ST lost his footing. The soft toenails on his paws were not strong enough to keep him from sliding down the bag, which was covered with something slimy like cooking oil. His body twisted and flipped as he slipped down the side of the bag which also contained broken bottles. His body finally landed at the bottom of the garbage bag and his head bounced off a broken wine bottle. The jagged edge sliced off a very large chunk of the soft skin covering the top of his mouth right beneath his soft, pink nose.

ST let out a screech, alarming all of the other cats, who had lost sight of ST after he jumped into the garbage dumpster. They had been patiently waiting in the cool of the bushes for ST to return with a prize.

They watched as he leapt out of the garbage dumpster like a flash of red lightening and race across hot black parking lot, across the road, and into the nearby woods. He never looked back.

Humans, tourists and employees, never noticed the poor kitten.

"It is so hard to be careful when we are young and curious," King thought to himself. He mournfully meowed several times to the other kittens and cats, urging them to gather around him for a conference.

"Should we follow after him?" King asked the other cats listening.

Not even one of the other cats showed an interest in doing anything like that. It was still too hot. Those who had been watching the event walked back to their spot in the bushes to lay out for a little nap until the sun finished setting in the sky. Avoiding the heat of the afternoon sun was much more important to them. Later in the evening, before dark, they would have more energy to search for ST.

When the older cats began the search they, without any kittens, scattered around the marina parking lot. The search was short. And, no one wanted to cross over the highway into the woods.

The wounded kitten had acted foolishly but would heal fast. He became a stronger, smarter cat when he got older.

The cats returned to prowl around the fishing boats after the last tourists had left. Most of the captains left after they finished cleaning the boats and their catch of fish. It was usually guaranteed that something would be lying around to eat, either from the boats or the restaurants.

And so it had been more than just another long, lazy, summer day at the docks. It had been more memorable than most.

It was two days before ST reappeared from the woods where he struggled to avoid snakes, raccoons, scorpions, wolves and other scary animals. How ST survived those two nights alone in the woods, no one ever knew. No one asked. ST never talked about it and he never asked why no one came to help him. There were many opinions and guesses about what happened. The most popular theory was ST had climbed a tall tree and spent the night in a squirrel's nest with other squirrels. Baby squirrels are also called kittens, after all.

The day ST emerged from the woods it was late afternoon. The kittens quickly got out the news when they saw him making his way across the sizzling hot parking lot. The pink pads on his paws burned and the pain was almost as bad as the wound on his mouth, but the embarrassment felt worse.

Everyone could see his injury as he got closer. Most of the blood was cleaned away from his mouth. A large piece of his fur was missing right below his whiskers on the right side of his mouth. His long front tooth hung from his jaw like a sword.

"Hey, buddy!!" one of the kittens shouted with glee and joy to see her friend return. "You look like just a really, real tough guy! That Snaggle Tooth looks tough!"

ST sprang past the group, ignoring the comment. His eyes shone with pride and happiness. He was so relieved to be back with his friends.

"You were amazing flying out of that dumpster!" said another cat.

"I am sooooo glad to see you!" mewed an adult cat named Oscar.

All the cats saw that he was weak, and his fur was a mess, but they were eager to make him feel better about his appearance. And on, and on, it went until finally ST stopped, sat on his haunches, and started to purr!

King was amazed at ST's composure. "Unbelievable," he thought. "This kitten is gonna be OK. He'll be a loyal cat in the gang of cats. He's already learned from experience that it is better to be happy than sad!"

"Hey, you. ST. Can we call you ST for short? How about something to eat?" called out a long-haired furry white feline. She was a fairly recently new adult cat to the docks and had been nicknamed Fluff by the adult cats when she appeared one day out of nowhere. Everyone assumed she was dropped off, like many others, by an owner. Even though she didn't like the name, she was glad to be accepted into the group. She was happy to get food and protection from the other cats and would rather not squabble about a name she did not like.

He struggled to answer from his injured mouth. "I don't have a problem with ST. I am pretty darn hungry." He was eager to put something in his stomach even though he knew it would be a challenge to chew."

Fluff and another adult cat named Fat Cat left to hunt for scraps and fish. All cats were relieved that ST had returned and was acting nearly normal. Everyone believed that he would be just fine.

ST learned to accept his disfigurement. He didn't like it and wasn't proud of it, but had no other choice. He was happy to have many friends who wanted to help him and always accept him even if the scar made him appear slightly ugly.

And no one asked any questions about the days he spent alone in the woods. He was glad about THAT!

CHAPTER 3: LEGAL, ILLEGAL, OR JUST FUN?

Besides the restaurant workers, tourists, and fishermen there was always another familiar face seen nearly daily at the docks. That was the face of the Florida Marine Patrol officer. None of the cats ever worried about him because this man paid no attention to them.

He was a few inches over six feet tall with legs that allowed him to walk in long, fast strides. When one of the deep sea fishing boats arrived at the dock ready to unload, he was there in minutes. Every fish dug out of the boat's deep hull ice cooler and thrown onto the dock was observed by the watchful eyes, hidden behind sunglasses, of the Florida Marine Patrol officer.

"He never talks, smiles, or turns his head to anyone or anything but the fish," King thought while he watched him one day from the bushes. "He stares down at the sidewalk like he is looking at his feet. Then he brings up the wooden clipboard that he is always holding and writes down something. I wonder if he will ever do something with that metal stick and the metal gun attached to his belt? I heard a gun at the docks before. I know that they are loud and scare everyone to scatter. If I ever see him reach for that gun, I can run fast!"

Oftentimes fishermen returned to their boats very late in the evening after refreshing and eating at home. It was easier to sleep on their boats overnight in the summer time in order to be ready for the early morning departure with the tourists who paid to charter the fishing boat captain for a deep sea fishing excursion out in the Gulf of Mexico.

Some fishermen were known to get into arguments late at night. The arguments were over many things, mostly related to work. Some things were not important and some were important. Even though it was supposed to be their time to relax and talk about the day's business, occasionally an argument would grow and grow and the only way to stop the escalation was a gunshot fired into the night sky.

The exploding sound carried in all directions across the water and would make all the cats scamper and scurry across the parking lot as fast and as far as they could possibly run. They were not sure what would happen next. They only knew it was safer to stay clear of the angry, loud voices of the men.

The fishermen and boat captains never seemed to notice the cats hiding in the bushes when the Florida Marine Patrol Officer was standing with his clipboard watching the boats get unloaded.

On this very hot day, ST and Fat Cat also patiently watched

from the bushes as a load of fish was tossed off the boat 'Star Chaser'. The captain of this boat was a thin, short man with a wide brim hat to hide his balding head. He had a big grin as he tossed out each fish to slide close to the feet of the Florida Marine Patrol officer. ST and Fat Cat were hoping that one fish would slide into the bushes.

They were hopeful because the captain of this boat, who liked to sing loud at night when the day's work was over, also happened to be very friendly toward the cats. Often he would toss a few bits of left over shrimp, octopus, or cut-up bait toward the cats as he sang from his boat. He would sing about the moon, the harbor lights, the stars and the sea winds while he watched the cats scramble to get the items he tossed over the side of the boat. The more cats that appeared, the louder he would sing until eventually another boat captain spending the night on his boat would shout out, "Shut up, Darryl! Will ya?!" Often this caused Darryl to sing more, and louder. No one would protest for a short time and then more than one voice would shout out again to him, "STOP! NOW!"

This last complaint was always his cue to bring out his brass tenor saxophone. He played the horn much better than he sang. It was a calm and soothing sound. Long flowing notes seemed to harmonize with the sounds of rippling water from a warm breeze in the late evening of a summer night. No one complained when he played the sax. He was good.

This was the kind of perfect ending to a purr..fect day, but not all days were so nice. Rainy days, or cold days, were an entirely different story. On those kind of days, Darryl Kay, the balding, singing, saxophone playing boat captain would play different tunes and only for a very brief time in the early afternoon. He was not as friendly to the cats, and there were no fish to toss over the side of the boat.

For the most part no one – cats, workers, or tourists – seemed to pay attention to the Florida Marine Patrol Officer as he did his work. He wasn't missed on the rainy days. He was always expected to be there on the sunny days when the fish were thrown out on the dock. Everyone seemed to do the work they needed to do.

BUT, then came the day that ST and Fat Cat thought that they would try to have a little fun trying to get their fish for the day. It needed to be something out of the ordinary. ST never wanted to stop having fun.

After his close experience with death chasing the mystery animal into the trash dumpster, ST never considered anything that included the dumpster. ST didn't like to think about trash dumpsters at all, even if there were a lot of fish remains that could be tossed inside. The trash dumpster didn't bother Fat Cat, but he remembered the day ST went flying back out of the trash dumpster with the blood all over him. He also knew any plan to have fun should not include the trash dumpster.

"Hey, ST?" Fat Cat asked smoothly to see if ST was alert and there was any interest from the cat that had not yet fully grown up and wanted to be forever young. "I know Darryl will be giving us our usual toss of trill off his boat in a few hours, but what about having some fun with that captain of the boat 'Lucky Two'?"

"Why?" ST asked, somewhat curious but cautious. Both instincts were a second nature for him. Was Fat Cat bored, or was he interested in something serious?

"Day after day the captain of 'Lucky Two' is the first one to shout 'SHUT UP' at Darryl when he starts singing."

"True," ST answered, more focused on the fish sliding close to the feet of the man holding the clipboard.

"I think that guy needs a little lesson in humility. He thinks he's the only one working hard to make a living! I heard him fussing at Big Joe about how much it costs to run his boat and the money Big Joe offered for his fish!"

The news surprised ST. The boat captains complained, but never to Big Joe. Fat Cat wasn't a bully, but he didn't like complainers. All of the cats showed some respect for each other for the daily struggles of finding shelter and something to eat before going to sleep for the night.

King was nearby listening to the conversation. He focused on the sky where the sun was once again slipping below the water's edge. The sky resembled a painter's palette, reflecting colors in the clouds that included strokes of smoky grey, wisps of pink and beyond the clouds an endless universe of deep purple, fuscia, baby blue, dark red and orange.

King thought of returning to his shed to cool off on the concrete floor. He could return to the docks later in the evening when the docks would be quiet. Even though the sun had gone down there was still a lot of activity around the marine. People roamed around the parking lots and sidewalk. Cats raced across the parking lot from car to car, hiding underneath them to get away from the people until it was clear again to run to the next car or to the bushes next to Smith's. It was a game.

For now King thought he would rather listen in on the game that Fat Cat was planning. He noticed that other cats, from various locations beneath the bushes, had stopped what they were doing to lick and listen.

ST said in disbelief. "So the captain tells the cook from Smiths how much it costs to run his boat and he would like more money for his fish?"

"If the big shot boat captain puts the cook in a bad mood, he'll tell his employees who already yell at us when they see us!" Fat Cat growled.

ST's ears perked up and he became more interested. "What are you thinking about doing, Fat Cat? I think you're right. It is time to have a little fun and play a little trick on the captain."

"Just wait and see," Fat Cat replied, very sure of himself.

They sat on their haunches near the corner of Smith's restaurant purring and swishing their tails with excitement. Fat Cat was devising a plan, sure to be fun, making the captain of the 'Lucky Two' a little less annoying to the cook at Smith's.

Much later that same evening, unknown to the gang of cats, the Florida Marine Patrol Officer sat alone inside his official green truck. Gold letters, FMPO, were painted on both doors and the rear gate. The truck was parked on the side of the road near the top of the bridge that crosses over the body of water known as the lagoon. From there he had a good view of the boats docked in the marina. He was not looking out the open window as he sat behind the steering wheel. It appeared as if he was asleep, but he was only thinking. He was thinking about how much longer he wanted to wait to see if any suspicious activity happened around the dock.

The Florida Marine Patrol officer's name was Casey Howard. His job was to be sure that all of the boat captains were obeying the rules and laws of the State of Florida. There were many rules on boating and fishing, but Casey's job was primarily to follow the amount, size, weight and species of fish being caught. For a long time Casey had been suspicious of the captain of the boat 'Star Chaser'. Darryl Kay could be breaking the laws of Florida, but Casey had not been able to catch him to prove it. Casey felt a need to prove it!

Casey had been working for the Florida Marine Patrol for eleven years and was getting a little bored with the job of mainly counting fish. He never doubted that it was an important job, but just counting fish being thrown out on the sidewalk was not very glamorous.

He was always at the dock the same time every morning, 5:30 a.m., to check the number of fishermen the captain allowed on the charter boat. Then he would return at 3:00 p.m. to wait for the boats to return. He had his own reserved parking space in the marina parking lot, but he still had to politely push his way through the crowd of tourists who would also be waiting to see the boats come back with the catch of the day.

Usually no one said anything, not even hello, to him. Occasionally a little child would call out, "Look, Mommy! That man has a gun!"

Casey was required to carry a gun for his job. He was trained to use it, but there was no need.

As a young boy he had grown up near Freeport, Florida, and had fished in the bays most of his young life. He loved the water, boats, and fishing. He also had shot guns many times while he was a young boy hunting in the pine forests of north Florida. Hunting and fishing were his first loves in his life.

At first he thought the job would be a dream job, the cat's meow, and one that would make him feel important. It wasn't long before the job he held became tedious and very, very boring.

Casey Howard was eager for a little action. He often found himself thinking about how he needed to find a way to move up into a higher level job. He thought the path to that higher level was through the captain of the 'Star Chaser'. He needed to earn praise and credit for a job well done. In Casey's mind, it didn't matter how he earned the praise. He wondered, as he sat slouched in the front seat of the parked Florida Marine Patrol truck, "When? How? What can I do to catch Darryl in the act of doing something wrong?" He turned his head to look at the fishing vessels gently rocking on the water and angrily thought, "I know he's fishing, trying to make a living like all the rest of them out there. My gut feelings tell me that he's catching more than he's allowed and he's hiding them. That's it!!"

As if he had just found the true answer to his questions of how, when and what, Casey sat perfectly still and began to plot and plan, just like Fat Cat, ST, King and the gang of cats were doing now. Unlike Casey, the cats were enjoying some time together talking about having a little fun.

The sun had disappeared and the color of the early evening sky turned from smoky blue-gray to blue-black. Above the horizon, near the two-lane bridge that crossed over the lagoon, a hazy, frosted line of white light appeared on the skyline marking the end of day and beginning of night. Above the white line a bright twinkling star appeared. It was the brightest light in the sky.

Darryl Kay, the captain of the 'Star Chaser', enjoyed this very moment, too. It was a special time of day for him. He was humming to himself as he sat on the highest deck of his boat and gazed at the night lights and stars.

Darryl wondered about what tomorrow would bring and if it would be a good day of fishing with the four men from Hoover, Alabama, who had chartered his boat for the entire day. Darryl was a cautious man and had heard on the radio that a storm was probably going to enter the Gulf of Mexico in the next day or two, but he didn't want to cancel the trip because the weather system was still far away and hard to predict. The men had been on his boat before. They agreed that they would quit early if the day turned out to be too rough. They would pay him after they finished fishing for half a day or a full day. They were good natured men, good sportsmen, liked to drink beer, and have fun. Darryl was usually amused by most of his customers. Sometimes they didn't know a hook from a sinker. Darryl could talk to anyone and wanted them to have a good time. He didn't mind if they got sick on the rough water or complained if they didn't catch many fish.

Meanwhile, the captain of the 'Lucky Two', Earl Keith, was sitting on a plastic chair on the bow of his boat with his feet propped up on the side. He leaned against the built-in seating and popped the top on an aluminum can of beer. He grudgingly watched the tourists walk into Smith's restaurant and sarcastically grumbled out loud, "Good night to you. Enjoy that fish you're eating!" He hoped someone would hear.

"Oh, I don't know why I stay here. There's got to be a better way to make a living, or a better place to live than on my boat!" Earl took a long pull on the can of beer and swallowed hard.

"Here I am, paying high-priced fees for this boat slip and putting up with those gawking tourists, the singing and squawking horn of that idiot Darryl two boats down, the eagle-eyed Florida Marine Patrol fish counter Clyde, or whatever his name is, and pea-picking sea gulls. For all of this what do I get? A can of beer!!!" He emptied the last of the beer into his mouth and crushed the can in his hand. "If I only had a few bucks I would go into that Smith's and eat the biggest steaks on the menu, drink a few good beers, rent a fancy limousine, ride up to one of those big night clubs, find me some nice looking girl to talk to and dance with her all night long!"

Earl was a dreamer. This dream to make a lot of money as a charter boat captain had evaporated in the heat after two long years. He was sorely disappointed over his life and luck.

He had named his boat the 'Lucky Two' after he arrived alone to start up the business on Panama City Beach without his girlfriend, Eleanore. He remembered the night he announced his plan to move from Pine Mountain, Georgia, to Panama City to become a charter boat captain. They'd been drinking at their favorite bar, Stumpy's Watering Hole.

"What!!?? Are you crazy!" Eleanore had screamed at him. "Is this what you think I wanted to do? Go ahead; move on and away from here."

And that's what Earl did. He wanted to prove her wrong, and always thought she would follow him. Maybe just show up one day.

But, Earl soon found out that working as a charter boat captain took many more skills than the luck he'd had fishing as a boy steering his own small boat on the muddy lakes in Georgia. First of all, steering a bigger boat in the choppy waters of the Gulf of Mexico was a lot different but he passed the tests and earned his captain's license in a few months. He was still ready.

He was not prepared for all the other responsibility. He had to learn how to keep records and learn what fish were legal. He didn't like that only certain fish could be caught during certain months, and they had to be a specific size, and furthermore they had to be a certain weight. The hardest part was always, always, being nice to the customers who were often grouchy and didn't think Earl had the talent to find the best fishing spots.

As Earl sat thinking about another day of fishing and what could he possibly do to increase his chances of finding an easier way of making more money, he saw two cats scamper across the parking lot making their way beneath the parked cars. He lost sight of them when they turned the corner around the back of Smith's.

Seeing the two cats, who happened to be ST and King, made Earl feel worse. He got up from his plastic chair and turned to walk inside the cabin.

"Not only do I have to deal with everything about this boat, but I have to see those crazy cats hanging around here all the time. How annoying they are too!"

The cats always reminded him of Eleanore. She owned a big, white Persian cat named Princess.

"Can't stand cats!" he muttered out loud again hoping that this time the cats would hear him. "Princess," he sneered as he said it. "Frilly name for a furball! Rather have a dog named Bull any day!" And he closed his cabin door to spend the remainder of the night alone, or so he believed.

So that is how the evening began for Casey, Earl, and Darryl. One schemed, one scowled and one sang after the descent of darkness and quiet settled on the boats at the Anderson marina docks. Each saw a different hue of colors in life.

For ST, King, Fat Cat and all the other cats, a night of fun was about to begin.

CHAPTER 4: A MOUSE IN THE KITCHEN

Their paws pattered swiftly, silently across the pavement that had finally cooled only a bit from the heat of the sun. The boats, tied to the docks with long ropes, swayed gently on dark water that sparkled, reflecting lights glowing from the inside of Smith's restaurant and the parking lot lights.

When they reached the bushes by Smith's they heard muffled sounds of human voices. The cats cautiously moved away from the windows and trotted along, close to the wall of the restaurant building toward the back door of the kitchen.

After turning the corner, they found themselves near the back door of Smith's kitchen. They could hear the sounds of workers pulling dirty dishes out of bus pans and loading them into the dishwasher. They would wait patiently, but if nothing turned up near the kitchen they would head over to the storage sheds near the locked-up fish processing rooms conveniently located near the docks.

Inside Smith's restaurant patrons were laughing, eating and relaxing after what was most likely a fun filled day on the beach followed by the spectacular sunset at the marina. The awesome fishing boats bringing in the catch of the day was a big attraction for tourists before going inside Smith's. It was a daydreaming, hypnotic, pleasurable type of atmosphere for everyone. It provided patrons the opportunity to enjoy the moment and forget about jobs, work or responsibilities. Occasionally a tourist would notice a cat, but it was not very often that the cats allowed themselves to be seen by a tourist.

The cats already had their chance to eat from the charter boat captains. They also knew from experience that there was very little hope that anything would come out of the kitchen's back door unless it was tied up inside a black plastic bag and thrown into the big metal trash dumpster. The same dumpster that ST had jumped into and came out with a permanent injury. No cat forgot what happened to ST. They were curious, to be sure, but learned a lesson the first time they saw something like that happen to a friend. No taking a second chance on something that could cause such a serious injury.

King was the first one to notice the Florida Marine Patrol truck parked up near the bridge off the road.

King wondered out loud, "What's he doing around here so late?"

"Maybe he fell asleep on the job!" Fluff offered.

King, Fat Cat, ST and Fluff were staying close together as a group on this night, as they so often did.

"Nah," Fat Cat piped up quickly. "Not possible for that guy. He's like all the other humans. They only like to sleep in a soft bed in a quiet room. Never sleep in a car. He's got to be up to no good sitting in that truck.   There's not too much going on around here. Mostly everyone has left. I can tell you that he is definitely not sleeping!"

"Wait, shush!" King growled low and soft. The other cats quickly stopped their chattering to listen.

The sounds of the evening always changed when the sky got darker.

The last tourists leaving Smith's walked through the parking lot to their cars speaking in quieter voices, tired with full bellies. Some staggered and stumbled in the dark after drinking too much alcohol with their meals. The rattle of car keys was a common noise as they stopped for one last look at the fishing boats lined up along the docks. It was a very different scene from five hours earlier when tourists had been crowded around the boats to see the fish being unloaded shouting out loudly 'look at that one!' among the hundreds of fish that landed with a loud slap on the cement sidewalk.

The restaurant employees, hostesses, waiters, waitresses, busboys, bartenders, kitchen crew, and dishwashers left Smith's in that order. Most walked alone, but some walked in pairs, and then some would gather together on the wooden benches to smoke a cigarette, or have a drink and talk about the evening's work. They were in a bigger hurry than the tourists to get to their air conditioned cars, turn up the radio volumes to a high blast, and leave the work night behind. When they revved up the car engines and turned the corner out of the parking lot, wheels squealed on the hot pavement. They did not notice the Florida Marine Patrol truck still sitting off the road.

All was quiet now. Not a slamming car door, or footsteps of a human, was heard. The four cats concentrated, sitting taut and keeping their ears perched forward.

The other three cats heard a noise too. Was it the same noise King heard? It was the soft shuffling sound of another animal's toenails scratching on the concrete step near the locked back door of the kitchen.   Their eyes locked onto the direction of the sound.

Big cockroach? Mouse? Rat? Lizard? Crab? Bird? Maybe even a small opossum?

Not one cat moved or muttered a sound. The muscles in their rear legs tensed, as they all prepared to pounce. They waited for another sound or a sign of movement. Nothing happened for seconds. The night crickets in the woods across the street were raising the level of the noise they make, a noise the cats were used to hearing all the time.

With very slow, careful, precise steps, one paw at a time, ST inched slowly nearer to the kitchen step. He was crouched so low to the ground, on all four paws, that nothing, not even a flat stick,

18

could fit between his lean furry belly and the concrete. His tail was straight behind his back, lifted off the ground, and his ears lay flat on top of his head. As ST inched slowly and quietly closer to the door step, the other three cats watched, keeping their leg muscles tight and taut to be ready to leap after anything that escaped ST's paws.

Shuffle, shuffle, scratch, shuffle. The sound was very close. ST stopped and tightened every muscle on his body. Even his whiskers were straight and rigid. The cats imagined a small animal.

The sounds continued, soft and gentle. The animal making the noises soon revealed a black nose above the concrete step. A pointy nose, held upward toward the breezes, swayed from side to side. The nose had whiskers like a cat's only shorter, and they twitched as the nose sniffed the air. Finally, after ten seconds, the rest of the animal's body emerged. A head with pointy ears smaller than the nose, a two-inch brown furry body attached to a four inch long skinny hairless tail, and four tiny clawed feet revealed the mystery animal. It was a small brown mouse. The tiny animal froze when it saw the giant cats. The sniffing stopped. The mouse quickly dashed around in a circle and leapt backward to the top of the step.

ST watched as the mouse scurried to safety. It squeezed its tiny body through a crack inside the kitchen screen door frame. The mouse's body shivered between the closed metal door and the mesh screen. Its small black eyes opened wide to focus on ST, who inched closer and closer to go nose to nose with it.

The stare down lasted minutes, but felt like eternity to the mouse.

Fearlessly ST said, "Your time will come," and he turned around to face the group of the other waiting cats.

"I should have been a little quicker! I would'a had him. That brown fur ball would have been my toy! Then, dead meat!"

"Yeah, well, it doesn't make a whole lot of difference," Fat Cat sneered. "Those little mice can put on a chase but they're not worth the effort. They all squeeze their skinny bodies into any hole in the wall hiding place. Then they sneak out later. Odds are always in their favor."

King chimed in on ST's effort, "Hey, and what do you think are the odds that we'll see an even bigger one than that? I've just gotten an idea!"

In a jealous tone Fat Cat asked, "Let's hear it, buddy." He actually was somewhat interested in hearing the idea. King usually had good ideas. Fat Cat learned that about King soon after he arrived at the dock. Fat Cat understood the value in respecting a good idea.

Excited,King talked fast."I know how we can give the captain of the 'Lucky Two' something to get mad about.

Fat Cat listened, hoping to hear an idea to teach the captain of the 'Lucky Two' a good lesson.

CHAPTER 5: DARRYL LEARNS A FISHING LESSON

One of Darryl Kay's favorite things to do on any given day next to fishing, or playing his saxophone, or singing, was to breathe in the nature that was all around him. He believed that he lived in a beautiful place. Sometimes he called it paradise. His senses were always aware of the birds, animals, marine life, and natural beauty all around him. Nothing bothered him one bit. The weather, or even a few miserable humans, may disappoint him, but never enough to make him angry or spoil his love for each day. A petulant human amused him when he watched their interactions with other humans. He was always in awe observing the interactions of animals.

He believed that the time he spent musing over the movements and actions of animals was always time well spent. He also believed that there was no better way in the world to make a living than to be fishing in the Gulf of Mexico in his very own boat!

"Oh, sure," he rationalized to himself every now and then. "The money is important for paying the bills and I'd sure like to make a little more money now and then. Maybe buy a better saxophone. Maybe improve the boat. Maybe buy a bigger boat one day. Yet, if I am eating and paying the bills, there is not a better place in the world for me to be right now. There is no better life when you love the work you're doing!"

Darryl's enthusiasm was expressed in all the things he surrounded himself with. Prominently placed above his bed was a yellowed, weathered large poster printed by the Florida Department of Commerce displaying all of the saltwater and freshwater fish that could be caught in Florida waters and the Gulf of Mexico. The collection of fish, at more than a hundred, and the variety never failed to amaze Darryl. The colors on the fish included every color of the rainbow.

The remaining walls inside the cabin of his fishing boat, where he lived, were covered with pictures of fish he had caught over the years. His favorite was a black and white framed picture of him holding a thirty-eight pound black grouper. He caught this monster sized fish on one of his early deep sea fishing trips. He was smiling, with teeth spread from ear to ear, and he still had a full head of hair that was long enough to touch his shoulders. There were also pictures of him in various poses with a hammerhead shark, red fin tuna, red snapper, a blue marlin, and even a ling. All of these fish had been caught by Darryl on his own boat, the 'Star Chaser'. All of them except for the ling.

One Sunday, many years back, Darryl read an article in the

local newspaper about the great number of Ling schooling near the beach city pier. It was the month of March.

Wondering if he had ever been fishing from the pier, Darryl asked another, more experienced, boat captain at the marina about it. "How can that be any kind of fun? The newspaper makes it sound like some great fishing event. You got hundreds of kids, women, and other amateurs out there crammed on a narrow platform that amounts to an oversized concrete sidewalk. Everyone there is casting into the water from the same spot. That makes for an accident waiting to happen. Light poles, people, pelicans and who knows what else will get in the way!"

Darryl did not get the answer he expected.

"Let's go, man!" the captain said enthusiastically. "It's darn good fishing this time of year! Come with me and try it out."

It was hard for Darryl to imagine any other kind of fishing better than trolling a long line over the wide open, aqua green waters of the Gulf of Mexico where there was no other sound nearby except for a brisk breeze and the occasional loud beeping of the fish finder when it located a big school of fish. In early spring time, there was a lull in bookings on the deep sea fishing charter trips, so Darryl was up for the experience

"Well, all righty then," Darryl said. You seem to have a handle on this. I'm skeptical that it is something for me, but your enthusiasm makes me curious. Maybe it could be interesting."

"We'll just have to find out, won't we?" the other captain answered. "Better go early. It may be a slow charter boat day for us, but it will be busy day on the pier. Lots of folks will be out there trying to land a ling."

"Can't be as busy as the fishing some guys do in the bars during the college spring break weeks!" Darryl joked. "What the heck, we're on!" Both men laughed together. They knew each other well enough and trusted they would have a fun, friendly challenge ahead.

They met in the marina parking lot at 5:30 the next morning feeling fresh and ready to go. They were used to early morning fishing, unlike some of the tourists who had been drinking at the bars the night before and showed up already looking seasick before they set one foot to board the boat. Each man took one fishing pole, a tackle box filled with necessary fishing lures, and a cooler of ice that they hoped would be later filled with Ling.

They arrived at 6:00 at the Dan Russell Pier. It was supposed to be the longest concrete pier in the Gulf of Mexico. Most taxpayers complained that if it was not the longest, it was probably the most expensive.

Darryl's face broke into a toothy smile when they approached the chain link fence blocking the entrance to the pier. He was starting to get excited. On the left side of the fence was a counter where they waited for an elderly man sitting behind a glass window to speak to them. A plaque with the word Snapper and a pink painted fish hung in the window.

"Got a Florida Driver's License?" the elderly man asked.

Both men nodded yes. They set their gear against the wall of the building and reached into their pant pockets to pull out their wallets.

"Two dollars each, please," said the elderly man.

"That's a deal," Darryl answered and handed the two dollars through the window. "Do I need any live bait out there?" Darryl asked, noticing the deep wrinkles on the man's tanned leather like skin.

"Can't tell you how to fish and we don't sell bait. Just walk on through that gate and good luck guys," he told them cheerfully.

"If that doesn't beat all!" Darryl joked as they entered through the fenced gate and began the walk down the long pier. "All I got to do is show my Florida driver's license, pay two bucks, and I can fish with the amateurs! This might just be more fun than that time I rode the go-carts at the Gator Race track!" Darryl was always in a good mood early in the morning. He began to think that he would have a little more fun than he expected in this adventure as he observed the various types of people of all sizes and ages. There were men, children and women, many rolling their fishing equipment on elaborate carts rigged with bait buckets, cup holders, tackle boxes, rods, and boxes loaded with various fishing supplies.

"Wheels," Darryl thought while carrying his rod in one hand and holding a handle of one side of the cooler that he and the captain carried together. "Not a bad idea!"

Darryl turned his head to look at his friend and said, "I think we are in the company of some serious fishermen."

"Oh, yes!" he said and then added abruptly, "Stop here!"

Surprised, Darryl stopped but soon felt the excitement. He felt vibrations in the concrete pier and then he heard someone loudly shout 'RUNNING'. Darryl turned his head around and his jaw dropped. A group of twenty, or more, men were running toward him. It was a stampede. Each man carried a fishing pole high up in the air. All were racing fast down the pier like a herd of galloping horses. No one slowed down as they darted around anyone and everyone and ran past Darryl.

The fishermen stopped ten feet away from Darryl and the captain. In unison they took a place at the rail and cast out into the choppy waters. Darryl bent to look over the side of the rail into the clear water below. He was awestruck and full of respect when he saw the school of Cobia Ling, hundreds, passing underneath the dock. Each individual fish, some up to two feet long, moved with the group. They appeared to be in a flawless dance of swaying movement, one way then the other way, casting a silvery radiant glitter off black and white stripes in the beautiful morning sunshine. Darryl's eyes widened and he gasped. Then he fumbled around for his fishing rod, excited and hoping to catch one. He realized quickly it was too late to cast into this group of fish passing underneath the pier but it was an awesome spectacle of nature to watch. He planned to be ready when the next group of Ling passed beneath the pier.

The beautiful Ling, framed in the picture on the wall of the 'Star Chaser', was caught off the city pier that morning years ago.

After that day Darryl realized the sport of *pier fishing* was just as serious as fishing off a boat. He was respectful of the pier crowd, as he forever called them. The experience had been way more than beyond his wildest imagination. It had also taught him a lesson. On that very particular day he learned something about himself. Whenever again he felt an instinct about something he didn't know anything about, he remembered the day he went *pier fishing*. Instinct was a good thing, but keeping an open mind and putting a check on prejudgment was also important. The Ling was his favorite photo. It grounded him in the present each time he looked at it.

It was late evening. Darryl left the top deck of the 'Star Chaser' and climbed down to the main deck. He put away his saxophone. He didn't play it every night. Sometimes he liked to only hold it. It was a pleasant reminder of how much he used to enjoy playing in a band. It was his former career, the one that he left behind before he became a charter boat captain. He looked around at the photos on the wall in his cabin as he did most every night before going to sleep.

In his former career Darryl played saxophone in a five piece rock and roll band called the Electrons. The beachfront property nightclubs they played in were very popular with the tourists, but many locals from town loved the band too. The style of music they played was popular dance music, turning any crowd into an energetic rhythmic wave of motion. He loved the effect the music had on people, making them laugh, have fun and forget their worries. But, he liked his new career as a charter boat captain for the same reasons.

He had been quite the ladies' man many years ago! His hair was long enough to touch his shoulders and wave around in the air to the beat of the guitars, drums and his own saxophone notes. He wore tight fitting clothes in dark shades to highlight the muscles in his legs and arms. The shirts were worn unbuttoned to show off his bare chest.

As he grew older, the fun of playing to a crowd of admirers in a bar wore off. He began to notice the worst kind of behavior in human beings who drank too much and could not control their emotions. In the late, wee early, hours of the morning the drunks would not want to leave the nightclubs. Fights ensued over something as simple as a woman talking to another man or a man talking with another woman. Drunken people would get in their cars and drive! Being in the bar was hazardous and too dangerous for him to justify playing on his saxophone with the Electrons.

The final straw came on the night during a break he was

23

mistakenly punched in the face and knocked off his chair onto the floor. "Boys," he announced to the band after they cleaned him off the floor, "I think you'll need to look for a new singer and sax player!" They thought that he was joking. He silently walked away serious about his decision. His good natured disposition allowed him to continue his work playing in the band, but he knew he needed to change his lifestyle.

His fishing hobby, relaxing from the stressful evenings at the bar, became a dream for his future career. He came to this conclusion late one night driving home in the dark thick fog hoping to arrive home safe. It took him five years of careful planning, studying and saving money to purchase his boat the 'Star Chaser' and get started.

He spent many days hanging around the marina. He talked with boat captains who would be willing to answer his questions about the business. Getting another person's perspective, Darryl thought, was a good approach to avoid mistakes. He wasn't so naïve not to expect that there would not be any mishaps, but it was much better to know about the mistakes others had made if they were willing to share.

The captains who were willing to talk about the business cautioned him about the difficulties. They told him about the laws, rules, captain license test, record keeping, and paying bills. He was never very good at these things before. He tried to be good at these responsibilities personally but never had to think about costs before. In the band he only thought about the music. The captains would also talk about the best things they loved about being charter boat captains. It was the thrill of seeing that fish come out of the water. It might be THE big one, whatever kind of fish that it would be. So he knew that he was making a good decision.

"Aw shucks, going to the bank, applying for a business loan, buying the fishing equipment and keeping track of the records is nothing. I haven't heard the first charter boat captain say anything about getting hurt on the job."

He loved playing music with the band and loved it when people enjoyed his music. He would miss the Electrons. On the other hand he was making a change that would make his life safer, better.

Darryl had worked as a charter boat captain for as many years as he had played the saxophone with the Electrons. He was happier now than when he played music with the Electrons. He let the mystical sounds of nature filter through his mind when he played the saxophone alone at night sitting outside on the deck of the 'Star Chaser'.

Jokingly he said to himself on this night, "I wonder if the cats running around out there liked that serenade? I know these guys around here don't like my singing, but I know they like the soothing tones of my saxophone. No one ever complains when I play it. Time to call it a night."

CHAPTER 6: GOOD SCENTS AT NIGHT

An unsettled stillness descended on the docks at the marina. A quieter variety of activities began to erupt.

The restaurant lights were all turned off. The outdoor lights on poles shined over the marina with a hazy orange phosphorous glow. Shadows from the masts of rocking boats swayed like giants across the black tarred pavement of the parking lot.

Nocturnal animals made appearances with usual certainty.

Strong scents floated in the heavy, moist evening air. The humidity of the early October night weighted the breezes carrying odors high and low. No longer were the exhaust fumes of diesel boats and gasoline automobiles the predominant odors. Gone were the heavy perfumes of sunscreen oils and after tan aloe lotions of the tourists. Greasy oil from the restaurants' left-over fried food dumped in the garbage dumpster was the dominant scent in the salty, thick air.

Any human would pinch their nose to close off the smells coming from inside the garbage dumpster. The smell was worse than a football sized field of rotting cabbage in the heated up soil of a Florida farm. The animals loved it. Those delicious, ethereal scents were in the landscape where the animals loved to play. The dumpster became a playing field for the hungry animals. Various animals emerged from their hiding places, energized and ready.

This was the best, and most interesting, time for the cats, too. They no longer had to race across the parking lot pavement to avoid moving cars, the stares of tourists, or burning their soft paw pads. They slowly eased their way out into the open and relaxed. All eyes were opened wide, shiny and glowing like the sodium lights. The cats stopped frequently in mid pose to lift their head and sniff the air, patiently waiting for the rats and other scavengers to emerge and make a journey into the garbage dumpster. All would appear within the hour, a dozen or more, giving each other space, charting their territory rights.

"What was that?!" ST hummed in a voice half way between a growl and a purr. It was a noise that only cats can make. No other animal can imitate the sound of a cat who is excited with expectation.

King and Fat Cat stopped and froze in their tracks. Only Fluff did not notice the flying blur of fur rushing speedily around the corner of Smith's restaurant. It ran past them and continued to run fast in the direction of the boats docked in the slips.

"Find it! Find it!" The words pounded in the hearts of each cat as they raced along the concrete sidewalk to chase after a small scampering animal. Each cat had their own idea of what the animal may turn out to be.

The chase finished quickly. In a few minutes they were back where they had left Fluff sitting. She never got into races because she knew she was slow and would only get left behind. Fluff watched the line up of three cats casually trot back toward her.

The cats returned empty handed. No one was carrying a prized animal in its mouth.

"I think that we've spotted the one thing we've had our hopes on all day!" ST gasped first. He was the most excited of all the cats whenever there was the expectation of a little fun and action. He was forever cautious after his dumpster experience, of course, but that didn't mean he wasn't one to get excited.

With his usual confidence Fat Cat growled, "Pay dirt!"

"Let's be careful and move fast," King said lastly with a sureness that meant there was no chance to lose the pretty prey they were hunting.

"Oh," Fluff said. "I get it!" She began to purr with the pleasure of knowing there would be more fun to watch.

"Shhhhhh!" The other three cats gently mewed in unison and circled around her. This was their signal to follow them quietly and quickly if she wanted to be included in the action. Fat Cat, ST and King were about to follow through with the plan they had discussed earlier in the evening.

The cats had spotted a long, fat, rat. Unlike the small mouse that had slipped between the kitchen screen door at Smith's, this animal appeared to be nearly eight inches long from the tip of his nose to the end of his long, shiny, skinny tail. The rat, like the cats, had a good sense of smell. It knew that it was being hunted.

The rat had just left the garbage dumpster after scouring through the bags filled with leftover table and kitchen scraps from Smith's. The last employee from Smith's to toss out a garbage bag had not closed the side door. After trolling through the trash and filling his belly, the rat was sluggish and could not run as fast as it normally would if it were being chased by any cat.

The rat scurried along the concrete sidewalk toward the boat slips. Rats kept safe hiding nests away from humans, birds and cats underneath the wooden planks at the dock. Normally a rat could easily pick up the scent and motion of another animal. Having a full belly, and not as alert, it was caught by surprise when the cats began the chase. The cats ran noiselessly on their soft paw pads. The three cats were at a very close distance, stalking the rat before it even noticed them.

Now there were four cats running after it, bellies and heads low to the ground, tails straight behind the body, and sixteen paws moving together in a fast, blurred motion.

Suddenly the four cats split up and formed a square, each one taking a corner to surround the rat. The rat was cornered in the middle of the sidewalk. The cats stopped, froze like statues, and stared. Then they slithered closer, closing in the square.

The rat's long whiskers quivered in its sensitive snout. The body shook and shivered. It ran in one direction, then halted and turned sharply in another direction. The tail of the rat dragged along the pavement, stiff as a board. The rat knew the danger of the enemies. With a strong surge of energy it leapt up about three feet and went airborne across a short strip of water to land onto the starboard deck of the nearest boat. It was the 'Lucky Two'.

"Oh great" said King breathless and exasperated after losing the rat. "I would like to believe that our mission is accomplished because we have chased this rat on to the boat of the one captain we like the least, but we all know that the mission is not accomplished until we leave a dead rat on the boat. AND, it will be a huge, smelly dead rat when 'ol captain Keith wakes up in the morning. His customers won't like that!"

The next thing the three other cats heard was "Here I gooooo.....!" Without wasting another minute, King shouted those last words and ran ahead. His rear paws propelled him airborne and he leapt onto the deck of the boat. He picked up the scent of the rat immediately after his four paws firmly landed on the fiberglass deck.

The boat was dark and quiet. Only a small wedge of soft yellow light glowed over the deck. It came from the cabin windows inside. Using the light King could see a separate square piece of fiberglass on the floor of the deck. Attached to it was a handle that, when lifted, would open into the hull. A crack in the deck, only inches wide, near the handle, is where King caught sight of the long tail of the rat disappearing down into the hull.

Inside the belly of the boat, where the engines sat quiet for the evening, the rat squeezed its way into a small, damp and smelly corner between pipes and plastic boxes.

King tried to think quickly. If only he could find another way below, inside the hull! He wandered around the deck looking for another opening big enough for him to squeeze his head through and get into the hull. King thought, "The strong smells of diesel fuel and engine oil will confuse the rat. Those smells will cover my scents, too. That rat won't even know it when I get on top of it."

He padded across the deck, staying close to the outside walls. He knew Captain Keith was inside the cabin. King did not want to be discovered if Captain Keith happened to walk outside.

"I'll just wait here a little while." he decided. "That rat won't stay down there all night in those awful smells! The other cats will find something else to do and will be happy to hear the rest of the story tomorrow. I'll get to tell them how I out-smarted and killed the rat."

The three cats hung around the 'Lucky Two' pacing back and forth on the concrete sidewalk in front of the boat, waiting for King to return. They believed he would reappear on the deck of the boat to display his prey, a large ugly rat dangling from the grips of his jaw. Then he would leave the dead prize's stinky body hidden somewhere on the deck.

Nearly an hour passed and King did not emerge. They retreated to each one's sleeping area. They knew it would be a long night for King, patiently stalking and waiting for the rat, but all were convinced he would be victorious.

ST looked into Fluff's worried, skeptical eyes and tried to reassure her. "King is a great hunter. He never loses a scent. It'll happen eventually. Go on and stay in King's castle. We'll have to wait until morning to hear about the outcome."

CHAPTER 7: LOST AND LONELY CAT

Earl Keith's former girlfriend, Eleanore, was sitting in her one room efficiency apartment in Pine Mountain, Georgia, feeling lonely again. She was so ready for a change in her life. Ever since Earl left two years ago she was lost. She struggled to find purpose in living without Earl in her life.

Eleanore was not interested in any of the men in Pine Mountain. There was no man, or anyone for that matter, as interesting as Earl. He was not around now to make life exciting for her.

Every Friday night she used to go to Stumpy's bar with Earl. Stumpy's was the happening, and only, place to catch up with friends. Back then being with Earl, after a long week of work, was all she needed to make her happy. Nowadays she would never dream of walking into Stumpy's alone. Friday night after work she went home, alone. Saturday she went grocery shopping, did housework and laundry and maybe another shift at the Kountry Kafe restaurant where she worked. Sunday was always a day of rest and sometimes church.

There were not many choices of exciting things to do in a town of only 1,200 residents. There was only one store and it carried the basic, necessary things most people needed to buy.

She knew all of the Kountry Kafe customers who were regulars and caught up on the news in their lives. She didn't talk to her customers about her life though. There were plenty of times to open a conversation when they asked her how she was doing but there wasn't much for her to talk about since Earl left town. It was an embarrassment to talk about her life.

Sometimes people asked her if she'd heard any news from Earl. As long as Eleanor knew him he had always been the talk of the town. And he was still the talk of the town. It was rumored that his family, who had been in Pine Mountain for several generations, had *old* money. 'What happened to all that money?' people would ask Eleanore. They wanted to know. The family had grown smaller and smaller over the years. If anyone would know what happened to Earl's family money it would be Eleanore.

Eleanore had no idea about Earl's family money. All she knew was that ever since grade school they had been sweet on each other. Earl had been her first kiss. He was a nice looking and she was nice looking. They went together like Jack and Jill. They went everywhere together and even up and down a few hills. Now they had been separated for two years.

Life in Pine Mountain without Earl was different. Eleanore didn't know how to get *normal* back into her life. She withdrew from everyone.

Eleanore had been too afraid to leave Pine Mountain when Earl announced that he planned to move to Florida. "I'll buy one of them big fishing boats and fish in the Gulf of Mexico where all the REEL fishing is," he announced one Friday night at Stumpy's after a couple of beers. She thought he was trying to joke around with her. Then he said, "I'm gonna name this boat 'Lucky Two' for you 'n me!"

She didn't think about where Earl would find the money to follow this dream. Money had never been something that he discussed with her. The rumor had always been Earl was born with a silver spoon in his mouth, so she let it alone and never asked him about money. She didn't think Earl had been drinking too many beers. He was good when it came time to stop at the last beer. But, she knew that Earl was dead serious. Earl liked to dream big. This was no joke about one of his favorite hobbies, something he was good at doing.

She swallowed hard and asked Earl, "How am I gonna fit into that scene?" emphasizing the word I.

Thoughts of the beaches in Panama City, Florida, crossed her mind. Thoughts of the flashing neon lights at the bars, the girls riding in the shiny new cars with the windows rolled down screaming at the men and vice versa, the oiled and tanned bodies of men and women wearing skimpy bathing suits, and the dance floors in the nightclubs where men and women acted promiscuously.

She had already moved past that point in her life. She liked the quiet life of Pine Mountain.

"No, absolutely not!" she spoke with as much convincing courage and determination in her voice as she could muster. "I will not go! You can go on without me. Name your boat 'Lucky One' – just one!"

Earl took a few moments before he told her that he wanted her to be happy too. She could get a good waitress job at some beach restaurant and make much more money in just three summer months. It would be more than an entire year at that small country style food diner in Pine Mountain.

Defiantly she said, "Well, Earl, I'm pretty darn happy here."

"Eleanore, you won't have to work if you don't want to! I'm planning to use the money my grandma left to me when she died. I'll buy a boat with cash, no debt, and make lots of money in the charter fishing boat business. I know I can make a better living down there. I love to fish. You know I can be good at it. You know that! I just can't stay here for the rest of my life here in Pine Mountain. It's just not got all that much to offer me," he hesitated, "or you, either."

She stared back at Earl with her lips pressed tight together.

Earl tried harder to coax the idea into Eleanore's head. He said, "Me and you, it's always been us the 'Lucky Two'. Get it?"

She tried to swallow but her mouth was dry. She took a deep breath. She wanted to say, 'Maybe in your mind right now, but not my mind', so angrily said to him, "No, Earl, I can't go down there with you. You can go and move away without me."

Eleanore never imagined that Earl would leave her and go to Panama City Beach without her. Earl was gone two weeks after the last conversation they shared in Stumpy's.

"Well, he never did ask me to marry him," she'd often think to comfort herself and justify the decision she made that night. "I guess he didn't care enough about my feelings."

A few months after Earl left Pine Mountain Eleanore made a spontaneous decision to drive to Panama City Beach by herself. Maybe she would discover that she might like living there. She planned to stay in a cheap motel for a couple of nights. Then she could make a decision. She knew she could find Earl if she wanted to find him.

The six hour drive had not been difficult, but as soon as she reached the main road on the beach, called by locals as front beach road, she found herself inching the car along in a sea of traffic.

"Must be an accident," she thought while nervously glancing around at the beach motels looking for one with a 'Vacancy' sign lit.

Traveling so slow in the line of cars gave her a chance to get a good look at people in cars passing her from the other direction and people walking along the side of the road. Car radios and stereos were blasting out loud, thumping, music. Cars were full with girls screaming and laughing and guys shouting back at girls, "Woo wooo! HEY HONEEEEEYY!" Nothing had changed, including Eleanore's feelings. She felt very uncomfortable to be driving alone down front beach road.

Along with the spontaneous decision to drive down to the beach, Eleanore made a last minute decision to bring along her cat, Princess. She did not want to leave her cat alone in the apartment. To bring Princess along had not been such a good idea. Princess was very distressed after the long car ride. Now there was all this noise!

"This is very strange, and I don't get it. How can this be fun?" Eleanore shouted above the noise trying to control her nerves and calm Princess. "Now I know that I was right about not wanting to move here! She continued talking in a very loud voice trying to block out all the other noise. "I'm thinking now I should not have come to visit. But I've driven all this way. I might as well try to find Earl before I leave to go back home. I'm going to ask him if he is happier since he left Pine Mountain!"

Eleanore passed by several motels before she finally found one with a flashing red light with the word *Vacancy*. She wasn't even sure that she wanted to stop after she pulled off the road. When she drove closer to the building she saw flaking paint and litter lying around on the ground. The words The Lamplighter were painted in large black letters above the office door. It was a one story building with small horizontal slatted frosted glass windows. The stucco walls were painted grape purple and the metal trim work around the windows and the room doors were painted bright yellow.

"Good grief," a tired Eleanore sighed when she parked the car in front of the motel. "I have never, ever, seen those two colors together on anything except an Easter dress or an Easter egg, maybe?"

The room price fit her budget. She did not mention to the desk clerk that she had her cat. She wouldn't ask if a cat was permitted. It was only common sense that a motel could turn her away if she asked about keeping a cat in the room. She had seen more *No Vacancy* signs so it was better to take the motel with an available room.

It was hard to get out of the car without Princess trying to escape. She was careful to park her little white car a short distance away from the motel office so no one would notice the white cat pacing, and jumping, from the front seat to the back seat and meowing loudly.

After Eleanore paid the desk clerk and got her room key she jumped back into the car. It was safer to take Princess on the ride to explore the beach and try to find a marina, Earl, and his boat, 'Lucky Two'. She couldn't leave Princess alone in the room.

Eleanore didn't really know where to start to look, so she asked the desk clerk at The Lamplighter for the names of some of the marinas and driving directions to get there. The closest marina was Captain Anderson's. It was also the largest. That's where Eleanore decided to go first.

Finding the marina was no trouble, but when she arrived she found a very crowded parking lot. She circled around three times and finally found a parking space. Eleanore was so distracted by the busy atmosphere, and the sheer size of the marina, she completely forgot about Princess, who's meowing had softened to background noise that Eleanore didn't notice. Eleanore's eyes took in the boats, restaurants, hundreds of cars, and people. Her heart beat faster than normal. Excited now with the thought of seeing Earl, and putting on a brave face if she did find Earl, she completely forgot about Princess. After turning off the car's engine she threw open the car door. Princess immediately jumped out the open door and raced away to huddle beneath another parked car.

Eleanore was frantic. "Princessssss!" she screamed.

Eleanore's heart was beating three times faster than normal. She did not want to call out for Princess again. She was aware that a few people turned to look at her when they heard her scream. No one stopped to ask what was wrong or if she was all right. It would be useless to ask a stranger for help because Princess hated strangers anyway.

She dropped down to her hands and knees. It had been only three, maybe four minutes and she already lost sight of her precious feline.

She repositioned her body to sit up on the pavement and with legs stretched straight in front she started to cry. She quickly stood up and climbed back into her car. She did not want any stranger to see her cry. That might bring attention to her, which she did not want during her moment of despair. With the windows down she sat in the car for nearly an hour, wiping tears away from her flushed cheeks and staring in every direction possible trying to get a glimpse of either Princess or Earl.

The strong smell of fried seafood suddenly made her hungry stomach growl, but a painful tight knot took control of the hunger. The tears had stopped flowing but her sorrow grew stronger. She had let Princess escape!

She found herself angry at Earl. She thought, "It's all Earl's fault this happened. The last year of my life had amounted to nothing. Nothing's right anymore."

She really did not want to get out of the car and be seen looking so disheveled. There was nothing more she could do but leave the marina, drive back to her motel room, get cleaned up and get some rest. She could come back later in the evening, after the crowds had left.

The marina was changed when Eleanore returned later that evening about eleven o'clock. No people. No cars in the parking lot. But, this time she did not feel safe to leave her car. It was too creepy to walk alone in the dark. Someone could be hiding in the shadows of a building! She sat in the car for fifteen minutes. Then her eyes caught sight of something move. There along the side of a large restaurant, on the sidewalk close to the boat docks, was a group of four cats sitting on their haunches, front legs straight, paws close together, like soldiers in a color guard. They turned their heads side to side, as if looking for something too.

Eleanore's eyes squinted in the direction of the row of cats. It was too hard to tell in the dark exactly what they looked like. She was pretty positive that not one of the cats was solid white. Her car was parked a few rows away from the sidewalk. She cranked it up and drove slowly forward, toward the cats. They promptly scattered when they heard the car's engine noise.

She sat in her parked car, windows only cracked open to let in a little bit of air and the car doors locked. She waited for a glimpse of another cat to pass by and desperately hoped it would be her own. For two hours she sat forlorn, thinking about her life, wanting to see either Princess or maybe even Earl strolling around, but she never got a glimpse of her furry white precious feline nor Earl. At one point she even heard a mournful meow in the distance, a voice not familiar to her ears.

She arrived back at The Lamplighter motel shortly after 1 a.m. and slept a fitful four hours before waking at 5 a.m. It was dark, but she remembered she was in the central time zone and it was 6 a.m. on her own body clock. It was not an unusual time for her to be awake when she worked the breakfast shift.

During the drive back to Pine Mountain she cried for nearly six straight hours. But now her tears were prompted by anger and fear of what would happen to Princess.

She worried for the cat's safety. "How will she survive? There are restaurants nearby so she probably won't go hungry. I wonder if it gets very cold in the winter? Well, of course it won't be as cold in the winter as it is in Pine Mountain."

Her wandering mind created chaos with her emotions. "Who would want to live in a wild and scary place full of strangers? My poor cat! Those other cats looked mean. They won't like a beautiful cat like my Princess. How will she survive?!?!? How is Earl surviving?!?!?! Oh, boo hoo, BOO HOO!"

Now she had lost Earl and her beloved cat Princess to this Gulf coast beach town.

The visit to find Earl had been a fateful disaster. Eleanore decided she definitely would not want to live anywhere near Panama City Beach even if she was unhappy living alone.

She reported back to work on Monday at the Kountry Kafe in the little town of Pine Mountain.

Yet she continued to think about Earl and Princess. When she found herself feeling unsure, angry, or afraid of her decision to stay in Pine Mountain she just prayed for the safe keeping of Earl and Princess.

CHAPTER 8: CASEY'S UNDER THE WEATHER

Casey Howard parked the Florida Marine Patrol work truck behind his personal car. It was a single-car uncovered rock driveway with a small stone path leading to the front door of his single story stucco house on a clay dirt road two blocks north of the beach.

He couldn't put his car in the garage for multiple reasons. First, there was so much junk in the garage. Boxes, tools and mostly useless stuff, blocked him from getting in, or out the door, if he pulled the car into the garage. Second, he liked to leave his car outside to give the impression that someone was always home. He did not want his house to be robbed. A car left parked in the driveway made it look like someone was home. Third, and he liked to believe this was the most important reason, his car was always covered in clay dirt or mud from the road and he didn't want to clean the dirt out of the garage. On the days he was off work he just parked the Florida Marine Patrol truck on the grass, what little grass there was, in front of the house.

He learned early, as a young boy, that he hated to spend time cleaning. His approach was simple. The best way to avoid cleaning was to prevent the dirt from getting there in the first place. Minimize the dirt in as many ways as possible was his code of operating. He did not want mud in his garage or his house.

He often grumbled about the politicians when it rained. "It's stupid. The politicians won't spend any money on the roads out here on the beach. The beaches bring in all the tourist dollars. Roads for tourists are paved, oh yeah, and then they got plenty of money to pave bridges and roads for themselves where they live on the other side of the bridge."

Casey also did not like to leave the truck parked outside at his house, but his job required him to keep it where he lived. If he was called to be somewhere to investigate something he was expected to be there fast. He lived too far from the headquarters so it was better for him to have the truck at all times.

On the other hand, a person who might hold a grudge against a Florida Marine Patrol Officer could follow him home, or even see the truck parked at his house. It made him feel like a sitting duck for anyone who might want to take revenge against the agency for enforcing a law they thought to be unfair.

So far he felt he had been very lucky. His feeling was that the first time a fisherman got mad at him for writing a ticket for a violation of rules it wouldn't take long before someone would follow him home and find his truck with big fluorescent letters 'FMP' stenciled on every side. It would take less than a few minutes for someone to slash his tires with a knife, pour sugar into his gas tank, spray paint over the FMP letters, smash the windows, or throw eggs and tomatoes all over the truck.

"Darn." Casey exhaled a deep breath of exasperation and sat down on his favorite living room chair. He turned on the TV to watch the late night weather.

Casey's job responsibilities included being aware of weather. It wasn't specifically in his job description. It was his own common sense that made him stay abreast of the daily weather forecasts. It was on the mind of anyone who made their living on water in the Gulf of Mexico.

"I wish I could figure out a way to nail that Darryl Kay on the 'Star Chaser'. If he is doing something illegal it could put him out of business for a while and it would help me get some recognition in my job," he thought.

Casey didn't know exactly why he had a premonition about Darryl or why he didn't like him. But, he badly wanted to catch him doing something wrong. Frustrated about the time wasted sitting in the truck parked on the lagoon bridge Casey said loudly, "There's got to be something about Darryl!!"

He glanced at the television weather reporters with little interest. A commercial interruption helped him keep his concentration on Darryl.

"All I hear from the other boat captains is about Darryl. He gets the best customers. Repeat customers. He gets the best hauls of fish. Everyone talks about his singing and then playing that horn at night. I am SOOOOO tired of listening to everyone talk about Darryl!"

Casey didn't want to deal with Darryl, but he knew that if he found a way to make it appear that he caught Darryl doing something illegal the other boat captains might give him credit for doing something about Darryl. It might also get him closer to his personal priority of rising up in the ranks in the agency. He was ready for a new set of duties. He'd spent enough time counting fish!

A never ending stream of commercials aired on the small television set. Casey started to think about his plan to go fishing on his upcoming day off.

Casey had his own personal watercraft. It wasn't as big as the deep sea fishing boats, but he could use it for some salt water fishing in the bays and bayous.

He optimistically named his eighteen foot fiberglass flat bottom boat 'The Reel Thing'. Casey wasn't trying to be ambitious but the name made him feel hopeful.

There were many laws about fishing, which Casey knew was the primary reason he had a job with the state of Florida. However he did not enjoy writing a ticket to a fisherman for catching a beautiful fish because it wasn't a legal catch during a certain time of year. On the other hand, he wasn't opposed to writing a ticket to the fisherman who caught an overabundance of undersized fish during the legal time of year. He strongly believed small fish should be thrown back into the water and allowed to grow into adults that produced more fish. Often, as he watched and counted some of the large beautiful fish thrown off the charter boats, he felt a tinge of envy in his belly. He would love to go far out into the deep waters of the Gulf of Mexico and catch the *big one*. He could not go out very far in his own small boat, but he could not go with one of the charter boat captains, the same people he was tasked to monitor and patrol. It just didn't work. It was called a conflict of interest in the agency manuals.

As a young boy, between the ages of eleven and fifteen, Casey had fished the same waters with his dad, and his dad's friends, on many a summer day when he was out of school. There were not many rules back then, over twenty five years ago, that regulated the size of the fish and when anyone could go fishing. That was before the state of Florida nearly doubled in population and inversely the fish population declined. Back in those days it was common for the guys to reel in a thirty pound black grouper, a twenty pound red snapper and beautiful, rainbow colored pompano. Trigger and sheepshead were considered trash fish, not suitable for eating and would be tossed back into the water. Casey would watch in amazement as a fish that had once been flapping and snapping its entire body like a rubber band, and gasping to breathe through gills, would just glide back into the depths of the water and quickly disappear after the hook was removed from its mouth.

Casey liked to fish for snapper, his favorite fish to eat. The two short fishing seasons for snapper were ten days in February and ten days in October. For weather reasons, Casey preferred to fish for snapper in October. The month of February was seasonally the better time to fish for the popular fish, which tend to like cold water and may be closer to land at that time of year. Chilly weather, cold water, spooky foggy conditions and rolling waves in February were not to Casey's liking. The weather in October usually meant calmer waters in the Gulf of Mexico, smooth like a sheet of glass, but it was still hurricane season too. The official hurricane season lasted from the first day of June to the last day in November. A storm could take weeks to arrive, or maybe evolve in a few short days. With the most favorable factors like warm water, low pressure, and favorable upper level winds, a strong hurricane could form in a shorter amount of time. It could take as little as only forty eight hours. Florida fishermen were always cautious before going out into the Gulf of Mexico in October. They had to go out further to find the bigger Snapper. They would go out with the knowledge that they may have only twenty four to thirty six hours to get back to shore before a storm brewed up in a short forty eight hours, but many were lured by the high price paid for snapper.

Casey knew that a deep sea fishing captain with a good boat, one with fast high powered engines, could make it back to the marina in time to beat an approaching storm. He knew that his boat 'The Reel Thing' was not fast, or big, enough to make it back if he went out very far.

By October most of the captains, weary from the five to six months of hot summer taking the tourists out on charters, were eager for a change. It was possible to make as much money catching snapper in October than a whole season of taking out summer charters. Casey knew these captains loved the sport and chance to make a lot more money with a big haul of Snapper in the short ten day season in October. In February most of the captains were too cash poor to spend any money on boat maintenance. Their tourist dollar from the previous summer had been spent on the basic living necessities for survival through the winter.

The law allowed each boat to take in two hundred pounds per fishing trip. That added up to a lot of money.

Officially, Casey was allowed to fish anywhere he pleased once he was off duty, but Casey was not interested in the money he could make. For him the snapper season was a sport and he could fill up his freezer.

He sat in front of the television but looked beyond the screen. His legs were stretched full length in front, toes pointed toward the ceiling, heels of his shoes planted on the floor, and his arms hung limp over the sides of his chair. His mind wandered on the details of his job.

The charts he kept were records of the maximum and minimum weights and the number of fish caught by each boat in the marina. It was a daily record that was boring and uninteresting to an untrained eye. Over time however, the details on the charts showed patterns, just like the number of storms and hurricanes during each month of the hurricane season recorded every year over time. Patterns and frequency sometimes help with decisions and predictions.

The 'Star Chaser' was bringing in the best haul of fish almost every day. For each year Casey had been assigned to Captain Anderson's Marina this statistic was a constant record. Darryl Kay appeared to Casey to be too much of an ordinary kind of man. Why did the records show such extraordinary results? Casey couldn't answer the question. It caused him to be suspicious. Was Darryl overfishing? Casey counted the fish that came off his boat. Was Darryl leaving some unaccounted in the hull?

"Well, maybe I am wasting my time worrying about it, but that captain Darryl is so darn annoying. How is it possible for him to be the best one down there at the docks?!" Casey grumbled.

As much as he tried to fight it, he felt an underlying respect for Darryl. "The truth is Darryl has the best customers. He gets the best charters. The people who come off the 'Star Chaser' after fishing with

Captain Kay talk about his ability to find the fish. What's wrong with that? And, they all seem to have the best time!"

Casey didn't think twice about talking out loud in his home. He did it often. He lived alone with no pets.

He didn't believe that he had the time or ability to properly take care of a dog, cat, or bird. At one time he considered owning a tropical fish tank since he liked to fish. After researching the costs of tropical fish and the requirements of maintaining the tank he realized that it was expensive and no easy matter either. All pets required attention and care. He once considered taking home one of the stray cats that wandered around at the marina however none of the cats ever came near him. Also, they looked too straggly and behaved too unruly to consider taking one home.

One cat in particular had a messed up mouth. Casey thought maybe it was from being in cat fights. This cat had the ugliest mouth, with the upper lip missing and one long fang, a tooth on the top gum of his mouth hanging out exposed over his bottom lip. This cat seemed more bold than the other cats, not minding as much to be around humans as if to show off his scarred mouth as a badge of pride and respect. When the boats docked, this particular cat would walk directly up to the fish laying on the concrete to sniff at them. Casey tried to make sure that he wasn't there long and sniff at the fish. One big stomp with his heavy shoe on the concrete would send the cat scampering back into the bushes.

Like Casey, the boat captains were used to this particular cat. The customers were sometimes taken aback by the sight of the cat and made off-handed remarks. The boat captains would make jokes about the cat to put the customers at ease.

One day not too long ago after recording a count of fish Casey noticed a beautiful long-haired, green eyed, white cat hiding in the bushes with two other cats. The white cat had inched its head out of the bushes to observe the unloading of a fish haul on the sidewalk. It was round-faced, calm, appeared to be perky, alert and did not act as skittish at the step of a human being. It weighed in heavy on the scale of possessing beauty.

Inwardly Casey thought, "Now, if there was a cat to bring home, that would be the one!"

Casey tried to sympathize with the boat captains for all the rules and regulations they were expected to know. Occasionally a boat captain would ask a question about a regulation. Casey thought they were just testing his knowledge. He tried to laugh it off and take it lightly. He did not try to make a case for whether the rules were fair or not fair. His job was to apply the same rules to everyone. He understood that the charter boat captains worked hard to make money every week, every year, at fishing which was a hit or miss endeavor. The business depended on finding a spot where the fish were schooling, finding a good crew to work on the boat, and finding customers willing to pay the right price. It depended on the weather.

Little did Casey know that the charter boat captains had mixed feelings about the work that Casey did. They could count on him to always be there when they arrived back to the marina after a long day of fishing. He kept his records and that seemed to be the only thing that he did. They believed he treated them all fair and equal. Some captains almost felt sympathetic about the job he had to do because they knew that fishing was in his heart, too. They were not the least bit worried about Casey unless, of course, he brought attention to something they were doing, which he never did.

He turned his full attention back to the small screen television. "I suppose it is not too much of my time to keep my eye on the 'Star Chaser' for a day or two more," he mumbled about the plan in his heart. "Too bad I don't have an extra eye in the back of my head. I should start to keep those boat captains, all of them, wondering about me and why I hang around." Casey half-heartedly attempted to justify the importance of his work.

Casey perked up in his chair when the weather reporter began to talk about the category one hurricane over the western part of the island of Cuba, and heading into the Gulf of Mexico. After sitting prone in his favorite chair he'd lost track of the time.

"Now why do these dam gum things just pop up out of nowhere?" he shouted with irritation at hearing the news.

He rose from the chair in jerky motions, like a blow up inflatable doll. He stomped over to kitchen only a few steps away from his chair. He found a frozen dinner to pop into the small microwave oven.

It took five minutes to heat up one of his regular favorite frozen dinners of fried chicken, macaroni and cheese, and corn. He kept listening to the television weather reporter, but by the time he sat back down in his chair holding the heated meal on his knees the local weather report was over. He switched the channel to the twenty four hour channel that carried only weather radar. He scooped a large portion of food on his fork and watched the radar.

"Yep, I see it coming. Never fails this time of year. Hurricane's a going to come this way in October and I wanted to take a day off to go fishing for Snapper!"

He let out a deep sigh, switched the TV channel to a comedy show and continued to slowly eat the TV dinner. He hoped there would be something on the show to make him laugh. It would be awhile, he had a feeling, before he had a good laugh again.

CHAPTER 9: CHANCE OR LUCK?

King waited, still and patient, in a dark corner on the deck of the boat for the rat to emerge. He remained focused on any and all sounds, especially any sound coming out from the inside of the cabin of the boat. Captain Keith was in the cabin. Why else would there be any light on?

Rats, like cats, know how to remain motionless for a very long period of time before moving swiftly and quietly. Rats, too, can leap three to five feet from one place to another. King knew that he needed to be very quiet and still in order to hear the rat come out of the hull if it wanted to leap or scurry away. Perked up ears would be able to sense the general direction from where the sound came. King believed that it would be very unlikely for the rat to take a leap off the boat this early in the chase. On the other hand, if the rat remained hiding, it was worse for King. He was not familiar with the boat and didn't know anything about a hull. He had never, ever, even been on any boat before! King kept hope the rat would try to make an escape off the boat. He would snatch it before it left the deck.

He cautiously crept close along the side deck wall of the 'Lucky Two'. The soft sounds of water lapping against the sides of the boat made him nervous. He worried about his ability to remain focused on any noise the rat might make. The boat rocked gently. He tried to tighten his footing with his soft padded paws, but his legs were shaking. He reassured himself that the boat was tied to the dock, which was tied to land!

His eyes grew more accustomed to the lighting on the boat. He could identify outlines of objects. It was all such a very strange territory for him. He thought of ST. "This is how he must have felt jumping into the dark dumpster after chasing the lizard!" The memory encouraged him. He must be courageous, too.

King had to maneuver around large and small unknown objects and tangled ropes pushed against the sides of the boat. Rope lay scattered around on the deck. Fishing supplies - hooks, filament lines, round bobbers, plastic bait and lures - poked out of the top of a plastic bucket near the floor hatch. He reminded himself to be extra careful. His reason for being on the boat started as a game. If he played the game right, the rat might take a chance on his luck and try to escape off the boat. King wanted to find the rat, but the hull was an open area in the bottom of the boat and inaccessible to him. King needed to be ready if the rat tried to escape. He hoped the rat wanted to be off the boat as much as he did. Perhaps the game now was who wanted off the boat the most.

His paws silently padded fast away from the stern and toward the bow. As he ran toward the front of the boat he stopped briefly at a set of three small stairs leading down to a door about five feet tall. King started to shake. He detected human sounds. Footsteps were coming closer from behind the closed door where a yellow glow of light appeared bright.

He nervously thought. "I must not get caught!"

He hurried away from the door, racing back to the stern of the boat, still hoping in his heart for a chance to find another access to the hull where the rat had disappeared. He did not want to be caught by Captain Keith. He reassured himself that it was unlikely, being a black cat, that Captain Keith would see him in the dark. This advantage in the dark night boosted his confidence.

"It doesn't matter whose boat I am on, I just don't need to get caught! I must remain calm." He reminded himself.

King stopped short, dead in his tracks, when the cabin door behind him suddenly creaked open. King froze in place and pushed his body flat against the side wall of the boat. He watched the young Captain Keith emerge from the cabin and close the door, leaving the light on. He fearfully watched Captain Keith walk down the side of the boat, passing within inches of King. Then Captain Keith hopped off the stern onto the concrete sidewalk.

The young boat captain was soon out of view but King could hear the man talking to himself. His voice grew fainter as he walked away. When King felt assured that Captain Keith was a safe distance away from the boat he took a deep breath and let out a sigh of relief. It felt good. Luck may be with him. He could continue the hunt for the rat. Captain Keith had departed. Maybe it would be awhile before he returned to the 'Lucky Two'.

After this scary close encounter, King sat alert patiently waiting but thinking about humans. None of the other boat captains, or workers around the marina, showed any kindness to the cats who lived at the docks except for one. It was Captain Darryl Kay.

The 'Star Chaser' was the only boat the cats would even dare get close to only because they knew Captain Kay would frequently throw a fish over the side in the late evening hours after all the other captains had turned off their lights. After this act of kindness, Captain Kay would pull out his saxophone and play it while he watched the cats run up to the dead fish, usually a small bee liner, and growl at each other until the first cat snagged it with its claws and dragged it away to the bushes to eat it. The cats learned over time that this was a game Captain Kay played with them. After one cat, usually Fat Cat, had his belly full the others would move in on the bony, smelly carcass, and pull and tug at it until they got a few chunks, all the while growling for the other cats to keep their distance. All cats got a turn at the fish, which was always big enough to feed the group.

Thinking about Captain Kay's past kindness calmed King. He crouched down low, close to his belly, on four bent paws. He was more focused, waiting, again for the sight or smell of the rat. His ears were perked up like two triangles. His long, shiny, slim black tail was curled around his backside.

The soft salty breeze curled through open spaces on the deck. He lifted his nose upward, twitching it, trying to pick up a familiar scent when the air brushed by his nose. He smelled nothing that would indicate a rat. Just the same old familiar salty humidity was all he could identify.

"Much better than diesel oil fumes!" he thought.

Should he dare to try to find a way to get inside the hull, where the rat was? Was there another way for the rat to escape from the boat without King being aware that the rat was already gone?

No sounds or smells gave King any hint of where the rat might be.

"He still must be hiding!"

King crouched close to the floor and crept along slowly. His paws padded silently along the fiberglass deck, up to the bow. The rat had found an entrance way into the hull from the stern, but maybe there was an opportunity to get inside the hull from another entrance point on the boat.

When King reached the bow he immediately became distracted by the large open expanse of water, as far as his eyes could see.

"Oh, Oh!" he cried. "I've run along the concrete seawall from Smith's to the boat slips before, but standing on the edge of this boat feels nothing like that!"

A two foot wide plank stuck out of the front of the bow like an arm. Below it was only water. It was a lot of water.

King straightened up and ran quickly. He held his tail up straight and twitched it back and forth. He ran past the plank and avoided looking at it. Once he rounded the curve of the bow to the other side of the boat the square shaped stern came into his view again. It was time to think of a new strategy to get to the rat.

"No use running in circles and getting distracted by things I know nothing about. I just know that rat is still hiding somewhere on this boat!"

He sat on his haunches staring into the black night. His front paws were side by side, stiff and straight in front of him. His eyes were black, too, instead of their usual aqua blue. As he turned his head from side to side his nose twitched to pick up scents drifting in the breeze, again. His ears picked up the sounds of rippling water.

Nothing was familiar. He wasn't going to give up. He waited motionless and silently. Every now and then one of his ears would twitch if a little bug landed on it, but he purposefully twitched his ears to pick up any new noise.

His animal instincts sensed someone was watching him. Turning his head toward the parking lot, his black eyes scanned the empty blacktop, searching and searching. The large glass windows of Smith's reflected the lights of the parking lot. The windows gave him a reference point to the bushes where the gang of cats usually hung out. In the shadows of the bushes he believed he could see glowing eyeballs and the silhouette of cats. It could only be ST and Fluff. He could count on their loyalty.

A noise from the parking lot alerted him. He twitched both ears backward and flat. He recognized loud footsteps coming closer. Someone was walking at a steady pace toward the boat. His eyes, black in the night light, focused in on Captain Keith not far away. He had not been gone a very long time after all!

The sight of the man sent a chill through his body. He did not want to be seen by this man, yet he didn't want to leave the boat.

King had no time to hesitate. He took a last glance at his friends in the bushes and darted toward the front of the boat. He avoided looking toward the plank jutting out over the water. He looked upward and then suddenly noticed a small window, cracked open. Maybe there was another way into the hull from inside the cabin. The window looked like it was cracked open wide enough for his body to squeeze through it. He made a quick decision to jump up to the window and to go inside the cabin.

The window ledge was very small, but he balanced his four paws on it. The opening was wide enough for his head and whiskers. He turned his head right and left to look quickly inside the room, adjusting his eyes to the bright yellow light. A fluorescent blue light from a clock drew his attention to a corner where he saw a table, a chair and a bed.

In one fast motion, King jumped off the window ledge onto a small table. He bounded off the table onto the floor, skidded under a chair and quickly hid in the corner where the table joined the wall.

"If a rat can find a hiding place so can I!" He didn't give a second thought to the fact that he was six times bigger than a rat. He had made it this far, gotten inside the cabin, and was not giving up!

He had to be perfectly quiet once Captain Keith made it back inside the boat. He crouched beneath the table and flattened his body against the wall. He was partially hidden by the chair. There he waited for what was a very short time before he heard the soft thump of the first step on the deck of the boat. Then he heard a loud thump of some large object thrown down on the deck. The footsteps came closer and closer until the sound of the slatted wood door opened with a creak that made King's fur tingle and his muscles twitch. King's eyes shone like glassy polished marbles. He didn't breathe for fear of making any sound.

Captain Earl Keith stood in the center of the small cabin room. He scratched his head with both of his hands and stared at the floor for several minutes.

When he finally lifted his head he angrily said, "Dang, I'd better close that window. Doesn't do me any good to leave it open all night in this heat. No doubt there'll be some animal in here. Got to be the reason I heard something crawling around in here earlier."

Disgusted with himself he slid the glass window shut and added "I am so dumb!"

Earl snapped the lock on the window, pivoted on his toes and turned his body back around. He made sure the cabin door was also locked. He reached above his head and tightly pulled down on a beaded chain hanging from the ceiling. The light bulb stopped glowing yellow, turning the cabin dark except for the blue light shining from the digital clock. Earl moved toward the table where the clock rested. If he looked straight down he would have seen black, shiny marble-like eyes staring up at him, only a few feet away, hiding beneath the table.

Balancing his body with one hand flat on the table Earl reached up and turned on the radio. King heard the muffled sounds of Earl's body roll onto the cushion of his bed. To think he was locked up inside the cabin with Captain Keith all night!

The voice of a female radio announcer filled the cabin, "We'll keep everyone posted on the latest weather update when we get it For now, let's hear some music from....."

CHAPTER 10: DEVOTION AND DETAILS

Earl Keith grew up in a family faithful to the important basics of life. They believed in themselves, their calling to the service of God, and in the principle 'if there's a will, there's a way'. His mother and daddy taught Earl to work hard, play hard, and life would be filled with rewards.

When Earl reached the age when he had to settle down and go to work, only a few years after becoming a teenager, he got the idea in his head that life in Pine Mountain was too much work and too little reward. Life was moving at a slow, boring pace. He began to dream. If only he could make a living doing what he loved the most during his play time, which was fishing, he could be happy. He was good at it. Fishing for a living made sense for a life of complete fulfillment.

Those dreams were soon erased by the reality that recreation in a boat on the clay colored rivers and lakes in the great state of Georgia was different than a life of recreation on the Gulf of Mexico off the coast of the great state of Florida.

Earl had grown from being a small-boned, lanky, skinny teenager into a lean, sharp-minded tall man with muscles in his arms, legs and belly. His long legs and arms were quick and strong for working on a moving vessel. "I have great sea legs!" he used to joke to his passengers. Lately, his legs were stiff and sore. It was now a chore to bait, cast, reel, and gaff or do anything else required of him on a deep sea fishing excursion.

He'd look in the small cabin mirror and see that his teenage good looks were fading worse than the blue canvas covers on the chairs on the boat. His blonde hair had grown to his shoulders. He pulled it into a ponytail and threaded the ponytail through the rear clip of his faded red and blue Atlanta Braves baseball cap. His hair, he knew, caught the attention of many a young girl walking the docks at the marina, but he paid no attention to them. He would love to be a lady's man. He also knew that the women at the docks were tourists. Those women liked a man with money and having a good time. Earl had very little money these days.

Something had gone terribly wrong with his plan to have fun while working. He felt tired all the time. All he did on his boat, 'Lucky Two', was work. The dreams he once had of being a Florida fisherman, to have fun at his work, and get rich at the same time were just faded memories.

He tried very hard not to think about how he had made a huge mistake leaving Pine Mountain. The biggest question in his mind was how to move his life forward in a positive way. Thinking about the past two years in Panama City Beach didn't help.

Still, as much as he tried to think of the future and move forward, he got stuck on life as it used to be. His thoughts would always drift back to better days in his past life, before he moved to Panama City Beach. He remembered how he used to be young and full of energy. He forgot how he had been restless and eager for a life that offered a little more action and was less boring.

On many nights, once darkness closed in and wrapped around him inside the lonely cabin, he would regret his decision to leave what had been a pretty decent home in Pine Mountain. On this humid fall evening in October Earl felt even more lonely and anxious. He fidgeted and paced the floor of the small room, going around in circles, back and forth, with his mind working full speed.

He thought about the times he drove his old black pick-up truck down highway 231 with Eleanore sitting next to him on the bench seat. He used to love watching her brush her long, brown hair hanging down her back. She would lean her head close to the open window so she could blow dry her hair after an early morning shower to get ready for a week end at the beach.

In the old days they would leave early on a Saturday morning for a week end of fun. Both of them would be relaxed, listening to their favorite country music radio station and anticipating good times in the sand and water. He would have his window down, his left arm out the window resting his hand on the side view mirror, his right hand on the steering wheel, tapping the fingers of both his hands to the beat of a song.

By noon they would reach the city limits of Panama City and drive along Highway 98 toward the Hathaway Bridge that crossed over North Bay. It would lead them to the island of sugar white sands of the World's Most Beautiful Beaches on the Gulf of Mexico. They would first stop at the liquor store where he'd buy a small bottle of whiskey from the drive through window.

A beachfront motel room was easy to find on the twenty-five mile strip of island that stretched from the Hathaway Bridge to the Phillips Inlet Bridge. All along the two lane road flashing neon signs hung in the windows of brightly tropical colored one story stucco motels advertising room vacancy. It wasn't a problem to pull into a motel parking lot and find a room without having a reservation in advance.

After carrying bags, chairs and coolers into the room, they would drink a few shots of whiskey, go to sleep for a midday nap, and save the rest of the bottle to get liquored up for a Saturday night on the beach.

He thought how Eleanore always looked beautiful and sexy wearing a colorful cotton top with cut-off blue jeans for shorts and flip flops. She would giggle and seem so happy just being with him out for a walk in the starry night on the sandy beach. She always gave him her full attention. To Earl she was perfect. She had long legs, and curves in all the right places often attracting the stares of many men that she never seemed to notice. When Earl walked along front beach road with her he felt so proud to be with her. The other beautiful women walking on the beach sometimes distracted him, but none were more beautiful to him than Eleanore.

Thinking back on those days in the not too distant past he now found it difficult to understand how, or why, things had changed. Eleanore had a beautiful face, a knock your socks off body, and a devotion to him that he never even felt from his own family. Everything was so different now. It seemed incredible to him. Now it made no sense to him why he ever got the idea to leave Pine Mountain.

Earl remembered how Eleanore once told him that he was like the sun and she was like the moon. His energy cast a light on her life that made her glow. "Boy, I could use a little radiance in my life right now!" he said gloomily.

Sitting alone in the cabin, in the chair by the table, rethinking his life as it had turned out to be, made him feel worse about his situation.

He was usually good about blocking out sounds and motions. But, tonight he felt more sensitive to everything. Living on the boat nearly two years and getting nowhere was getting on his nerves. The gentle night time sea breeze, usually a relief from the daytime heat, contributed to the constant noises. It caused the constant clatter of wires and lines on the boats. It carried the echoes of car engines driving over the lagoon bridge, the idle chatter of the final tourists leaving Smith's restaurant late at night and the noise from the man he nicknamed Captain Horn Blower two boat slips away. Constant noise and motion was not something he had anticipated when he started out the plan to work as a deep sea fishing captain. He knew hard work, but had been used to the quiet life in the woods. At first he believed this was going to be a fun career after he studied the books at Sea School to pass the test he needed to get his license and business permit. Never had he given thought to all the other annoying details that go with the business.

"I should have been born into it," he sighed heavily. "No daddy, or mamma, to tell me at the get-go that my idea was all wrong for me."

His anger over his situation kept growing until he found his ears tuning in to a familiar noise that needed attention. He was listening to a sound he had heard often and hated it more than anything. It was the sound of an animal running around deep inside the walls of his boat, down below in the hull. Small scratching scurrying nails on a fiberglass floor.

"Oh blazing heck!" he said with disgust. "I've got to tune all of this stuff that's in my head out of my head."

Earl got up from the chair and reached up above the table to turn on a radio attached to the wall by two brackets. He seriously hoped the country music station he left it tuned to would be playing one of his favorite songs. He desperately needed a song that would change his mood. He wanted to hear a song that would give him hope. He wanted to hear a song about starting over, or leaving the bad times behind. Unfortunately the announcer was giving a weather update.

"Seas will be increasingly choppy in the bay for the next six to eight hours as the winds pick up speed. Waves at the second buoy are now at eight feet and wave action is five to eight seconds," said the announcer.

"Jeez!" Earl reacted to the news with both genuine surprise and fear. "It's after midnight and this is what I am hearing on the radio? No music? All I get is a bad weather report! Can it get any worse?"

Though he was aggravated, Earl's voice reflected a tone of seriousness and concern. Earl knew that you can't be a fisherman and not pay attention to the weather.

"Boaters should definitely exercise caution and tomorrow will not be a good day to be out on the water," the announcer finished the weather report and followed by saying, "Next, coming up after this commercial break, we'll have one of our favorite songs for you by Keith Urban."

Earl stood up from his seat at the table.

There wasn't enough room to walk around in the cabin with such a strong urge to go for a walk to clear his mind. There was always the deck outside with the wide open sky, but it wasn't like going outside back in Pine Mountain. Back there, in the country, in a wide open field away from the tall canopy of pine trees, you could see millions of stars and even the soft creamy wisp of light called the Milky Way. The stars cleared his mind and made him think of the big picture.

There had been one night that he strolled around the parking lot noticing the cats and wishing they were stars. On that night, he imagined that he even saw a cat that looked like Eleanore's cat, Princess. "All cats look alike," he reminded himself.

"Princess," he remembered the name and dreamily thought again of Eleanore. He shifted his weight to one foot then propped the other foot on the chair he just emptied. He crossed his left arm across his chest and held his right arm underneath his chin.

"I can't just take the boat out for a quick spin like you would a car back in the old days in the woods of Georgia," he thought gloomily. The radio station cut into a commercial for a local steak restaurant. It was one that he had heard too many times. It was played on every TV and radio station, over and over every day, during the summer season.

"Man, oh man!" he shouted and stomped his propped foot back down to the floor. He sharply pushed another button on the radio. "I am so sick of hearing that commercial! I've probably heard it fifty times a day!"

All of the buttons on his radio were preprogrammed to a country music station. There were so many area stations playing country music that he could have preprogrammed more than the six buttons on the radio.

Even though seafood was popular for tourists, many of the fishermen who chartered his boat loved the sport of fishing but enjoyed going out to eat steak after a long day on the water out in the sun.

Earl thought, "A two-inch thick twenty ounce steak grilled to perfection over a hot open pit fire would hit the spot for me right now."

The new country music station was playing an older song that brought back memories of a summer night walking shoeless in the soft white sand with Eleanore. A full moon shining bright that made the dark rippling waves sparkle with stars jumping across the water. His eyes welled up with tears.

"Another steamy summer love song," Earl thought as he stood listening to the entire song while staring out the small cabin window that he called his porthole. He stared at nothing in particular and allowed his mind to float, letting his feelings drain to empty, like the needle on a gas tank.

When the song ended Earl whispered, "Man, my name should have been Keith Urban instead of Earl Keith. I could be singing for a living instead of fishing. Well, I'm not a good singer, so it's best that I stop dreaming. This life, my life, is real."

Earl turned the radio off and walked one full circle around the cabin that held all of his essentials for living. His eyes surveyed the few things he owned.

"That's all I got. Is this enough?" he asked himself.

Earl had a ship to shore radio that scanned the police reports and he could use it to call for help. He did not use a cell phone after discovering he could not afford the monthly payments. His ship to shore radio was required by Florida law for all commercial boat captains who took charters. In spite of all the grudges and complaints running through his mind about the rules, procedures and regulations, Earl knew that this one was good for his own protection and safety.

"Why does all this crap have to cost so much?" he asked himself for the thousandth time. He picked up his baseball cap, wallet and keys off the table. Next he turned off the radio.

Earl exited the cabin door and didn't notice the black cat hiding on the deck watching him. Earl stepped off the boat and journeyed across the black asphalt parking lot to the pay telephone on the wall near Smith's front door. He hoped the phone call would be the first step, first move forward, toward a better future.

By the time Earl left the 'Lucky Two' it was almost one in the morning. No one was around. This would normally be the time he desperately tried to get a few hours of sleep before the alarm clock buzzed and the early morning fisherman who chartered the boat would arrive, eager to get started to go out fishing.

"No sense in getting any sleep, anyhow," Earl grumbled out loud. "Don't look like any boaters are going anywhere tomorrow. I'll bet nothing that those two guys will show up late tomorrow morning and ask for their money back."

Earlier that day two men stopped by his boat asking if they could charter the 'Lucky Two' for a half day trip. His boat was not well known and he didn't advertise. The two men had seemed like so many others he had taken out on a deep sea fishing trip. They looked like inexperienced people who were looking for a cheap thrill and liked his boat's name. It was a catchy name. Maybe they would actually catch some fish. They were just another two tourists who didn't have the big bucks to book one of the other better equipped charter boats.

At one in the morning anyone loitering in the parking lot was cause for suspicion. All the boat captains agreed to report to each other if they saw anything or anyone who appeared to be up to no good. Earl soon discovered, however, that not all of the boat captains shared good information about their hired help and deck hands. Just like so many of the other beach and tourist businesses, the employees working on the charter boats would come and go. Some would come back to try and steal equipment or supplies before they left for good. It was a continuous seasonal problem for all beach businesses.

When he first noticed the dark object about sixty feet away he stopped to pause and get a better focus on it to be careful before proceeding. Was it something dead, alive, or even moving? After a good look, Earl decided it wasn't alive and walked on. His interest was piqued. At first he thought that it may just be something that fell out of the back of someone's pick-up truck. People were always losing hats, towels and shirts and sunglasses. This object looked bigger than any of those items.

When Earl got closer he was surprised to find a single, black, rubber knee high boot lying in the middle of the parking lot. It was a type of boot any deck hand or fish cleaner would wear. They were not too expensive, but then again not cheap. Nothing was cheap anymore in Earl's mind. Earl tried to assess the value of it.

"Someone will want that boot back if they need it for work. It's got to belong to someone who works at the docks or the owner of a business. If someone was trying to steal a pair of boots, they only got one. I can put a note on it and sit it out on the sidewalk by the 'Lucky Two' in the morning, or maybe I can use it for something."

Earl picked it up and continued to walk carrying the black rubber boot by the toe, slightly swinging it to and fro.

Earl stopped at the phone booth. "Change. Did I forget to bring change?!" he suddenly thought. He reached into his pocket. He needed at least a quarter and a dime. He found five quarters and a few pennies. He dropped all five quarters into the coin slot. He still knew the phone number. After he dialed the number a tin like voice of a woman announced, "You have eight minutes."

He heard the phone ring three times before he recognized the sleepy voice of Eleanore say hello.

"Eleanore?"

"Yes. This is Eleanore...whose calling?"

"Eleanore. It's Earl. Don't you recognize my voice?"

"Earl!" she shrieked, clearly more awake. "Where are you? What are you doing?"

"Well," he started slowly, realizing he had not given any thought of what he would say to her when he called. "I'm still down here. You know, in Panama City Beach. Here with the 'Lucky Two'."

"Oh? Do you know it's one in the morning? You're calling me at one in the morning and I haven't heard from you in two years. Are YOU okay?"

"Sure. I mean yes." He tried to sound sympathetic and collect his composure. He detected the anger in her voice, but didn't know what to say next.

Sternly Eleanore asked, "And just WHY are you calling me in the middle of the night?!"

The sharp edge in her voice unnerved Earl, but he needed to try to soften the tone of the conversation and get it to go somewhere.

"I'm, I'm....I'm just a 'thinking of you right now. You're the other half of the 'Lucky Two', remember?" he urged her.

"EARL! Well, yes, why wouldn't I remember? I can't believe you. Here it's in the middle of the night and you haven't got anything better to do than call me to tell me that? You are unbelievable, Earl. You're just the same ole' crazy Earl!"

In a soft voice, Earl agreed. "Yes, I know. Right now I'm standing at a pay phone holding a black rubber boot and talking to you for the first time in too long."

"Stupid idiot. Are you drunk? I am not talking to you right now."

"NO, wait, Eleanore."

"Good bye Earl!"

"Eleanore....?"

After a moment of silence with two hearts beating fast through the space of a telephone wire Earl said, "You know what I think, Eleanore?" He didn't wait for an answer. "I think I've made a huge, HUGE mistake in my life. I'm a highly trained...."

"Four minutes left," interrupted the tin voice.

Earl gulped a dry swallow and continued "...boat captain who spends his time hanging around at the docks, waiting for customers and if they don't come then I have to make sure the boat is tied up strong to the dock when a storm comes a blowing its way through the Gulf of Mexico to take it all away."

Breathing hard to get through his controlled emotional

outburst, Earl waited for Eleanore to respond.

"What's that mean, Earl?"

"Weather's looking bad and a hurricane is probably coming. I want to believe, hope, that the mistakes I've made in my past can be changed but I know that I can't change the past. I can only change the future."

Eleanore's voice became harsher, "And, you just decide to call me?"

"Sweet Jesus, Eleanore. I think I'm in a big mess right now."

"Earl, I think that's the first time that I ever heard you admit that you made a mistake. But, you know what, Earl?"

Earl didn't ask 'what' because it was more like a statement and she didn't pause for Earl's answer.

She continued in a strong, gruff voice that started to crack with emotion like she was going to cry.

"It would have meant a lot more to me to hear you say 'I should have never left you for some wild dream of becoming a boat captain down there in some playground they call the Gulf of Mexico.' Fishing and doing what you love, is more than you ever loved me."

Eleanore paused for a second to catch her breath. Hearing her talk in such a way he'd never heard before took away Earl's breath. He tried to think clear. He could only think of her beautiful body standing at the other end of the phone line.

"You used to just be the boy with the fishing pole up at the lake standing on the dock," she continued after a small sob.

Earl's fingers twitched on the phone handle when he sensed the softening in her heart. He said, "And I remember you would holler at me, 'hey you boy. Boy with the fishing pole!'"

"Yeah, I used to love to watch you back then. You were so handsome, tanned, sure of yourself and relaxed," she barely whispered and then paused a few seconds. "Then you come up with this wild idea to leave all of the people here in Pine Mountain who loved you. You left us, Earl. You left us for fishing! GAWD, Earl."

"Eleanore, you're right."

"Yes, Earl. I am right. This conversation is over. I loved you and wanted you to be my friend and lover. It sounds like you're in a bad way now. I don't want to see you get hurt, but you'll have to get out of this on your own."

"Eleanore, I'm OK. I'm just needing to....."

"Earl, forget it. I don't care what you need! I don't even want to hear anything about your problems. I've got to get up early in the morning and go to work. I'd appreciate if you'd just leave me alone and do NOT call me back again tonight!"

"Eleanore! WAIT!.....I won't call you back"

"Well, then, good....GOODBYE Earl!"

Earl heard the click and the line went dead before the tinny voice could interrupt again. He held the silent receiver and stared at it for a few seconds before replacing it to the cradle. He stared at the black rubble boot he had placed on the ground near his feet, thinking whether he wanted to carry it back to the boat. "Why did I pick that thing up, anyway?" he said feeling depressed after the conversation. "Oh yeah, that's right. Everything has a value. What might I use this for?"

He picked up the boot. He carried it limply and slowly walked across the quiet parking lot back to his boat. He was deep in thought over the 'if onlys' and the 'might haves' that could have worked for him. He thought "If only I had worked harder to convince Eleanore to come with me. She would have been a lot of help. She's a lot stronger than what I gave her credit for and might have helped me become successful in the first place. She might have liked it here. She could have even brought her cat. There are lots of cats here, but she once told me her cat didn't like water. I'm sure cats don't like to be on boats."

When he stepped over the side and onto the boat he absently tossed the black rubber boat into a corner of the deck near the other supplies. The black rubber boot would be more valuable than Earl could ever imagine. What Earl also couldn't imagine was a black cat with shiny eyes hiding inside the cabin.

King suppressed a loud meow when it heard the sound of an object hitting the deck with a loud thump.

CHAPTER 11: CONFUSED CAPTAIN

Casey finished his meal, scraped leftover cold food into the garbage can and set the utensils and plate into the stainless steel sink. Even though he frequently ate frozen dinners he still preferred to eat his food from a real plate, not something metal or plastic. Normally he could eat everything on his plate. Tonight his heart and thoughts ran at such a fast pace he couldn't eat.

Bad weather always generated an excitement that led to distraction. It was a chance to escape from his job of the tedious and mundane, but the anticipation of a crisis made him nervous. There was always a fool born during a storm.

He went into his bedroom and sat down on the bed. How early should he set the alarm clock he thought. He wasn't really very tired, and knew he would have trouble falling asleep now, but he knew that he would need to wake up earlier than the usual 5:30 a.m. The national weather service would probably start issuing storm warnings for boaters in the Gulf and protected waters before the 6 a.m. update.

He needed to be dressed and ready to get down to the docks for the boaters. Most captains were very good about what needed to be done for preparation for a hurricane. Others needed help and advice about what to do to secure their boats, or where to move them if necessary.

The most experienced boat captains always had a plan in place. The largest party boats, or head boats, that carried forty to fifty passengers would tie down loose cargo and be ready to pull out of the marina before 6 a.m. The head boats were owned and operated by a large corporate office. The owners had many employees and other crew to help with the effort involved in getting ready for an evacuation.

It was the small, private boat captains who took longer to decide on a plan. Before leaving the marina they had to stock up on diesel fuel and food supplies in addition to storing their fishing supplies. The younger, more inexperienced, and sometimes careless, captains needed the knowledge he could provide.

Casey decided to set the alarm for 3:30 a.m. knowing full well that he would only toss and turn trying to get the sleep he needed for the busy day ahead of him.

A short time later he was backing his truck out of the driveway in the dark morning hours. Casey gave a fleeting thought of his own boat. It rested on a boat trailer parked next to the side of the house. His boat would have to stay put. There was nowhere else to move it.

People who could afford it kept their personal watercraft in one of the huge storage facilities at the marina.

The largest storage facility was across the lagoon from the Anderson Marina. It was a large metal structure that enclosed up to five hundred boats. Each boat rested on a v-shaped metal rack. Above each rack was another rack. Boats were stacked one above another up to the ceiling. The walls of the facility were lined with row after row of boats.

Casey's boat was not worth enough money to pay for a monthly, or annual, storage fee. Many of the owners of the boats kept in storage were from other states like Alabama, Tennessee, Kentucky or Georgia. A single year's rent to keep his boat stored in the metal building would almost cost him as much as what his boat was worth. He needed the money to pay the rent on his small two bedroom house.

Casey knew the boat storage facility manager. If there was an empty slot for his boat Casey believed the manager might allow Casey to store his boat during the weather event. But for now Casey didn't have time to worry about his boat.

When he thought about money, his thoughts always drifted back to his ex-wife. They'd had ugly fights about money. She wanted to spend money on different things than he did. Maybe the marriage had only been about money, he often wondered. He had worked many extra overtime hours to earn extra money, but the less he was home the unhappier she seemed to become.

"Can't win for losing," he thought with bitterness. "Can't let myself think of her," he quickly corrected his slide into negativity. I've got some work to do!"

Casey's drove his truck onto south Lagoon Drive. He turned his head occasionally to catch glimpses of the lagoon in between the houses he passed. The water still appeared to be at a normal level, but he knew that a strong storm would push water easily up over the banks onto the yards of all the beautiful waterfront homes. Sometimes he envied the people who lived in these homes because they could enjoy the gorgeous sunsets and balmy breezes from the Gulf of Mexico. He wondered if the people living in these homes argued about money.

At a time like this he was concerned for them. He knew this was not the time to argue about money. Safety was on his mind and he hoped that it was on theirs too.

The marina was at the end of north Lagoon Drive. While he waited at the signal light to cross over Thomas Drive into the Anderson Marina parking lot Casey noticed he had not yet seen a single car on the roads.

"Not even a drunk driver on the road," he thought. He knew all this would change by daylight.

In the summer time there would be a drunk driver on the road every night. October was not as busy a time of year for vacationers.

"Yep, end of the season," he muttered with a hint of contempt for the weather. When the light changed he crossed through the intersection and into the parking lot. Under the glow of the high density parking lot lights Casey could see a few crewmen were already sitting on benches or standing near the boats. "Good, getting ready."

Casey pulled his truck into a parking space closest to the dock's main fish cleaning house and hopped out without bothering to lock it.

"Got your radios on?" Casey yelled to the first crewman he saw when he approached the docks. The first fishing boat was the 'Aqua Girl', a twenty year old sixty-five foot head boat. It was Ralph Hood, a man with weather worn skin who appeared many years older than his mid-forties. Ralph was standing on the stern of the 'Aqua Girl'.

"Yup," Ralph responded.

Their eyes exchanged knowing looks. The many years Captain Hood had spent in the hot, harsh Florida sunshine had left his skin wrinkled and leathery, almost like a gorilla's skin, but his sparkling blue eyes had not changed. His passion for the water and fishing reflected in the spirited look so many of the boat captains had.

"It's starting to build up in the gulf pretty good, ain't it?" Ralph hands became busy again while he talked. "Is it named?"

"Don't know for sure," Casey answered. "If it does get a name, and I am sure it will, it will be called Louise."

Amused, Ralph chuckled. "Ahhhhh, a girl. Always dangerous."

Casey stepped up to one of the round concrete tables near the sidewalk and boat slips. The tables were used by customers and marina workers. He lifted his foot to the concrete bench beside the table and rested his forearm on his knee while he scanned the area to get a look at the crewmen already at work.

Ralph asked casually, "Where's it located about now?" Ralph knew approximately where the storm was, and the direction it was predicted to move. He asked the Florida Marine Patrol officer to show his respect for Casey. He knew that eventually Officer Howard would get the storm updates directly through his truck radio. Ralph viewed Casey as a friend now more than an enforcer of the rules.

Casey answered, "I don't know any more than what I heard last night. This morning I had the radio on and it has not changed. It's just been sitting out there gaining strength during the night."

Casey looked up at the early graying light spreading through the cloud speckled sky.

"Well, last night when it was sitting a couple hundred miles south of us I was kind hoping that it would take a turn to go to south Texas or even cut further west to head to Mexico. They all need the rain, don't they?" Ralph asked with a more serious tone in his voice.

"No such luck. It's going to head more north than west. They been talking on the weather I saw last night, pretty late, about a high pressure system holding it back," Casey answered in a professional voice.

"It needs to cut west."

"Yeah, but....it is what it is." Casey knew that he would have this same conversation with everyone he encountered at the docks.

Case shifted his weight and planted both feet on the concrete sidewalk. His eyes searched across the lagoon to the boat storage facility located at the Treasure Island Marina on the other side. He noticed a little activity in the distance.

Ralph went back to his work making preparations on his boat.

The eastern smoky gray sky became striped with shades of red, pink, yellow and gold. The colors appeared brilliant. White laser beams from the rising sun on the horizon streaked through the colors like a fan. Casey patiently watched the sun ascend above the horizon until a tip of crescent red first appeared. It only took minutes before there was a huge, completely perfect circle of yellow glowing fire, too bright for his eyes to look at directly.

Casey was awestruck, once again, by the sight of the sunrise. Like the sunsets on the Gulf of Mexico, the sunrises stirred his respect and belief in the greatness of the Creator of the earth.

The sky slowly changed to a deep blue hue, but the bands of the storm could be seen developing. The air temperature was around eighty degrees, but it would easily get hotter by late afternoon and climb into the nineties even though it was October.

He allowed himself to enjoy the moment to watch the sunrise, but soon began to think how strange it seemed to know that a huge storm was churning in the Gulf of Mexico waters so far away, over two hundred miles southeast of where he was standing. The weather he was experiencing now didn't give any hint of a hurricane threat. Casey enjoyed the low humidity and fresh salty breezes. He suspected all of the moisture in the air was being sucked into the swirling cyclone cloud so far away.

Casey eyes shifted down to stare at the sunlight's reflection on the water. He imagined tiny jumping stars along one single, straight, long line of light, breaking across the lagoon, streaking across the water like gold glitter. It was a beautiful sight to behold.

"Hey, there!"

Casey thoughts were interrupted. He turned his head toward the sound of another man's voice and recognized Earl Keith, the newest captain at the marina. He knew him as the man from Georgia who had bought the used boat 'My Girl' and renamed it 'Lucky Two'. It was not a name that made much sense to Casey in the world of deep sea fishing boats, but he understood that every boat was given a name for the owner's own personal reasons.

"Yup?" Casey called back acknowledging Earl. He watched Earl approach with deliberate quick footsteps.

Earl was wearing blue jeans, white screen printed T-shirt and a pair of flip flop sandals with the word REEF printed on the straps.

They were the clothes he had worn the day before and slept in last night.

"What do you think?" Earl pointedly asked when he reached Casey and abruptly stopped within inches of his face. "I mean do you think we'll be able to ride this storm out in our boats here, or what? I mean, I know I should know about this stuff but, really.... I really don't know. And, I don't think I can take my boat by myself up into the intracoastal or the bay or somewhere else."

The intracoastal, a system of waterways, some natural and some manmade, between the Gulf of Mexico and land was unknown territory to Earl but a valuable resource to many boaters. Instead of going out into the gulf to travel from one part of the state of Florida to another, boaters could reach the intracoastal through bays and rivers and other natural inlets allowing boaters to navigate in much calmer waters during a storm.

"I think many captains do well riding out a storm on the intracoastal." Casey looked directly into Earl's eyes. He tried not to reveal any sign of emotion that expressed concern or worry. It was a careful, well-practiced, answer he repeated many times over the years.

Casey continued, "It allows you to go a long way on a short amount of diesel fuel. But, you've got to know the channels. Sometimes, during rough seas, there's trees and stuff under the water surface that can possibly give you some trouble."

Earl asked, "I've never been up there before. How long does it take to get there, say, in a boat like mine?"

The young captain appeared nervous and anxious. Earl shifted his feet from side to side and pulled his hands in and out of his jean pockets. He had dark circles beneath his tired blue eyes from lack of sleep the night before.

"Oh," Casey paused and said in a calm voice, "You probably need to allow maybe two, three hours to get from here just beyond the west bay bridge. That's over by highway 79. There's a few inlets up in there where you can anchor your boat and be pretty safe, I would think. Usually not too many other people around there either. Just regular guys like you," he added thinking this might calm Earl a bit.

"Probably a safe plan then?" Earl's voice cracked.

"Oh, yeah, sure." Casey said.

"Well," Earl hesitated. "Well, what about leaving the boat here?"

Casey hoped he had reassured Earl and did not want to be asked this question. He didn't want to engage with the young captain in an important decision that involved personal property, but he answered as best as he could.

"Well, I cannot know for sure what could happen if you leave your boat here. I can say with certainty that if the storm comes here, and if you decide to leave, today is the day to pack it up and do it. Once the weather start's to turn worse you've got to stay put." Then

Casey said with more emphasis, "The national weather service will probably be issuing warnings later today. Once it's dark you can't do anything but tie down and stay put."

"OKAY, man. Thanks! Thanks a lot." The enthusiasm in Earl's response was obviously false.

Earl stuck both of his hands deep into his pant pockets and turned his head upward to stare at the same sky Casey had just been admiring. Earl was not wearing the usual baseball cap. His long blond hair was bound by a rubber band into a pony tail to keep it away from his face. In contrast, Casey was in his official work uniform with gun, baton, badge and a small CB radio hooked to the epaulet on his left shoulder. Casey stood alongside Earl and turned his head upward at the sky as if trying to find what Earl was looking at. He watched Earl from the corner of his eye. Then Earl looked directly at Casey. Casey felt the eyes upon him and turned his head back to face Earl directly.

Casey asked, "Something else you want to ask about?"

"Well, man, it's like I haven't been into this deep sea fishing, rental boat thing for a long time. Now I can't get my head together and think straight about this situation that I'm in. I'm feeling a little stretched financially, mentally and emotionally. I don't know what I want to do in this situation." Earl's mouth quivered and his shoulders twitched.

"It's not a good situation for any of us," Casey stated flatly turning his head away so that their eyes wouldn't meet. He felt the conversation going in a direction that would take more time than he had.

Earl's voice cracked, "I'm pretty much out of money, man."

"Money's pretty tight for everyone." Casey said.

Then Earl pleaded, "Listen, I need to leave the boat here and shut it down as best I can. Will you be back around here to check on things after the storm? I'm thinking of leaving town."

"Your boat's not my responsibility," Casey said, but he quickly found himself becoming a little more interested in hearing just a little more of what Earl would say next. One part of his brain was telling him that this man was talking crazy and he shouldn't waste any more time talking to him. The other part of his brain was registering another side of Earl. He felt himself being pulled to stay and hear more.

Casey's impression of Earl, when he first noticed the new name on the old boat 'My Girl', was that this was another man who wouldn't make it through one fishing season. Earl was not a boat captain Casey needed to pay much attention to, or worry about regulating, because Earl didn't know the business. Guys like Earl were dumb dreamers. They came down to go on a couple of deep sea fishing trips in the gulf and got lucky with a good captain. These guys had just enough money to set themselves up and think they would get rich on tourists. Next thing they knew they were in trouble. These guys didn't realize it didn't happen in one, or even two seasons. There weren't too many who tried. Yet Casey remembered a few staying more than five years before calling it quits. The seasoned captains knew the business by growing up in the business.

Captain Kay briefly crossed Casey's mind. How was it that Captain Kay become such a success?

Casey returned to the moment. "Leaving it here, huh?" He asked cautiously. "You got insurance for any damages?"

"Insurance? Oh, sure." Earl lied. He didn't remember the last time he paid the insurance premium.

"Well, then leave it. It's your decision. But even if you tie it up, you won't see nothing left of it if a category three or four hurricane blows water and wind up into this lagoon. You'll find pieces in the parking lot, and if you're lucky a cracked up hull to identify the boat."

"Huh?!"

"Yup. Listen. Good luck to you. I've really got to go now." Casey turned on his heel as if he planned to walk away down the sidewalk and toward the larger deep sea fishing party vessels.

Earl's shoulders slumped and he sat down on the concrete bench. He folded his hands behind his head, stretched his back straight and tall and stared blankly at the water.

Casey saw the look of human dejection and hopelessness. He turned his body back toward Earl and said, "If you don't have anyone to help you, listen here. I can maybe try. I won't be back here checking on the status of the marina until after the storm passes through wherever it lands. If you decide to leave, go ahead and give me an address where you will be, or a cell phone number."

"Don't have a cell phone. I'm thinking about going to Biloxi."

This was an even crazier idea than jumping ship on his business. People did not drive along the coast in the same direction the hurricane was moving. The goal was to escape from it.

Casey responded to Earl's answer in a gruff tone. "Well, usually I hang around here to be sure everyone who moves their boat has enough supplies to get out. Diesel fuel, food, water, ropes, stuff like that. I generally don't pay heed about the boats left behind. I see what happened to them and let the owner know. But I can offer a piece of advice to you if you are leaving the boat behind. If I was you I'd be heading back to Georgia. Isn't that where you came from? Biloxi won't be safer than here."

Earl woke up. "I'm from Georgia. How'd you know that?"

"Tag on your truck. I know your name is Captain Earl Keith from the log sheets I keep on fish catch. You know my name? Captain Casey Howard, right? You know that?"

"Yes." Earl answered. He slowly let his hands unlock from behind his head and released his arms, letting them drop down to his side.

Casey extended his hand to shake Earl's hand. He thought it might wake him up from the trance Earl appeared to be in. The two men briefly shook hands. Earl's hand was moist and his grip was loose.

Earl was tired from a night of no sleep. The memories kept him awake: the scratching sounds of a little critter; a muffled thump; the conversation on the phone call to Eleanore; and his imagination going wild. It was not the first time his imagination kept him awake or got him in trouble. He remembered his dream of becoming a deep sea fishing boat captain. He wasn't sure that he liked the idea of going back to Pine Mountain. Fishing on a lake was not a big dream.

"I know it's probably safer to head north, but there's nowhere for me to go. I have no one to go to. I figured I'd take what little money I got left in my wallet and go to the casinos. Not going to make any money as a charter boat captain this week. Maybe never!"

Casey thought Earl was really scared and dumb. He said, "Biloxi will be open. Lots of hotels with rooms for you, but I'm telling you, son, if the storm doesn't come here it'll be going that direction. Guess it's your call. And what are you planning to play in the Casinos? They can take your money quick."

In a wispy voice Earl said, "Oh, I guess the slot machines. I've never been any good at cards. I don't understand those other game tables. What are they? Roulette? Craps? Or maybe I'll play the game of finding a woman and falling in love."

This last comment struck a chord in Casey's heart. This man was just as human as he was and he shouldn't forget that. "Know what you mean about that. Just think about my advice. Good luck, brother!"

Casey turned around and began to walk slowly down the sidewalk toward the large party boat vessels. It was difficult to stop thinking about the conversation he just had with Earl. "Maybe the guy is smarter than the rest of us, leaving his boat here. Maybe he'll be back. Maybe he'll win a lot of money and come back here. He'll get another chance at making the business profitable. Maybe he'll be back to sell the boat and the name will be changed again. It will still be the same boat. The more things change, the more they stay the same. Isn't that the way it goes?"

Casey wanted to stop thinking about Earl.

Earl stretched his arms above his head again. His neck and shoulder muscles ached. He held his arms high above his head, locked the finger of his hands and stretched to release tension. The bones in his back and neck made popping sounds.

He let his arms drop to his side and turned his head to look over his shoulder. He noticed a pair of white leather athletic shoes tied together by the shoelaces hanging from a hook on the T-board. Trophy fish were hung on the T-board, hooked on a nail through the eye, so a photographer could take a photo of it with the proud angler who caught it.

"Not my size," he mumbled about the athletic shoes. "This whole place is just not my size."

Earl didn't want to go back to his boat just yet. He wanted some coffee. He wanted something to eat. He felt a sense of urgency to move on and get out of town. A new surge of energy and determination that he had not felt in a long, long time came over him. "Guess my flip flops will do just fine. I'll be good. I just know it."

Earl was convinced that his decision to leave the 'Lucky Two' behind and go to Biloxi was the right choice. He started to walk across the parking lot to his truck. By the time he got to his truck he was smiling.

A couple of the stray cats wandering around the garbage can by Smith's Restaurant caught his attention. "There's that cat that looks like Eleanore's cat, Princess, again," he said out loud. Seeing the cat and thinking of Eleanore sealed his desire to hurry up and leave.

However, once he reached the truck he realized that he probably needed to get some of his stuff out of the 'Lucky Two'. Surely there was something in there he should take with him.

He cautioned himself. "Man, my mind is running way too fast."

His shaking right hand gripped the truck's driver's side door handle and opened it. He slipped onto the seat and held onto the steering wheel tight. He noticed the cars driving over the north lagoon bridge.

"Where are they going?" he wondered out loud. "I'm going nowhere. No! That's not right. I am going somewhere!"

He took a few deep breaths to try and calm down. Looking over to the passenger side of the seat he saw his sunglasses, a phone book, a small black notebook, and a pile of receipts. He looked out the passenger window and saw nothing but woods, a line of oaks and tall pine trees. "Wonder if the cats go there during the hurricane," he thought.

He suddenly jerked his body back out the open door of the truck. "I'm confused, but one thing I am sure about. I am getting out of here and out of this business. I don't know what I'm going do with my life, but I know anything else will be better than this. I am so sure!"

"HEY again!" he yelled across the parking lot to Casey standing next to the monument placed to honor the namesake of one of the founding pioneers of the marina, Mr. Max Anderson. The monument was erected to honor the man. Mr. Anderson was a fisherman and also started a dinner cruise which delighted tourists who liked to be out on the water but didn't want to fish.

A bronze plaque on the monument described the founder's efforts in establishing the marina and building the charter boat deep sea fishing industry. Max's father, Virgil Anderson, had arrived to the area in the mid 1800's and started a community on North Bay. Mr. Max Anderson had started his fishing career in the early 1900's in St. Andrews. He and his brothers, Walter, Lambert and Virgil, moved operations to the lagoon to be closer to the Gulf of Mexico. The first fishing party boat was named the 'Miss Panama'.

Casey heard Earl call for him again. "Yeah?" Casey reluctantly answered.

"Hey, man. I want to leave you with the keys to my boat!"

Earl approached Casey, who held up his hands to stop him.

"No, man. I can't do that," Casey said loud enough for Earl to hear him from the distance.

Earl already had the keys out of his pants pockets and jingled them in the air as he continued to walk toward Casey at a fast pace. They were only thirty feet apart and it didn't take long to reach Casey.

"Like I told you, I am not supposed to assume responsibility for someone's property here," Casey repeated.

"No. Oh, no. I AM leaving you the keys. I am not asking you to move it. I am giving you the keys. Just hold on to the keys, will you?"

Casey was speechless.

Earl continued, "I know you'll be around after the storm and when I get back, IF I get back, I can just get them back from you."

"Why don't you just take your boat keys with you, sir," Casey said with authority. He was not asking Earl a question. The tone of desperation in Earl's voice was evident. It seemed like he had more problems than the approaching hurricane. "I think you'd feel better knowing that you have them with you once you leave here."

Earl's voice squeaked. "Don't know if I'm coming back. Ever coming back! NO, NEVER coming back!"

In his calmest, most reassuring voice, Casey said, "What do you mean? Everyone comes back after a hurricane evacuation."

"Nah, nah, nah. I am ready to leave for good," Earl stuttered. "Sooooo red-deeee to quit this fishing life!"

Earl fidgeted with the keys in his hands and shifted the weight of his body from foot to foot in a rhythmic way, as if he was hearing music.

"Just hold 'em for me. If the boat's still here after the storm I'll get them back from you," Earl said and cut his eyes away from Casey. "Yeah, I'll get 'em back. Right now, if I leave here with these keys in my pocket I'll feel like I have a noose hanging round my neck. I've got to loosen that noose and get away to clear my mind for a few days. No one else around here I'd trust to give 'em to but you. You, I trust!"

Casey's mouth was parted open in disbelief.

Earl held his arm up and straight out and dangled the keys between his thumb and forefinger in front of Casey. Earl was shorter than Casey, so he gradually lifted his arm up high to the level of Casey's face and continued to dangle them, waiting for Casey to take the keys.

Casey didn't notice the noise of the keys so much. The look in Earl's eyes reminded Casey of a deer caught in the headlights about to get hit by a car. He gently and slowly took the key ring dangling in front of his face. He slid the ring of keys into his own pocket and then he said to Earl, "I'm going to give you my card. Listen, you make sure that you keep it in your wallet. Don't leave it anywhere lying around. I don't want you to lose it."

Earl was breathing heavy. His face expressed a crazed look of happiness.

Casey twisted his right arm around to his back pants pocket. He felt like he was losing a little of his own composure. Nothing like this had ever happened to him before. This situation was not like any he'd read about in his training manual. He began to feel that he really wanted Earl to be on his way and out of there. Casey knew he would have another problem to deal with beside the storm coming if Earl stayed.

"You got everything loose locked up on the inside of your boat?" Casey asked Earl as he handed him his business card.

"Oh yeah." Earl fumbled with his hands before reaching out to take Casey's card. He didn't look into Casey's eyes

"You're going to get back in touch with me? Right?"

"Right."

Casey said in a stern voice, "You put this card in your wallet right now!"

Earl did what Casey told him with a jerky quickness.

"If the storm comes through here it'll take two or three days, at least before you can get through to me on a phone. In fact it could be more. So you wait wherever you are. I want you to keep trying. When you get back you better call me. Tell me you'll do that for me?"

"Hey, listen, man. I can't thank you enough for helping me out here."

"I am not doing nothing but holding on to your keys. That's all. You take care, you hear me now?"

Earl's head bounced up and down indicating a strong yes. Without saying another word he turned around and walked with a brisk animation, his arms slinging back and forth, back to his truck. Casey watched as he climbed into the truck, cranked up the engine and slowly, carefully drove through and out the parking lot.

Casey thought, "Man, I've never given advice to a man who wants to abandon his boat. That's like a fisherman abandoning his life."

CHAPTER 12: PRESSURED DECISIONS

Fluff watched Earl Keith, the captain of the 'Lucky Two', walk to his truck for the second time. She had rushed from an open spot on the sidewalk to the bushes beneath the windows of Smith's, the prized seats for customers who enjoyed watching sunsets over the lagoon. She'd ventured out to sit on the sidewalk in front of the 'Lucky Two' after Captain Keith walked to the truck the first time. She waited alone, trying to catch a glimpse of King, hopeful he'd emerge from the boat.

The bushes grew low and thick and made for the best hiding place. It was space where there was soft cool dirt, fresh open air, and a cat could easily watch the action without being observed by humans. They were the favorite spot for cats to spend time during the day.

Besides the bushes each cat had their own private hiding place. King and Fat Cat had very nice hiding places. King had shown her his storage shed, his castle, and Fat Cat had showed her his covered corner beneath a large deck.

She laid down flat on her side and panted to catch her breath after the run away from the sidewalk. Her pink tongue curled and hung out the front of her mouth. She didn't take her green eyes off Earl as he walked toward his truck. That man stirred strange feelings in her, but she didn't know what it was. None of the cats liked Captain Keith, but for her it was something else about him. It was more than a dislike. It was as if she had seen him before. If she sniffed him maybe she could make a connection to her feelings, but she wouldn't dare get close to him, or any humans.

Whenever Fluff gave in to her fear of humans she felt a wave of sadness sweep over her. She recalled her owner, Eleanore, who had shown her so much love. Eleanore had not treated her badly, except for that long ride in the car. Fluff had been afraid in the car. Fluff now knew she had made a huge mistake running away from Eleanore.

The day she jumped out of the car and ran away, across the scorching hot parking lot, was the scariest day of her life. It had been a long day of coming into contact with rude, angry people who "shooed" her away; wild-eyed cats who hissed and growled at her; and the first time in her life that she didn't have food to eat when she was hungry.

She loved her human owner, Eleanore, but now that love was lost forever. Fluff missed the days when Eleanore always spoke to her in a soft, sweet tone of voice and called her Princess. Fluff missed being petted, brushed, and cuddled. She remembered the comfort of sleeping with Eleanore in a soft warm bed at night, the pleasure of playing with a soft furry toy and the convenience of finding food and water in her own dish.

Fluff quickly learned living at the docks was not as luxurious as Eleanore's apartment. Reality set in on the first day. Life at the docks was difficult. She adapted to her new life of having only basic necessities, new friends and new name.

A few days after her arrival the other cats allowed her to follow them, at a distance, as they prowled around at night hunting for food. Being a wild, feral cat at the docks was a dangerous, yet exciting, lifestyle. She learned where to find food, safe places to hide, and a safe place to sleep. She learned to play with small creatures such as cockroaches, bugs, lizards, mice, ants and spiders.

After King chased the rat and followed it on the 'Lucky Two' Fluff sat along with ST in the bushes, watching and waiting for King.

Her green eyes nervously locked on Captain Keith when she saw him leave the boat and wander across the parking lot in the dark. When he returned to the boat both she and ST decided to leave their hiding place in the bushes. It had been hours since they'd seen King. The unfinished business of the night would have to carry on the next day.

She worried and said to ST before giving one last look at the 'Lucky Two', "I hope he is tucked away somewhere safe on that boat!"

Fluff retired to her safe hideaway between the storage shed and the building where the fish were cleaned. The fit was tight, but she had managed to create a space where she could sleep comfortably if she curled her front paws and hind legs beneath her body and snuggled her nose into her belly. The smell of fish was the big attraction on that first night alone when she searched for a safe spot to hide. She managed to find some fresh fish guts washed into the cracks of the concrete sidewalk. She licked at the crack for a long time, hungrier than she had ever felt before. It became a habitual comfort she enjoyed every night. King slept in the storage shed he called his castle next to her. It made her feel safe and secure knowing he was next door. This night was the first that King was not there.

In the early morning daylight Earl and Casey woke up Fluff. They were talking outside of her safe hideaway not far from the concrete bench. She waited until she no longer heard their voices and believed that they were gone when she decided to venture out to the bushes by Smith's.

She watched the man who always carried a gun and wore a uniform walk over to the bronze monument where oftentimes crowds of tourists gathered to read the inscription on the monument.

"So unusual," Fluff thought. "This is not the time of day for him to be here."

She saw Earl walk to his truck, sit inside, then get out, and run after Casey. She curiously observed Earl dangle the ring of keys in Casey's face and the man with the gun take the keys out of Earl's hand. Both Earl's and Casey's quick movements startled her. Frightened, she watched Casey walk to the 'Lucky Two', stop and step onto the stern of the boat.

She shuddered. "Why is HE getting on the 'Lucky Two'? That's where King is!"

Fluff cautiously moved one front paw forward, then her rear leg, and slowly took short steps out of the bushes. She turned her head sideways and upwards toward the glass windows of Smith's restaurant. The bottom frame of the window was level with the top of the bushes. Sometimes Fluff had seen faces of people peering out of the window, but there were none there this morning.

She sat on her haunches and scratched her ear, then licked both front paws. When she felt confident that no other human were nearby, she ran down the sidewalk, past the long benches where passengers would sit and wait to board the three decked dinner boat, and skidded around the corner of the sidewalk where she saw the rest of the boats lined up in full view, bobbing on the waters of the lagoon.

A two story building, the ticket office for the dinner boat and large head boat charters, sat on the corner of the end of the sidewalk. She was in open territory, in full view of anyone, but she was also close to many hiding places here. There were benches, tables, garbage cans, decks around the fish cleaning area, and other shops.

Being foolish was not an act of bravery. She nervously wondered, "Where do I want to hide while I wait and watch for King?" It was necessary to make a good decision.

"Here, Kitty, Kitty!" came a voice from above. It was Darryl standing on the 'Star Chaser' looking down at her.

Fluff crouched low and froze. She attempted to growl in defense. Darryl, she remembered, was the only captain who was kind to the cats.

Darryl pursed his lips together tight and made a noise sound between a squeak and whistle. "What cha doing down there? Are you trying to find somewhere to hang out before the storm gets here? Well good luck with that little one. Hope you find something to eat. I'm sure that there will be plenty of rotting food around here after it's all over." he said.

Fluff sensed a caring tone in his voice. She relaxed her muscles and didn't attempt to jump, run, or hide just yet.

"Hey! Casey!" Darryl's attention suddenly switched. He yelled to Casey who was standing on the stern of the 'Lucky Two' two slips away.

Startled, but not scared, Fluff stayed where she was.

"Hey!!! Caaaaseeeey!" Darryl hollered louder, getting Casey's

68

attention this time. "Where's the storm? When's it gonna get here?"

"Good question," Casey hollered back. He stepped off the 'Lucky Two' with ease and walked toward the 'Star Chaser'.

Casey stopped in front of Darryl's boat, laughed and said, "Have you been talking to cats again?"

Fluff scrambled away to hide behind a garbage can nearby.

"Oh, you know me." Darryl rolled out the words through a huge toothy grin. "Sometimes it's easier than trying to talk to some people."

"Yeah, I guess," Casey agreed.

"Saw you standing over there by the iconic Captain Max's plaque talking to Earl. Then you go on his boat. What's going on?"

Casey looked directly at Darryl but didn't know how he should answer. He folded both arms across his chest and locked his feet together. It was ironic he was getting friendly with the boat Captain he wanted to snoop on last night. He was dealing with a new set of issues today.

Casey knew what Darryl meant by the reference to Captain Max Anderson and found the word choice for the marina's namesake a little odd but not disrespectful. There was never any dispute about the fishing ability of Captain Max. Casey didn't take a bit of offense. Casey believed that this was Darryl's way of showing his fondness and respect for the great Captain Max and the family of deep sea fishermen.

Darryl felt the eye-balling he was getting from Casey. "Yep, Earl. He's a strange duck in these waters," Darryl said.

"You're telling me?!?" Casey's face revealed his shock.

"So what's going on with him? Has he got some plan for his boat? Why'd he drive off? Does he have any idea what to do?" Darryl's words burst out of his mouth like water gushing out of a busted water pipe.

Casey hesitated a moment, then said, "No. He just drove off in his truck. He told me that he just didn't want to be in this business anymore."

Stunned by what Casey just told him, Darryl reacted. "Whaaaatt?!" Then he broke into a loud laugh. "Right! I can believe that! When the times get tough, the tough get working. The weak run and hide."

"You won't believe this. He gave me the keys to his boat."

Darryl was even more stunned. "WHAT?!?!?"

"I gave him my business phone and told him to call me after the storm passes, but he walked off like he didn't care."

"You. Are. Kidding Me!" Darryl said each word slowly and distinctly.

"I know. Way, way too weird." Casey shook his head side to side and looked past Darryl over the lagoon.

"He won't be back," Darryl stated then abruptly swiveled his body around and made his way down the ladder from the captain's perch where he had been standing. He wanted to get a closer look in Casey's eyes, where he always believed the truth was found.

Casey didn't need to deny Darryl's comment about Earl coming back. He believed it was true, too. He also thought it was better to stop talking about Earl before the conversation took a bad direction.

Before Darryl could say another word Casey said, "Speaking of coming back, there's a bunch of cats like the one hiding over there. The one you've been talking to. They're all going to need a place to run," Casey chuckled. "Especially that ugly one with the missing lip! You could talk those cats into coming on your boat for a hurricane party."

Fluff was offended. "What? Is he making fun of us? He doesn't like us? Why?" Fluff thought. She sat crouched behind the garbage can. She wanted to run fast and far away from the mean man, but her instinct told her she needed to stay.

"Yeah. I have to admit I got a thing about cats," Darryl said. He stood on the deck of the 'Star Chaser' grinning at Casey without showing his teeth. It was a wide, laughing type of grin that made his eyes crinkle at the corners. "Don't know why but I've never have been a big dog fan. I like dogs and all that, but just have a little more respect for the cats. They show a lot of cleverness. I like to watch them eat a fish so delicately, licking and licking, until nothing is left but the bones. They stealth around here watching all of us and we can't even see them most of the time. I'd have one on the boat with me all the time, but I know that most cats are not fond of water splashing near them. They're not good...."

Before Darryl could finish his rambling Casey interrupted, "So what preparations are you making to get ready for the storm?"

Casey felt an urgent need to leave. He knew that he was in trouble if he stayed. If he hung around Darryl would trap him into listening to him talk and ramble on and on for another twenty or thirty minutes. This was a time when everyone needed to be thinking about preparations for the hurricane. Darryl was too nonchalant and easy going.

Even though he had been cut off in mid-sentence, Darryl easily switched to the changed subject. He didn't skip a beat. "Well, you know, I've been through it before." He removed his baseball cap from his head and ran his hand across the dome of his balding head. He had acquired the habit of running his hand through his hair whenever he was nervous. Even with no hair on the top of his head now he still unconsciously did this.

"I'm going to probably wait awhile to later today. It's at least twenty four hours away. I want to see if it takes a turn, weakens or gets stronger," Darryl said in a serious voice.

"Think you'll take your vessel somewhere?" Casey asked, keeping Darryl focused on the serious subject.

"Only if it gets up to a category four."

Casey whistled and said, "That's a hundred sixty five mile per hour winds!"

"Yep." Darryl said, trying to sound nonchalant.

Casey's attention was waning by the second. Darryl was not the type of fisherman who wanted advice. Darryl had his own thoughts and opinions about anything, and they were usually much different than what one might think of as normal.

"Hey! Guys!" A booming voice from a very large man carried across the parking lot. It was Big Joe, the kitchen chef from Smith's.

"Good morning!" Darryl yelled back.

"Yeah? What's so good about it?" Big Joe shouted back.

Big Joe had a reputation for being a short-tempered mean man. Many of the kitchen employees complained about the way he treated them while they sat together on the benches after work and the restaurant was closed. They smoked cigarettes, had a drink, and shared work stories before making the drive home. Big Joe had worked at Smith's more than twenty years. He'd seen a lot of employees come and go. He knew that they complained about him and he didn't care. Big Joe liked to believe he was a good chef and worked hard at being the best chef he could be. He worked hard in the kitchen, spending ten to twelve hours a day on his feet, walking from coolers to stoves to sinks, station to station, lifting heavy boxes and pans of food. He liked to eat what he cooked. Although he worked very hard, he steadily gained weight year after year. His short brown hair and pale skin had an ever present oily shine from working around grease fryers. His hands, arms, and legs were oversized, just like his big belly. Anyone who saw Big Joe for the first time sensed right away that he was not a joking person.

Casey attempted to be friendly. "Well, hey there Big Joe. What are you doing here so early?"

"Boss said to clean out the kitchen coolers," Big Joe answered.

Big Joe's boss, the restaurant owner, trusted Big Joe to take care of everything that had to be done with kitchen operations. Joe did an excellent job of keeping things running smooth in the back of the house. And, Joe wanted nothing to do with the operations in the front of the house. His personality worked best in the kitchen where he never failed to please a customer with the food he prepared. Spoiled food was not on the menu. If the power went out with the hurricane, which was likely to happen, there was no sense in saving any of the food. It was better to remove it now, before it had a chance to spoil and stink up the coolers.

Innocently Darryl asked, "Got a lot of food left in there?"

"Food order comes in on Thursdays, and we had a real good week end, so it's been worked down pretty good."

"How many did you feed last Saturday night?" Darryl asked, genuinely curious to know.

Big Joe was always proud to brag on the volume of food that was prepared in his kitchen. "I think we served at least six hundred people. Boss said we turned almost all of the tables at least once.

Not too bad for October."

"Wow, that's great. That's a lot of fish!" Darryl exclaimed.

"Yep. I don't think I'll need any fish in the next few days. Tourists won't come down in this kind of weather. Locals will stay home too. I need to call the food distributer and see if they can hold the truck delivery one more day to see what happens with this storm."

"I wouldn't expect truckers heading out on the road to drive south now. All they'd do is turn back around and get in a line of traffic evacuating north," said Casey. "Shouldn't be any problem postponing the delivery."

"Yep," Big Joe agreed. "Even if the truck is already packed and out on the road, they can hold the food in a refrigerated truck."

"Where's your delivery truck come from?" Darryl asked.

"Jackson, Mississippi," Big Joe answered then turned his back to Darryl. He wasn't in the mood to answer any more of Darryl's questions. After years of interacting with Captain Kay at the docks he learned that the man was just too chatty.

"What do you hear about the storm?" Big Joe asked Casey.

"Just what I heard on the radio this morning and saw on TV radar. Still pretty far out there, but it's big, gaining strength, moving fast and the weather conditions are just right for it to come this way."

"It now stretches over two hundred miles of water!" piped Darryl.

Casey said, "Yes, I know that." He felt himself becoming annoyed with Darryl too.

"How late do you think the authorities will wait before they give the orders to evacuate?" Big Joe directed his face and question to Casey.

Casey gave a thorough answer. "I don't know, maybe early afternoon today! As you know, these storms can do anything they want, but we've got this large high pressure moving in that's going to collide with the thing and it just depends on how fast these two weather forces move."

Both Big Joe and Darryl listened intently, four eyes fixed on Casey. Both men hoped in their hearts that this man with the Florida Marine Patrol uniform would be able to tell them something they didn't already know. Tell them something to reassure them that they were not going to be in any danger in the near future. Casey worked for the government and he should know what was going to happen.

"Hey guys, you both know the captain who owns the 'Lucky Two'?" Casey suddenly changed the subject.

Big Joe and Darryl shook their heads as if to shake the fog out of their brains.

"Oh, yes. Yes, of course," Darryl said first, with a hint of sarcasm.

Big Joe nodded his head yes. He was not a big talker and always a little suspicious about offering too much information about someone else unless it was something going wrong in Smith's kitchen. But, he did have something to say about Earl.

"Funny guy. When I was leaving work late last night, after locking up the kitchen, I noticed him walking across the parking lot by himself. He was carrying this rubber boot. I thought that was just a little odd."

"Tell you what's really odd about him," Casey jumped in before Darryl could speak a word. "These keys." Casey pulled the keys to the 'Lucky Two' out of his pocket and dangled them. "These are the keys to his boat. He gave them to me less than thirty minutes ago. He said to keep 'em. Said he was leaving town. He couldn't deal with the storm coming."

Big Joe was interested enough in this bit of news to hang around for more details. He knew how much work he had to do to clean out the kitchen coolers, but it could wait a few more minutes.

"Gawd dog," Big Joe said. His eyes squinted with disbelief and suspicion.

Big Joe knew Darryl could take over a conversation in a split minute. Big Joe was a man who never wasted any time, which was also the reason why he was so good in the kitchen.

"Let's cut to the chase," Big Joe said. "What exactly did he say? Where is he going?"

Casey shook his head. "He said he was going to Biloxi. He acted kind of spaced out, like he must have been awake all night and didn't get any sleep. He didn't make any sense to me." Casey added, "His eyes looked pretty weird, too."

"Never could handle the business here," Darryl slipped in.

"Pretty damn weird," was all Big Joe could muster from his mouth.

Casey continued, "He said he wanted me to look after the boat! Like he wanted me to keep it!"

"No way?!?!" Big Joe exclaimed.

"Oh Yeah!" Casey said, nodding his head.

Casey rolled his eyes upward to the sky. "As if dealing with the weather, locals and tourists aren't enough," Casey said.

"Yeah, tell ME about it," Big Joe's voice boomed with exasperation. "Listen, I gotta get this food out of the coolers. You guys want some?"

Without hesitation, or thinking ahead, both men said yes. Big Joe was not known for his patience.

"Let me check the ice machines to see how much ice we've got then," Big Joe said.

"You guys aren't going to try and run generators to keep the food from spoiling?" Casey asked, thinking it was a safe question.

Generators were a good back up source of power for the kitchen at Smith's, but they would be good for only one or two days maximum. If a big storm with the potential of a strong hurricane came through the area it could be a week, maybe longer, before power was restored to the beach. Not many people lived on the island as year round residents. Most of the people lived on the east side of bridge, on the mainland in Panama City. If power was lost the power would be restored on the mainland first. Food did not last more than a week in the coolers anyway. It spoiled quickly. In October the kitchen coolers were not as full with meat and seafood. It would cost less to give it away than to try and keep it from spoiling.

"Nope," he said. "Boss wants it to go to charity, or the Red Cross. They'll need the food if the storm comes through here. And, there's not as much as there could be. Especially if we have the truck order stopped. You guys come on over in about an hour. I'll have things sorted out by then. I need to go and get on the phone."

Big Joe lifted up his large hairy left arm to check his watch. "Wow," he said with a hint of irritation. "It's already 7:30. See you guys later."

Big Joe lumbered his large body around and started to walk to Smith's. Turning his head back to them he said, "Just come around to the back door if you want some steaks to grill. I think I got plenty."

"I'd like to get some of that stuff!" Darryl grinned at Casey and turned his head toward the 'Lucky Two'. "You going back on that boat and see what's loose in there?"

"No, I don't think so. I'm too busy," Casey said and shoved the keys back into his pants pocket. Then he said in a strange voice, "I'll see you maybe later at Smith's. If I don't see you make sure you get some extra ice from Smith's and stock up on food and supplies. If you plan to take the 'Star Chaser' up to the bays or intracoastal you better get a move on."

Casey turned around and hurried away from Darryl.

"Later," Darryl said to himself.

Darryl already felt tired. He sat down on the concrete bench, rested both of his elbows on the concrete table, and cupped his chin into the palms of both hands. He stared over the rippling water of the lagoon and thought about how much he loved to fish and live on his boat. He didn't want to leave the boat at the marina. He knew he couldn't stay at the marina in a storm as big and bad as Louise had the potential to be. It was all a matter of timing: if and when was the big question. He remembered the four men from Hoover, Alabama who wanted to go out with him to fish. "They aren't going to show up today. So, there's no pressure for me to stay around. Might as well leave," he thought.

He turned his eyes away from the water and looked down at the cracks in the sidewalk, staring at the dried fish scales and tiny bits of paper trash. In the corner of his eyes he picked up a flash of movement. Darryl lazily moved his head out of the cupped hands and turned his body half circle toward the building where fish were cleaned. White fur was barely visible behind a nearby trash can. The white cat he'd been talking to earlier was hiding. It would never come out in broad daylight with him sitting there so close. Nevertheless he loved every opportunity to talk to a cat. It felt better than talking to a human being sometimes.

"Hey kitty, it's you again. Want to go for a ride on my boat?"

Darryl stood up and stretched his arms above his head. "Better get ready for the storm. One way or another, it's going to affect us. Better go find yourself a hiding place." The warning was for himself and Fluff.

Fluff stared intently at Darryl as he idly walked back to his boat. The soft tone in his voice reminded him of Eleanore who used to talk to Fluff in the same caring tone of voice. Fluff fought the emotion to walk out of her hiding place and rub her body against Darryl's leg. She had learned from the other cats that humans couldn't be trusted, but Darryl was different. He was the kind boat captain who threw scraps of food to the cats.

Her mind raced. After listening to the conversation of the three men Fluff was more anxious about King. Captain Keith was gone and it sounded like he wasn't coming back. Casey was gone too but would he come back to the boat? She didn't trust Casey.

She inched out from behind the garbage can one paw at a time, crouching low and slowly forward. She was ready to make a dash. Fluff raised her head and sniffed the air. The air felt different. Her fur stood straight up on her back.

She felt an urgent need to find King. "He needs to be warned. Those men talked about a dangerous storm coming and I think I heard fear in their voices! A boat does not seem like a good, safe hiding place. Captain Darryl warned me, I need to warn King! This cat and rat chase is over."

The idea of being safe with King gave her new courage. She arched her back, held her tail high, wagged her hind quarters and quickly sprinted toward the 'Lucky Two'. Using her rear legs to propel her body she leapt high and stretched her front paws straight, far out in front of the rest of her body. She flew through the air. In seconds she landed onto the boat.

"Oh, my gosh. I'm on the boat!" She exclaimed as she skidded across the deck. She slinked along the fiberglass wall to be out of view of the humans she had learned to fear.

The fears she faced on the strange boat would be small compared to the fears she faced when the big storm to be named Hurricane Louise arrived the next day.

CHAPTER 13: EARL'S MEMORY LANE

The volume on the truck radio was turned up very loud. Earl drove with his windows down. He was traveling north on highway 79, crossing over the West Bay Bridge and didn't even glance to either side to take a last look at the water. He felt free and was not the least bit interested in looking at the water.

That feeling of freedom was interrupted by painful tight squeezes accompanied by loud growling noises coming from his stomach. Earl realized that he had not eaten anything since yesterday. Was it afternoon or evening that he last ate? He wasn't sure. Today he didn't have the usual plastic wrapped pastry along with a cup of coffee for breakfast. The morning had come and gone too fast.

Last night's dinner for Earl was a can of spaghetti warmed up in a plastic bowl in the microwave oven. The best part of dinner was the two beers, a bubbly tonic that washed down the food. Even though his stomach was in knots, the reminder of such a meager meal made him feel better about leaving.

His body had changed quite a bit in the time he'd spent on the 'Lucky Two'. He wasn't happy about those changes at all. He thought he was downright ugly now. In just a little over two years he had become skinny with muscles protruding through tanned taunt skin on his thin legs and arms. He was not the beefy muscular chick magnet that he used to be back home in Pine Mountain.

Thinking about the past didn't help, but he couldn't help it. He had hit rock bottom. He had wasted his time and money. He really didn't want to go to Biloxi but going back to Pine Mountain was not going to be easy. Eleanore did not even want to speak to him on the telephone last night. Earl searched for a way to somehow comfort his mind while he drove.

"Dang! I had it pretty good in Pine Mountain," Earl groaned out loud. "Granny. Yeah, Granny. I'll think about her."

His grandmother had been the one woman in his life who always showed her love for him. She never got angry at him. She always believed in him.

"I let you down, granny. I'm going to change and make it better." Earl choked as he said these words.

Earl was her only grandchild. She gave him everything he asked for and treated him like he was her favorite thing in the world, which he was. When she died, no one in the family and the entire town of Pine Mountain was surprised when she left Earl all of her money, which was a sizable sum. She left her jewelry, land and home to other members of the family, who she knew would be better off with those items. Most people took it for granted that Earl would just waste away the cash, spending it on nothing of real value.

People in Pine Mountain were quite surprised, though, when Earl announced quite suddenly not long after the death of his grandmother that he was leaving town to become a businessman running a deep sea fishing charter boat in Panama City Beach.

After his grandmother died, Earl spent a week-end alone on Panama City Beach and chartered a deep sea fishing trip. He experienced the thrill of his life after catching more fish than he'd ever caught before. He picked up a Sunday newspaper before leaving town to return home. In it he found a boat for sale in the classified ads for less money than his inheritance. That's when the whole idea began to form in his head.

He loved the excitement of seeing more than two hundred pounds of fish being caught in a single twelve hour trip by a group of four men. So many fish that he couldn't remember all the names. It was dizzying fun. It seemed to him the ideal way to make money.

Earl didn't wait more than a day to call the telephone number in the classified ad. He arranged for a meeting with the seller of the boat the following weekend. Earl fell in love with the boat, 'My Girl' and thought immediately of Eleanore. He closed the deal that same week end.

When his friends in Pine Mountain heard the story of his plans they knew it would not be as simple as Earl dreamed it would be. Earl was known to be quite a dreamer. The only person to argue with him was Eleanore.

Before that night when he announced to her that he had bought the boat Eleanore had pleaded with him, many times, to use the money his granny left him to go to the local community college. That should come first, she had told him. Learn some business skills. Then they could move to Atlanta where all the good paying jobs were. He could enjoy weekends going to the beach and fishing whenever he wanted. The big city would be more exciting, she had told him, than going to the beach all the time.

As it turned out Earl needed to spend six weeks in Sea School studying for his captain's license to operate the deep sea fishing boat. The test was not difficult and he easily passed it. The most difficult part for Earl was the wait. He was ready to start fishing, have some fun, and make money. He was motivated to have fun and make money.

On the last Sunday Earl spent in Pine Mountain he went to his church where he'd spent many Sundays when he was growing up. Recently his attendance had dropped off to Easter and Christmas church services. But, he wanted to say goodbye to everyone in town and make sure that everyone knew his plans.

As he sat in the pew that morning, Earl's heart was filled with hubris and confidence. He was humble and thanked God for his riches. Earl prayed for His help to make him successful in all the plans for his future.

The preacher's sermon on that day was centered on chapter sixteen, verse thirteen, from the book of Luke in the New Testament. The preacher spoke feverishly, waving his hands in front of the congregation of worshipers, about mammon. Not knowing what the word 'mammon' meant, Earl ignored the words in the sermon and daydreamed about his new future. It was awaiting him.

The memories saddened Earl.

His stomach growled again and the hunger pains grew stronger.

"I'd better get something in my stomach if I'm going make this long drive," he said out loud, deliberately trying to clear the memories. Earl tried to keep beef jerky in the box compartment inside his truck but didn't check it. He knew the search would be time wasted. "What I could really use right now is a good, brewed cup of black coffee!"

Earl remembered there was a gas station and small convenience store after he crossed the West Bay Bridge. There had been one or two occasions when he left the beach traveling on highway 79. If he turned right at the convenience store and headed east on county road 388 he could reach highway 231 and be heading north, back home to Georgia.

"No, I am going to Biloxi first. I want to win a little money. Gamble on the machines. I can't go home broke."

Earl wondered exactly how much money he had left and he suddenly remembered the two men he took money from who asked for a half day charter. They were supposed to be on his boat today. He realized that he had more money to spend in Biloxi than he thought.

He groaned with guilt and said to himself, "Those men need the money just as bad as me. They were digging deep in their pockets to pay for the trip. It's too late to turn around and go back to the marina to find them and give it back. I'm messing up everything. Maybe someday I'll get something right!"

A solid line of cars moved over the bridge at a slower pace than normal.

The loud music on the radio, which had been only background noise in Earl's ears, was suddenly interrupted by the loud voice of an announcer who said, "We're going to give an update on Louise. The tropical storm has now formed into a hurricane. Winds are now well over seventy four miles per hour with gusts of nearly ninety."

A startled Earl yelled, "Why does this have to happen to me? I've spent almost all my money in just over two years' time with nothing' to show for it. Got a boat that will be worthless in about a day. No insurance to cover it if it's destroyed, which I dang sure bet it will be. Nothing! And, I feel like a thief for taking money from someone I don't even know!"

Earl pounded on the steering wheel with the one hand he'd been using to steer. The truck, now at the crest of the bridge, veered and swerved toward the center line. Earl grabbed wheel with both hands and steered the truck back on the right side of the yellow line. Luckily no one was coming in the opposite direction.

Earl took a few deep breaths to calm down his racing heart. "Don't need an accident now."

The radio announcer continued, "Hurricane Louise is expected to remain on the track it's on for the next twenty four to thirty six hours, drifting west, northwest, at ten miles per hour. It is expected to gain more speed during the day. Again, those coordinates for you to keep track on your maps are twenty seven degrees north and seventy nine degrees west. We'll be bringing you updates every hour, on the hour, helping you keep track of this potentially dangerous storm. Remember, the hurricane is expected to make landfall on the northern gulf coast somewhere between New Orleans, Louisiana and Port St. Joe, Florida within the next forty eight hours. At this time the forecasters in the hurricane center in Miami are predicting it is possible for this storm, because of the warmer waters, size and movement, to become a category three hurricane reaching one hundred and forty mile per hour winds when it makes landfall."

Earl wanted to stop listening to the announcer. The predictions scared him. It also convinced him that he was doing the right thing,

Lastly the radio announcer finished the five minute hurricane update saying, "Residents living all along the gulf coast and in low lying areas are being asked to make plans now for when possible mandatory evacuations are ordered, which will be issued for specific areas in the next twenty four hours."

"I did the right thing jumping ship," Earl said.

Earl eased his sadness about his failure with those words, but he felt the wistful tug at his heart about leaving the 'Lucky Two'. He took a quick last glance over the concrete side walls on the bridge. The walls were placed at eye level to prevent people from getting distracted. Many people loved to look at the scenery as they drove over the bridge. The height of the wall did not prevent a person from climbing over it and jumping over the side, which some had tried. Earl couldn't think of killing himself despite his despondency about leaving his hope and dream.

Finally Earl's truck descended the steep slope of the West Bay Bridge and made it to the first destination. The 'One Stop' convenience store and gas station was there at the end of the bridge. The strong smell of fried chicken drifted from the building and through the truck's open window. The smell took over his senses when he rolled into the parking lot and pulled the truck up next to the gas pump.

Earl's stomach let out a loud noise that couldn't be ignored any longer. It was the painful rumbling gurgle of raw hunger. It was real pain, not just an annoying fluttering tingle in his belly. The kind of gurgle that you hear and you know that it's your own. Anyone else standing within five feet of Earl would have heard it too.

The smell of real food, not canned food, gave his mind a single focus. He threw the gears of the truck into park and reached around to his back pocket for his wallet. He remembered how Eleanore used to serve that fresh fried chicken at the Kountry Kafe in Pine Mountain.

"Don't smell as good as the KK in Pine Mountain. That smelled a whole lot better. This'll do for now. I am God awful hungry for something good to eat! It's been a long time! This will be a blessed change from what I've had to eat lately!"

Earl looked around the parking lot and saw no other cars or trucks. For a moment he wondered if the 'One Stop' was even open.

He stepped out of the truck and walked up to the dirty glass door filmed over with road dust. He pushed on the metal bar to open the door.

"Hey! I wouldn't have smelled fried chicken unless they were open," he reassured himself. Inside the building a lit neon sign advertised cold beer. Earl briefly noted that a beer would taste good with fried chicken. "Better stick with the black coffee," he thought.

At first Earl saw no one inside. In a few minutes a young looking woman, with greasy long brown hair pulled back behind her pale white ears appeared from a back room doorway. The woman wore a sky blue loose T-shirt and tight blue jeans. A large belly jiggled beneath the loose cotton fabric of the t-shirt and thick thighs rippled inside tight fitting denim. Earl grimaced as he thought of this very over weight young woman eating too much of her own fried chicken.

"Can I help you?" she asked in a genuine friendly voice oozing a southern Alabama accent. Southern accents of people vary by the state that they live in. Earl recognized that drawl was not from Georgia.

"I'm gonna fill up with gas and I'd like to get something to eat. Smells like you got some fried chicken cooking," Earl answered, trying hard to be genuinely friendly too.

"Yes sir. Got some frying in the back right now...it's nearly done. I can check on it to see how much longer before it'll be ready," she replied. "You said you want gas too?"

"Yeah, I need gas," Earl said.

"OK. I'll open up pump number two if that's your truck out there, the black one?"

"Yeah," Earl nodded his head to his truck, the only one out there.

"OK. You paying cash?"

Earl forgot that his wallet was still in the truck and said, "Oh, yeah, sure I am. Money's in my truck."

"I'll need to know how much gas you want," she said.

"I'll go get thirty dollars for the gas and how much for the chicken?" Earl asked.

"Chicken depends on how many pieces you want. We got a six

80

piece special for four dollars and seventy nine cents. It includes tax. Or, you can get an eight piece with two biscuits or four small rolls for six ninety nine."

Earl thought about the number of pieces he could eat for a minute. He was hungry. He remembered the coffee he really wanted. "Got any fresh coffee ready?"

"Of course," she answered politely.

"I'll have a large cup of coffee and the six-piece special. How much will all that add up to?"

The round faced sweet girl wrote down the numbers and answered Earl, "So, thirty dollars for gas, six-piece chicken and a large coffee will be thirty six dollars even."

"I'll be back in a few minutes with the money," Earl said.

Earl turned around to push open the glass door and thought, "Why do some women stop caring about their appearance and how they look? What makes that happen?"

Earl opened the passenger side door of the truck and picked up his wallet off the bench seat. He quickly counted the cash, all the money he had left. There was none in a bank account. He felt a little tinge of fear. How long would this money last? He had enough to pay this bill, but how many more days could he live on what was left? A trip to Biloxi might be a losing gamble, too. He noticed the price of the gas on the pump and felt worse. Last week the price had been only a dollar eighty nine and now it was two fifty nine a gallon.

"Why did that happen?" he wondered.

Earl took the money out of his wallet, counted the money he needed and dropped the wallet back on the seat. He didn't want to open his wallet, with a thick wad of green bills, in full view of the girl's eyes.

"Here's the money. Nice even number like you said," Earl said to the girl as he handed over the money. "Where's that coffee?"

"Over there on that counter to the right."

"I'll go gas up and be right back."

"Your chicken will be ready by the time you finish pumping your gas," she called to Earl as he turned to walk out the glass door.

"If you have any packets of honey, throw them in the bag too," Earl said and pushed the door open for a second time to go outside and pump the gas. When he finished Earl went to get his chicken and coffee.

"Here's your chicken. I threw in a couple of extra rolls since we ain't got no honey," she said nicely.

"Well thanks a lot," Earl said a little sarcastically. "I'd prefer honey and cheaper gas."

"Well, I know that the gas is high. Always goes up when a storm is coming. Will this be all?" the girl replied flatly. She'd dealt with difficult customers many times and didn't see a need to waste any more time trying to be nice to the man who at first seemed to be a decent sort of person.

Earl felt bad as soon as he snapped at the counter girl who he knew didn't have anything to do with the price of gas.

"What's your name?" Earl asked her.

Shyly she answered "Grace." Her face blushed red.

"Grace, I know it ain't your fault about the gas. I'm sorry," he said.

"Which way you headed?" Grace asked Earl.

"I don't know for sure," he answered thinking she wouldn't be half bad looking if she lost maybe seventy five pounds. "I was thinking about Biloxi, but maybe I'll head back north to Georgia. Know of any good places to stay in Biloxi?"

"The only place I've ever heard people talk about is the Windjammer," Grace answered wistfully as if wishing she was going with Earl. "Yeah, someone I met told me they went there."

"Well then! Maybe I'll try it!"

With those final words Earl nodded his head to Grace and went through the glass door for the last time.

He set his box of warm fried chicken down on the bench seat before he slid in behind the steering wheel, still holding his cup of coffee in one hand. With his free hand he shut the door. He slipped the styrofoam cup into the plastic cup holder mounted on the door next to the window handle. He turned the keys to start the engine and paused, uncertain about what he was about to do next.

Eat or drive? Drive and eat? Drive, but where?

Earl shifted the truck into gear, placed two hands on the steering wheel, tapped his right foot lightly on the gas pedal and very slowly drove away from the gas pump. He stopped to look at the road signs.

He remembered Casey Howard tell him the storm may head west to Biloxi. The money in his wallet would be enough to go to Pine Mountain.

He reached inside the bag to grab a piece of chicken. It was a wing.

"Wings are for flying," he smiled at the thought.

He turned the truck north on highway 79. He had more time to drive north before deciding to go east or head west.

"Darn, forgot to pick up some napkins," he muttered after he took the first bite and hot grease dripped down his fingers. "Not bad," he said when the flavor of seasoned chicken meat fried in grease hit the taste buds on his tongue. It was the first taste of fresh, hot food he had put into his mouth in a long time. Earl chewed the chicken slowly, savoring the flavor.

He swallowed the first bite of food and aggressively took another bite, chewing it more quickly. He picked up the cup of coffee, which had cooled down a bit, and took big gulps to wash down the bites of chicken he was eating more rapidly.

He hadn't been on a road trip since he moved to Panama City Beach. It felt different to be happy traveling north. As a visitor he had always been happier when he was heading south toward the beach and gloomier when he was heading back home.

He felt freedom. Free from the daily worries of operating his business. Free from people. Free to do what he wanted without worrying about how someone else felt about it. It had been too long since Earl had felt this happy about being free

He recalled Granny Keith's words of advice to him. "She was one special woman. She always made me feel special," Earl remembered. "She told me 'Earl, don't let anyone tell you what to do with your life or how to run the affairs of your life. You always think for yourself and have confidence when you decide on what to do. Think big dreams and don't short change yourself. You're a good boy and granny loves you!' Now my Granny Keith was special. Her words meant more to me than money she left me. Her words of kindness and encouragement keep me hopeful. Right now I can't see what what's in my future. Eleanore's not. She made that clear on the telephone last night that it's over."

Earl talked loudly over the music on the radio. He threw the second bone of the chicken out the open window. His hunger for food was satisfied, but not the hunger for an answer to the direction for his life.

"I'm fleeing from this hurricane Louise but I'm really fleeing that boat 'Lucky Two' which will be worth nothing if it gets destroyed by the storm. If it doesn't get destroyed, I'll have to sell it. I can't support myself working on it. There's no future for me in Pine Mountain. I'll keep on going west, past Biloxi to Texas, or California or Oregon. I'll try something new."

Earl looked at the dashboard to check his speedometer. He had not noticed a speed limit sign. He could see cars in the distance ahead. He noticed no cars in the lane going south. The gas gauge was almost to the full line. How far could he drive on a full tank of gas? What towns besides Biloxi would be a good place to stop? He wanted a good night's sleep in a good bed in one of those fancy casinos. He just might just be a winner in Biloxi. Leaving his failure, and the past, felt good.

"Yes, Granny, Biloxi here I come. I'm going to discover my opportunity out west! Just like a cowboy. Yeeeehawww!" Earl shouted inside the cab of the truck.

Earl glanced up at the rear view mirror. He saw a long line of cars from far behind.

"Okay, were going keep everyone up to date on Hurricane Louise, but for now it's gonna be a little country with a lot of soul. This is what we play to get you through the day on your radio station....."

Earl didn't hear the rest. The radio announcer's voice drifted into the wind. With the word *country* fixed in his head Earl began to think about the drive to a new state far out west. He was dreaming big about a new life and a new home.

"Dream big and don't find yourself living in the shadow of someone else's dream!" Granny Keith's beautiful voice sounded in his head again.

CHAPTER 14: CATS ALONE HIDING

King pried his eyes open. His ears perked up straight. His normal senses were dull. The early morning light shone dim inside of the boat cabin where he had slept through the night with his body curled up into a flat ball against the wall. His muscles ached.

When Earl woke early, King feared he would be noticed. King was tremendously relieved when Earl left the boat soon after he awoke. The night before had been nerve racking after Earl returned to the boat, shut the window and talked loudly in a bitter, angry voice.

King's nose twitched. He took short breaths, trying to find fresh air inside the closed cabin.

During the night King woke up several times to hear the scratching of the rat's feet inside the hull beneath him, in the belly of the boat. Like Earl, King was annoyed when he heard the rat, but not for the same reason. King knew the rat was likely going to find a small crevice somewhere to squeeze his body through, escape and jump off the boat. The rat would be gone. The game of chase it, catch it, and to leave it dead for the boat captain to find was over. King knew he had lost the game.

The game was different now. How was he going to get off the boat now that he was locked up inside?

The tip of his tail switched back and forth like a pendulum on a clock. It was a movement he could not control. It switched and twitched while he sat pondering his problem.

Shortly after Earl left, King heard the muffled voices of men talking outside. They were voices he thought he recognized, but he was not sure. It didn't matter. He only needed to be on alert for Earl's return.

King did not hear a noise when Fluff jumped onto the boat deck or when she raced on her soft padded paws along the starboard side to the bow of the boat.

He stared at the small window through which he had entered the night before. He could not wish it open. He knew that. He turned his head to the slatted wood door to the cabin, also closed to his escape.

"No way out unless..." Something distracted King. His eyes detected motion by the window. King's body stiffened. He crouched low.

In amazement and in stunned surprise he saw Fluff like a white cloud, a white fluffy ball of fur, staring at him through the window. He made a soft gurgling noise, something between a purr and meow.

With two quick leaps, one to the table and one to the window ledge, he found his face nose to nose with Fluff's.

They paced taking short steps. Fluff on the window ledge and King on the table, stopping often to bring their faces to the window and to look at each other eyeball to eyeball, nose to nose, through the glass window. King, so happy and relieved to see Fluff's familiar face, desperately wanted to be out of the locked cabin as much as Fluff wanted him out too.

King sat up on his hind legs and pawed the window with his two front paws. He rolled on the table to his side and tried to slip his paw, claws extended out, beneath any crack in the window track. Fluff stretched her body and extended it to the top of the window, trying along with King to find an opening. It was a frantic effort.

Frustrated, Fluff stopped her pawing and watched King, lying weak on his side, continue to fruitlessly paw and grab at the corner of the window. They both knew if caught at the right spot in the groove of the track the window would slide open. If only one claw could hook into the smallest gap.

Exhausted, King finally stopped. Fluff turned and walked away.

"Where is she going?" he thought. He started to feel hopeless. He was so tired from the sleepless night. All the energy left in his body was nearly gone. He jumped back down to the floor and flopped down. He stretched his front paws straight forward and hind legs straight back. All four limbs vibrated with his stretch. Then he tried to lick his front paws. His mouth was dry from not drinking anything since the night before.

The air inside the cabin was stale and stuffy. He opened his mouth and panted to cool himself. The fiberglass floor of the boat was not nearly as nice as the cool dirt beneath the bushes.

King closed his eyes and laid his head down between his two front paws on the floor. There was nothing else he could do except listen for noises from the outside world.

The noises made by the rat scampering below had stopped. The water splashing against the sides of the boat and the creaking of the boat caused by the motion of the waves added to his anxiety. He knew it did not help to worry, but he still didn't have any idea when he would get another chance to escape from the boat. He couldn't remember the last time he had not been in control of his comings and goings.

Fluff cautiously pattered back to the stern where she originally jumped onto the boat. The marina parking lot was back in plain view. She did not want anyone to see her on the boat. She crouched down low. She held her four paws close to her body and her belly touched the deck.

"It's a good thing that my fur is white," she thought. "Few humans are out there, but if they look this way it will be more difficult to see me against the background of a solid white boat deck."

All she could do was think about King's predicament. How could he be freed?

She wondered, "Why have no boats left their slips at the marina. By this time in the day most of these deep sea captains have their boats already out by now. Why even the large head boat is still here. That's the one that always leaves with the most fishermen."

From where she was crouched she also had a view of the parking lot. "The parking lot is almost empty. Only a few cars are parked out there."

Too many things confused her. She wondered why things did not seem normal at the marina. "If it is pouring down rain then the parking lot is always empty, but we've seen boats leave during occasional rain showers! I heard Darryl and the other two men talking about bad weather, but when?"

Fluff was overwhelmed with worry. King was locked up inside the boat. What happened to the owner? That mean guy. Nobody leaves their boat locked up and empty on a good day for fishermen.

The bravery she felt when she took the leap on the 'Lucky Two' was gone. Fluff forgot for a moment where she was and meowed so loud that the sound echoed across the water. Fluff cut short the urge to release a second meow. "I should leave now and find another cat. Maybe Fat Cat can help. He may laugh. But, if I stay here alone what am I going to do next?"

Within seconds the sound of heavy footsteps of a large person approaching the boat interrupted her thoughts. It was actually the sound of footsteps from more than one person getting closer and closer.

"Oh,OH! How can I get off the boat now?" she cried, despondent. She flattened her ears close to her head and crouched low. Her tail was glued flat down on the deck. "It's too late! I could run fast and take a flying leap to the sidewalk, but what if I land in the water?"

The thought of landing with a splash in the smelly water below was too repugnant. There was no chance, or way, she could climb up the round, wooden, slippery pilings or a concrete wall. She knew she couldn't swim all the way to the shoreline beneath the lagoon bridge. That was much too far. She had seen a cat fall into the water once. The cat's head bobbed up and down, in and out of the water, while it slowly swam toward the bridge. Even though the cat had survived, it wasn't a pretty sight to watch. It was a bad memory.

"I have to find a place to hide somewhere on this boat!"

Fluff jerked up and swiftly scampered away. Her paw claws were extended for traction and nosily scratched the deck. Near the stairs leading to the cabin door laid a large black object. It was the rubber boot that Earl picked up in the parking lot the night before. Fluff scurried over to the boot and crawled behind it. The opening was large enough for her to fit inside. Anyone that came onto the boat, would never think to look inside of a rubber boot.

Half contentedly she said after hiding, "I'm still with King."

87

CHAPTER 15: CHARTERED AND CHEATED

Two young men walked across the black asphalt parking lot and stopped next to the concrete table in front of the 'Lucky Two'. In unison they turned their heads left, then right, and then shifted their bodies around, in opposite circular turns to look around the parking lot. Finally the two men turned their heads in the same direction to face the lineup of quiet charter boats bobbing in the brownish water.

"Well," the taller, huskier man with a sharp nose and dark hair spoke up first. "This is the boat, but I don't see anyone here on it." His voice had an angry edge as he spoke to a small framed man whose wide eyes, freckled faced, and strawberry blond hair, made him appear like a fearful, nervous puppy dog. The smaller man swallowed hard before he spoke.

"Vince," he spoke in a softer voice. "What now? Who else would be around here who could we talk to about getting our money back?"

Both men wore a typical tourist uniform of cutoff jeans and new spray painted t-shirts. The skin not covered by their clothing, which had the rumpled look of sleepwear, revealed the color of ripe red tomatoes.

The bigger man's cold dark eyes glared at the boats before he turned to look at his companion and answer.

"Well, Ricky. I can blame myself right now. I didn't get a receipt or even get a business card or nothing. I am gonna have to figure out a way to make this right. I had a bad feeling about this guy yesterday."

"So did I Vince. A baaad... feeling." Ricky tried to be agreeable and energetic. He sensed anger beginning to build up inside the husky body of Vince. "But what else was we gonna do? We wanted to go fishing and he was the cheapest boat for a half day. It's so dang expensive around this place for anything. I don't know how other people can afford it!"

Vince stomped his foot on the concrete. "We shoulda been watching the weather channel at the hotel room last night instead of that dang TV channel with all the commercials about what to do and where to go on the beach. Heck, we knew we was gonna get up early and go fishing! This guy's taken off with our money. I wonder if he's left for good or if he's gone to get some supplies and coming back to get the boat."

"Maybe he's already gone for good and leaving the boat here. The boat looks all locked up," Ricky said, hoping to be helpful.

"So here we are and he's gone off with the money we gave him. We can't hang around here too much longer ourselves. If we want to get back home safe we'd best get on out of town," Vince spat on the ground. "Preferably with our money."

"Yeah," Ricky spoke softly, responding to Vince's mood. "Maybe if we walk around a few more minutes we will see someone we can ask about this guy. I don't remember his name, do you?"

Vince spat again. "Walk where? We got to ask someone if they know the guy who owns this here boat. 'Lucky Two'. YEAH, real lucky for us."

As the two young men carried on their conversation, trying to come to terms with the loss of their money and decide whether to wait around to find out if it was possible to get a refund from the missing captain of the 'Lucky Two' before they left for home, three individuals were close enough nearby to notice them and take an interest in them.

Fluff was on the 'Lucky Two' and wondered if she would need to crawl inside the black rubber boot to hide from these new visitors if they boarded the boat.

Casey was still hanging around the corner of the fish cleaning house trying not to think about the 'Lucky Two' and trying to focus on doing his job. He watched the white truck with the two men in it slowly pull into the parking lot, park, get out of the truck and walk toward the 'Lucky Two'. He hoped the two men would not approach him and ask him for help. Casey had a gut feeling that these men were looking for Captain Keith. It had to be something about getting money back from the boat captain. People always had a complaint when it came to their money. If asked, he would tell the men that he knew Captain Keith had left town. That was all he would say if they asked him.

Darryl was working on his boat the 'Star Chaser' trying to get it hurricane ready. He was never one to be at a loss for words if there was someone he took an interest in talking to. Noticing the two men standing nearby, overhearing the conversation, he decided it was time to take a break. This was an occasion when he was interested in the problem of these two men.

"Hey! Guys!" Darryl yelled over to the two men.

Both Vince and Ricky turned their heads toward Darryl, who was already stepping over the side of the 'Star Chaser'. They stood and stared at him as he casually strolled toward them.

"Sounds like you guys got a problem," Darryl said when he stopped and faced them both.

"You know the captain who runs this boat?" Vince asked with a slight hint of friendliness and hopefulness.

"Yep, sure do. A little, I guess. Hey, it looks like you two spent a day in the sun without sunscreen."

Vince and Ricky turned their heads away from Darryl and looked at each other. Their eyes silently traded a message: this was not the best guy to be talking to about the refund. Their *silent secret look* of communicating began back in the days when they first became best buddies. It was a simple message. A 'he's not all there in the head' or 'he don't know who he's dealing with' look.

Vince spoke first, using a sly tone of voice that Ricky recognized. "Yeah, man. A little too much sun. Probably better that we're not going out in the gulf fishing today. We bought a half-day trip from the operator of this boat yesterday. That's before we knew about this bad storm coming."

Darryl laughed and said, "The storm's name is Louise. Yup, she's a coming this way. You won't find the man who runs this boat around here today. He's already headed out of town."

For about ten seconds Vince and Ricky stared at Darryl with mouths hanging open. They were not prepared for the bad news and the cheerful, enthusiastic way Darryl delivered it. Then they locked eyes with each other again. Their glassy eyes and red skinned faces shone with anger after hearing that their suspicions were confirmed.

"Headin' out of town, huh?" Vince's words erupted angrily.

"You guys got a receipt for what you paid?" Darryl innocently asked, genuinely curious. Some businesses on the beach ran their operation as a cash only business. Mostly all businessmen, like Darryl, kept paperwork and tried to run an honest business.

Earl Keith had never socialized with the other boat captains. He rarely even said hello to anyone. Most of the captains, while not overly friendly with each other, took a keen interest in the business other captains were getting. It was an informal, professional business association without the annual association rules, dues, official officers, and executive committee. The best way to find out business trends, and monitor the reputation of the industry, was to occasionally talk to other captains. All wanted to be represented by captains who served customers in a professional manner and treated customers with honesty and respect. Each boat captain served a certain clientele, or customer. These two men appeared, on the outside, a good match for the personality of Captain Earl Keith, but in Darryl's opinion no one should be cheated out of money.

"Heck, he didn't give us no receipt," Vince's voice snapped at Darryl like the crack of a whip. "I tell you what, Ricky. Sometimes there just ain't no justice in this world."

"Yeah," Ricky agreed and pulled a pack of generic label cigarettes from the front pocket of the new t-shirt. He tapped the package on the forefinger of his left hand and a single cigarette slipped out. He stuck the cigarette in a small parting between his lips, and then pulled out a plastic lighter stuck inside the cellophane wrapper of the pack of cigarettes. After the cigarette was lit, he inhaled a deep pull and let go a relaxed blow of smoke directly into Darryl's face.

"Where are you boys from?" Darryl smiled and acted unfazed by the smoke. While the manner in which Darryl acted struck Vince and Ricky as slightly out of range, they were far from knowing who Darryl really was.

Darryl believed that he was a very good judge of the character of people. He was getting the distinct feeling that these boys were not of very good character. They were probably on the not too nice to be around if angered or upset list. Yet Darryl couldn't blame them about being upset over losing money. He decided to ask them a personal question to make them feel like he cared about them and their money. He thought he could loosen them up a bit.

"Where you boys from?" Darryl asked again when neither man answered his question the first time.

"Gimmee one of those cigarettes," Vince drawled out to Ricky in a loud, cocky voice.

Ricky was nervously spinning the metal gear wheel on the plastic lighter. At Vince's command he immediately jerked the package of cigarettes out of his shirt pocket and placed it in Vince's outreached hand. Vince extended the palm of his other hand and Ricky slapped the lighter in the dead center.

"Opp," Vince finally answered Darryl's question before he slipped a cigarette into his mouth. "Opp, Alabama."

"Pretty good drive from here?" Darryl asked.

"Not too bad, I guess," Vince lit his cigarette, took a drag and also blew out smoke directly into Darryl's face. "Maybe four hours 'cept that there's probably gonna be a lot more traffic now with this weather situation," Vince snapped. "It'll take a whole lot longer."

"Ooooh, not too friendly yet," Darryl thought to himself. "Need to find an exit out of this circle."

"We got a rattlesnake festival there every year," Ricky chimed in. "Ever hear about it?"

"No, can't say that I've heard about that one," Darryl chuckled.

Darryl could carry on a conversation with anyone; however he had enough good sense to know when it was time to shut his own rattletrap. His safety and well-being always came first.

"It's a pretty good one, huh Vince?" Ricky looked to Vince for agreement. Vince was looking past him and Darryl. Vince's eyes did not appear to be focused on any one thing in particular.

Vince suddenly came to life. He directed his eyes at Darryl and said in a voice that sounded as evil as the rattle of the buttons on a rattlesnake's tail, "That rattlesnake festival is more fun than hanging around here with the snakes who steal our money."

"Well, well," Darryl said in a smooth, calm voice. "I suppose even the best laid plans get changed by the weather. Heck, even William the Conqueror beat the French in the year 1066 because the frogs, meaning the French ya know, couldn't get their boats across the English Channel the night they were supposed to invade England. The weather was so bad."

In confusion, Ricky's jaw dropped. Vince's eyes blazed in anger. They both continued to smoke their cigarettes while Darryl rambled.

"Well hell's bells," Darryl was smiling as he continued. "You plan for something and it doesn't work out the way you planned. Things happen that you haven't planned for. You can't plan unless you take the weather into consideration and back in those days, in 1066, they didn't even have weather forecasters."

At the mention of the word weather, Vince squinted and shut his eyes so tight that his eyebrows touched. Vince's anger, fueled by the stimulation of the nicotine circulating through his blood to his brain, became apparent to Darryl as he watched the frown on Vince's face turn the red skin on his forehead into thin, white lines.

Vince growled at Darryl. "Whoa, whoa, man. You're talking about things that are nothing I care to know anything about. I may be from the south, and talk a little slow, but I ain't no fool. Ain't there somebody around here like the law? I just want my money back from the idiot who runs this boat!"

No more fun stuff. This was a straight shooter. Darryl knew quickly what to say next.

"Well of course we have the law around here. I don't know where he's at right now. He was here just a few minutes ago." Darryl turned his head to scan over the nearby buildings, parking lot and boats with one eye looking for Casey. He tried to keep the other eye on Vince.

"Do you know where this guy was heading? Which way?" Vince asked in the same growly voice.

Darryl knew exactly how to answer the question.

"Nope, sorry. Hope it all works out for you guys." He tipped his forefinger finger to the brim of his hat, turned around, and walked quickly back to the 'Star Chaser'.

For a moment neither Vince nor Ricky said a word to each other while they watched Darryl take leave.

"Yeah, right! Sorry, all right!" Vince snorted and a puffy cloud of smoke exploded from his nostrils. "Someone's gonna be sorry!"

The two men remained, shifting their feet, while they looked around for people at the marina. There was nothing else to do but wait to find someone else to talk to about getting back the money.

Casey Howard kept his eye on the two men he suspected were Earl Keith's customers. While Darryl talked to them Casey decided to take his truck and park it in the neighboring marina parking lot at the Lighthouse Marina, one block east of the Captain Anderson Marina. His Florida Marine Patrol truck would not be as noticeable to these two men. Customers on a day like today would only have complaints they would need to take to other law enforcement. Casey had other things that pressed on his mind.

Vince sucked the cigarette to drag more smoke into his lungs. "Time to get to higher ground," he said bluntly. He exhaled the smoke through parted lips. Thin wispy curls of smoke slowly descended from his nostrils. There was less than half an inch left to the burning cigarette he held between his thumb and forefinger which were stained yellowish brown from his habit.

Vince abruptly flicked the cigarette butt to the ground and walked up to the 'Star Chaser'. Ricky said nothing. He had no idea what Vince meant by higher ground. He trotted behind Vince like a faithful puppy.

"What's he driving?" Vince yelled out at Darryl.

Startled, Darryl lost his footing and stumbled a little off balance. He had not noticed the two men walk up to his boat.

"What's who driving?" Darryl hollered back.

"Hey, c'mon man. Don't talk to me like I'm an idiot."

"Well, I really don't know who you mean. Are you talking about the law or the boat captain?" Darryl asked.

"I know what a freakin' cop car looks like!" Vince shouted at Darryl.

"Oh, right," Darryl said with a sheepish grin.

Darryl nervously thought to himself, "It was a rather dumb question to ask. Better stay calm and cool with these two."

Darryl assumed they would leave as soon as they found out Earl was gone, but they were still hanging around. They made him feel edgy, which was not his nature. Darryl said, "It's a black, older pick-up truck. I think it's a Ford. It could be a Chevy, though. Not too sure."

"Solid black?" Vince asked.

Darryl answered "Yes. Solid black."

"Well that ain't tellin' us a whole lot. So, tell me, how long has it been since he left?"

"Oh, maybe ten, fifteen minutes ago. It's not been very long," Darryl felt comfortable telling them that. He knew that it had been at least that long. "He's probably heading out of town the same way everyone else is going. The only way to go out of town from here."

"Is that up highway 79?" Vince asked.

"Yep." Darryl answered.

"Okay, man. Thanks for the info," Vince said more calmly.

Darryl was relieved to see Vince calm down. He figured Vince would be excited to get some information to lead him on the money trail.

"And listen man. We're not mad at you," Vince said. "Ya know it just seems like every place around here on this beach you feel like you're getting ripped off with the price of things. You get charged for everything from water to sitting down on a beach chair and now this jerk's gone and ripped us off our money."

Sympathetically Darryl replied, "I hear ya buddy. I hear ya." Darryl knew it was best to agree with a complaining tourist. He could not disagree with their complaints, but he was glad these two, who exhibited exceptionally bad karma, were leaving soon.

Darryl blurted out, "Ya'll remember what this guy looks like, right?"

Ricky looked at Vince, who nodded his head slightly and said with confidence, "Yeah, we do."

Neither man wanted to admit that they really didn't remember very much about the boat captain of the 'Lucky Two'. Did he have brown hair or blonde hair? Was he skinny or muscular? He wore sunglasses so they didn't know the color of his eyes.

"That's good," Darryl said. "I can't remember if he's driving a Ford or Chevy truck, but I'm pretty sure it's black and I know he has one of those glass blue dolphins hanging from the rear view mirror."

Vince and Ricky, hands inside their pants pockets, listened to every word Darryl said hoping to get a better description of Earl or his truck.

Darryl imagined he saw their tongues hanging out of their mouths. He knew he had caught them, like a fish on a hook, by surprise. He had their attention. He went on.

"It's a pretty good sized blue dolphin. You'll notice it if the sun catches the glass just the right way when you're driving up from behind. It may help you find him."

"Yeah?" Ricky said in disbelief.

"There's a lot of legends and superstitions tied to the blue dolphin," Darryl went on. "Dolphins are highly intelligent creatures. They're mammals you know, like you and me. There's a legend that they were crafted from sailors who jumped ship after being chased by snakes on board their boat. So they are considered the sailors' protectors for those of us who still try to make a living from the fruits of the sea, so to speak."

An angry look returned to Vince's face. "Fruits of the sea, huh!?" Vince's voice rose up to a new level. "I'm gonna find that captain and show him how to put a little fruit in my pocket. He's gonna know what it feels like to be chased by a snake!"

Darryl was glad he was losing his captive audience. He didn't even try to make his long story short. He'd rather talk to anyone than get prepared for the approaching hurricane however these two men felt more dangerous than the approaching storm. His voice fell quiet.

"We got to get going if we're gonna catch up with this guy." Vince continued before allowing Darryl to say another word. "So there's two ways to get outta this town, right? I know there's highway 79. That's how we can get back home to Opp. But, if we want to go up that other highway, what is it? Highway 231? Yeah, 231. How do we go to get to highway 231?"

"Well." Darryl dragged out on the word. "Gotta go east over the Hathaway Bridge. Always a lot more traffic going that way. I really think you're better going west on highway 98 and then north on highway 79."

"Let's go Ricky. Thanks." Vince turned his back to Darryl and started to walk to his truck.

"Hey, thanks man," Ricky said politely. "And good luck with your boat and the storm and all." Ricky's flip flops squeaked when he quickly turned to catch up with Vince.

Darryl watched them walk back to the white pick-up truck spotted with dents and rust stains. "I've never been very good with the models of cars and trucks. Now ask me about a fish. I can identify a fish!"

Darryl heard the truck engine rumble and went back to the tedious work of pulling in his fishing gear and locking it up.

It was necessary even if it felt like a waste of time. The last few hurricanes predicted to land on Panama City Beach had missed. It was only a fool who didn't prepare and take precautions. Earl Keith had definitely acted foolish. "Earl's not going to be prepared for these two guys either if they catch up to him," Darryl thought. "I need some music."

Darryl stepped over to the cabin door, stretched his arm inside, and flipped on the radio switch.

Instead of music Darryl heard the voice of a male announcer. "A hurricane watch has been issued from Cedar Key, Florida, to New Orleans, Louisiana.

"Jeeze," Darryl wheezed. "What doesn't it cover?"

The announcer continued, "Hurricane coordinates at seven a.m. central time were twenty-seven point three degrees north and eighty-five point two degrees west, placing the storm two hundred and fifty miles south, southeast, of Apalachicola, Florida. Louise is moving faster now, west, northwest at twenty miles per hour. She is expected to continue on this path for the next twelve to twenty four hours. Sustained winds are clocked at ninety miles per hour with gusts of winds up to one hundred and fifteen miles per hour. Right now Louise is classified as a Category One storm, but conditions are favorable for the storm winds to strengthen, making this a very dangerous storm. A new storm advisory will be updated at ten a.m. central time."

Darryl's mood turned somber. He stepped inside the cabin and flipped the radio switch off. "No use listening to that stuff over and over. There's going to be continuous coverage until the storm arrives. It'll be non-stop talk about roads closing, shelters opening and evacuation plans."

Bending at the waist, he reached down and pulled out a leather suitcase from beneath a table. He laid the box on top of the table, flipped open two hinged brass clasps attached to the lid, and opened the box. Lying inside, like a trophy on top of black velvet lining, was the shiny instrument that soothed his nerves and made his pulse beat to a rhythm of peace and calm. It was a dance he had to take to get ready to be swept away by the upcoming hysteria of wind and water colliding. Wind and water creating a force and tension like the instruments in a band.

"Yep, a dance with nature's elements and it'll be all orchestrated by our merciful God," Darryl thought. He picked up the instrument, held and stared at it tenderly, like it was a baby.

CHAPTER 16: CATS ON ALERT

Fat Cat and ST sat on their haunches on a small triangle patch of cool dirt near the boat slips and seawall. It was a convenient bare spot for them to sit, offering a view of the surrounding marina parking lot, Smith's restaurant, and the nearby bushes where they could make a fast escape if needed.

"Chatty, chatty, what's the big word for chatty?" Fat Cat mewed to ST. "Loquacious!" Fat Cat meowed the answer before ST had time to think about the question.

ST had been meowing better than fifteen minutes, nonstop. Fat Cat began to wonder if the silly cat could breathe during all the meowing.

ST knew what Fat Cat was referring to. "I can't help it. There's something wrong and I can't help it."

ST was worried about King, who never returned with the rat. King had not been seen since last night and it was getting late in the morning. Fluff was missing too.

"The parking lot is almost empty. No cars. No people. And over there, at the back door of Smith's I saw Big Joe filling up big coolers with ice. The kind of coolers the boat captains take on their fishing trips. Then we have that Florida Marine Patrol guy already here. He's never hangs out here until the boats unload. I saw him already. He drove his truck across the parking lot and parked it by the Lighthouse Marina. Darryl's here too. He was talking to two men a little while ago but they didn't go on his boat to fish. Darryl's on his boat just puttering around. He's normally gone fishing by now."

ST could have gone on longer talking except Fat Cat took a quick swipe with his paw, claws barely extended, and caught the side of ST's face where the upper lip was half missing. It didn't hurt ST. He realized Fat Cat was getting edgy and impatient with him. It was time to keep quiet now.

Fat Cat felt uneasy too. Something didn't feel right but he couldn't think with ST being so noisy. He was distracted by what he didn't hear.

Normally he paid attention to the important sounds and movements around the marina, like the wheels of Big Joe's fish filled wheelbarrow with the front wheel going whump, whump, whump rolling across the cracks of the concrete sidewalk. Or, like the screened back door of Smith's Restaurant squeaking open and shutting with a loud bang. Or, like the cars carrying kitchen crew and tourists. As ST pointed out, the fishing boats were still there, rocking on the water tied to the boat slips.

96

The hair on Fat Cat's back stood up straight. The tip of his tail switched back and forth, stirring up the dirt like a broom being swept over a floor. He was tense.

Uncontrollably ST began to meow low, throaty, mournful sounds.

Fat Cat let him go. It didn't matter. No human would notice them sitting out in the open even if the cats made a lot of noise. There were hardly any humans around.

It felt like a normal hot and humid October morning, but something was different.

They were sitting out in the open, deep in thought, when a loud bang startled them both. Fat Cat and ST jumped up and scrambled around to face the sound echoing across the lagoon water. It was a familiar noise, the sound of the back door of Smith's kitchen door slamming shut.

Big Joe came out of the kitchen. His hands and arms were full of wrapped packages of meat. They watched Big Joe place the packages inside coolers.

"It's Big Fat Joe," Fat Cat sneered. "He's coming out of the door where all the excitement with the rat started last night. It's unusual that he's here now. Usually he's here later in the day."

They listened to Big Joe talking to himself out loud.

"Who does all the work around here? All the time it's me to show up to do the work. I've got all these coolers to clean out by myself. All those other dogs out there are jumping ship to take care of themselves."

"Not talking about us, is he?" ST sniffed his nose and cocked his head in the direction of Big Joe. With a mischievous twinkle in his eyes he added, "We're cats, not dogs."

The comment pleased Fat Cat. He liked jokes. Humor helped calm him and stay focused.

Both cats sat back down and perked up their ears while they watched Big Joe pack the cooler. Next to the cooler was the famous wheelbarrow. They watched Big Joe scoop ice out of the wheelbarrow and pour it on top of the packages of meat.

Big Joe continued to talk loudly. He didn't notice his audience listening to him. He stopped shoveling ice and let the shovel drop. He crossed one thick ankle over the front of the other. His heavy arms were crossed across his huge chest. Beads of sweat rolled down his fleshy, greasy face and streaked through his two-day-old beard stubble.

"Guess I'd better load up another ice chest. Problem is they're way too heavy for me to push, shove, lift, drag...oh, whatever!"

Big Joe exhaled a deep breath of air out through fat lips. He shifted his weight from one leg to the other leg. He reached into his pants pocket, pulled out a cell phone and began to talk into it.

"HEY! It's me. I'm going need some help down here!" Big Joe shouted into the phone.

Big Joe slapped the phone inside his pocket and walked back inside Smith's kitchen.

ST and Fat Cat stared at the kitchen door. Thirty seconds, a minute, two minutes passed and nothing happened. No sounds came out of the kitchen.

Fat Cat stood up and trotted toward the bushes. ST followed him close behind. Once they reached the bushes they crouched low behind the branches of leaves, kept their sharp eyes on watch for Big Joe, or anyone, to come out of the back door or around the corner of the building.

"Speaking of rats," ST spoke up first. "I wonder if King captured the rat last night?"

"Doesn't matter now," Fat Cat replied with little interest. "I remember the last time things were like this around here we got some really bad weather. Really, really bad weather. Not just a day of rain. I've got this feeling that all kind of rats are jumping ships before they sink."

"Well, I remember when the parking lot was empty on a really rainy day, too. But, it's not raining today," ST said. "I'm confused Fatty Cat. What are you talking about? Rats? Sinking ships?!"

"You're not old enough to remember what I'm talking about. You weren't even around here then," Fat Cat said using a sharp voice of authority. "Big Joe is here working and he's complaining about the dogs jumping ship. That's his employees he's talking about."

"Oh, really? I wouldn't have guessed that. How'd you know that?" ST asked. He was really confused. He had no idea what Fat Cat was talking about.

Fat Cat didn't answer ST's question. He continued to talk, as if trying to get a grip on the situation that was developing. Unlike Big Joe, Fat Cat had an audience as he spoke his thoughts.

"Not sure what he's going to do with those coolers. Last time when the bad weather event happened they didn't bring food out of the kitchen. They left the stuff here, inside the kitchen."

"Maybe we'll get lucky and get some fish out of the coolers!" ST said. The thought of eating an easy meal of fresh fish excited ST.

"Not a chance," Fat Cat snarled. "Listen to me. He's taking those coolers somewhere. He's not going to throw it in the dumpster and he's not taking it back into the kitchen."

"So, what's this all about then?" ST nervously asked. He was becoming more concerned, too. He didn't like the tone of Fat Cat's voice. This was something more serious than finding King and Fluff.

"I'm pretty sure that it means whatever bad weather is coming, it's coming soon!" Fat Cat growled.

"Golly, Fat Cat. When's this bad weather event going to start? How long does it last? You're not mad at me for calling you Fatty Cat are you?" ST asked. Fat Cat knew other cats called him Fatty Cat behind his back, but ST innocently let it slip out.

"No, I'm not mad at you. Look up high in the sky." Fat Cat

instructed ST. "You can see clouds up there. They're moving so fast that they don't block the sun."

ST squinted into the brightness of the sky. A strong wind blew into his eyes and through his whiskers. The wind stopped, then came another gust. The next breeze blew in a puffy marshmallow mass of white cotton that sailed above his head. Close behind came a dark mass of cotton, a pale shade of grey.

Feeling dizzy, and thrown off balance by the strong gust of wind, ST lowered his head and said, "Those clouds are moving too fast!" Bending his head backward to look straight up high into the sky was awkward. He was not used to looking up. It was completely different from looking straight ahead or down on the ground.

"Exactly!" Fat Cat said.

"What do you mean by exactly?" ST asked. A sky with breezes and scattered puffs of white, smoky grey, clouds did not translate in ST's mind into a rainy day, or terrible weather event.

Exasperated by ST's question Fat Cat said, "It's something serious coming. Believe me son! Trust me! I don't know when, but it's coming!"

In as few words as possible he recalled the last hurricane that came through the marina. He described to ST the details of the experience. Fat Cat explained how it was an adventure that he never wanted to ever experience again. He knew ST's cautious approach about living his life after the scary escapade chasing a lizard in the dumpster and becoming permanently scarred for life. Ready or not, ST needed to know.

ST trusted Fat Cat's story. Now the questions they both considered was how soon would it be before the bad weather arrived, what could they do to prepare, how dangerous would it be, and what to do to help the other cats who didn't know what they faced.

ST craned his neck back to look upward at the sky again. The clouds were almost interesting and fun to watch. There were white, light, airy clouds not at all like the dark black ones that rolled and swirled across the water, sometimes growing into large behemoth giant shaped mushrooms that shuddered with thunder and shot bolts of horizontal lightning. These clouds glided high above in bands, forming shapes and figures that he imagined were fish, bugs, birds, frogs, lizards, crabs or any other animal he could dream about. Flying high near the clouds he saw seagulls and terns swooping and gliding along with the gusts of wind.

Fat Cat stood up. He stretched his front paws forward as far as possible and shook off some of his stress.

"Come on. Follow me," he said to ST.

ST didn't ask questions. Fat Cat had ST's full respect after hearing the story about of his experience with the last bad weather event. ST was ready to listen up and follow instructions.

The two cats hopped out of the bushes and trotted along, close to the wall of Smith's. Occasionally their bodies bumped against the cool, stone block. There were no bushes to hide beneath at the back of the building. Tall grass created a border between the building and a seawall that separated the land from the water. ST followed Fat Cat through the tall grass to the seawall. There they stopped near the edge of the foot wide concrete wall. Both cats sat on their haunches and lifted their noses up to the air.

"I smell so much trouble," Fat Cat murmured.

"You smell another rat?"ST asked.

"No rat," Fat Cat said flatly despite feeling emotionally overcharged. He wasn't annoyed by ST. He felt some comfort in having the company of ST. If he was alone he would become more distracted by ominous thoughts. He had to keep his composure to be the leader. After all, he was Fat Cat! He was the cat all the other cats respected!

"Look at the water," Fat Cat continued in a calm voice.

"Okay," ST obediently gazed below, beyond the seawall.

"Does it look any different to you?"

"Maybe. I'm not sure. Well, yeah, probably." ST stared down at the murky, yellowish brown water rippling with white foam. It was not the blue-green aqua color like the Gulf of Mexico. Most of the time it was clear enough to see small fish swimming around, or crabs walking on the sandy bottom. Stringy seaweed, paper trash and bits of broken white styrofoam floated on top of the rippling water.

"Can't say that I see anything much different than the usual stuff," ST finally announced. Staring at water was not his favorite thing to do. He was one of those cats that did not like to get wet. Watching the motion of waves for too long made him feel a bit sick to his stomach.

"You should be called ST for Side Tracked and not Snaggle Tooth!" Fat Cat hissed, impatient with ST's answer. The two cats locked eyes again. ST's golden yellow eyes were a strong match for Fat Cat's light grey eyes. Two sets of eyes with black vertical slits were focused only on each other.

Fat Cat broke the stare first and turned his eyes back on the water. "It's nothing in the water moving around," he said to ST with an air of self-righteousness. "Look at the concrete wall. Do you see how high the water has risen above where it normally should be?"

The concrete wall was built near Smith's to keep the water away from the walls of the restaurant and to keep the sand in place. There wasn't much land between the restaurant and the lagoon on the western side of the building. Opposite the building was the bridge that crossed the lagoon. It was the same bridge where Casey Howard had parked his truck the night before. During low tide a small strip of sand was exposed at the bottom of the six foot concrete wall. The water level never reached more than three feet up the concrete wall at high tide. Now the water level nearly touched the top of the seawall.

100

Tides changed from low to high at different times of day during different times of year. It was a science that the captains of the deep sea fishing boats learned so that they would easily know when to steer through the narrow channel of the lagoon to make their way to the pass to the Gulf of Mexico.

Cats never thought about the tides.

"This water rising so high confirms it. I know something bad it going to happen. That bad weather event that I described. The humans call it a hurricane."

ST's ears perked. He'd never heard the word before.

"This is where the water gushed up over the wall and filled up the parking lot. Not just covered the parking lot, but it was inside the buildings and so deep in some places our paws couldn't touch the ground."

"No way!" ST jumped backward to get further away from the wall.

"I tell you, it was one miserable time for more than just a day or two. There was no one around here. There was nothing to eat or drink. I had to live with stinky, wet fur for days. The stench of rotting dead fish was tremendous. It was just a miserable time."

Fat Cat turned away from looking at the water and headed back. Both cats walked back the way they came through the tall grass and along the wall of Smith's. They approached the corner of the building very carefully to be sure that they did not run into Big Joe. Seeing no one after they turned the corner of the building, they continued along the sidewalk in the direction of the fish cleaning house.

When they reached the corner of the sidewalk Fat Cat stopped and said, "We're going to need to find a place to take cover and hole up. We'll need a place that is high and dry."

"In the restaurant, maybe?" ST asked.

"It's not very likely that we can get in there," Fat Cat answered.

"Where then?" ST asked.

Fat Cat said, "Let's see if we can round up some of the others and get some ideas."

No sooner were these words spoken by Fat Cat when a golden colored striped cat known to everyone as Dog Ear dashed around the corner of the fish cleaning house as if he were being chased. His ears were lying flat on his head and his four paws barely touched the ground as he managed to skid to a stop in front of ST and Fat Cat.

"Guess what I just found out?! There's a problem with Oscar!!" Dog Ear panted. ST and Fat Cat both hoped to hear news about King and Fluff, but Oscar was part of the gang. The mission to find a safe shelter was put on hold.

CHAPTER 17: ARE YOU OUT THERE NUMBER 17?

Casey Howard kept his ears and eyes open. His body jerked in reaction to the static on his CB radio attached to the epaulet sewn on the shoulder of his green cotton shirt. The CB radio was part of the uniform. He listened to the static with half his heart. He hated hurricanes. He hated them worse than anything.

Hurricane Louise was supposed to have weakened when it reached Cuba and swept westward across the island's chain of mountains. It had been only a minimal hurricane when it reached Haiti and slammed into the island inhabited by people probably poorer than the people in Cuba. It hit Haiti with the tropical force winds of sixty five miles per hour. After Haiti it churned up the Caribbean waters and landed on Cuba in less than a day.

Louise had taken everyone by surprise. The weather experts in Miami forecasted that when Louise reached Cuba as a tropical storm it would skirt along the southern coast of Cuba, then bump into the Cuban mountains, then steer into a more easterly direction. This forecast was driven by an upper level high pressure in the atmosphere pushing downward on the tropical storm winds.

Instead, Louise quickly passed over the most eastern edge of Cuba in six hours, bumped off the mountains and steered westward to find favorable eighty six degree waters off the Florida Keys. The warmer waters fed and grew the spinning funnel while at the same time the high pressure weakened and drifted north instead of south. Louise was not confused. She took this opportunity and churned her way through the middle of the Gulf of Mexico, sucking up warm water, growing stronger and stronger. She drifted west, then quickly wobbled back east. Everyone on the west coast of Florida living south of St. Petersburg stayed glued to the radio and television, nervous as cats. With no upper atmosphere winds to push or pull her, Louise just continued to wobble, drift, speed up and drive north. She revved up her engines and then put her foot on the gas pedal. The forecasters predicted it would take under thirty six hours for Louise to arrive, somewhere, on the northern Gulf Coast.

Casey's call number on his CB radio was seventeen. The radio static made him jumpy. It always made him nervous whenever he heard the scratchy voice call out a number. This time it was not his number being called.

"Not me," he thought and let his shoulders and body relax. He leaned back against the cushion of the truck seat. "Dang, we're probably going to get a hurricane tomorrow morning!" Casey recalled hearing about the tropical depression the night before. He was getting snippets of new updates over his CB.

Casey thought, as he often did, about the number of years he spent working at this job. He'd passed eleven years. How many times had he prepared for tropical storms and minimal hurricanes? Only once, during his time working for the Florida Marine Patrol had there had been a bad storm to reach Panama City Beach. It was a major one and the mess it created was a major problem for months afterward, almost up to a year. The roofs of buildings were ripped off. Water flooded homes and streets. Hotel rooms on the water's edge were filled with sand to the ceilings of the first floor. Televisions, beds, furniture, appliances, and equipment had been all been pulled out of hotel rooms and pulled out with the storm's surge to be left lying half buried in the sand or sunk out in the Gulf of Mexico. To make matters worse the debris from trees and structures torn apart from the raging winds littered the water and land. Debris didn't discriminate where it went. It littered canals, parking lots, yards and streets. There was so much damage that it was difficult to know where to start cleaning up. Casey, and anyone who worked in law enforcement, had to take care of the public first. Safety mattered first and no one wanted to find anyone hurt after the hurricane was over. It was all just a really big mess that not a single soul would wish for anyone.

"Guess I won't have to complain about counting fish thrown from boats for a little while," Casey mused.

He reached with his long right arm behind the front passenger seat and pulled a wood clipboard out of the pocket attached to the back of the seat. He looked at a list showing the names of the boats in the marina with a Florida boat license. These were the boats that rented a slip at the Captain Anderson marina. This was Casey's assigned territory to monitor compliance with the Florida Fishing and Marine laws and regulations.

Experienced fishermen often predicted that the fishing would be quite good after a strong storm blew in. The water would be so churned up and murky and the fish would become confused about where their regular swimming habitat was.

"How can fish be confused?" Casey wondered, and then tried to put his thoughts in order. His objective was to observe the condition of each boat. "Oh yes, today I won't be counting fish. That's for sure. I need to inspect each boat before it leaves the marina."

If a claim of hurricane damage was filed on a boat, insurance companies would ask for the records he logged on his clipboard. The government sometimes got involved in damage claims as well. He would most surely be asked for the information recorded on his clipboard to corroborate a claim.

Boats were often left in the marina during tropical storms. The boat captains would secure their boat to the dock pilings as best as they could. Then they would stay in town at a hotel, a shelter, a relative or friend's home, or if they had the money to afford a home they would stay at their own house. With a serious storm like hurricane Louise boat captains preferred to leave the marina and head inland into protected bays, leaving through the lagoon channel and toward the Intracoastal Waterway.

Casey's forefinger slid down the list of registered boats. It stopped at the name 'Sentimental Lady'. This name stirred up the memory of his ex-wife. The name was the title of a song that was popular and played on the radio. It had been their favorite song.

"If only I had one of these big fishing boats I could name it 'Sentimental Lady' and maybe we could get back together." Casey's eyes clouded. "Dang! I need to put a stop to this thinking, there's already a boat with that name registered! Stop it now. This is crazy. What's wrong with me?"

Casey rarely lost control of his feelings but the keys of 'Lucky Two' inside his pants pocket made him feel edgy. "That's it!" he nearly shouted. "I'm holding onto these keys for an idiot and thinking I'm the new owner of that darn boat and day dreaming about getting rich, and even my ex-wife."

Casey reached down inside of his pant pocket and rubbed his fingers around the key ring of the 'Lucky Two'. He allowed his mind to fantasize about being a boat captain.

"Captain Casey, yes sir. Now that has a nice ring to it." It sounded lyrical and wonderful. "Captain Casey, yes sir," he whispered again. Then suddenly he shouted it. "Captain Casey, YES SIR!" The loud shout jolted him back to reality. He was acting like a fool while sitting inside the truck owned by the state of Florida.

"Good grief. Anyone see me sitting here shouting inside of my truck is going to think I'm crazy. I think I'm a little crazy playing this game in my mind. These hurricanes make everyone a little bit crazy."

Casey turned his head left, then right, in one swift jerky motion to see if anyone was nearby. He was relieved to not see someone who may have heard him. He took in a deep breath and let out a heavy sigh.

He took quick, short, deep breaths, hoping it would calm his jittery nerves and muscles. His fingers twitched uncontrollably on the hand resting on his pant leg, only inches away from the pocket containing the keys to the 'Lucky Two'. He bounced his right leg up and down, using his toes on the floor of the truck for leverage. He jerked his head right, then left, then right, sucking in air and blowing it out through a crack between his tensely pursed lips. Nervousness won. It took over his mind and body. Emotions, like the weather, were not in his control.

He reached into his pants pocket with the keys and pulled them out. His eyes connected with the keys belonging to Earl Keith's boat. The light of the morning sun reflected off the shiny metal. Casey's mind was in a hypnotic state, locked onto owning the boat. He totally lost control of sane thoughts. The thought of becoming an owner of a deep sea fishing boat captured his soul. The task of checking the list of boats on the paper attached to the clipboard was merely a lost memory. He unconsciously laid the clipboard, with the stack of papers, down on his lap.

"I'm a boat captain. I've got the keys right here in my hands to a genuine, real, deep sea fishing charter boat. Now, let's see. I don't really care for the name 'Lucky Two'. Soooo, I think the first thing I should do is rename the boat 'Happy Hooker'. Yep, I always liked that name for a boat!"

He grunted and repeated the name 'Happy Hooker'. The words echoed inside the cabin of the truck. The spirited sound and tone of his voice pleased him.

Casey continued holding the keys in his right hand, occasionally clasping his hand around the keys, gripping the ring tightly, then loosening the grip to pop up two keys and let them fall against each other. The sound made by the keys rang out like wind chimes. While he played with the keys, clipboard lying on his lap, eyes staring at nothing in particular, he dreamed about becoming the successful captain of the 'Happy Hooker'. His lips moved slightly, forming words that created the fantasy in his imagination that he believed might become a reality.

Only fifteen minutes had elapsed since the time Casey had moved his truck to the Lighthouse marina parking lot to avoid the two disgruntled men, the cheated customers of the 'Lucky Two', who were talking to Captain Kay. Only fifteen short minutes and the alter ego, the new attitude, emerged and raged inside of him. It took control of every thought. He struggled with it at first. He tried to fight it off. The stress of the impending twenty four hours with a hurricane creating chaos was an overload on his usual mental self-control. The sight of the boat keys in his hands awakened the fantasy of a lifelong dream to be someone who lived in glory and envy of the average working man. He would become someone rich. He would be free to do what he wanted, whenever he wanted by his own choosing. No boss would be telling him the rules and the rituals. No more documentation of every move or decision he made.

Normally, Casey dealt with the daily rituals of his job quite well. He rarely had direct contact with other workers in his division except for the occasional meeting at central office or job training in the field. He had been promoted to dock duty in less than one year. At the docks he silently worked on his own with little supervision. He was not required to speak to the tourists or boat owners. He just recorded numbers on his clipboard and at the end of the week drove to central office to turn in the forms to be entered into an electronic data base by another employee. Thinking was not required.

Thinking caused him stress. Stress triggered thoughts about the *what ifs* in his life. What if he had stayed married to his wife? What if he had tried harder to be a good husband? What if he had children? What if he had tried harder in school? What if his father and mother had been rich? What if he had chosen another career?

All of this negative thinking made him angry and charged his energy like a starving lost dog afraid, lonely and only sensing one goal: find food and a safe place to hide.

"I'm not going to be a loser this time," Casey said out loud.

He turned the keys still dangling from the truck's ignition to start the engine. He picked up the clipboard off his lap and tucked it back into the folder on the back of the passenger seat, not even giving it another glance. He placed the key ring holding the keys to the 'Lucky Two' into the manufactured cup holder on the console next to the driver's seat. He gave the keys a loving look, smiled and shifted the truck into reverse. When he looked into the rear view mirror he gazed deeply, near drunkenly, into his own sea green eyes and chuckled, admiring and congratulating himself for being a strong, handsome, decisive man.

He chuckled and said, "Yep, I'm not a loser anymore."

Casey never lacked confidence in his appearance. He was tall and muscular. The light freckles on his nose and cheeks accented his fine, light brown hair and helped to soften his bulbous nose. His mother had always told him he looked like his grand daddy. He felt that he possessed good boyish charm that went along with his strong southern roots.

Those thoughts led Casey to say."Oh, yeah. I got the charm working for me today. Yes, SIR!"

Casey checked the rearview mirror for objects behind the truck before setting the gear into reverse. He turned the steering wheel and pushed the gas pedal slightly. When the truck was turned around to face the Captain Anderson marina he shifted it into drive and maneuvered slowly across the Lighthouse marina parking lot and back toward the docks of the Captain Anderson marina a couple hundred feet away.

Casey gazed across the lagoon water to another marina. Treasure Island marina was home to hundreds of boats kept in covered storage.

"Not a quitter. No. Not a quitter. I'm a go-getter," Casey rambled. He did a quick search for the two angry customers, but as he expected their truck was already gone.

"Now, they're the losers! HA, HA! Not ME. I am a responsible member of the community! I'm not a loser. No sir! That Captain Keith. What a loser he is too!"

As his mind raced out of control Casey grinned, mouth gaping wide open, almost laughing. He pulled his truck alongside the sidewalk instead of inside the angled white striped lines of the parking lot. He wanted his walk to the 'Lucky Two' to be short and quick. His eyes had become bloodshot, demonized by deprivation not only from lack of sleep from the night before, but unfulfilled hopes.

He grabbed the keys to the 'Lucky Two' out of the console cup holder and stepped outside of the Florida Marine Patrol truck. He looked briefly around and saw nothing out of the ordinary. Workers were preoccupied with readying their boats and property for hurricane Louise. Not one took notice of him.

Casey quickly walked toward the 'Lucky Two' and stopped directly in front of it. Once again his eyes scanned the other boats and parking lot to see if anyone was watching him. If anyone was watching him he could explain that he had a legitimate reason to check on the boat. After all, he had the owner's keys right there in his hands. It was his responsibility under the law to protect citizen's property.

Casey stepped gently onto the stern of the 'Lucky Two'. Toe down first, then heel gently down. He made no sound. The boat rocked only slightly, rippling the water below the hull. He stood for a few minutes and mentally absorbed the features of the vessel. The color, the contour, the equipment, and size of everything he could see on the boat from where he was standing. He let his mind wander. He wondered what it would feel like when he turned the engine on for the first time; to hold on to the steering wheel; to push forward on the throttle,

"I am rescuing this boat," he thought. "It will never, surely never, survive any measurable wind or water damage sitting here, tied to the dock, and unsecured. I need to haul it out of here."

There was a hitch on Casey's truck, but he needed a trailer to pull the boat out of the water. He wondered if the manager he knew at the boat storage facility at Treasure Island marina would let him borrow a trailer. Maybe there was a chance that there was a space inside to keep the boat during the hurricane. If not, what would he do?

Casey was a simple man. He was not driven by greed for money. He was driven by greed for glory. He wanted, so very badly, to save this boat. The events of yesterday evening came back to him. The idea that he would catch the captain of the 'Star Chaser' with an illegal load of fish seemed unreasonable and out of touch. Saving this boat was a grander idea to him.

A dark version of greed had become a part of Casey's life after spending years counting fish day after day. The quest for glory was his goal. His job with the Florida Marine patrol gave him little chance to seize power and grab the opportunity for glory.

The list of boats on the clipboard inside his truck was forgotten, in the back seat of his memory. He could not forget about the CB radio, still clipped on the epaulet of his shirt, because it suddenly sounded off with static.

"Twenty-one to seventeen. Come in seventeen." It was the call center supervisor.

The sound jolted Casey. He was seventeen.

"Seventeen here," he answered robotically.

"We're checking in to find out if you are at the marina yet."

"Yes. I'm here, checking on the boats at the marina. They all seem to be getting prepared for the storm, Casey answered in a controlled voice."

"Ok, seventeen. Let us know when you think you're ready to leave. You don't need to hang around there long once the boats are all accounted for. Twenty-one checking out."

Casey grabbed the knob on the radio to turn the sound to its lowest level. He suddenly remembered the gun still strapped on his belt. That was more important than the clipboard. He may need the power of it later.

Despite having less than five hours of sleep Casey felt energized. He was not at all tired. He didn't even feel like the slow moving grumpy Casey like he did last night. Every muscle in his body felt tight, taunt and ready to move fast.

"Is this what happiness feel like?" he asked himself. He stood stiff and motionless on the stern of Earl's boat. He tuned out the CB radio and all other life around him.

"That man is goofier than any words I can find to say," Darryl mumbled to himself, "and I'm not usually at a loss for words."

Darryl stopped what he was doing to watch Casey. He'd heard the engine of Casey's truck when he drove up and parked near Earl's boat.

Darryl thought, "That's not a normal looking face. Casey looks different. That guy can be a little scary."

Darryl went back to work on the 'Star Chaser'. It made more sense not to bother a man like Casey Howard. Still, Darryl couldn't help but wonder about Casey. What was Casey thinking about doing? He had the keys to Captain Keith's boat and was standing on it.

"I've never kicked a dog lying down, but I know there are some men who will climb over the hilltop just to get the spoils left by the dead who sacrificed for the living," Darryl mumbled, remembering lessons in history. He tried to keep a watch on Casey from the corner of his eyes.

Soon Casey stepped off the 'Lucky Two' and walked in long, fast strides back to the green Florida Marine Patrol truck.

"Anybody and everybody out there should keep a watchful eye out for Casey Howard," Darryl said to himself with conviction.

Little did Darryl know how true his words would become.

CHAPTER 18: HARDENED HUNGRY HEART

Eleanore sat at the small kitchen table in her faded blue jeans and a loose white t-shirt. The table was not exactly in a kitchen. The small apartment she rented above a garage was a single room that served as kitchen, bedroom, and dining room. There was another small room, the bathroom, which had a real door for privacy. She rarely used the door since she lived alone. Her landlords, an elderly couple, lived in a wood two story house separate from the garage. They rarely used the garage space below the apartment for anything except for storage of tools. It was a very quiet place to live. Even more quiet without her cat Princess.

She rarely had visitors or invited guests up to her apartment. She was embarrassed by the size of her living accommodations and meager furnishings. She spent her time at home reading books, listening to music on the radio, sewing crafts, and occasionally watching her small television that picked up two local channels. She tried not to allow herself to get bored, knowing that it would only make her feel lonely. She went shopping only when she needed something. She mostly felt contented with day to day life, but knew that she wanted something better for her life. Just what she wanted, she could not decide.

After Eleanore ended the phone call from Earl at one a.m. she sat down at the table where she answered the call and cried. The apartment was not designed for luxuries like a telephone next to the bed.

Her fingers lightly massaged her hairline and scalp. She thought of Earl and herself when they were a couple together. She allowed herself to get angry. They were close as a couple could be until he got his big ideas. Now it was all lost. They'd been young and physically attracted to each other. They also enjoyed the time they spent together. Their conversations were basic: Where do you want to go eat? What movie do you want to see this week end? I'll talk to you tomorrow. The world seemed easy, small and simple. Now the world was big and complicated. Hot tears rolled fast down her cheeks. She cried because she was lonely. She cried for what she lost. She cried because she was confused.

She finally decided to say a prayer. It was simple, direct and she said it out loud with her hands folded beneath her chin. "Dear Lord, I know that I'm a sinner. I know that your will is my path in life. Please help me to live according to your will. Bless me, and please have mercy on me. Amen!"

After saying this prayer she looked at the watch she always

wore on her wrist. It was three thirty in the morning. She'd already been awake for more than two hours!

Eleanore blew her nose, splashed water on her face from the kitchen sink and crawled in between the sheets on her bed.

She woke up in the dark after a disturbing dream and kept her eyes closed until the first grey light of morning. She could not go back to sleep. Thinking about the past and her future kept her awake A full sunrise forced her out of bed. She sat at her kitchen table.

The past never changed. The future could become a reality instead of a fantasy if she could only decide and take action on a plan. Her only plan thus far was in her hope, and belief, she would soon meet a man who she would fall madly in love with and he would fall madly in love with her. They would be so madly in love that nothing else in the world mattered. They'd get married and set up a comfortable, neat, cozy home. It didn't have to be a large home. It would be everything they needed if they remained loyal and devoted to their love for each other. That's what Eleanore truly believed. It was all that she needed. But the more she thought about it the more she felt despondent. It felt too out of reach. Her heart felt shriveled and dying in the unhappy home she lived in now.

The empty coffee cup was like a big, blank, shiny eyeball sitting on the table staring back at her. She thought, "In my life, sometimes events happen so fast that there's just no way to take control or stop them. They just happen and then you're left asking yourself what happened? Why did that happen to me? Why did Earl leave? Why did Earl call me in the middle of the night? There are times when you want something good to happen to you. Want it so bad that it hurts. You desperately try to will it, but nothing happens. You're just at a lifelong waiting point. So now what do I do? What am I supposed to do? How can I make something good happen to me?"

She picked up the cup and turned it from side to side, absently studying the curves and design. She'd already drank three cups of coffee. It was ten o'clock and she was supposed to be at work at the Kountry Kafe where the lunch crowd usually started to arrive at ten forty five.

The daily routine for the waitresses was simple. Three always worked the lunch shift. Two waitresses could easily handle the prep work that included rolling silverware inside paper napkins, setting paper placemats on the table along with the salt and pepper shakers filled the night before, opening boxes of ketchup and mustard, making coffee and iced tea, filling up ice in glasses to be ready to pour the tea into, lining plastic bread baskets with paper napkins, filling table racks with sugar packets, and wiping down chairs and tables. The final task for one lucky waitress was to wipe clean the glass front door, which was always fingerprinted by the first customer to open it. Three waitresses were needed to serve the customers.

110

Eleanore didn't want to be late. She knew how it felt when someone else didn't show up on time. If there were only two waitresses to do the prep work there wouldn't be enough time for a five minute break for a quick cup of coffee before the real work began. If she arrived late, just in time for the first customers, she would get the cold shoulder from the other two waitresses.

All three waitresses were given the same number of tables on rotation when customers walked in. The waitresses worked equally hard. Most customers ordered the special of the day, called the *blue plate*, with a glass of sweet iced tea. The tips they had in their pockets at the end of the shift depended on the personality of the customer and how much they liked the waitress, food, or service. Take the order quickly. Get it back to the table fast. Serve it with a genuine smile. There were so many mundane details, but taken all together, no detail could be left out if a waitress wanted to make money.

If Eleanore was late for a good reason the other two girls would understand. She hoped that her story would be a good enough reason for forgiveness. She thought, "If being woken up at one in the morning by a telephone call from Earl isn't a good reason, well, I don't know. Wait til they hear the details of the conversation. They'll understand why I'm so distraught and tired!"

Eleanore recalled the things Earl told her last night. He was out of money. There was a bad storm in the Gulf of Mexico heading his way. His life was in danger!

"Why am I worried about Earl now?" she asked herself. "Last night I didn't want to hear him talk. I practically hung up the phone without saying good bye to him. Now, I am paralyzed and don't know what to think. What's changed besides it being a new day? Why are my feelings so different now?"

Hot tears welled up in her eyes again. She sat up straight in her chair, held her chin high, and firmly planted her feet to the floor. She was not going to let fatigue get the best of her. She had fought the emotional battle over Earl many times. The battle had been going on for too long.

"I believe we are not entitled to everything that we want, but I am sure motivated to work hard for what I want. I am motivated!" Eleanore said emphatically. "I'll make up for the prep work I didn't do and I'll stay to do all the extra cleaning after the lunch shift. Mop the floors. Take out the garbage. Sanitize the tables!"

She would offer to do all of it and that would earn her forgiveness.

Eleanore walked to the telephone, lifted the receiver out of the cradle and held it to her side while pressing the seven numbers to the Kountry Kafe.

There were two telephones at the Kountry Kafe. One was at the front counter where the cashier sat. The cashier would not be there yet. The other phone was on the wall in the kitchen. The cooks never wanted to be bothered by a telephone ringing at this time in the morning. They were too busy getting the meats and side dishes ready for serving when the front door opened in less than an hour.

Eleanore lifted the phone to her ear. She knew that she had to let the phone keep ringing. It would take more than eight rings before one of the cooks would loudly yell 'someone answer the dang phone' and the dishwasher, or a waitress, would stop what they were doing and slide over to the wall as if they had just discovered the telephone ringing.

Eleanore anxiously gripped her phone. "Come on. Answer it."

"Thank you for calling the KUN...TREE Kafe. Can I help you?" The upbeat woman's voice stretched out the words Kountry Kafe with her southern drawl.

"Thank goodness it's you Kathy!" Eleanore nervousness dropped a level. Kathy was the older, kinder, more understanding and soft-hearted of the other two waitresses.

"Yup, it's me," Kathy snapped back immediately recognizing Eleanore's voice. "Is that you Eleanore?"

Eleanore caught her breath and said, "Yes, this is Eleanore."

As if the wind suddenly shifted to a new direction Kathy asked in a softer voice, "What's going on? Are you okay?" She'd learned a long time ago it did no good to waste time getting too angry at people. Either they had good reasons or no reasons for being late to work.

"Yeah, I'm okay. I'm just running about fifteen minutes late," Eleanore answered knowing that it was probably going to be more than fifteen minutes. "Will you let Johnny know if he comes in early?"

"Sure. I will if I see him and he asks but he ain't gonna like it if you're late again."

"Hopefully I'll get there before him and he won't know. I'm getting dressed now and I'll get there as quick as I can. Tell him...."

Kathy cut off Eleanore's sentence. "Just you get your butt down here. Make it fast!"

Eleanore heard the click in the telephone ear piece, but knew that Kathy understood emergencies. Kathy wouldn't be mad as long as Eleanor got there before the first customer walked in the front door. Once seating of the customers started, it was too late for anyone not to be mad at her. It was a game. They'd look at you as if they were happy to see that you'd walked in the door, arriving to rescue them from chaos. After the shift was finished, and the last customer was gone, they'd be mad at you for being late. The questions would come from the kitchen crew, not the waitresses. "Hey, Eleanore! Why wuz you late today?" She did not want to tell the kitchen crew. She'd wanted to tell Kathy on the telephone she was late because of the call from Earl last night at one o'clock in the morning, but Kathy did not ask why she was late. Kathy and the other waitresses just wanted her to show up for work.

Eleanore gently laid the receiver back into the cradle of the telephone. She walked past the table and shoved the chair she'd been sitting in back to the table. She left the coffee cup on the table, walked into the bathroom, turned on the shower, and turned around to open the dresser drawer within arm's reach of her bathroom door. The top drawer contained her undergarments. The second drawer contained her folded up work clothes. She pulled out a clean pair of blue jeans and a white t-shirt with the name Kountry Kafe embossed in blue ink on the front right corner of the shirt. The back of the shirt had a photograph, also in blue ink, of a picture of the Kountry Kafe. That was all there was to her work uniform. Her work clothes were nearly the same as her daily street clothes.

Ten minutes after the call Eleanore was showered, dressed, and her hair was tied up into a pony tail. She never applied make up. She discovered it wasn't good for her to look better than her customer, customer's wife or customer's girlfriend. She knew that she had some naturally good features and qualities, but she tried not to accentuate them at work. Fortunately the shower washed away some of her worry.

She grabbed her purse off the floor by her bed and stuck her hand inside to find the car keys. They were always on the bottom of the purse and hard to find. After a couple minutes of feeling around her fingers felt the lucky red dice, a single one, hooked on to the key ring through a hole cut in the middle. She'd found the dice lying in the floor of a restaurant on one of the visits to Panama City Beach.

Reminded of Earl again she huffed, "It's just the luck of the dice."

She took a deep breath, as if trying to suck in energy, and said, "It's not what we get to pick and choose. It's what's thrown in our paths. We've got to make the best with what we're given and what we're dealt. We've got to use our ability to play the best with the cards we're dealt or the number rolled on the dice. A simple twist of fate can change everything we planned for. Twist our plans into wreckage if we let it."

Eleanore took one last look at the room before she turned the lock on the door handle and shut the door. It was a habit. She didn't want to forget anything.

In spite of being tired, she bounded down the twenty wood steps of the staircase located on the side wall of the garage. She counted them once, as she sat at the top, when she first moved in. It was a lot of steps to walk up when she carried bags of groceries or her basket of laundry. She never took the steps slowly going down. She was eager to leave the apartment.

The old, four-door, white compact car she bought with her first paycheck and money saved while she was in high school was parked alongside the wood garage. It sat there like a loyal friend. The driveway was a rutted, two lane orange dirt path the same width as her tires. It was carved through a lawn filled with a multitude of lush green weeds that sometimes bloomed with colorful, cheerful tiny flowers. She always parked close to the bottom step to be safe. Eleanore had to be careful not to hit the wooden rail when she opened the door on the driver's side. On morning she was late for work she forgot about the wood railing. She slammed the door into the wood railing, causing more damage to the rail than the car door.

"Not my fault that the stupid driveway is so close to the staircase," she sniffed when she glided into the front seat and wiggled into a comfortable position behind the steering wheel.

Once the keys were in the ignition her mind went into autopilot. Hear the engine turn, shift the automatic gear into reverse, tap her foot to the gas pedal, and steer the car out onto the paved road. She had made the drive so many times that oftentimes she would arrive at the Kountry Kafe and not remember a thing about the drive. The scenery never changed. It was always the same old pine trees, paper trash lying in the tall weeds alongside the road, three stop signs, five wood houses with peeling paint, two red Georgia clay brick houses with grey mortar, four churches, one hardware store, one drug store, a grocery store, and the same old dogs lying in the ditches panting with their tongues nearly touching the dirt. It was not worth her time to notice these things every day. She'd think, especially this morning, about finding happiness and love.

Usually she listened to a country music station on the radio during the ten minute drive to work. The music stirred her soul into a happy mood for work. The radio speakers automatically pumped sound when the engine turned. This morning the sound seemed more like loud, annoying noise.

"You're my friend, but I just can't take you right now," she said to the car radio and turned it off. "I need quiet time to set my mind at ease. Why am I talking to myself out loud?" she asked herself. "That's scary," she said out loud again.

Eleanore tried to order her mind to go blank, but having no thoughts now was impossible. She recalled the fitful dream she'd had during her short night of sleep.

Run! Run! Run to higher ground! Run from the rising water. The wave is surging toward you. Look up! There's the eye of the storm. It's coming! The eye is coming right at you! It's full of water. The eye is full of water. The water is full of energy. It's looking at you. It wants to release energy on top of you. It's coming! Racing! It breaks apart everything in its path. The funnel is wrapped around the eye. It will suck you up and separate you from everything. The energy is fierce! It's racing toward you! Run! Where? Meet me again if you want to be a lucky one, or two. If you are brave, if you have no fear, race ahead of the wind, rain and the black funnel that sucks you up. Race! Escape! Stay away from the water. Don't go near the water. It's coming closer! It's rising! It's looking for you. It's a big eye. The dolphin has disappeared. Where's the whale? It was here. I heard it.

Save yourself! Quick! This is a dream......oh! Oh, NO! I'm gone.....

Eleanore sat in her car after she turned the engine off. She was dazed, afraid and shaking after remembering the dream. She hesitated to get out of the car and go inside. She forced her eyes to look out the car's windshield. They focused on a blurry figure standing in the back door of the Kountry Kafe. The eyes of a woman were staring back at her through the screen door where the workers entered and left.

Eleanore squinted hard and realized it was Kathy. The expression in Kathy's eyes had the tell-tale look of bad news. Eleanore quickly scrambled out of the front seat of the car, grabbed her purse and slammed the car door shut with her hip. She bounded to the kitchen screen door and grabbed the metal door handle. Kathy stood like a stiff soldier guarding the door.

"YOU are oooh, soooo much in trouble!" Kathy barely whispered through a clenched jaw. Kathy's face was inches away from Eleanore's as they faced each other through a screen. There was a severe, serious look on Kathy's face.

"Johnny's here. He's been looking for you. He asked me where you were, so I told him you called me and was running late. He said to me, 'When has that girl ever been on time?' I know you're a few minutes late a lot, but today you're really late and that's not good. So then he says to me 'Well, this is the last time she's going to be late!' I couldn't say anything else to him Eleanore. I didn't think I should. I think you'd better go in there yourself, right now, and tell him why you're late. It'd better be a good reason. Maybe you should punch the time clock first."

"Punch the time clock?" A strong male voice boomed from behind Kathy.

Eleanore had seen Johnny walk up behind Kathy, who did not know he was standing there. There was nothing she could do except let Kathy keep talking until he finally spoke up. When he did, Kathy jumped like she'd seen a rat. She quickly turned her head down to the floor, stepped around his back and headed in the direction of the kitchen where all of the employees had one eye on their work and the other eye on the screened door.

Johnny took one step closer and moved his face up to the screen door. "Eleanore, I like you. In fact, I like you a lot. You're a good worker when you're here but I need to you be on time. The other employees here see you coming late and next thing they think they can be a few minutes late every day too. I think we can get along fine without you today. You go on home now. You can come back and get your check on Thursday."

"Mr. Johnny, please," Eleanore pleaded. "I'm really sorry I'm late. I can explain what happened."

"What happened, Eleanore?" Johnny's southern drawl hinted of fatherly concern. It was natural for him to speak this way to his employees.

"Well, I was woken up in the middle of the night. I got a phone call from Earl. It was about one in the morning. He was telling me he was in trouble because there was a hurricane coming and he didn't know what to do any more."

"A phone call from Earl? You're telling me that's why you're late?" It was apparent that Johnny was in disbelief and getting impatient.

"Yes, sir!" Eleanore answered respectfully, but nervously.

"Just go home today. We're covered. I don't need you today. I need you here on time. It's not fair to the other waitresses when you get here late and don't do your extra prep work. Do you understand?"

Eleanore pleaded again. "I really, really need this job Mr. Johnny. I love working here, too. I'm really sorry. I guarantee I won't be late again."

"Nope," he stated in a matter of fact voice and turned to walk away from the screened door. He stopped, turned his head and looked back at her "Call me next week. Call me on Monday."

Johnny knew that Eleanore was a favorite waitress for many of his customers. She was young, cute and friendly. It was not the case with most young women her age. If they were young they soon wanted to move on to better things. Often, the longer they worked and older they got the less friendly they became. Johnny knew her personal circumstances and that she would give one hundred percent as long as Earl was not in town. He wanted to keep Eleanore, but it was time for her to learn a lesson about getting to work on time. He also knew the customers would be asking him about her if they did not see her at work.

With a sharp turn on his heel Johnny turned away from the screened kitchen door and walked into the thick, steamy air of the hot kitchen.

"I'm tired of the same old people in this town thinking I've got to do this and that for so and so because she was friends with Earl's grandmother...or something like that." Johnny grumbled, knowing it wasn't true. Everybody liked Eleanore for who she was. Nobody felt happy about Earl leaving Eleanore alone.

"Go down to the beach, get some sand in your feet and then you think you're in love. Ha! Every heart is hungry for love. That don't come first when the belly is growling for some food to eat," Johnny said loud enough for all the kitchen staff to hear. They'd all been listening to the conversation at the screen door.

Johnny picked up a spoon and stuck it into a ten gallon pot simmering over a gas burning flame. It was filled with bubbling tomato based vegetable beef soup. He dipped the spoon into the reddish-brown, steaming, dark broth and brought it up to his lips. Johnny gently blew on the spoon before putting it into his mouth. After he pulled the spoon out of his mouth he smacked his lips and said loud enough for everyone in the kitchen to hear, "Tastes a whole lot better than love!" He laughed. The cooks behind the serving tables joined him in laughter.

Eleanore drove directly back to her apartment. She didn't give a second thought to what she was going to do. She would collect some belongings from the apartment, as much of her clothes and necessary items that would fit into the back seat and trunk of her car. That would be mostly everything that she owned. A few household things would have to get left behind. The little bit of food would get packed.

She couldn't afford to stay in the apartment if she didn't have a job. Johnny told her to come back next Monday but that didn't guarantee that she'd still have her job. She wouldn't go to her mother for help. She'd have to listen to her mother's 'I told you so' hateful words and lecture about poor behavior and bad choices.

There was only one thing to do. She was going to drive to Panama City Beach to find Earl.

Eleanore had enough money in her wallet, cash she earned in tips, to pay for gas. The balance in her checking account was nearly zero. The credit card still had an available balance on the limit. She could use it if she needed it. All of these facts took little thought. A full tank of gas would get her through the six hours of driving and that would give her plenty of time to think. She would get there, pick up Earl, and together they would escape from the hurricane.

Bad decisions made in times of uncontrolled emotions may become good decisions later on. Sadness, anger, happiness, confusion, hate, love are the emotions that become the soul's inspiration for the decision.

In less than an hour Eleanore loaded up the car and left town without saying good bye to anyone. She turned on the car radio before she backed out of the drive way.

"Oh, sweet music is so good for the soul. Melody and words feed energy into the folds of the brain. This is my food. This is the sustenance of my life," she thought as she drove, blazing a trail toward a new history. "There's a treasure in this choice. I know it. I will keep on looking for the treasure in this trial I am about to face. I know that a life is well lived only if there is love. Love to give. Love to receive. Love to share."

Outside the town limits two long, two-lane, country roads stretched through field after field of farmland. One road led north to south. The other road led east to west. All roads crossed through the cotton, peanut and corn fields. Forty five miles south was a connection to the four lane highway 231, the road to take to Panama City Beach.

Eleanore's journey on the four lane road would take her places she never dreamed about.

CHAPTER 19: LIFE'S NEW MEANING

A glass blue dolphin, the size of a minnow, swung side to side from the rear view mirror of Darryl's small white pickup truck. If the sunlight passed through the front windshield at the right spot the dolphin shimmered like a fish swimming in the water. Darryl loved having the dolphin in his car. It was a symbol of his spiritual connection to the water.

Darryl latched on to a love for dolphins soon after he bought the 'Star Chaser'. He knew they were social, like him, and were very protective of their families, the weak and defenseless. Beside the snake chasing legend he'd told the men looking for Earl Keith, he also read that dolphins were recorded in ancient history books to have acted as guides, helping ships to safe harbors and shores. The dolphins in the Gulf of Mexico were a favorite attraction for tourists, fisherman and local residents, especially when they performed a synchronized water ballet, gliding up and out of the water.

"Hoooonnnnk!"

A loud, continuous blare from the car behind him caused Darryl to jump up in his seat. His right foot remained firmly on the brake.

The sound screamed, non-stop, like a flock of geese in the sky. Darryl realized that it was not just one car, but many cars lined up behind his. The car horns were much worse than the noise of geese.

A dark emotion swept over him. His heart began to beat so fast that it felt like it would explode out of his chest.

Darryl moaned, "Give me a freaking break!" He locked his teeth together.

The red light turned green, but no cars in front of him moved forward. Where was he supposed to go? Darryl disliked people like the ones in the cars behind him. They were thoughtless and selfish.

"The world is full of them so I'd better keep my cool. Just so long as nobody like those two guys at the marina looking for their money don't get in my face today." Darryl remembered the two men searching for Earl. "I can't handle another encounter like that one. Those two hot heads were enough for one day."

Darryl soothed his emotions by removing his mind from the madness around him. He looked up and scanned the storm clouds in the sky with one eye, looking for clues about the weather. He knew that in the next twenty four hours there would be many, possibly worse, encounters with irate people. It wasn't going to be easy. He'd have to find a way to cope.

Darryl began to chant his favorite mantra. "Put on a happy face!"

"Ha, ha," Darryl laughed out loud. "I told those guys that Captain Keith had a blue dolphin hanging from his rear view mirror. Just like mine!" Darryl reached up and touched the glass ornament. "Well, I sure hope he does have something to guide him. That man needs all the help he can get whether or not those two guys catch up with him."

In what seemed like a few seconds the light turned yellow, then red. Long honks, not polite short beeps, started up again. He lifted his foot up off the brake and let the car idle.

Darryl grinned. "Dang. I hope no one thinks I'm going to move the cars in front of me." He pushed down softly on the brake pedal again to brighten the red rear brake lights.

Darryl could see up the road far ahead. The right turn lane from Thomas Drive onto highway 98 was blocked by a line of the cars, bumper to bumper, already on highway 98. It was going to take a long time even if a patrolman came to direct traffic standing at the intersection. With thirty or forty cars in front of him a long while could mean an hour.

Darryl thought, "Settle in and enjoy. This developing situation is progressively going to get worse. Think of happier times!"

His first memory went back to his first deep sea fishing experience in the Gulf of Mexico. It was on a boat named 'Justin Case'.

The owner of the nightclub where The Electrons played invited a bartender and Darryl to go out for a day of fishing on his boat. The experience, which happened many years ago, was as vivid in his memory as the day it happened.

The three men were enjoying their time on the water when they noticed the azure blue sky was swiftly changing to a black colorless sky in the distant east. A huge obelisk shaped summer thunder cloud, moving like a hot pot of densely thick bubbling water, was growing taller and taller, moving closer to the men in the boat. The cloud seemed to join the water and the sky into one black wall. As it moved closer, the wind picked up speed and turned gentle waves into white-crested three foot rolling hills slicing through the water and roughly rocking the boat.

"Not going to be a problem," Lou, the owner, kept shouting to the two men, who became quieter as the black cloud loomed closer. "It'll be passing over us in twenty minutes. Hard rain, that's all it'll be."

Out in the Gulf of Mexico, more than two miles offshore late in the afternoon, too late to quickly return to the marina, the men were left with no choice but to sit out in the elements of nature. There was no cover or an inside cabin on the 'Justin' Case'. The three men pulled their poles out of the water, stacked them side by side on the deck, and huddled with their arms covering their heads. There was nothing left to do but wait for the storm to wash itself out and pass over the boat while the three men sat anxiously, patiently, waiting for a fresh start to begin fishing again. The first splat-plop drop of rain brought with it a crackling flash of bright white light directly above their heads. Immediately after the white light, a bang of thunder sent all three men bouncing up off their bottoms and then landing back on the padded seat.

Darryl remembered feeling glued to the marine vinyl boat seat before he bounced up in the air. He remembered his surprise when he felt the hair on his arm rise straight up and his skin begin to feel prickly and raw, like someone just rubbed a fresh picked nubby cucumber all over it.

The flashover, where the skin resists lightning, happened fast. The current of energy had passed directly overhead, but the skin on Darryl's arm resisted the current of powerful electricity. 'Justin Case' rocked and listed slightly, favoring one side more than the other.

Soon after the first one, another flash followed. Each new bolt was as surprising as the first. Then a third and fourth and the rain beat down with a forceful wind. The rain stung like needles pressing into Darryl's skin. The clothing the men wore was no protection. Their shirts stuck like fresh wet plaster against their bodies forming a fresh new skin.

The bright white vertical streaks of lightening, and torrential rain and thunder lasted what seemed like an eternity. It weakened with each passing minute and finally ended, like Lou said it would. When the rain stopped completely the clouds made room for the blue sky. Bright patches of lilac and pink colors appeared, like spray paint, inside white wispy clouds propping up a stunning rainbow.

During the torrent of rain the three men said nothing. Each huddled and shivered, clutching their body for hope and comfort.

After the last raindrop fell Lou looked at Darryl and said, "Well, if that doesn't make you feel small and humble. We were just like little fish in a big pond. Thank God we weren't sitting on metal! "

Lou continued, "God has a plan for each of us. Look at that arm of yours Darryl! Now you know the reason my boat is named 'Justin' Case'. Better to believe just in case you need to ask God for help to keep you out of hell. It'll be a fire worse than that burn of yours!" Lou chuckled.

For Darryl it was not a laughing matter. To suddenly realize that he had spent so much of his life not believing scared him. To know how lucky he'd been, protected for some unknown reason, meant he had a lot to do to catch up. God had a plan for him and he needed to spend more time praising God.

Darryl examined his arm for a sign of a burn from the lightning that struck him. 'Wow, Thank you God!" Darryl didn't say it just in case there might be a God. Darryl knew, at that moment in his life, that there had to be a God to create such an event. "He creates everything, even spontaneous healing. He knows we're down here, all right!" Darryl proclaimed emphatically affirming Lou's words.

A superficial burn, spread out on his left forearm, shaped like a fern seemed to be disappearing right before his eyes. By the next day, the burn was completely gone.

The flashover on the 'Justin' Case' taught him that he was not in control of everything in his life.

The decision to leave the band became stronger after Darryl discovered new spirituality in his life. He was living on a big blue planet rotating in a celestial sky filled with bright shining stars that could only be seen at night. He regretted all of the nights he'd spend playing in nightclubs and missed seeing the stars. All during the day he was aware that those stars were up there, unseen, waiting for him to sat on the deck of the 'Star Chaser' at night.

Darryl's flashback to the flashover put his mind at ease. He daydreamed about being a seagull. He could just fly over the line of cars, gliding and swooping his way to a safer place. Then he wished that he had one of the steaks Big Joe tried to give him. Grilled steak with a huge salad and a baked potato would be so good to eat right now instead of sitting in his truck sweating, hearing car horns blowing, and listening to the hurricane broadcasters on the radio.

He didn't feel protection from the glass dolphin while he drove. The presence of God, the spirit of the Holy Ghost, was all that mattered to get him through the ordeal he had to face.

'Dear God," he began, blocking out all other sounds, "I know that I have been a sinner. I'm still a sinner because I'm a human being. Please watch over me and all of these other people. Right now, in this here town, today, tomorrow and forever how long it takes. I ask for your help to get us all through what's about to happen when the hurricane passes through. I know that it will be a mess we don't need. I know it will be scary. I pray that no one will get hurt. With your strength and guidance we will all be okay. I believe in you and live by your will. Just help me to do the right things. In Jesus name I pray. AMEN!"

After praying Darryl immediately felt calmer. He wasn't scared. He turned on his truck radio. He didn't have a clock in his truck and constantly checking his watch was annoying. The radio announcer would keep him posted on the time.

"Oh, here we go, John." The sound of a perky female voice came through the radio speaker. "We've just received word that the shelter at Mosley High School has been opened. People who are in need of a safe place will be allowed inside. You are asked to bring your own sleeping pillows, blankets and any other comfortable items for rest. Mosley does have mats they can provide to a limited number of people, but not for everyone. They also say you should be sure to bring any medications that you take, or if you have special diet needs to bring those items with you."

"That's right, Jennifer," said John. "People should bring only those things that they cannot do without. And, we have been asked to remind our listeners that smoking is NOT allowed at the shelter.

This is a smoke free shelter. In addition, pets are not allowed at this shelter. One thing people with pets can do, if they must leave a pet, is find an area in their home where they think the pet will be safe and be comfortable. It's hard to leave a pet at home, I know!"

"Jennifer and John," Darryl let their names slide off his tongue. He rolled his eyes and took a deep sigh. "Nice name for a couple. They are extraordinary to do this work, repeating this information over and over!"

"Hey!" Darryl jumped at the sound of a car horn. He removed his foot from the brake and guided the truck with one thumb on the bottom of the steering wheel. The truck rolled along, straight ahead, at the pace of child walking in the park.

The mention of pets opened a soft spot in Darryl's heart. "Those poor animals," he thought. "Pets can really get short changed. Look at all those cats that got dropped off at the docks by thoughtless owners. I wonder how they're going to protect themselves during a hurricane. How do they even survive?"

Darryl didn't like the idea of innocent cats getting hurt. His eyes settled back on the blue dolphin hanging from the rear view mirror. He thought about the story he told the two men looking for Captain Keith. He didn't like making up stories, but there wasn't any harm in that one. The two men seemed to him to be just a little dangerous. Maybe they wouldn't find Captain Keith, whose boat he left in charge to Casey Howard.

"That man, Casey, he's a real hard person to figure out. He worries me sometimes and especially now that he's got the keys to Captain Keith's boat." Darryl wasn't worried about other drivers who might see him talking to himself in the truck while he inched along in the slow line. "If anyone thinks anything about me talking to myself, that's their problem. There are bigger things to worry about right now."

Darryl kept thinking and talking out loud. It made him feel busy on such a slow, boring ride.

"I'm never sure if Casey's mind is on his work or if his mind is on something else. Something about his eyes and the way he looks at you. I sure never want him to be thinking about me. Not that I got anything to hide, but still.... the way he was walking around and looking at the 'Lucky Two'. Well, I don't know. There ARE a lot of rules in the deep sea fishing business and operating a charter boat. Casey knows all these rules, supposedly. But, and a big BUT, it was just very odd this morning. Casey took those keys from that kid, Captain Keith. As if it was just a natural, normal thing for him to do as a way to help. The kid just handed him the keys to his business. Casey didn't say no, or even say thanks but no thanks. The kid just gave it up. Probably a forty thousand dollar boat and gave it up like it was nothing. I just don't get it. OKAY Darryl! Stop thinking about it! It's not for me to worry about."

The sound from other car radios drifted through the air from open windows. Drivers turned off their air conditioners, trying to conserve gas. Yet it was eerily quiet out on the open road. It almost felt like being out in the open waters.

Darryl eyed the glass dolphin again and suddenly remembered that Casey was in a commercial on television about protecting the dolphins. "There's something good that Casey did!" he thought.

It was illegal for people to feed the dolphins because feeding them made them more dependent on humans for survival. They wouldn't know how to take care of themselves. If they couldn't take care of themselves they may die. People loved to see dolphins and the easiest way to see them was to throw food out to them. It was a pretty basic law of nature. Feed an animal and they will come back to the hand that feeds them.

Darryl looked at the glass dolphin and said, "Dolphins are man's friend without humans feeding them food."

"The latest coordinates for Hurricane Louise are..." The words from Jennifer, the radio announcer, through the car speaker sounded like blah, blah, blah in Darryl's ears. He knew the storm was coming and it was going to be a bad one. Nothing was going to change the fact. Not even an update of the storm's path every two hours from the national weather center.

"In reality, hurricanes are very unpredictable," Jennifer continued. "The eye of the storm, where the strongest circular winds are, will wobble. In the last two or three hours the strength of the storm could cross land at a spot thirty or forty miles away from Panama City. A little wobble to the east and Louise could come in at Carrabelle or Apalachicola. That would be devastating to the oyster, shrimping and fishing communities. A little wobble to the west and Louise could come in at Destin or Navarre Beach, our beautiful tourist destinations!"

"Wobble, wobble," Darryl thought. "Years ago we had that hurricane Elena. Another hurricane named after a girl. She wobbled back and forth, crisscrossing in the gulf, before making landfall. It was an entire week of wobble!"

A song began to play on the radio. "Finally! The sweet sound of music. I need something besides that chatter. The same stuff over and over." *We can make it if we try* a man sang out the words with a smooth, reassuring voice.

Darryl laughed out loud. "Well, now how appropriate is that right now! We'll be trying to make it with a hurricane named Louise. I think I even sang that song a few times in my nightclub career. Funny, it was dedicated to a different girl each time I sang it."

Darryl's saxophone, lying inside the velvet lined black leather case, was on the floor. It was the most valuable, precious thing in his life. The 'Star Chaser' came second to the saxophone.

When he bought the saxophone it was the best he could find. It was something that he wanted, and planned, for a long time to buy. The yellow brass professional tenor saxophone cost nearly four thousand dollars, brand new. It took years, playing in the Electrons, to make the money and make the payments. He wanted to own a saxophone since learning to play his first one in middle school. He loved the sounds that he could make with it and he was never lonely when he played his saxophone. In the band or on the boat, the saxophone was like a best friend. The instrument was more important to him than his love of fishing, even though he was happier fishing than playing in a band at night in the club.

Darryl was aware that there would eventually be a day when he would not have the strength, or health, to be the captain of the 'Star Chaser'. It took a lot of energy to make the long off-shore trip. When he could no longer cater to his customers he would stop being a deep sea fishing boat captain. He liked the idea of possibly playing in a band, again. It couldn't be the same as the old days, though. Maybe he could join a concert band or a church band. He'd never give up his saxophone. Playing music comforted his lonesome heart.

We can make it you and I the smooth voice sang through the car speaker.

Darryl grumbled, "So, maybe there is a girl out there for me. I just haven't met her yet. It's hard to meet a girl working off a boat every day. Not too many girls hang out down there. I never met a woman in the nightclub that I thought I wanted to know better. Those girls only see a man who can play an instrument and sing. They don't want to know me. One day, I'll find a girlfriend. For now I'll just have to deal with Louise."

He turned the radio off and looked at the blue dolphin again.

"Wonder what Casey has in mind for 'Lucky Two'. I think that's a good name for a boat. Maybe the guy had a girlfriend. Awwwww, Darryl. Didn't I just tell myself to stop thinking about finding a girlfriend? Okay focus, Darryl. What's Casey going to do with that boat?"

Up ahead Darryl saw the traffic light turned green. The line of cars inched forward. Darryl stretched his neck high above the steering wheel and saw red and blue lights flashing beneath the green traffic light.

"Cops up ahead! There must be an accident."

The cars continued to move after the traffic light changed colors again from green to yellow to red.

"Good! We finally have someone in charge of directing traffic. Darryl said and soon his truck was on highway 98.

At a slow and steady roll he approached the steep incline of the Hathaway Bridge. Boats in the bay came into view. A large fishing boat was moving north out of St. Andrew bay toward the bridge. Once it crossed underneath the bridge it would enter the waters of North Bay where it could continue on to the intracoastal waters.

"That's what Casey could do with the 'Lucky Two'," Darryl thought. "There will be less tidal surge up there than in the lagoon. There'll be rising water to be sure, but the protected waters are a lot

124

better than leaving a darn boat tied up at the marina. Too bad I had to leave 'Star Chaser'. Just don't have the extra money to put it into dry storage. I'd need another person to take it through the intracoastal and manage it through a hurricane. Hopefully I've got the 'Star Chaser' secured and will see it again. Casey might be able to find help taking the 'Lucky Two' through the intracoastal. I wonder who he would ask to help him?"

Darryl felt his throat get tight. He was almost thirty five years old, but a lifetime of hard work made him feel older. He prayed the hurricane didn't destroy his boat. One day he would be faced with the decision to move on to different work, but he wasn't ready just yet.

"Ok, think positive. So maybe I can't be gazing at the stars at night from the water if I lose my boat. I'll find another line of work, or location, and still find a way to let my eyes gaze at the stars in the night sky."

Two lanes of cars crawled up the incline to the crest of the bridge. Instead of picking up speed on the descent, the cars slowed down. There were two more traffic lights to get through before the road widened to four lanes. Once off the island, two lanes took traffic east and two lanes led north. Darryl hoped traffic would move at a faster speed.

On the way down the bridge Darryl got a better view of the broad expanse of circular bands of clouds in the eastern sky. He felt a gust of wind nudge and lift the truck. Then another stronger punch of wind shook the truck.

Darryl vowed, "Okay, if the 'Star Chaser' disappears in the hurricane I will make it my goal to find a new band and perhaps a girlfriend!" He gripped the steering wheel tighter.

When Darryl pulled into the Mosley High School parking lot he joined a large number of cars arriving, filling up spaces. He'd lost track of the time after turning off the radio. He didn't even remember driving past the Panama City mall after he turned off highway 98 and headed north onto highway 77. He parked the truck and walked down a wide sidewalk to enter the building. Once inside, Darryl shuddered. He felt a chill go through his body, like a cold day. He couldn't imagine going to school again, much less in a building that didn't have a single window.

"Ahhh, concrete walls. A necessity for a hurricane shelter," he reminded himself. He tried not to think about the amount of time he would have to spend in this building. "Can I still get a good spot? Maybe a corner near the hallway, but not too close to the bathroom? Anywhere in this place will be noisy. All these concrete walls will echo!"

"Checking in?" a dark-haired, middle aged lady with droopy, tired eyes, sagging shoulders and strong body odor greeted him. She sat behind a six foot folding table at the front door entrance.

"Naw," Darryl thought. "Yup," he said as cheerfully as possible.

"Name?"

"Darryl. Mr. Darryl Kay."

"Address?"

"Slip number 37, South Lagoon Drive."

Her hand stopped scribbling. Darryl felt the woman's eyes penetrate the paper for a moment.

It didn't feel awkward to give the marina as his address. Checking into a shelter, a gymnasium, felt strange. It was like he was being processed into a the hospital, or some similar place.

"Telephone number?"

Darryl wondered why the shelter needed his phone number. "None," he answered.

"Medical conditions, or any special needs?"

"None that I know about right now."

Darryl noted the woman's lip slightly twitched when he answered her question about medical conditions. Was she scowling or suppressing a laugh? Darryl hoped that this would be the end of the questions. He was getting impatient, standing at attention, in front of this woman volunteer. He wanted to get inside the shelter.

"I sense you getting impatient Mr. Kay, but these are questions that I am required to ask," she said with an air of importance. "I'm just going to go over the form to be sure there's nothing else I need. Then I'll give you a check-in number. You'll need to remember it."

She lowered her head, then finally looked up at him and said, "You'll be number eleven."

"Oh, wow, a cool number. I like it!" Darryl said enthusiastically. He was genuinely pleased. He really did believe number eleven was a lucky number and maybe the low number meant he was early enough to get a good spot to spend the night. Happy to be finished with the check in procedure he wondered if he should ask what the significance of being assigned a number was, but he didn't want to waste any more time.

"The rules of staying here are to keep order for the benefit of everyone. They are written on a board, on the wall, inside the gym. You'll see it first turn on your right. You can't miss it. You may come and go as you wish. If you leave the building please remember we lock it once we know the storm is within six hours of landfall. We'll probably get full. You'll be responsible for all of your belongings. We only ask that you respect the rights of other evacuees while you are here." The words were spoken in a flat, methodical tone with the speed of an announcer reciting the bad effects of a prescription drug during a television commercial.

Darryl mumbled "Thank you," and turned to go inside the gym.

He eyed the cave of the gym. "I wonder if I should ask about playing my saxophone while I'm here? 'Not a good idea, Mr. Kay' is likely the official answer. She can be the captain of the gym, and I can be the captain of the 'Star Chaser', but none of us will be the captain of Hurricane Louise!"

Chapter 20: Best Friends

Ricky tried to sit still on the seat of the truck. It was impossible on a wild ride. He fixed his stare on the black road straight ahead.

Vince was driving, if it could be called that, with his hands gripped so tight on the steering wheel that the skin on his knuckles turned paper white. He was aggressively guiding the white pick-up truck in and out of the solid line of traffic, accelerating speed, changing lanes, braking quickly, and tailgating vehicles until he could pull around with a quick jerk of the wheel. He drove through yellow lights, honked his horn through red lights, and uttered curses out of lips that spewed spit with each word.

Every now and then Vince cut his eyes sideways to look at Ricky, which made Ricky nervous. Ricky knew how Vince's mind worked and felt the anger growing inside Vince's heart. Heart and mind were heating up with hatred.

Neither man turned their head to look directly at each other, yet their instincts made them aware of the other.

As they sat in silence Ricky imagined the case building up in Vince's mind. Somehow Ricky was going to be blamed for the loss of money taken by the boat captain of the 'Lucky Two'.

Vince growled more than once, "Not even his name on a business card." It could have been an expression of anger with himself, or an expression of anger at Ricky. Ricky wasn't sure.

Taking no chances Ricky responded by saying, "You're right, Vince!" as if he was speaking to his boss.

Vince and Ricky had been friends since the first grade. Now they were grown men. Vince knew Ricky better than his own momma, who didn't stay home to raise him and see him grow up to be a man. By the time he was playing on the schoolyard playground Vince was already an angry child who felt cheated. His mind was filled with a jealousy that fermented greed and unconscionable behavior leading many people to believe he was slightly ignorant instead of a cold and calculating child looking out for himself. He was known by all the other children and teachers to act like a wild pit bulldog if he was aggravated by anything.

Ricky, who had a momma that loved him, became Vince's friend more by chance than choice. Always a follower, he needed someone strong and aggressive like Vince to help him make his decisions when he was in school and then after they left school. But Ricky also knew that he never wanted Vince to be mad at him.

Because he was such a loyal follower Vince trusted Ricky to be with him, but Vince still struggled to treat Ricky with kindness.

"You're gonna wish you was sitting in the next ditch on the side of the road instead of next to me in this here truck!" Vince suddenly barked at Ricky.

Ricky squeaked, "Whaddya mean, Vince?" He nervously fanned his knees back and forth and pressed his feet flat, gluing them to the floorboard of the truck in case Vince decided to slam on the brakes and shove him out the door. It wouldn't surprise Ricky if Vince did this.

Vince snarled at Ricky, "I can see the way you been cutting your eyes at me, looking over here at me like I'm crazy and all. I ain't no stupid fool! You think I'm stupid, don't you Ricky? You're just sitting there, quiet, not saying a word."

"Vince," Ricky pleaded. "I don't think you're stupid."

"You'd better believe that, Ricky!"

"Vince, I DO! It was my idea to go fishing and give that guy cash in advance." Ricky couldn't remember if this was true. "I just don't feel good talking about it. You know I'm mad, too, about what happened." Ricky felt the tension inside the truck lift a little. He knew it would please Vince if he took the blame. Ricky continued to stare straight ahead.

"Everybody wants a piece of the pie, Ricky. Some people just want a bigger piece. They take more bites. I'm gonna get my fair share, and more if I can." Vince's anger never went away.

Ricky glanced at Vince's knuckles, still white, gripping the steering wheel. He was desperate for Vince's anger to focus on something else. With each word Vince spoke the truck jerked.

"Man, there's a lot of cars," Ricky said, trying to sound as upset as Vince. "You're doing real good getting us ahead in the line." He praised Vince like he used to do in the first grade elementary school cafeteria line.

"I'm gonna catch up with that thief! We're lookin' for a black pick-up truck, but, we don't know what kind. If I see any black trucks I'm gonna honk my horn real loud at them so they turn their head when I'm passing. Then you get a real good look at the face. Okay, Ricky? Think you can remember what the face on the fishing jerk looks like, Ricky?"

Ricky lied, "Oh, YEAH! You bet I can Vince!"

Long, heavy minutes of silence passed after they agreed on the plan. The truck's engine roared.

Suddenly Ricky said, trying to maintain a controlled voice, "Your turns coming up."

"What?" Vince shouted back.

"Your turn's coming up at the light up ahead," Ricky repeated.

"How'd you know that?"

Vince had been too busy racing his truck west on highway 98 to notice any signs.

Ricky said, "We just passed a sign for highway 79. Back there a little bit."

"Well, that's real good Ricky. I like it when you pay attention."

Car horns blared at Vince when he made a sharp turn to the right lane, cutting close in front of another car.

"Oh, don't get your cookies shook," Vince sneered and laughed.

Surprised by the laugh, Ricky said "Everybody's anxious to get out of here, Vince, ain't they?"

"Yeah, right, Ricky. But we're going to get outta here before they do and hopefully with some money in our pockets."

Ricky wanted to be helpful again. "I been looking but I ain't seen no black trucks, yet. We're still on his trail."

"That means he's still ahead of us further up the road," Vince said as he slowed down the truck enough so not to raise the attention of the patrol officer at the intersection of highway 98 and 79. He turned right onto highway 79.

Although it was getting to be late morning, the two lane highway was not yet closed to southbound traffic. Once Louise got closer, and the possibility of it making landfall on Panama City Beach stronger, the authorities would order mandatory evacuation. Under mandatory evacuation the southbound lane on highway 79 would be closed and opened for northbound traffic too.

Very few people were heading south to the beaches with a hurricane brewing in the Gulf of Mexico. Fewer cars allowed Vince to pass four and five cars at a time. When he approached an occasional curve he swerved back into the northbound lane at a high rate of speed, cutting off the car behind him and slamming on the brake to avoid hitting the vehicle in front of him. He didn't worry about being reported to the Florida Highway Patrol or Sheriff. If someone called the authorities it was not likely they'd try to chase a reckless driver. Their priorities were managing major traffic flow problems.

It was a good day for Vince to drive like a maniac.

The fifteen mile drive after the turn onto highway 79 to the bridge that crossed West Bay and across the intracoastal took Vince eleven minutes. Neither man paid attention to the darkening sky above or the brown churning water below when they reached West Bay bridge.

After crossing over the top of the bridge both men noticed the sign for the One Stop gas station and convenience store. As if programmed by an alien mother ship to speak simultaneously both men said, "I wonder if he stopped there for gas?" Big toothy smiles erupted on their faces. They looked at each other square in the eyes.

Ricky said, "I know what you're thinking!"

"Yup," Vince said cheerfully.

Vince slowed the truck to a safe speed to pull into the One Stop. Ricky yanked his door open before the truck came to a complete stop, jumped out, and pushed his way inside through the glass door. He approached the same young, overweight girl who had sold fried chicken to Earl less than fifteen minutes earlier.

Grace was sitting on a four legged wooden stool at the cash register behind the counter with her arms crossed in front of her chest. Before Ricky could speak she said, "If you're getting gas you pay me first then go ahead and fill it up."

"Hey," Ricky said. "I'm wondering if you can tell me if a man driving a black truck was in here a short time ago." Ricky was unaware of how stupid that might sound to the store clerk.

"A man in a black truck," Grace said with a hint of sarcasm. "I've have had a few customers and maybe one in a black truck."

"Do you remember what he looked like?"

Grace said, "No, actually, I can't tell you that I remember anything. Are you getting gas or food?"

Grace was suspicious of many people who came into the store. She had seen a lot of characters come and go. Ricky definitely fit the appearance, and profile, of a character. Some people came into the store and took care of their business. Other people came into the store acting strange and talking about strange things. Ricky was behaving strange. She didn't allow strange people much time inside. It was easier to get through a day if she could move the characters out of the store as fast as possible.

"He's pretty young," Ricky said quickly and suddenly thought that he remembered what Earl looked like. "He's maybe in his twenties. Kinda long blonde hair, skinny, tan. A real good tan. Probably wearing shorts."

Grace had enough sense to say as little as possible.

Ricky continued talking. "He was a friend of my twin brother who got killed two years ago down in Panama in a bar on the beach. He knew my brother. I came down to visit and wanted to see him. I found out we just missed him leaving town on account of the hurricane that's coming." Ricky let the words come out of his mouth breathlessly.

"Your twin brother got killed? Gawd, I'm so sorry," Grace said in a soft voice. The subject took her guarded thoughts off track. She had a weak heart for people who lived through tragedy.

"Thanks. I miss him a lot," Ricky said.

Their conversation was interrupted by a loud, long honk from Vince's truck outside in the parking lot.

Ricky rushed. "Listen, I gotta go now. That's my ride. Can you tell me if someone who looked like that stopped here not too long ago?"

Grace had not forgotten Earl. He was fresh in her memory like the fried chicken that was still hot and smelling good to her. She remembered Earl had asked her name. Customers never did that. What had it been, five or ten minutes earlier? Now this guy is standing in front of her acting just as edgy as Earl. They almost looked like they could have come from the same family. Cousins' maybe. Both had blonde hair, skinny, and a scared look in their eyes. She felt comfortable believing the story Ricky told her.

"Well, yes, I had a man looking like the person you described come through here maybe five, ten, minutes ago. He was driving a black truck."

Ricky got so excited he began to jump up and down. "Which way was he going? Did he say where he was heading? Which direction?"

"I remember he said he was heading west to Biloxi or north to Georgia. Seems odd to me to be heading west, but hey, I don't give advice to customers. Maybe he is on the right track to dodge a hurricane. Maybe he will win some money at the casino in Biloxi. That sounds good too."

"No way!" Ricky said in disbelief, surprised that this was the exact information he and Vince wanted.

Grace responded, "Yeah, it's not what I would do, but then what do I know? Here I am standing at this counter while everyone else is going somewhere. The Windjammer. I believe that's the name of the place he mentioned." Grace gave the name of the casino she suggested to Earl.

"Great! Thanks!!!" Ricky shrieked. He could barely contain his excitement. He quickly turned and rushed outside.

"And, thank you for your business, too mister. Guess you don't need any gas." Grace mumbled to herself. She watched Ricky scramble back into the passenger side of the white truck.

"Weird, weird, weird." Grace worked on correcting her negative first impression of Ricky. "Now how unlucky can that be to lose a twin brother?"

She tried to remember back to two years ago and any murders that happened. So many weird things happened to people who came to visit the beach. Anything was possible.

"I hope that he finds the friend of his twin brother. I can't imagine losing a twin. How sad and awful it would make someone feel." Grace's heavy eyelids drooped nearly closed as she sorrowfully dwelt on the tragedy of such a personal loss. "It's like that verse in the bible in the book of Acts, number four verse thirty two, 'of one heart and one soul and all things in coming'. That's what it must feel like to have a lost a twin. Must feel like loving Jesus, he's in your life, and then losing Jesus in your life. That's too much pain. A loss I couldn't bear to suffer."

Then Grace mumbled to herself, "The Windjammer. I think that's what that man said. Or did I say it? That casino does so much advertising."

"You told that chick in there that you had a murdered twin brother?" Vince looked at Ricky with an incredulous, wicked grin. He couldn't believe what Ricky just told him. "Did I really hear that?"

Vince was elated. He was hot on the trail of Earl.

He jerked the truck out of the parking lot, tires screeching and smoking, and cut into the steady line of cars. The first car quickly braked and set off a line of flashing red lights behind it, like a string of lights on a Christmas tree.

Vince laughed uncontrollably and then started to choke. He laughed so hard he couldn't get enough air inside of his lungs. His face, scorched red from the day on the beach yesterday, turned a more fiery red and his eyes popped outward while he gasped for air.

Deep white creases on his forehead, framed by yellow puffy ridges, gave his face the appearance of a scary clown. The only thing missing to make him look like a real clown was a red ball painted on the tip of his nose.

"Are you gonna be okay?" Ricky asked Vince in a timid voice.

Vince shook his head vigorously up and down. He sucked air into his lungs, but couldn't speak yet.

Ricky continued his story. "I wasn't sure I was gonna get her to talk. Then the idea about the dead twin just popped into my head. You should have seen her face. She got this look on her fat face, like real sad, and came right out and told me. Popped right out of her mouth!"

Vince was impressed with what Ricky just accomplished. He always thought Ricky had a very limited imagination. The hormones released from the laughing spell relaxed Vince. He was happy, too.

"It's probably a good thing that we didn't go out deep sea fishing Vince. Your face is really red right now."

The round of laughter had turned Vince's face to a purplish shade of red. Vince didn't need to be reminded about the fishing trip that didn't happen, the lost money, and the pain of the sunburn. Vince's anger started to boil again. His mood changed to serious.

"So you say he was heading which way again?" Vince asked.

"She said west. She said Biloxi. He's going to a casino."

Vince yelled back at Ricky. "You gotta be kidding me! I mean, gawd, you GOT TO BE KIDDING!"

Ricky felt real danger in Vince's voice.

Vince asked, "Did the chick mention which casino by any chance? Did she give you anything more specific?"

Ricky's bottom lip protruded into a pout. He felt like crying. "I don't think she woulda told me, Vince." He couldn't remember the name of the casino Grace mentioned. He lost the confidence he felt a few minutes earlier. He turned his face halfway toward Vince and slouched down on the seat. If he let Vince find out that he forgot the information he would suffer. He didn't feel guilty about lying. He only hoped he wouldn't get caught.

Vince relaxed his grip on the steering wheel, but his eyebrows were pushed together in deep thought. Finally he said, "You're right Ricky. How would she know? That guy wouldn't have a reason to tell her."

Relief flowed through Ricky when he heard those words from Vince. He was off the hook, like a released fish swimming freely back into deep water.

Vince silently resumed his speeding and wild driving, passing cars.

Ricky thought about all the years he and Vince had been friends. "How long have we been friends? Well, first grade! We've been friends for twenty years. I love him like a brother. It's just when he slips into these angry moods. They can last for days. Sometimes it takes a long time to break the spell. I hope this spell don't last long."

Vince's parents were separated by unusual circumstances when Vince was very young. His father made a half-hearted effort to take care of Vince properly. Vince's father had two major problems, or maybe one. He didn't know when to stop drinking alcohol and he couldn't keep a job for very long. The joblessness was really a result of the drinking problem. Being abandoned by his mother and having a father who showed very little strength of character gave Vince few good examples of how to exercise self-control over his own emotions.

"Crap," Vince rolled down the window to spit.

"What's that mean?" Ricky was carefully watching out for a black truck and keeping his eyes on the road.

Vince answered. "I don't like anything about where we're heading. I mean, it doesn't make sense. But we don't have a lot of choices."

"Yeah?" Ricky tried not to sound confused. He wanted to agree with Vince, but wasn't sure where the conversation was heading.

"We could head east, west, or keep on going north. Any which way we head, we're gonna be running into real trouble with the weather. So, we might as well head on west to Biloxi. We can stop at a bunch of casinos to find this guy. Just drive around looking for a black truck. We can't be that far behind him. I'd like to catch up with him and teach him a good lesson and then head on to a casino myself. Get more than our money back."

"Look up at those clouds, Vince," Ricky said, finally noticing the clouds. "We're definitely going to get bad weather anywhere we go."

At Ricky's suggestion Vince twisted his neck sideways to look up. Then he looked down at Ricky slouched in the seat next to him. The truck jolted to the right. Vince corrected the truck back to the center of the road.

Ricky fearfully looked at Vince. Vince's dark brown eyes pierced into Ricky's. Ricky felt the hair on his arms rise despite the heat and humidity inside the truck. He did not like to look directly into Vince's eyes when he was angry. Vince had an extra brown spot in his left eye. The spot, the shape of a crescent, was on the white part of his eye. It looked like a second pupil. When Vince was angry Ricky felt like he was looking into the eyes of a reptile, like one of the rattlesnakes at the festival in Opp.

Vince hissed, and asked Ricky again, "You don't remember if the girl at the gas station told you the name of the casino?"

Ricky felt his throat tightening. Like a bolt of lightning the name of the casino came to him. "Oh, now I do remember she did say something. Well, she said she couldn't be sure. She said maybe it was the Windjammer." He choked on the words, "Yeah, the Windjammer."

"Windjammer! Well, alrighty!" Vince twisted his head back to look at the road. "Well, ain't that some kind of coincidence, since

we're gonna do some jamming in this here wind. Ha!" Vince's foot
slammed down on the gas pedal and Ricky's head jerked back
against the seat with the truck's fast acceleration.

"Ya, man. A jammin' good time!" Vince drawled out the word
jamming. Then he sang the words jamming, jamming good time,
over and over again.

"Cool," Ricky managed to say and then suddenly he shouted,
"Hey, Vince! There's a black truck up ahead! See it?!"

The highway had been mostly straight and flat, but a slight
change in curve and slope allowed Ricky to notice the black truck.

Vince squinted. The expression on his face had the eager
anticipation of a child opening a gift.

"Up where? How far?" Vince asked.

"Up the hill," Ricky stuttered with excitement.

"I think I see one, maybe ten or twelve cars ahead of us. Is that
the one you mean?" Vince asked.

"Yes! Yes, Vince!"

A big white toothy smile spread across Vince's face. "You think
it could be him, Ricky?"

"I don't know Vince. The funny guy down at the marina did tell
us it was a black truck.,"

"Yup, jamming." Vince's sharp voice growled like a dog. He
jerked his head to the right to look at Ricky's face. "We're about to
get this cheating thief!" He shouted gleefully, happy to get his
revenge. He hammered his fisted hand on the steering wheel.

Ricky had his eyes fixed on Vince's left eye. He thought he saw
flashes of light coming out of the crescent spot. Imagined, or real, he
had seen the flash before. Many times before. It always made his
body tingle.

An unnatural quiet descended inside the cab of the truck. As
Vince maneuvered around vehicles, passing and speeding up closer
to the black truck, the only sounds were the rumbling roaring
engine, rubber tires whirling on the road, and racing winds outside
the windows.

Fear overtook Ricky. His stomach churned. It felt like a clothes
dryer with sharp rocks tumbling inside of it. His jaw ached from
clenching his teeth tight together inside his closed mouth. He feared
what would happen when the speeding truck he was riding in came
to a stop.

Vince was no romantic when it came to people. He had a high
opinion of his natural instinct to get what was rightfully his.

Vince chuckled as they got closer and closer to the black truck.

"Ready for some fun, Ricky?"

Ricky answered cautiously, "You bet, Vince."

CHAPTER 21: CATS IN DISTRESS

Dog Ear didn't stop to rest when he skidded on the sidewalk to report news to ST and Fat Cat. He nervously paced in front of them and circled around them. The other two cats tried to act nonchalant.

"Are you being chased?" Fat Cat casually asked Dog Ear, not giving away a hint of concern. Fat Cat believed if he used measured control in his voice it gave others the impression of confidence and authority.

ST knew to only listen and not butt into the conversation between Fat Cat and Dog Ear.

"No!" Dog Ear panted, still trying to catch his breath. He paced in front of the two cats with his tail held straight up in the air. His tail was puffed out and covered with dust.

"NO! I am not being chased!" he said again. Dog Ear had a habit of repeating himself to be sure he'd said the right thing.

Fat Cat remained sitting, patiently waiting. ST licked and groomed his body while waiting for Dog Ear's answer. He licked every part of his body, first licking his paw and wiping it behind his ear and over his face. Then he licked under his armpit, his tail, the skin between his translucent toenails on his two forepaws, over the bottom of his mouth and across the top of his snaggle tooth. His whiskers twitched when he finished licking.

"I can't find Oscar. I haven't seen him since last night!" Dog Ear wailed. "I just saw that mean, sassy Putty Paws. She told me she saw Oscar climb up inside a black truck last night. The truck the boat captain of the 'Lucky Two' drives. His truck is gone!" Dog Ear panted his news in serious, distressed gasps.

Like all of the other cats, Dog Ear and Oscar had been hanging out in the parking lot the night before enjoying the action of watching the rat being chased by King. They both left soon after the rat, and King, jumped aboard the 'Lucky Two'.

Dog Ear was born, along with five other kittens, in an unused tackle box near the storage shed King called his castle. Dog Ear had no memory of who raised him. However, he believed that Oscar was his brother, the last of the kittens to survive along with Dog Ear. Oscar and Dog Ear only knew a life of hanging out with other cats at the marina. No other family history filtered their philosophy about how to live. Dog Ear was distressed because his brother was missing.

Dog Ear earned his name when he was only five weeks old after he ripped off the tip of his soft, peach fuzz, thin skinned ear trying to squeeze his head into the jagged opening of a small round tin can that had held small, round sausages. He had been very, very hungry that day. The smell coming from the can was a wonderful, fresh smell of some kind of meat. A small piece of meat, left in the bottom of the can, floating in fatty juice, was much too much for Dog Ear's growling belly to resist. He squeezed his entire head, small enough at his young age, completely inside the can. Immediately he felt the can so tight around his head that he could hardly breathe. He tried to remove the can by taking wild jumps, pushing at the can with his front and rear paws. He rolled around, but he could not loosen it off of his head. His entire head was covered by a tin can smaller than a tennis ball. Despite his efforts to remove the can, all he could do was flip and flop around with the can tightly attached to his head.

Soon a young teenage girl working in one of the marina gift shops ran out of the store upon looking out the window and seeing Dog Ear in distress. He was worn out from body convulsions and close to unconscious from lack of air. He didn't put up a strong fight when the young girl picked him up, but he found energy to bare all of the claws on his front and hind legs and instinctively dug into the girl's hands and arms. In one sweeping motion she quickly yanked the can off the kitten's head and tossed Dog Ear and the can to the ground. Her good deed ripped off a piece of the kitten's ear. The can, covered with blood and a chunk of skin from the kitten's ear, rolled away.

"Yikes!" The young girl let out a piercing scream from the pain of being scratched and the sight of blood spewing from the kitten's head

The screams scared Dog Ear as much as the painful injury to his ear. Dog Ear made a jack rabbit run and slipped through a small gaping hole beneath the deck attached to the gift store. The same deck where Fat Cat kept his home.

Once he felt safe Dog Ear wasn't sure if he had been lucky or unlucky. One thing he knew for sure. He learned that he would always be more careful when he hunted for food. The pain from his torn ear was worse than the hunger pains.

Luckily for him the ear healed quickly. Fat Cat and the other cats gave him guidance on how to lick his wound clean every day. Fat Cat brought food to him during his healing time, but he never fully recovered from the trauma. He lacked confidence and depended on Fat Cat and other cats to help him through any crisis.

He was called Dog Ear, after that day, but later nick-named Dear by Fat Cat, who once tried to say Dog Ear too quickly and it came out Dear. The nick name caught on with all of the other cats, who used it affectionately when they wanted to calm down Dog Ear's jittery, excitable personality.

"NO? Is that all of it?" Fat Cat asked Dog Ear with measured patience. "Can't find Oscar? Is that all? Why are you still panting?"

"Fluff is missing too!" Dog Ear blurted out.

"Slow down! Stop pacing in front of me!" Fat Cat said gruffly.

The mention of Fluff's name perked him up. He was keenly interested to know more about Fluff.

"Dear, we're here for you. Don't worry," ST finally spoke up sympathetically after patiently listening to Fat Cat ask the questions.

Clearly Dog Ear was distressed and ST understood Dog Ear better than any of the others. They were close to the same age when their accidents happened almost a year ago. ST never forgot his accident when he foolishly leapt into a situation without thinking of the consequences. The scar on his upper lip was just as noticeable, or obvious, as Dog Ear's. The difference between ST's and Dog Ear's scars came from pride in the hunt, not hunger in the hunt.

"When was the last time you remember seeing Fluff? Was it late last night? Where was it?" Fat Cat asked.

Dog Ear stopped pacing and flopped down on his side. The panting continued. His belly moved rapidly up and down with his quick breaths. His tongue hung out of his mouth quivering with each pant. The pink tongue contrasted against his orange fur. It was not a particularly appealing color combination. His greenish yellow eyes darted from ST to Fat Cat.

"Here, last night, in the parking lot, by the boat King jumped onto when he chased the rat." Dog Ear said.

"We know. We remember last night." Fat Cat responded, and purred, "Dear."

"Dear," Fat Cat repeated. "Do you remember when and where you last saw Fluff?" Fat Cat's eyes shone. The tone of his voice was sharp, and a little less patient. He wanted to know Fluff's whereabouts.

"Well......" Dog Ear stopped panting and closed his mouth.

Fat Cat tried to cut to the chase. "Did you see her today?"

Dog Ear panted again. "Last time I saw Fluff?" He repeated the question. "Well, uh, she, uh...so, yeah. She was hiding in the corner of the building where the fish cleaning goes on, near the rinsing sinks."

"You mean that gap of the building where the fish cleaning and the souvenir store connect?" Fat Cat asked.

Fat Cat was familiar with Fluff's hiding places. He frequently kept on eye on her comings and goings. "You mean you saw Fluff today?

"Yes, yes. That's where I last saw her. Yes, I saw her today. But, I have not seen Oscar today," Dog Ear moaned in despair.

"He's probably still sleeping inside one of the cars," ST mewed. "I bet Fluff's still hiding somewhere over there too."

Both Fat Cat and ST were restless and anxious to get back to the business of finding shelter. The news Oscar brought was disappointing. They'd both hoped it would be news related to the hurricane. On the other hand, Fat Cat was interested in finding Fluff. He knew that she couldn't take care of herself or be alone if a hurricane was coming. If King was not around to help Fluff he wanted to know. Maybe she would be more interested in him, more than in King, if he offered to help her.

Fat Cat asked, "What about King? Has anyone seen King?"

"Nope." Dog Ear answered. Dog Ear calmed down. He sat up on his haunches, swished his tail and twitched his good ear. He was finally breathing normal.

A loud bang startled all three cats. They quickly jumped up on all four paws and scrambled away to hide.

The back door of Smith's restaurant had been slammed shut by Big Joe. The same door where all the excitement began the night before.

All three cats ended up in a short patch of shrubbery beneath the bronze plaque of Captain Max Anderson.

The tired eyes of Big Joe caught the motion of the animals scattering away. He stared in the direction of the bronze plaque.

"They're going to have quite a rotten time of it," Big Joe thought. "Wonder where they'll go. Hope they'll make it through this storm."

In spite of Big Joe's nasty moods from working long hours in a greasy, sweaty, hot kitchen, he held a healthy respect and soft spot in his heart for the cats. He respected their ability to survive under the harsh circumstances in which they lived. They were not ordinary home bound cats who ran up to the yard when the owner's car pulled into the driveway, or heard the sound of a can opener, or heard the noise of dry cat food shaking in a box. These cats dealt with the same kind of daily struggle for survival like Big Joe. He wished now that he had not stored all the fish from the freezers into coolers. He wished that he could leave some behind for the cats who would be staying at the marina during the hurricane.

Big Joe remembered the story he read in the newspaper about the six toed Hemingway cats that lived in Key West, Florida, and felt better. "If those cats can survive storm after storm that crosses across that island then I believe it's going to be okay for the cats here." Big Joe swiveled his huge body and walked back into the kitchen. It was time to lock up.

"Maroww" Dog Ear couldn't help himself.

The loud, deep throated, mournful sound jolted Big Joe. "I gotta hurry up and get out of here. Leave behind these worries about what's going to happen. I need to worry about myself. Leave as soon as possible."

"Mouwww!" Fat Cat shot back, louder and deeper than Dog Ear.

ST turned his head from one cat to the other. He was as distressed as the other two cats, but wasn't going to make any noise.

"I'm not hanging here," Fat Cat growled. "We've got to move on." He circled around the other two cats, and leapt out onto the concrete sidewalk. His ears perked up straight and tall. The short hair on his tail was fluffed out, an outward sign of his agitation. He needed more valuable information. He needed to know more about the hurricane and needed to know more about Fluff. He needed to find shelter.

Fat Cat had a suspicion that Fluff was with King or at least somewhere nearby. So the big question was where was King? If he was still on the boat, how could she be with him? How much time did he have to find Fluff and take her with him, or convince her to go along with him? He could convince her if he could find her. He was sure. All he had to do was describe to her all the scenes and details he told ST. And if it was all going to happen during the coming night she would go with him.

Dog Ear and ST followed as close distance behind Fat Cat. The three cats quickly, steadily and skillfully ran on the sidewalk, under wooden benches, concrete tables, around signposts, scattered boxes, trash cans and buckets. The three nervously looked around as they ran, turning their heads frequently to avoid any dangers.

When they turned the corner around the gift shop, fish cleaning house, and fish market, they stopped in front of the 'Star Chaser'. Few boats were left tied to the docks in their slips, but the 'Lucky Two' was there, bobbing and rolling in the choppy, rising, foamy water.

While the three cats trotted down the length of the sidewalk, Fluff nervously cowered inside the black rubber boot lying on the floor of the 'Lucky Two'. She was afraid to move out of it, worried that Captain Casey would show up again. Hiding behind the boot was easy when the two men talked to Captain Kay on the sidewalk. The sound of angry voices was not troublesome as long as they stayed away. Then the big footsteps of Casey Howard approached the boat. When the first footstep rocked the boat she scrambled inside the boot before he could notice her.

She heard the loud meows, thinking that she recognized the meow of Fat Cat and suspected the other was Dog Ear.

She liked Dog Ear. "Dear," she murmured. The sound of saying the name comforted her nerves. She did not want to be near Fat Cat. She believed he was responsible, maybe the sole reason, for the predicament King was in. Both she and King were prisoners on this boat.

"King. Oh, where is King now? How is he?" She tried not to worry, but it was impossible. "He just had to be so brave. He thought he was going to show all those other cats that he could outsmart the rat."

"Thinking this way is not productive. It is only makes me feel worse and sad," Fluff thought. "I have to admit that Dear and ST are not such bad fellows, even if they hang around Fat Cat all the time. It's just that Fat Cat always has to act like the boss of everyone. He thinks he's better than the rest of us. Humpf! We're just as good as he is."

She wanted to meow for King, call for him, but she knew better. She didn't want the other cats to hear her meow and discover her, either. She wanted to get through this terrible, scary experience with King. She couldn't leave until, together, they found a way off the boat.

After her accidental arrival at the marina, where she was forced to take permanent residence, she soon learned to be careful about bringing attention to herself. She should do it only when necessary and under the best circumstances. It was so different than living with Eleanore

If only Eleanore had not made her get into the car and come with her on the drive down here. She hated riding in cars. Didn't Eleanore know that? She liked staying inside the small apartment, stretched out in the window sill and looking out the second floor window at the activities in the trees and the yard below. She liked watching and waiting for Eleanore to return home. She always heard Eleanore's car engine at least a block away before it even pulled into the driveway. Fluff could meow all she wanted for Eleanore. She would jump down from the window sill after Eleanore exited the car and began to climb the staircase. Fluff heard every step Eleanore took coming up the stairs, but Fluff still meowed at the door for Eleanore until the door finally cracked open and Eleanore began to talk to her. She loved Eleanore that much. When Eleanore got inside, Fluff would stop her meowing. She wished Eleanore was there right now to talk to her.

Fluff wanted so badly to meow for King the same way she used to meow for Eleanore.

It wouldn't have mattered if she did. King was half asleep on a semi soft square vinyl seat pad inside of the boat. He was too tired and exhausted from the night before, where he laid against the wall of the cabin, wide awake all night, watching Earl. King was thirsty and hungry.

After Earl left the boat, and a safe amount of time passed, King jumped to the tabletop and stretched until his front paws could grip the window sill. For a long time he looked out of the closed window from which he could not escape. King tried to jump up to the ledge of the window. He desperately tried again to slide it open with his paws. Nothing he did would move the window. He was certain Fluff had left the boat hours ago. There was nothing she could do to help him.

He'd felt the boat gently rock when Casey stepped onto it.

King felt hope. "I can get out of this predicament. I just have to be patient and wait for the door to open. Then I'll make a mad dash through the open door. Next time whoever opens the door won't have a chance to catch me."

Time passed. He wasn't sure how much. Finally he laid down, curled his tail around the perimeter of his body, tucked his four paws beneath his tail, snuggled his nose into his soft belly, and cuddled himself into a deep slumber. It would take a strong jolt to wake him.

CHAPTER 22: LUCKY CHASE

The fried chicken that had tasted so good and satisfied Earl's hunger was not sitting so well in his stomach now. Another, different kind of rumbling sent sharp piercing pains up from his stomach crawling through the lining of his esophagus inside his chest. A hot, harsh blast of air came up and from the back of his throat and through his nose. It left a nasty taste in his mouth. His head throbbed. The first sign of a severe headache began to frame his consciousness.

The happy sense of well-being he felt only an hour ago was waning. Leaving the 'Lucky Two' and responsibilities, filling up his gas tank and his belly, getting on the highway to escape Hurricane Louise, felt like the world of worries were gone forever. Suddenly he felt the sensation of a dark shadow hovering in the cab of his truck alongside him. It was present with him. It darted in front of his face, blurring his vision of the road ahead. He looked to the side view mirror and the dark shadow darted out of the window, opened to let in the breeze of fresh air.

"Darn," Earl grimaced. He sucked in a full breath of air, puffed his cheeks, and briefly closed his eyes. He tried to blow the bad taste out of his mouth and relax.

He glanced up into the rear view mirror to check to see if a dark shadowy cloud was following close behind him. What Earl saw instead was a white truck, not less than five feet away from his rear bumper.

Two men were sitting in the front seat. The truck was so close that Earl could see their faces. The driver's face exposed a toothy grin. It did not look like a friendly smile. It was the smile of someone obviously crazy. Only a crazy person would be following him so close.

A sudden sense of alarm and danger ignited Earl's stomach into a fiery blaze, sending bursts of gaseous pain into his mouth. It was stronger, worse, than the general feeling of being uncomfortable that enveloped his senses seconds before. It felt like evil creeping inside the cab of the truck.

Earl glued one eye on the rear view mirror and tried to keep the other eye on the road ahead. He gripped his steering wheel and slowed down a little to put some space between him and the car in front of him. He waited for the white truck to pass.

"What's the deal with them?!" He wondered and worried. He squinted at the rear view mirror, watching the truck and the faces of the people in it. Why they didn't try to pass? The lines in his forehead deepened. "No one's getting out of here any faster than the guys of ahead of me. This is really going to piss me off if I have to put up with them. As granny used to tell me, 'we're all getting out of here in our own due time'. WHATEVER! I'm trying to do sixty. How fast do they want to go?"

The sharp pains in his stomach and head intensified with his growing anger. Now he had to deal with another aggravation. Hadn't he had enough? This was a very unpleasant distraction. The happiness he felt with his freedom had been too short lived.

"Christ Almighty!" Earl screamed as loud as he could. He slammed his right fist on the steering wheel. He flipped the radio switch on and turned up the volume as loud as it would go, hoping it would be a better distraction. In a moment's time he angrily switched the radio switch off.

Sorrow and pain swept over him when he realized the words he had just spoken in anger were not meant to be said that way. The name of Jesus should be used with reverence, thankfulness and respect. He was definitely heading toward more trouble, which is what he was trying to escape when he left the 'Lucky Two'.

Where was the dark shadow now? He avoided looking in any of the truck's mirrors, but knew he would have to look sooner than he wanted.

"Son of a bitch!" Earl screamed when he saw the truck following him even closer. It didn't seem possible.

He never felt the same shame when he uttered those words, but he knew they were bad. It was not the same as taking the Lord's name in vain. He was a believer. In God. In Christ. He couldn't control himself sometimes. He didn't understand why these words would pop out of his mouth when he knew he only felt remorse and guilt as soon as he said them.

The two men's faces seemed to stare at him, through the back of his head and into his eyeballs. A memory flashed in his head. Did they look familiar? The driver had a wide, sinister looking, grin and the other man just looked dazed with his eyes fixed straight ahead.

"Dear Lord, I'm not going to make it to the next turn," he moaned low. "Please help me."

As if in answer to his request Earl noticed in the distance two hundred feet ahead on the right side of the road a very large sign. From the distance it appeared to be a sign for the entrance to a Florida state park. A brown wood sign painted with bright yellow letters and a green pine tree.   He was approaching it quickly.

"Can't be," he murmured. "Not out here. Not in the middle of nowhere. A state park?! Divine intervention. Thank you, Lord!"

Earl didn't plan to put on his turn signal until he got closer to the sign. These guys were following him too close. His instinct told him they were up to no good. There had been many opportunities for them to pass Earl's truck, but they didn't. Earl thought of the people riding in the cars behind them. They would need to see his turn signal. He feared a messy pile-up of crashed cars if he didn't use his turn signal. He didn't want anyone to get hurt in an accident. He slowed down to fifty miles per hour. He hoped, in one last hope, the driver of the white truck would pass him. If he didn't, or couldn't because of an on-coming car, which was unlikely, Earl could dart into the entrance of the state park and be out of their way. The driver would be off his tail.

The white truck slowed down to hug the bumper of Earl's truck. Other cars sped up and passed around both trucks.

Earl was close enough now to read the brown wood sign for Pine Log Forest State Park. A short entrance into a stone gravel parking lot was up ahead only forty yards. He looked again into the rear view mirror and decided to turn on his right turn signal. He gasped for air to fill his lungs. The white truck's right turn signal started to blink too!

"Oh...my...God." Earl spoke slowly, emphasizing each word equally. "Oh...my...God. Why are they following me?"

Earl turned into the park entrance. He couldn't think of anything else to do.

There were too many other vehicles, a solid line, going north on highway 79 for someone to take notice of two vehicles pulling into the park's parking lot that was close to the road but unremarkable.

The white truck carrying the two men speedily pulled up alongside Earl's black truck, leaving a cloud of dust and gravel flying behind it.

The two men looked vaguely familiar. The dark shadow passed in front of Earl's eyes again. With keen awareness of danger in this predicament, Earl recalled these were the two men who made arrangements, and paid him yesterday, to go deep sea fishing on the 'Lucky Two'.

Vince violently pushed open the door of his truck and jumped out of his seat. He did not shut the door. With the engine of his truck still running, he jauntily ran around the front of his truck up to where Earl was sitting in his truck with door closed but the window still wide open.

There was an intensity in Vince's dark eyes that Earl did not like, nor thought he had ever seen before. The eyes that were fixed on him were boring hate into Earl. It was a hatred that made the blood running through Earl's veins feel hot. His heart beat at a racing pace. He felt like his heart would explode inside his chest. The pain he had been feeling in his stomach was gone, replaced with knife stabbing fear. The bad taste in his mouth was gone, replaced with a mouth so dry his tongue was stuck to the roof of it. His lips quivered when he tried to speak.

"Hhhhhaa...hhhhey," Earl made a feeble attempt to speak while he focused his eyes on the black eyes staring at him through the open window. The eyes reminded Earl of coal in a barbeque pit, black and smoldering, spewing out sulphur smelling thin lines of grey smoke. He could not break his eyes away from Vince to catch a look at the other man in the white truck. He did not even know what Vince looked like besides the eyes.

"Remember me?" Vince growled at Earl.

"Nnnnn....nnnnn....." Earl's throat choked on his fear. He could not speak.

"No? Are you trying to say no?" Vince said in a tight, controlled voice.

"Nnnn...nnnooo," Earl stuttered.

"Nah, nah, nah, nah. No?" Vince grinned, feeling amused like a cat that had cornered a tiny mouse and felt playful before striking with fangs at the helpless animal.

Vince waited a few seconds in silence. He watched Earl attempting to take deep breaths. Both men's eyes were locked like magnets.

Earl finally found his voice. He spoke clearly but not firmly. "No, can't say that I do remember you." Immediately Earl didn't feel good about the lie.

"Don't you have a deep sea charter fishing boat down there in Panama?" Vince barked back.

"Well, I used to." Earl answered without hesitation. This was a truthful answer.

"Used to?? USED TO?" Vince shouted angrily.

Vince dug the toes of his feet into the gravel and leaned forward into the window. He was so close to Earl's face that Earl could feel the vibrations of Vince's vocal cords and the heat of Vince's breath. Earl looked past Vince's beet red face for a second and caught a glimpse of Ricky sitting in the truck next to his. Ricky was staring straight ahead.

"Look at me! Look at me!" Vince screamed.

Earl's eyes darted back to Vince's hating eyes, the dark pieces of charcoal. An imaginary thin, wispy line of smoke was curling upward in the air in front of him. And then Earl noticed the crescent shaped brown spot on Vince's eye. It was creepy. Earl thought he saw flashes of lightning and then some smoke seeping out of the crescent.

"You got some money that's mine! MY money. And maybe more for the trouble of getting it back." The tone of Vince's voice was different. It was low. He growled like a leopard. It was more menacing than a scream.

Earl understood that Vince was not a man to play mind games with, but he still tried to summon up the last drop of courage in his belly to test the rules of the game he was playing. He was resolute, confident, about his answer that he did not own the boat.

"I haven't got a boat anymore and no money left either." The words blew away with the smoke. Before uttering them he immediately knew they sounded like a lie.

Vince's right arm rose up to the open window of Earl's truck.

144

His hand, gripped into a tight fist, was two inches away from Earl's face.

Earl shifted his focus off Vince's eyes and on the glint of an oversized, odd shaped, shiny silver ring.

"Say again?" Vince bellowed the words, like hot air flaming from a fire, directly into Earl's face.

"No boat. No money," Earl said again, with false courage, like he had been dared by a bully on the playground. He knew that he was losing the fight.

With lightning speed in one quick fluid motion, Vince threw the length of his entire bare-skinned right arm through the window toward Earl's jaw. Earl moved forward slightly to dodge the thrust, but the chunky ring on Vince's fist struck the temple next to Earl's left eye. The full force of the fist, with ring attached like a steel knuckle, split the thin skin. Blood immediately spurted from a small gash and trickled down the side of Earl's face. Both of Earl's eyes, although open, became glassy. His eyelashes fluttered a few times. Then his body slumped forward and his forehead slammed with a loud thud on the top of the steering wheel. His head bounced, then tilted right, as if to take one last look at the enemy.

"Sweet Jesus," Earl softly mumbled through slightly parted lips.

Vince's heart raced. He felt a pounding inside his chest, pumping, pumping, pumping blood through his lungs and tightening up every muscle in his body. He stared at Earl a few seconds. His coal black stony cold eyes bored into the slumped body of Earl with his head strangely propped up on top of the steering wheel. Vince knew that Earl was not going to move soon. Maybe never, ever again. Vince didn't care about Earl.

"The money. That's what I need to find!" Vince grunted with eager anticipation of his reward as he stood at the window of Earl's truck.

The money, the sole purpose of his chase and the confrontation with Earl, was first and foremost on his mind. Get it back. The small twenty two caliber handgun he stored in the glove compartment back in his truck flashed across his mind. "Do I need the gun? Nah!" Vince's menacing grin stretched ear to ear while his eyes cut back to take a quick glance at Earl again.

"Vince!!" Ricky's loudly whispered shout floated across the space between the two parked trucks. Ricky had not moved a muscle while he listened to the short conversation between Earl and Vince and watched the scene unfold between the two men. Only his eyeballs darted back and forth from the road to Vince during the fast few minutes that passed after Vince exited their truck.

Vince loudly shushed Ricky, never turning around to look at him, and kept his eyes locked on Earl's still body. He stepped slowly away from the window and took long steps around the front of Earl's truck to the passenger door. He opened the passenger side door without hesitation and quickly scanned the seat for a wallet or anything that looked like it would have cash in it. He poked his head further inside the cab, briefly looking up through the driver's window to check the steady line of cars moving north on highway 79.

No one slowed down. No one would find it unusual to see two trucks parked side by side in the parking lot, with one door, the driver's side door, still wide open. From all appearances it would be just two men having a chat and making plans for evacuation. Earl's body would have looked normal, as if he was leaning over the steering wheel to take a rest.

Vince reached over the greasy bag of chewed chicken bones and thought, "Well, now. This is much, much too easy." He grabbed the wallet Earl left on the seat.

"Tooooo dang easy!" He laughed and hummed while his fingers picked through the folds of the brown leather wallet for the cash he sought. He saw the symbol of the State of Georgia on the driver's license and it sent a message to his brain. "Georgia boy. Dog!" Vince grunted and sneered. "Well, now, mama, old lady. Ain't I making you proud right now. Wouldn't this make you proud of your son! Your son just caught a thief from Georgia."

Vince did not know if his mother was dead or alive. He only heard bitterness in his father's voice when he often told Vince, during one of his drunken escapades on the rare occasion when he saw his son after the parents had separated, that his mother was from Georgia. But, she ended up with some poor Alabama boy from Opp.

"Yeah, MAMA! Your son's getting his money back from Georgia." At a time of victory Vince felt his soul burning with the spirit of the mother who abandoned him. It filled his heart with happiness whenever he had the chance to think that he felt her spirit.

After emptying the wallet of all the green backs, Vince slapped it down on the seat. He rolled the thick cash and stuffed the wad of money into the front pocket of his shorts. Then he reached over to lightly touch Earl, whose head was still facing the driver's window. Earl's body felt hard, stiff, and completely lifeless. Vince grabbed the wallet again. He stepped back, pulled his head out of the cab of the truck, and scanned the landscape away from the road and past the parking lot. Thirty feet away, beyond the parking lot, he saw clumps of weeds, sawgrass, palmetto bushes, and forty foot tall pine trees. He took one step back and power pitched the wallet as far as possible into the woods.

Ricky smiled nervously when Vince calmly slipped back inside the driver's side of the truck, slammed the door shut, and shifted the gear shift back into drive, all in one fluid, smooth motion. "Got the money?" Ricky asked timidly, knowing the answer to the question he just had to ask. The irritability in Vince's face had disappeared.

"Oh, yeah! Got it all. It's all good now!" Vince began to sing. "Sweet Home Alabama. Coming home to see you."

Vince swerved out of the parking lot and cut into the line of oncoming cars without a blip on anyone's radar. The old, rusty white pick-up truck blended into the long line of cars heading north.

"That was real good, Vince. REAL good!" Ricky was relieved that the chase was finally over. Now they were going home.

"We got our money back, Ricky, old friend! And then some," said Vince, touching the wad of bills in his pocket. He hoped that there was more money than what they paid Earl for renting the charter boat. "We can't go fishing with this money. Wanna go to Biloxi?"

Ricky was shocked by Vince's suggestion. Vince was just singing about going home to Alabama. "Go west? Mississippi? Are you sure it's safe?" Ricky asked, trying not to sound worried.

Vince laughed. "Why not, Ricky? We can try some gambling. We might get lucky. Heck, we got lucky today, didn't we? Didn't get to go fishing on a boat named 'Lucky Two' but we got our money back to have fun doing something else we haven't done before."

Ricky reluctantly nodded his head yes. He thought they were leaving Panama City Beach because there was a hurricane. Didn't they need to go home, or at least somewhere safe? On the other hand, he liked the idea of going somewhere new. Maybe they would have a little fun. After all, they had another day off before they had to be back at work.

"Yahoo, Vince. Let's go! Our luck ain't gonna change now!" Ricky hollered.

CHAPTER 23: BOATS IN STORAGE

Casey needed a little time to clear his mind. In the three hours since he first arrived at the marina that morning strange things had happened. Things not typically expected in preparation for a hurricane. It was time to take a drive to Treasure Island Marina and see what was happening on the other side of the lagoon.

As he drove over the Grand Lagoon Bridge Casey remembered the plans he had last night. Sitting alone in his truck on the side of the road in the dark, eating the simple frozen dinner alone at home and watching the weather on TV was boring compared to what had happened today. Today was much more interesting but difficult to digest.

It occurred to Casey that life was like a maze. There was always a new corner to turn. At the end of one path, which you thought was the right path, you often found another corner to turn. There was no going back to find out where the last turn would have led. There was just another unknown to choose. The only choice was to move forward, not backward.

The two lane bridge, a short low-rise span over the lagoon, gave Casey another chance to catch a glimpse of the water he so loved. The tired lines beneath his eyes did not betray the worry in his mind. A lack of sleep the night before and years of working outside, squinting in the sun, made the crinkled crow's feet at the corner of each eye made him look much older. When he wasn't wearing sunglasses people might think that Casey smiled a lot. That was not the case. Casey rarely smiled.

The sun was not shining now but Casey squinted as he looked at the choppy, brown, frothy water below the bridge. Small white caps on the waves of water, unusual to see in the lagoon, churned up foam that was collecting on the shoreline. Recent years of increased boating and fertilized lawns from the homes built along the water's edge had all but destroyed the water quality in the lagoon. Casey was told that many years ago the water in the lagoon had been crystal clear and the same aqua green color as the Gulf of Mexico.

"Don't know how any creature can live in that water," he grumbled. "Rarely see a fish or even a blue crab in the lagoon any more. The water's definitely rising, though. This isn't looking so good."

Casey was aware how the combination of a rising tide and a high tide driven by the phases of the moon could make even a small hurricane potentially more serious and dangerous. Louise was no small storm and picking up speed faster than any previous hurricane he'd ever known. Highly trained in all aspects of his law enforcement duties, Casey knew he had little time left to take care of the 'Lucky Two'.

"Last night I was thinking Darryl was the one I should be watching," Casey shook his head in disbelief. "Then this guy, Captain Keith, comes across as THE real strange one." Casey thought he was a good judge of people's character, but this incident had him quite perplexed.

The keys to the 'Lucky Two' pressed against the skin of his thigh through his khaki trousers. Feeling them troubled his mind. After crossing the Grand Lagoon Bridge he carefully made the sharp left turn into the parking lot of the Treasure Island marina.

The Bahama blue color of the corrugated steel building blended into the sky and loomed large in front of Casey after he shut off the truck's engine. He imagined the view inside with five stories of row upon row of boats resting on carpet covered steel v-shaped pads.

Casey looked out of the truck window and spotted Sharkey, whose real name was Bob Smith, walking past the door of the building. Sharkey was no relation to the owner of Smith's Restaurant. He was always asked, and he always answered, "Smith's a very common name. I don't have any ownership in the restaurant. Wish I did, though."

Bob picked up the nickname Sharkey after he caught what was, at the time, the largest hammerhead shark ever pulled out of the Gulf of Mexico. It made him feel pride whenever someone used the nickname. The name Bob Smith made him feel very ordinary.

Casey hopped out of his truck and walked toward Sharkey.

"Yo, Casey," Sharkey grinned when he saw Casey. His white teeth appeared like a row of pearls against the dark, tanned, leathery skin on his face. "Gonna be a real wild day coming up. What do you think?" Sharkey was genuinely pleased to see Casey.

Sharkey had a career deep sea fishing on charter boats but stopped when he became too old to handle the long hours. The years Sharkey spent operating the marina helped him better understand the difficulty Casey had enforcing the laws on charter boat captains. Sharkey knew some of the deep sea fishing boats owned by private owners brought in illegal fish. Casey never asked Sharkey the questions he asked the charter boat captains. It was not Sharkey's job to report what the private boat owners did. Casey respected Sharkey's job to manage operations at the marina and maintain the privacy of the owners who kept their boats stored there.

Casey returned a friendly smile and said, "Got that right." He extended his right hand. The men exchanged a tight-gripped friendly handshake, a gesture of respect and trust.

"Can't say that I'm quite ready for this." Sharkey's lips formed a circle and blew out a breath of tired exasperation.

Casey shook his head. "Never!" he said, echoing Sharkey's

feelings.

Both men had been acquaintances for at least ten years of the eleven Casey had been working with the Florida Marine Patrol. They shared much in common in their family, work background, and appearance. Both men had stout, strong muscular legs and shoulders and possessed a quiet demeanor, a good attribute for a good fisherman spending long quiet hours bobbing on waves waiting for the perfect bite. Both were born and raised in the north Florida panhandle and claimed many relatives from south Alabama, just across the state border. Both were divorced and lived alone. Neither of them had children. Both loved to fish and ended up working in jobs that barely supported their living expenses. Sport fishing in the Gulf of Mexico was a rare luxury for both men who didn't have the equipment, money or the time.

"Pretty full in there?" Casey nodded his head toward the cavernous blue building.

"Nah." Sharkey turned his head and looked toward the storage facility. "Got quite a few empty racks in there," Sharkey added.

The owners of the storage facility had planned for the distant future when they built the metal structure to hold up to five hundred boats. It took time to fill it up with permanent renters. An event like Hurricane Louise would bring in extra revenue from people who wanted to protect their boats in dry storage, even though it would not be a permanent rental.

"Got a space to hide a freebie?" Casey sheepishly asked. He looked past Sharkey's shoulder to avoid direct eye contact with him. Casey was embarrassed to ask.

Sharkey narrowed his eyes. One eyebrow arched up higher than the other. He pursed his lips tightly while he thought about the question for a few minutes. Then he said, "Is this your boat we're talking about? I can't remember that you had a boat. What kind of boat you got?"

"Yeah, I got a small boat. But, it's not for my boat," Casey looked directly into Sharkey's eyes.

As a prior deep sea fishing captain working out of the marina Sharkey knew Casey well enough that the details of where, who, or how the boat was in Casey's charge was a matter for Casey to deal with. Sharkey asked, "You're checking for someone else I take it? Seems kind of odd for you to be asking for a freebie for someone else, but then when a hurricane is coming there's no telling what people try to do," Sharkey eye-balled Casey back. "Whose boat is it?"

Sharkey folded his bronzed arms across his chest.

"It's one of the boats from Anderson's marina. It's called the 'Lucky Two'. Captain left me the keys," Casey explained.

"I don't think I've heard of that boat. What's the captain's name?" Sharkey asked.

The fear of losing his possession of the 'Lucky Two' prevented Casey from divulging too much information to Sharkey.

"Not too sure. I can't remember at the moment. He's a young kid and hasn't been here very long. I could get the name off the records it I have to. Right now I couldn't even guess to tell you his name," Casey lied.

"Can't remember his name, eh? What are you doing with the boat?" Sharkey began to feel suspicious of his friend.

"Pretty strange kid, he just dropped the keys in my hands and said he was done with being a boat captain."

Sharkey was dumfounded. "Just as simple as that!?" Sharkey shot back. "Didn't he say where he was going and when he was coming back?"

"Didn't say where he was going or when he was coming back. He did mention Biloxi at one point. I started thinking now here's a crazy man."

"You're kidding me, right?" Sharkey asked.

"No. It all happened so fast. At first he asked me about leaving the boat at the marina. I recommended that he take it up to the intracoastal. He didn't have a clue how to get there. He got in his truck to leave, got back out, and dropped the keys in my hands. I gave him my phone number, business card. Told him to try and get back in touch with me. He pretty much peeled out of the parking lot. Didn't say anything about what I was supposed to do with the keys or the boat. I don't know if the kid's going to make it back or not."

Casey went on, "Then I saw Captain Darryl Kay. He's the horn blower who lives on the 'Star Chaser' playing his saxophone almost every night. He's on his boat talking to the cats again. I told him what happened and he agreed that the kid just kind of flipped out. This all happened a little over an hour ago."

Sharkey began to relax and chuckled after hearing the story. He knew about Darryl. He'd heard from people who chartered his boat. The fishing excursions usually turned out great with a lot of fish to brag about.

"Bet Darryl must have got a laugh out of that!" Sharkey shook his head side to side in disbelief.

"No. Not really. You should have seen this guy and the desperation in his face. He was nervous as all get out. He didn't have a clue about what to do with his boat with the storm coming. You would have felt sorry for him. All Darryl said to me was the kid never talked to anyone. He kept to himself. Darryl went back to getting things on his boat battened down."

Sharkey wasn't surprised to hear that Darryl reacted the way he did. Not many boat captains liked to get involved with the work Casey Howard did. It was his business, not theirs.

"Well," Sharkey drew in a long deep breath. He was thinking about choosing his words carefully. "I don't feel so sure about doing this, Casey. I'm not the owner of this facility, you know."

Casey didn't wait to second guess what Sharkey would say.

"How about taking a chance? I'd sign paperwork if you got any. I don't know what else to do, but I don't think it's a good idea to leave it untied and bobbing around and smashing into the docks and everything else," Casey pleaded with a smile on his face.

"Let's go on inside and look," Sharkey said. He turned his body around and began to walk toward the entrance. "How big is the 'Lucky Two'?"

"It's pretty good sized, maybe at least thirty nine foot bow to stern. It doesn't have a high crow's nest. It'll fit in there somewhere, I'd bet." Casey walked alongside Sharkey.

Both men stopped at the open doorway, inside of the building.

Another man was driving a small forklift, used to transfer boats, down the center of the building. The concrete floor was the length of a football field. The rumble of the forklift's engine bounced off all four metal walls. It sounded as if four or five machines were all moving at the same time.

Casey turned his head right, left, then upward. His eyes quickly scanned the rows of boats suspended in mid-air. It reminded him of bats in a cave, hanging upside down, row upon row. Each boat was settled on a set of steel beams, like model boats inside a display case.

The metal walls were creaking. Gusts of increasingly stronger winds slapped at the corrugated steel walls making them shake. The open door gave the wind an opportunity to generate more energy inside the cave. A strong gust of wind blew Casey's hair and slapped the cloth of his trousers against his legs. The wind reminded both men of the urgency of time.

"It's amazing to see all this money in one space, huh?" Sharkey asked, watching Casey for his reaction.

"Must be millions of dollars," said Casey almost jealously. He was awestruck to see all the wealth under one roof. "Looks like there's space for more money in here." Casey gave his friend a trusting look and thrust his head upward in the direction of the empty rows above his head.

"Our insurance won't cover us unless the boat is registered to be here with us." The tone of Sharkey's voice shifted to business. "Our form to lease space requires us to have the name of the boat, the state registration license number and the signature of the owner."

Casey eyes rolled up to the ceiling, then around the metal walls, then down to the concrete floor. His head moved slightly with the direction of his eyes. He tried to calm his nerves before making eye contact and speaking to Sharkey again. His head tilted slightly to the left, as if trying to hear something, but he was thinking about the dilemma in his heart. Should he save the boat and falsify a report? Should he protect his future with the job he had now? If he was caught falsifying a report it would put his career in jeopardy. If he protected the boat he might be protecting his future. He could take a risk with the prospect of becoming the owner of a bigger boat and living the life of a real boat captain. He thought about how all of his life he had to answer to someone else. He could seize the opportunity to call the shots. He didn't have time to think about the situation much longer. There was not much time left in the day.

"What's the difference if that boat's in the water tied to a dock and gets busted up with no insurance, or if it's in here with no insurance?" Casey finally said defiantly.

Sharkey's personality was like most men who worked on the docks. He accepted the comment, posed as question, with a laid back attitude. Rather than be offended by what could be construed as one-upmanship, he understood the point Casey made. He saw no reason to start a philosophical discussion.

"What's one more boat going to matter with the millions of dollars stored under the roof now?" Sharkey said with a smirk and a glint of glee in his eyes. "If the roof blows off this place it won't make a whole lot of difference where the boat is. Can't get you the best spot in the house but I'll let you get in the door without paying a cover charge. Let's just go ahead and let's move this thing in here!"

Sharkey turned around and proceeded to walk toward an extra fork lift parked against a corner wall in the building. Before he started the noisy diesel engine he said to Casey, "Meet you at the boat ramp. How long do you think it'll take you to get it here?"

Casey opened his mouth to answer. Before he could get out a single word the crash of heavy metal silenced him. The sound bounced off the metal walls.

"Holy jeeez!" both men yelled in unison.

CHAPTER 24: PARKING LOT MEETING

It wasn't very long after checking into the hurricane shelter in the high school before Darryl's spiritual wellness began to deteriorate. He missed the elements of living on the water. The flapping wings of a pelican, cry of a seagull, salty mist coating his body, tourists' chatter as they walked along the sidewalks admiring the boats, fishy smells rising from the lagoon waters. Heck, even the cats!

He closed his eyes and tried to imagine those things that he loved, but the assaults on his senses, nose, ears and eyes, in the high school gymnasium were too much competition for his imagination. He felt heaviness much like the weight of being buried up to his neck in sand on the beach. The heaviness was settling deep inside his chest.

His mind went back to a cold winter afternoon in January when the charter boat business was at a standstill. He was sitting alone on the top deck of the 'Star Chaser', enjoying the gentle bobbing rock of the boat. No one was around at the marina. It was normal for the parking lot and docks to be quiet and empty that time of year. The major restaurant, Smith's, was closed for two months until the warm weather attracted the tourists back.

Visiting the 'Star Chaser' in the winter was an escape from being shuttered into a small space at the motel room converted into an efficiency apartment he rented for the entire month of January. It was too cold to stay on the 'Star Chaser' because the boat had no heater. He had a standing contract with the motel owner every year. He paid very little since few tourists rented in the winter. In the summer months Darryl repaid the owner the favor of his cheap winter rent with fresh summer fish.

He needed his visits to the 'Star Chaser" to refresh his soul. Even though it was the coldest month of the year, to sit on the top deck on his boat felt like the perfect thing to do. He would promise himself to sit there for a least an hour. He could handle the outdoor cold better than the cramped room of the motel.

Some days, if the wind was not blowing too strong and the skies were clear, he ended up staying until the purple haze that preceded a dark night appeared in the eastern sky and the last glow of orange tint on the western horizon melted into the water line. The lagoon would be as smooth as a pane of glass, reflecting the boats tied up at the marina. It was so easy to relax. He loved the quiet, calm, peaceful time.

The wailing scream of an unhappy baby in distress shattered

the calm images in his daydream. His eyes popped open. His stomach twisted up like a wet towel in the wringing cycle of a washing machine. He was ready, like a wet towel, to flap in a breezy wind to dry out.

"I've got to get out of here and get outside," he huffed.

Babies didn't bother him. Darryl liked babies a lot. They were small human beings who could only cry to express themselves. He had a problem with the adults who did not know how to calm their babies

He rationalized. "Ok. Maybe I need to give the parents a break. Babies know when things aren't going right."

Darryl sat on the cot covered with a thin blue mat, kept his two feet firmly planted on the floor, and eyeballed his corner of the world for at least the next twenty hours or more.

He forced a chuckle and thought, "Hopefully not more than that! At least I got my own pillow."

Before leaving the 'Star Chaser he stuffed a backpack with a pillow, a few clean shirts and two pair of shorts. It would last a few days. He also brought toiletries and a good towel. The backpack was shoved underneath the cot.

Darryl reminded himself of the information heard repeated several times on the radio, "Shelters are the refuse of last resort and not the most pleasant place to be. You must bring your own blankets, toys, games and special food needs."

"I've marked my territory here. You keep a watchful eye on it for me. OK, baby?" he thought. As if he'd transported the thoughts to the wailing baby on the opposite side of the gymnasium, the baby suddenly stopped crying, as if it had heard Darryl's thoughts.

Darryl often felt that he had positive connections with people. It was the key to his successful charter boat business. It started when he was playing his saxophone in the nightclubs, but it translated into all the other things in his life. He called it having it *good vibes* .

His parents, who were both deceased, taught him three basic simple rules in life that contributed to his success in managing his finances and staying out of trouble with the law. Be respectful, obedient and disciplined. Being prepared for the unexpected was something he learned on his own, like the day he experienced the lightening flash-over on the 'Justin Case'. His parents never taught him anything about how to be a survivor in the spiritual world, including falling in love. The day he connected with God's almighty power was his turning point to connecting to people and happiness.

He walked out of the gym and continued at a steady, sure pace down the concrete block hall. At the end was a large opening with a red exit sign hanging above it. As he made his way toward the exit sign he thought about Earl. Life at the marina was never far from his thoughts.

"I didn't have much connection with that kid who abandoned his boat. I should try to pray for him He seems like a lost soul,"

Darryl thought. "Casey Howard. I should pray for him too. Now there's a soul I can't quite put a number on. He goes whichever way the wind blows. Put my finger up and here he is in front of you and smiling. Put my other finger out and there he is with a frown on his face."

Darryl couldn't help but notice that the concrete walls were painted a shipyard grey. Emerald green and tangerine orange highlighted the classroom door frames. The bulletin boards, covered with paper notices and signs, were accented in the same orange and green colors.

"Yuk. No windows anywhere and this is all these kids have to look at? Someone needs to paint a beautiful mural of white waves crashing on the shoreline of the white sandy beaches. Maybe add a dolphin frolicking above a wave. That would liven up this place."

As if his wish were his command, a life-sized, bottle nose, blue dolphin, appeared in front of him. The dolphin was painted on the wall and draped in a ribbon bunting of emerald green and tangerine orange crest. Written above the dolphin's body were the words *Home of the Mosley Dolphins*.

"Hmm." Darryl hummed. "My wish came true. It's just missing the aqua green water, rip curls, sea oats, shells and sugar white sand."

Darryl picked up his pace and made a right turn at the hallway opening. He found himself entering another hallway. At the end of the new hallway he saw a set of solid double doors. He hoped they opened to the outside world. Standing near the doors was a deputy sheriff, wearing a green uniform. When Darryl reached the end of the hallway the deputy sheriff spoke in a deep voice in a tone lacking emotion.

"Can't go out these doors."

"Well, OK sir," Darryl said avoiding sarcasm. Then he asked the obvious question. "Why can't I go out these doors?"

"They're locked."

"OK, so how do I get out of this building?"

"Same way you came in," the deputy responded.

"Well, I'm sorry, Sir. I didn't know this was the wrong way to exit. Everything in this building, the walls, the doors, all look the same to me," Darryl said, trying hard to not get aggravated with the man in uniform.

The deputy stood silent and stone faced, looking past Darryl and down the vacant hallway, not paying attention to Darryl.

Darryl swirled his body around to switch direction. He hoped he was walking the way he came into the building. He had only asked the man in the uniform for directions, a simple question. It seemed appropriate, under the circumstances, that the deputy would give better directions.

"Must be too busy," Darryl thought, "What's happened to people trying to be more helpful? Well, maybe he's got the hurricane and safety of everyone on his mind."

Darryl was patient. If he gave it some serious thought, and he had plenty of time for thinking, he would find his way out of the building.

Darryl's mind used to speed in circles, like a song repeatedly playing over and over, when he didn't understand why things didn't happen the way he thought they should. Before his experience with the lightning flashover on the 'Justin Case' Darryl allowed himself to get angry and frustrated in situations that seemed so absurd and stupidly simple to remedy. Now it was much easier to live by a simple rule. If he was not in control, he endured. His goal was to enjoy each moment as best as he could, and don't worry too much about what might come next. That was yesterday, this is today, tomorrow is a mystery.

So Darryl easily dismissed the deputy from his mind.

He hurried, walking at a fast pace to put the encounter with the deputy behind him. The rubber soled shoes he wore squeaked with each footstep on the hard floor, echoing against the concrete walls.

He back tracked and finally found the end of the correct hallway. At the end was a set of double metal doors with steel lined windows. When Darryl reached them he forcefully pushed the horizontal metal bar with both hands. He greeted the fresh air and parking lot with a huge smile that disappeared when he saw groups of families peering into the trunks of their parked vehicles. Bags filled with supplies of questionable contents were being unloaded into waiting arms of children and adults. One person held a leash with a small dog on the end.

"Now that's sad. That dog's going to spend the stormy night in the car all alone. I don't know if that's better than inside the house or not. Oh well, to each his own solution," Darryl thought as he headed to his vehicle.

Leaving the high school and getting back on the road was easy. Another car quickly took his parking space.

He drove the Lynn Haven neighborhood streets to highway 231, first traveling north on Highway 77 and then turning right on Highway 390 to go east. He had no specific plan of where to drive. He was taking a break away from the gymnasium noise and going to enjoy the last few hours of daylight. He rarely went to the northern section of Bay County. It wasn't long before Darryl realized that he'd made a very stupid choice.

"This may have been a huge mistake," he thought. "Everyone is heading out of the county. I am crawling in a line of traffic again. Didn't I already do this once today?!"

In spite of the inconvenience, Darryl smiled at his foolishness. The slow moving traffic allowed him more time to stare at the blue glass dolphin hanging from the rear view mirror. Being in the quiet of the car, with no radio on, just observing nature around him reinforced his decision to leave and find peace outside of the gymnasium.

When he reached the end of Highway 390 and approached the intersection at Highway 231 his jaw dropped. His right hand held the bottom of the steering wheel, guiding the small pick-up truck at a slow roll into the parking lot of the gas station located at the corner of the busy intersection. The sight of so many cars lined up waiting to get a turn at the gas station pumps was unbelievable. At first appearance it seemed like foolishness. So many people, like little ants, were moving slow and trying to escape. They were barely going anywhere. He saw urgency in the faces of people who sat in their cars. There was a fierce, strong hurricane moving in their direction. It was real and they were scared. The damage that Mother Nature would cause surely could be devastating to the lives of so many.

Darryl inhaled air through his parted lips.

"Think positive and happy thoughts," he coached himself. He slowly let the air back out of his lungs through his nose.

He checked the needle on his gas gauge. There was three quarters of a tank full of gas. Darryl thought about what he would do if hurricane Louise did make a direct landfall on Panama City Beach.

"I probably have enough gas to drive to Dothan, Alabama. Maybe even Atlanta, Georgia. What would I do there? Should I get in one of these lines? It'll probably take most of these people thirty or forty five minutes for a turn at the gas pump. At least ten cars are waiting in each line. I will probably burn more gas waiting."

Darryl decided not to wait in a line. He turned his truck to park at the convenience store associated with the gas pumps, but saw nowhere to park. He drove to a neighboring parking lot of a fast food hamburger restaurant across from the gas station. There were spaces in the parking lot and a long line of cars waiting in the drive through order window.

"I'd best turn back and head to the high school gymnasium," he decided.

Before he could turn the truck his eyes were suddenly drawn to a young, pretty girl, standing all alone and leaning against the front hood of a small white car. Both of her arms were folded across the front of her chest and her face was tilted toward the sky.

For no particular reason and without giving any thought to why, Darryl decided to drive in the direction of the girl to get a closer look. As he inched his truck closer he wondered if she was alone. No one else was sitting in the car.

"Now what am I doing?" he questioned his actions but continued to drive the truck toward her.

He passed directly in front of the girl, slowing down to get a closer look at her face. It was not the face of someone who appeared to be waiting nonchalantly for another person to return to the car. Darryl believed he was the kind of man who was experienced in

158

understanding, and reading, the emotions of others. This girl's face had distress and sadness written all over it. The crossed arms in front of her chest were not expressing anger. They expressed a need for protection.

Darryl stopped his truck in front of the standing girl. Out of the open window he asked, "Need any help?" He smiled and tried to show a look of sincere concern on his face.

Soft, chocolate brown eyes, the shape of a doe's, looked back at him with a quiet sadness that he'd never seen before.

Eleanore sucked in a breath, reaching inside to find her voice. She swallowed before opening her mouth to answer Darryl. Her eyes locked like a magnet on a pair of turquoise blue eyes. They were eyes that she instantly felt could be trusted.

If eyes are the window to a person's soul, Eleanore and Darryl felt, at that moment, a simultaneous connection to each other's kindred spirit. Two pairs of eyes found confirmation of honesty, compassion and hope.

When Eleanore finally spoke, Darryl's brain was captured by a new dimension of power beyond his control. It consumed him. The sound of her voice filled his body with the same emotions he felt when he listened to the evening sounds of summer sitting on the deck of the 'Star Chaser'.

Both were suddenly oblivious, unconscious of the cars and people all around them. The discontent they felt in their personal circumstances was forgotten. Their feelings became electrified, like the flashing lights on the rides at a carnival.

"I'm not from around here," Eleanore tried to speak in a calm voice. "I was planning to drive down here for the day, or maybe a couple days, to try to find an old friend of mine." Her voice took on urgency and words flowed out quickly as she continued. "I was actually planning to drive down to Captain Anderson's marina today. My gas tank is nearly empty now. Didn't realize how serious the hurricane might be until I got pretty far down the highway. I really didn't expect all of this." She unfolded her arms and waved them in circles toward the two parking lots. She let her arms drop to her sides in a dejected gesture of hopelessness.

Darryl asked cautiously, "You need some money?" He sensed she could really use his help, but was surprised to hear her mention the name of the same marina that constantly occupied his mind.

"Not really," she returned sullenly.

"Do you know how to get to Captain Anderson's Marina?" he asked.

At first she hesitated, then she said, "Well, not really."

Darryl detected a change in the tone in her voice. He decided that meeting her was not just a coincidence. She was beautiful and needed to find a friend at the same marina he called home. He put on the friendliest face possible and let the next words spill out of his mouth without thinking.

159

"I have a boat at Captain Anderson's Marina. I was planning to head that way myself to check on it. You're more than welcome to ride along," he said, hopeful that she would accept the offer. He didn't want to drive back to the gymnasium.

"That sounds like a nice invitation," she half smiled. "You look like someone I can trust."

Overcome with excitement Darryl clumsily said, "You and me too!"

CHAPTER 25: DARRYL'S DARING DRIVE

Eleanore had enough time alone with her thoughts and memories during the drive from Pine Mountain. When she glided her car on a near empty fuel tank into the gas station parking lot on highway 231 she was ready to go along with whatever happened. She'd built up a steely resolve to accept what may be a new beginning or the final day she'd ever spend with Earl Keith.

She'd thought about their beginnings together; when they first met in school. Being from a small town they had known each other practically all their lives. They really met, so to speak, on their first date. Earl invited Eleanore to go with him to the movies. It was some scary movie that she could not remember the name of to save her life. She'd thought on that detail for a long time before giving up.

What she did remember was how, in the darkness of the movie theatre, Earl first rested his arm on the back of her seat and then let it slide down to rest around her back with his hand cupped over her shoulder. That felt fine, but before the movie ended she found herself picking his hand away as he tried to move it over other parts of her body. He finally grabbed her hand and held it throughout the remainder of the movie. She allowed him to do that, since she expected it on a first date.

Eleanore was critically insecure when it came to her physical appearance. Compared to other girls she saw many flaws in herself. Her hair was too thin and straight as a board. The color of her hair was a dull light brown, not the same shiny vibrant brown like the other southern beauties in her town. Her face was just okay, an average looking nose flanked by common brown eyes. Her teeth were stained a little, on the yellowish side, and were mostly straight except for two turned overlapping teeth on the bottom row. She felt she was nothing spectacular to look at. She was nothing like the girls in the advertisements in the newspapers and magazines, and certainly not as good looking as the girls who lived in more expensive homes in Pine Mountain.

Anyone else who took the time to truly look at Eleanore would enjoy the image of beauty that she really was. Whenever she did notice the attention of others it annoyed her. If the attention came from a group of girls in the high school, she felt their critical stares. She was never quite sure what is was, but she often felt their jealousy or envy for something that they wanted to possess. If she attracted the attention of a boy, she believed it meant only a sexual craving for the opposite sex.

She wanted a deeper purpose to her life than to just have a

relationship with a man and start a family. What she wanted more than anything else in the world was to create something special. Growing up, her mother lectured that she must learn how to take care of herself. No one else would take care of her. Her mother passionately drove this in her head in a voice pitched with anger and hostility. From her mother's point of view, there would be no man who could be trusted to take care of her.

"If you find a man, always go for the one who has money. Otherwise he'll work you to death," were her mother's recurring words. "It's easier to love a man with money than to love a poor man."

Eleanore's mother told her to work hard in school, get a good education and then she could get a good job to support herself. It was a very simple formula. Added to this advice were more spiteful, hurtful words from her mother that Eleanore still hung onto in her heart: "You're on your own when you leave home. Don't expect any help from me. I've already done enough for you."

Eleanore tried, and earned, very good grades in school. Encouraged and inspired by the compliments of her teachers, she steadily grew to believe that she would be able to take care of herself when she finished school. She soon discovered that, without other advantages in the social world, she faced a life of hard work. The daily struggles of life compounded the simple formula she'd been taught by her mother. It was not as simple and easy as her mother had explained. There were more pieces to the puzzle than knowledge from bookwork, which of course always remained in her brain.

After high school Eleanore struggled to keep a roof over her head. She never seemed to have enough money and often skipped a meal. It was a challenge to prioritize what was important and be organized.

She had trouble finding people who she could trust. She believed that it was right to give everyone a fair chance to prove themselves. To be the person they claimed to be. She thought it wasn't right to judge a person by their appearance. She soon realized that it was often people who were the best looking and well-dressed who got the most attention, if only for those two reasons. She wanted attention and be judged for her knowledge and actions. These were the qualities that made a person fully acceptable.

There was one principle, one belief, that Eleanore stood firm on and would not budge. She knew her mother would argue against it.

Eleanore believed that love counted more than money for her to live a life of true happiness. She realized she could not live on love alone, but money was not the only thing that mattered in this life. She understood that love did not put money in her pocket, the roof over her head or the food on a table. She was willing to work very hard for the basic necessities, and maybe some luxuries. She did not expect anyone else to provide for her. She knew that there were many people in the world who possessed more money than they needed and were not happy because they lived without love. She wanted love to be the priority in her life, not money.

Eleanore would always choose the goal of happiness in loving someone over the goal of money. She believed opposite philosophies about money hurt a relationship.

Her ideas about money, and her ideal to be accepted and respected for who she was, was the foundation for her decision to not follow Earl to Panama City Beach. His dream to become rich being a deep sea fishing boat captain, doing what he loved, was fine. She didn't go with Earl because she never expected that he would make a decision that big without involving her in the choice. That night at Stumpy's he announced his decision. He never asked for her opinion, or how she felt.

Now that Earl was out of money, or so she thought, she would find out if he really loved her. Why else did he call her in the middle of the night? She hoped this would be the day she would find Earl ready to give her his heart and take her love.

Eleanore gave the inside of her small white car, packed with her few possessions , a last look before stepping into Darryl's truck. She heaved a heavy sigh when she sat down.

Darryl looked at Eleanore before starting up the engine. "You'll have to pardon the black case if it's in your way Got what you need?" Darryl words came out of his mouth like a gentle breeze.

She moved her feet to the side and said, "For now, I suppose," she answered calmly but gripped her fingers tightly around the straps of her purse, the only possession she took. She left everything else in her car. She believed she would be back soon.

"Seems really crazy around here right now," she said to Darryl when he eased his truck into a line of cars waiting to turn out of the parking lot.

"You're right! But, it's going to get crazier before it's all over," he replied. He nodded his head in agreement without looking at Eleanore. He didn't want her to see that he was more than a little nervous. It had been a long time since he had invited a girl to accompany him anywhere. "However, the good news is not too many people will be heading west, the way we're heading now."

"And so why are you going in that direction, then?" She fixed her eyes straight ahead. She felt suddenly felt anxious sitting in the truck with a strange man.

"I just didn't like the idea of hanging around a hurricane shelter all day," Darryl said in a matter-of-fact way. He hoped the tone of his voice didn't reflect the grumpy feeling he had about the gymnasium.

"Is that what you're going to do?" Eleanore's Georgia southern drawl was strong. She was suddenly surprised to hear this piece of information. "Spend the night at the hurricane shelter?"

"Well, it will be safer. I can't stay on the boat that I own at the marina. It would be way too dangerous. I just needed to drive around before I hunker down in my corner suite, or my corner cot, at the high school gym. I've been through this routine before. It's not pretty and it ain't fun. But, there aren't a whole lot of choices." Darryl's mouth was like a small motor, words flowing fast. He turned his head towards Eleanore's face to read her reaction and saw a pretty face innocently taking in his words with concern. He quickly changed the subject.

"Guess it might be good to introduce ourselves to each other. My name is Darryl. Darryl Kay. And you are?"

"Eleanore." she stated in a quiet voice, barely loud enough to hear.

"No last name?"

"Yeah, but...." She hesitated, unsure if it was the right thing to tell this stranger her last name. Then again, he had told her his last name. "Eleanore Mungo," she said with confidence.

"And, you're from out of town. Where would that be?"

"Pine Mountain. Pine Mountain, Georgia."

Darryl grinned. "Pine Mountain. I've heard of that place. Heard that's it's a great place. Pretty small, but a nice little town."

Eleanore felt herself relax. She couldn't find a particular reason but suddenly she felt safe in the company of this strange man. For the first time since walking out the door of her upstairs studio apartment she had not stopped thinking about finding Earl and what would happen when she did, until this very moment sitting in the truck with this man.

"What time you got?" Darryl asked without noticing if she was wearing a watch.

Eleanore looked at her watch and answered, "Three thirty."

"I bet you haven't set your watch on central time. Its two thirty," he angled his head slightly in her direction, chuckled and resumed his attention to the road.

"Oh my, that's right," she laughed, embarrassed after he corrected her. She made a mental note to advance the hour on her watch. After a long night and long drive she was tired. She needed to be aware of what was happening around her and thought she should have paid more attention to the weather too.

After a few moments of silence Darryl asked, "Was it a very long drive down here? How long did it take?"

"I was just checking," she said and glanced at her watch again.

Before she could answer Darryl's first question he asked another question. "How long have you been standing there at the gas station?"

"Oh, not long. Not sure, but not long." Eleanore said.

"Been standing there not long, or not long to drive down here?"

They both laughed. The laughter eased the tension and helped them feel less awkward with each other. It was as if they were old friends who had not seen each other in a few days. The substance of their conversation turned to other topics.

"Been down here many times?" he asked.

"A few. I guess maybe three or four times," she answered.

"Love the beach, do you?"

"Oh yes. It's a lot better than swimming in the lakes or creeks back in Georgia. The water is salty and warm and the waves are nice too."

"Gotcha," Darryl said. "But, you know what? I like Georgia. People there are nice. The countryside is nice. Lots of green in the mountains up north and they got a small coastal area around St. Simons Island. I hear that the fishing is good there, too. I'm guessing it is anyway."

"Yes, I think you're right, but I've never been to that area. I'm not one to fish much myself." Eleanore tried to keep up with Darryl.

"Have you ever been fishing?" Darryl was fishing for an answer that might spark her to open up a little more and tell him about herself.

"A couple times, yes, but only on the rivers."

"Did you fish in a boat or on the banks?"

"In a small Jon boat. I've always wondered why they call them Jon boats," she said.

"Don't know myself," Darryl answered. Her curiosity intrigued him. "Did it have a motor?"

"Yes." Eleanore felt a smile spreading across her face as she thought of the silly questions this kind man was asking. It felt good to feel a little happy. "It was a small motor. We generally don't need a big motor for going up and down the river. Maybe it was thirty five horsepower. I don't remember."

"Catch any good fish?"

The smile erupted into a small giggle. "I really can't remember!"

"Ever been out on a boat in the Gulf of Mexico?"

"Nope," her giggle died. The soft spoken, quick answer, made Darryl suspect something dark behind the answer.

Darryl joked, "Well, how'd you like to go out fishing with me one day? I can take you out on my boat one day. Just not today!!"

Both Darryl and Eleanore laughed together again at the absurd thought of going fishing on a day like this one.

"Lord have mercy. Look at all of these cars," he quickly changed the subject. Something about her expressions impressed him. He had a feeling that her spirit was troubled by a deep hurt, sadness, or fear that she was hanging on to. Violations against a person's heart are hard to reconcile.

Darryl knew he might not be able to heal an aching heart, but he decided to press on. "I asked you about fishing. Are you afraid to go out on deep sea fishing boats? Some people I know are afraid."

"I'm not afraid to go out on a boat," Eleanore whispered. Her emotions were going adrift like a small raft on a sea of rolling waves.

She turned her head to face the open passenger window. She couldn't help herself. The tears began to silently roll in a steady stream down her soft white cheeks. Never mind that she was sitting next to a stranger, a man who may not even be a person she could trust with her safety. She struggled to choke back the sound of sobs that crept like a long worm crawling to the back of her throat. Then she heard the next question.

"Think you'll be willing to take a ride on one of those big deep sea fishing boats that go way out, maybe ten miles, out into the Gulf of Mexico? That's the best way to catch some really fine eating fish!"

"Noooooaaahhhhggg," she sobbed. The word came out like a long burp of air starting from her stomach. Tears trickled down her face. Loud sniffles to stop the water dripping from her nose were as loud as the sobs.

Darryl tried not to get excited but he was caught off guard. "Okay! Okay! Okay!" He didn't want to create a commotion in the car. He knew a sob like the one he just heard was a serious matter. It might take some time before Eleanore calmed down. He knew that women did this crying to calm down in their own way and in their own time. He just hoped that it didn't get worse. He wondered if he should say anything else. Fishing, or boats, were definitely not good topics.

Darryl was used to one-sided conversations. Many of his deep sea fishing trips on the 'Star Chaser' featured a silent group of four or six sleepy men, groggy from a party on the beach the night before. He thought talking helped the men forget about the hangovers, or the seasickness. If he ever got a chatty customer he held on to the wheel and let the giddy man, or woman, chat and ask as many questions as they wanted. He understood why people were quiet. Either they listened and responded, or they tuned you out. It didn't matter to Darryl. His job was to take them fishing!

This situation with the stranger sitting next to him today, as he held on to the steering wheel of the truck, was much different than being on the 'Star Chaser'. Darryl was no quitter, even in this strange uncharted water. Eleanore continued to cry with an occasional snort and sniffle.

After a few minutes, Darryl tried again. "Pretty bad news, huh?" he said. "Come down here and then find out you're facing a hurricane!"

She sobbed. Her face was still turned away from Darryl. "No. NO! That's NOT it at all," she finally blurted out. Her shoulders shook.

"I'm sorry there's no air conditioning in this truck," Darryl said as casual as he could, as if nothing were wrong.

Eleanore's faucet was beginning to slow down and dry up. "I'm okay," she finally said without a sob. "I'm sorry."

She grabbed, controlled and built a steel wall around her emotions and feelings. She dismissed the ugly, thoughts she had in the car driving from Pine Mountain. Going back to Pine Mountain now, or ever again, under the circumstances she left were not on her mind. Those thoughts were not helpful. It was no use to worry about

Earl or her precious cat anymore. There was no hope in finding a cat that had been lost so long ago. She needed to focus on her life at this moment. Now she was facing a new problem: a hurricane. Could she live through that, too? It was better to focus on the moment. Who was this person, stranger, she was riding with in the truck, going to the marina? It would be smarter to find out more about Darryl.

"Sorry about the air conditioning," Darryl repeated himself, not knowing what else to say. It was enormously unusual for him to be at a loss for words. "I'm usually pretty good at coming up with new things to talk about. I thought maybe saying the same thing again wouldn't hurt."

His voice cut sharply into her thoughts like a boom of thunder after a bolt of lightning. The hair on her arms tingled. She began to fidget nervously with her hands as she sat in her seat. She was embarrassed by her loss of composure and wanted to restart and get to know this man.

"Oh, yes," she said, now looking at him with interest. "Oh, I understand how cars can be trouble. Mine is not in the greatest shape, either. I like the fresh air. Wind blowing in my face and blowing through my hair and all that."

"Great! I'm so glad to hear that! Not about the car trouble, of course!" Darryl laughed. He was relieved to hear Eleanore speak normally again. He vowed to not bring up the subject of fishing, or say the *boat* word again. This was going to be difficult. He loved to talk about fishing and his boat the 'Star Chaser'. There was so much he could tell her. Instead he said, "It's going to take us quite some time to get there at this pace. Want to listen to the radio? We probably won't hear much in the way of music. There will just be a lot of talk about getting ready for hurricane Louise. Things like get water, get gas, get canned food, and get money from the ATM machines before the power goes out because the machines don't work when the power is out. On and on with that kind of stuff."

"No, I'm not interested in the radio. I heard a lot of radio news and static on the drive down," she replied.

"Wow, it's incredibly hot here," she blurted out without thinking about his air conditioning problem. "I'm sorry! I didn't mean anything about that. I hope that I didn't offend you!"

"Oh, no. That's just fine. It's not so much the heat as it is the humidity in the atmosphere. It gets that way right before the hurricane gets here. If I could drive a little faster the wind could blow on your face!"

They both laughed politely about the circumstances.

They rode along in quiet, occasionally wiping beads of sweat from their faces. Wet stains formed on their clothing. A polite cough or a deep sigh was the only noise inside the truck for a long time. The sky above them was covered in a mass of dense clouds in various shades of white, grey and black. The riders in the truck, both nervous about each other, didn't notice the turmoil in the sky.

Darryl concentrated hard on something to talk about that wouldn't upset Eleanore again. He didn't want to hit the wrong nerve and make her cry again. It was just so unlike him not to be able to strike up a conversation with someone. He reassured himself that he knew he could do it. He kept his eyes on the road as he thought about the girl sitting next to him. Eleanore's voice finally broke the quiet and startled him.

"I like that blue dolphin," she said. The blue glass dolphin hanging on a filament fishing line from the rear view mirror swayed slightly.

Darryl felt his heart pounding. It was bursting with relief. "You do?" he said with heartfelt enthusiasm. Her mention of the blue dolphin was the springboard. Dolphins were one of his favorite topics.

"Hey, you know what? There's legend that dolphins bring good luck to fishermen. Oops, talking about fishing again." Darryl abruptly stopped.

"No. It's okay. Tell me the story of the dolphin."

He quickly started again. "It's a story about safety. There's a Greek legend about dolphins. This may be a myth, maybe true, but I can't be sure." He wondered if she should continue or change the subject. It involved fishermen.

Before he could say more Eleanore spoke up. "There are probably a lot of cool stories about fishermen, fish or even animals for that matter. There's so many different kind of animals in the world." Her voice drifted.

Darryl wasn't going to let her drop off so fast and prompted her. "Please go on. This traffic is crawling. I'd be going faster if I was a four legged animal."

She laughed, "That's funny. If you really think about it there must be thousands and thousands of different fish in the ocean."

"Can't even imagine a number to put on it," hiding his surprise that she used the word fish in a sentence again. "You'd think that as slow as I'm driving I wouldn't have to pay much attention to the road, but this constant stop and go, stop and go, makes driving more difficult."

"I agree. And dolphins," she continued. "I think I've read that they come in different colors, right?"

Darryl grinned. They were on a good track. "I've heard of pink dolphins over in China, I think. I think one was sighted once in Lake Ponchatrain."

"Where's that?" Eleanore asked.

"Over in Louisiana."

"No way!" she exclaimed, with interest.

"Oh, yeah!"

"You know what I think?" she went on. "This storm is coming and everyone around us is scrambling to survive. What do you think

168

all the creatures do to survive a hurricane?"

She really has a charming curiosity Darryl thought before answering. "I've been thinking about that too. All animals have instincts. They can feel the change in the atmosphere, like something isn't normal. I've heard the same thing about animals sensing earthquakes before they happen. They go a little bit crazy, I guess, so to speak. Then they try to run, but every animal, just like a human has a sense of fear when they feel cornered and have nowhere safe to go."

"I saw that look of fear in my cat's eyes," she lowered her voice. Then continued in a strong voice, "It actually happened down here at the marina, where we're going."

Eleanore was a bit surprised that she could talk about this event and not feel the sadness that swept over her earlier.

"Oh? R-e-a-l-l-y?" Darryl stretched out the word as far as it would go. It took him by surprise. She had been to the marina before today.

"Yes.....I was down here about a year ago. Oh, I guess a little more than that. It was in the summer. I had this beautiful white fluffy cat. It had green eyes. She was just beautiful. I was parked at the marina. She jumped out of my car when I opened the door and ran. I couldn't find her."

Darryl was puzzled by the information she just told him, but decided not to ask her questions that might make her cry again. "I can bet you that the majority of cats, at least the ones I've known, do not like to ride in any type of vehicle," he said.

"Oh, I cried and cried out for her but she was gone so fast. I didn't even see which way she ran."

"Cat's name?" his interest was genuine.

"Princess." She answered tentatively, a little embarrassed.

"Cool name. Sounds fitting from the way you described her."

"Oh, she was beautiful!" Eleanore was relieved to hear that he liked the name. "And, she was just only a little spoiled!" Eleanore smiled. The memory of her cat and Darryl's sincere reaction made her feel happier.

"So is it a friend, or the cat, the real reason you came back down here? To find your Princess or a Prince?" He laughed. "Now that's me!"

Eleanore burst out laughing. Her cheeks, already red from the heat, turned a darker beet red. Darryl's joke caught her off guard.

"I tell you what," he continued after their belly chuckling stopped. "All of those cats I've seen down there at the marina know how to take care of themselves."

"Would you know? Have you seen a cat that looked like Princess?" she asked breathlessly.

"I think maybe I have," he said haltingly. He gave the question some honest, serious thought. "Yeah, maybe, but don't get your hopes up. Those cats don't hang around us guys, or people for that matter, except when all is quiet at night. There are too many people around during the day with all the cars, noise, and traffic. When it's dark at night it's hard to tell if I've seen a white cat or a grey cat. If I have any extra fish from my trips I throw it to them from my boat."

"You feed the cats?!" she practically shouted, excited to know that her Princess maybe didn't starve to death.

"Wait, wait, wait," he raised his voice too. "Don't be thinking that you'll find Princess." He didn't want her to get hysterically hopeful about her cat. "Yes, I feed the cats, but food's the only interest they have in me."

"I am so sorry," Eleanore sincerely apologized. She noticed anxiety in his voice for the first time. "I know it sounded terrible the way it came out just then. I am just so excited now. Hearing you say you have the boat down at the marina. I mean, what's the word I'm trying to think of?"

"Don't have a clue," he said more calmly. He was trying hard not to worry about what word might come out of her mouth.

A few minutes of silence passed. Then she finally said triumphantly, "Serendipity! That's the word, serendipity!"

"Okay," Darryl stretched the sound of the letter 'K' into a long melodious note in a deep baritone voice.

"I've met you! Darryl. RIGHT?! And now I believe you may have seen my cat Princess and that's wonderful. And, you may even know another thing. Have you ever heard of a man named Earl? Earl Keith? He's supposed to have a boat down there at Captain Anderson's marina."

Darryl felt the hair on his arms tingle. His heart raced extra beats. This news was jolting. The only word he could think of was spooky, but the sweet word serendipity sounded so much better. He needed to come up with an answer quick or she might suspect that he knew something more. He needed to be careful and give serious, considerable thought before answering any more questions about Earl Keith during the rest of the long ride to the marina.

"Well, maybe. There are quite a few boat owners at Captain Anderson's marina. I think I met an Earl," Darryl said forced a laugh. "And there might even be a Duke, a King, a Prince and a Princess down at the docks. For now it seems that fate has brought us together. What else could make this day more interesting than a hurricane named Louise?"

CHAPTER 26: SOUND IN SPACE

Hurricane Louise, a spinning funnel that grew tighter and tighter, stronger and stronger, churning water into tall waves in all directions methodically grew bigger. The large sinister mass spanned across three hundred miles. Location didn't matter. The tides forced the waters to rise in the Gulf of Mexico, bays, bayous, and rivers. The barometer pressure was falling, dropping lower than any time in any recent record book kept by a weather center.

The boats at Captain Anderson Marina bumped along with the waves. Fluff's stomach was doing flip turns inside her shaking body.

"I need air! Space! Something!" Fluff's thoughts screamed inside her mind.

When she'd heard Casey Howard's footsteps getting closer to the 'Lucky Two' Fluff scrambled from hiding behind the black rubber boot lying on the deck to leaping inside of it. When Casey stepped onto the boat she backed up deep inside to the toe and nervously waited until he left. She felt the boat rock when he departed. When she no longer heard the noise of Casey' footsteps, she crawled out for air.

Nervously, slowly, she moved one front paw to the top of the black rubber boot and extended her claws, gripping the outside of the boot. She pressed her ears down flat on each side of her round face and gradually, inch by inch, extended her head until her glassy eyes were level with the top of the boot. She observed the landscape, fearful Casey might be returning. Her long white whiskers, bent against the inner circle of rubber, twitched. She extended he second paw and dug her claws tight onto the inside rim of the boot, ready to leap or lash out.

Fluff bolted forward like a guided missile. Space and freedom! She skidded across the deck of the boat and then turned her head to look back at the rubber boot lying on its side. The same boot she had spent cramped up inside for what felt like forever.

Fluff eyed the boat's deck. A small white plastic bag lying near the black boot caught her attention. She crouched and crept to it, belly dragging on the boat's deck, and sniffed at the plastic. She nervously licked and chewed at the plastic for minutes, feeling relaxation as she did it. She was ashamed to be doing something so silly, but it helped her nerves. Cramped in that black rubber boot was too much for her.

Fluff worried. "What now? I need to think clearly. What is King doing inside the cabin? I can't hear him at all!"

She perked up her ears. Her little heart was beating fast inside of her chest. She thought of licking or chewing on the plastic bag again, but there was nothing left of the bag for her scratchy, bumpy tongue to savor. The bag was already full of holes.

The sound of the waves splashing against the side of the boat caught her attention. The stink of the water made her stomach churn. She was not at all hungry, but a lick of fresh water, just one drop, would feel so good on her curly pink tongue right now.

"I can't think of being thirsty. Poor King! I bet he is so thirsty too. I could meow softly. King would answer me. I know that he would."

Suddenly a loud noise made Fluff jump. She screeched. Her mouth opened wide revealing her sharp fangs.

The sound of heavy metal crashing against heavy metal carried fast and loud across the open waters of the lagoon. The noise bounced off the waves, returning the sound to her ears multiple times.

Another new fear obscured Fluff's thinking. She reacted to the noise by bellowing out loud meows.

"KING!" The word spewed, fangs bared, with a strength she'd never used. "KING! I'm not afraid. I can handle this. I'm here. I'm alive. I can survive. I need you KING!!!"

She dug deep to find strength and think positive. She remembered her first day alone at the docks. She always regretted the day she jumped out of the car and left her beloved Eleanore. King had helped her to survive without Eleanore. She could not bear the thought of losing King.

A noise came from behind the cabin door. "I'm here."

Fluff heard the resolute, muted but strong, meow of King.

"Oh, King! It's you. I hear you! Are you okay?!" She meowed loud and frantically, giving no thought to who might hear her now. She buried her brief memory of regrets to focus on the moment.

"Yes," King meowed back.

"Did you hear that loud crash just a few minutes ago?" Fluff asked.

She paced on the deck, sniffing at the bottom crack of the door. She wanted to hear every snippet of sound from him. "KING," she marouwed.

"SHHHHH," he growled back at Fluff. "You might bring attention to us on the boat. I'm glad you're still here. I wondered if you had left. But, I don't think it is a good thing for you to stay on this boat."

He meowed a little more softly and continued, "Yes, I heard the loud crash. I'm not worried about it. I am worried about something else. I can't explain it, but I have a feeling that something else is going on. It's something bigger than any crashing noise. My fur is standing up on my back and my head is pounding."

"What do you mean? Why do you say that? Don't you want someone to come and open the door so you can get out of there and be off of this boat? Don't you want to be OFF of this boat?" Her feeling of hope and happiness began to dissolve.

"Yes! Of course I want to be off this boat!" he answered without hesitation. He knew he needed to be off the boat for many reasons. He wanted to reassure her, but he felt danger.

"After all that rocking and rolling on the water last night I'm so ready to be out of here." he tried to say with a small laugh. "I'm pretty tired of being locked up in here. There's no running room. I was afraid of Captain Keith. He got real angry after listening to the radio. He was saying crazy things to himself about bad weather coming. He turned the radio off and left, but then came back a short time later. His mood was rotten, worse than before he left. I couldn't believe it. He left early this morning and I don't think he is coming back. Right now, I doubt any human will be coming back to this boat. I have to figure out a way to get out of here."

King hoped what he told her did not cause her to worry. He wanted her to stay calm. But, he didn't want to give Fluff any false hope that everything was going to get better any time soon. He didn't know how she could assist him in getting out of the locked up cabin.

"Listen," he said, drawing on the last bit of strength he had. "Most of those humans don't' care much about us cats. But, right now I wouldn't mind if one of them hopped on this boat and started chasing me with one of those shovels they use to load up the fish in the wheelbarrow."

"Oh, that's not like you. You've been locked up too long!" Fluff giggled at the idea of King being chased with a shovel.

She knew there were humans, like Eleanore and the captain on the 'Star Chaser', who liked cats. She knew King had been mistreated and unwanted by his former owner. She hoped King would understand that there was goodness to be found in some humans. Just as it is difficult to look deep into the rock to find the diamond, the character and moral soul of a person lies deep. Not all humans treated animals bad. Some people loved their pets more than they loved other humans.

"Where are you?" she changed the subject.

King answered, "Sitting under the table. Where are you?"

"I am crouched next to the wall near the door. BUT, just a minute ago my head was sticking out of a rubber boot."

"That's funny," King purred. "Thanks for that laugh! I sure did need one. Why were you inside a rubber boot?"

She responded, "Sure, pretty darn funny. I was scared. Casey Howard came on the boat a little while ago. That's why I was hiding in the rubber boot. I'm afraid of him and didn't want him to see me." Fluff stopped, waiting for King to comment on the visit by Casey.

King didn't know what to think about Casey being on the boat. He thought he felt the boat drop lower a few minutes earlier, something different than the roll of a wave.

Fluff went on, "I'd like to see you, but I am afraid to jump up near the window again. Someone might see me on the boat."

King asked, "Can you see anything happening out there? How's the weather?"

"I don't know about the weather. I've been too worried about you, not the weather. It feels the same to me as always, hot and humid. Well, maybe a little more humid than hot. It's a little windy too."

"And where did that loud crash come from?" he asked.

"I don't know. It was really loud!" Fluff answered. "Sound travels quickly over water. It could have come from anywhere."

The cats fell silent and concentrated on hearing new noises.

Not far from the marina two drivers not paying attention to their duties behind the wheel of their vehicles met in an unfortunate way. A sporty black car had crashed into the driver's side of a minivan trying to cross the road. The impact of the black car caused the van to flip over on its side. The driver of the van, a middle aged woman, sat pinned inside with her seatbelt still locked. She was crying and yelling, "My dog, my dog!"

The driver of the black sports car was crouched on his hands and knees in a pile of shattered glass. He peered inside the driver's side window of the van. His face had a stunned look. His eyes darted wildly from the woman to the dog. His own vehicle had spun out of control but landed upside on the side of the road not far from the collision with the van.

In the back of the minivan a mixed breed medium sized dog was trapped inside a dog carrier cage, alternately yelping and panting.

"Oh my, those noises sound terrible," Fluff cried to King.

"I am not a fan of any dog, but I have to feel sorry for that one!" King replied. "It was such a loud crash. They must be really hurt."

"I believe it!" Fluff said with conviction. "Oh, King, I am so afraid to leave this boat, but if you are to get out someone has to open the door to the cabin!"

"I know. It feels hopeless," King said gently. "Have you seen any of the other cats roaming around or nearby?"

"Nooooooo!" Fluff moaned.

Like Fluff, King's nerves were stretched thin. He was tired. He was thirsty. His hope and plan to escape plan looked weak.

"Listen to me Fluff," he said in a stern voice using all the energy he could muster. "Stay calm. I think you should stay on the boat. I think you will be safe here and I'd rather have you stay with me."

"I am glad to hear that," she answered in a shaky voice.

To reinforce his decision he added, "We are better off staying on this boat anyway. If the weather gets bad, like they were talking about on the radio last night, we are in a better place on the boat. All those other cats are looking for hiding places too. You can bet on it. We've got the best hiding place here and there's no one around to bother us. Those other cats will be running across the street to hide in the woods. This boat is going to be a whole lot safer than some hole dug to barricade themselves against wind and rain. Or worse, clinging to a branch in a tree!"

After listening to the reasons for staying on the boat Fluff felt somewhat reassured. It made sense. It sounded better than the other options.

"You know about this kind of bad weather?" she asked, trying not to sound scared. She had something new to fear.

"Yes, I do." King answered in a firm tone. He remembered stories he'd heard about cats clinging with all four paws to a large oak tree branch for hours while winds, heavy with stinging rain, furiously beat against them for hours. It could be done, but it was the worst, scariest way to survive a hurricane. Ironically he felt lucky, despite his thirst and hunger. He and Fluff would be together, comforting each other.

He paused, and then continued. "Some storms are worse than others. It depends on things I don't know much about. The wind could be the worst part. The wind rips up buildings and sheds, like the one I live in. The water rises. Four legged furry animals like us don't do well in rising water. We don't swim too well. I'd have to say that a boat is a pretty darn good place to be in rising water. I consider myself lucky right now."

"Oh, King. That makes me feel better. You are so right!"

"You should just curl up, close your eyes and pretend that you're just going to take a nap and sleep through the whole thing."

Fluff laughed. "Right!"

Fluff and King chatted with each other through the thin space at the bottom of the slatted wood door of the boat cabin. They chatted about the humans working at the marina, including Captains Keith and Kay. They chatted about the other cats and wondered what they planned to do to be ready for the bad weather coming. They did not talk about the rat chase escapade of the night before.

While Fluff and King chatted on the 'Lucky Two', ST, Fat Cat, and Dog Ear, tried to herd all the cats together for a meeting. Where was a safe place to stay during the storm? There were so many cats, counting mamma cats and kittens, who called the marina home. There were older cats with legs that couldn't jump or run as fast as the younger cats. All of these cats concerned Fat Cat. If they didn't come to the meeting they would be left out to fend for themselves alone.

"Over there," Fat Cat growled to ST. Fat Cat tilted his head in the direction of the three story metal boat storage facility at the Lighthouse Marina. He lifted his muscular body on four strong legs and started to walk across the parking lot. ST followed closely by Fat Cat's side.

The Lighthouse Marina, the parking lot was where Casey parked his truck hours ago, was also busy with hurricane preparations to secure the building. The building was smaller than the Treasure Island marina and stored a few hundred private boats. A few deep sea fishing boats were still docked in the boat slips.

Fat Cat said to ST "I'm going to check the corner door. I snuck inside one time. It's like a cave in there. It's wide open but there are quite a few boats, stacks of boxes, and big blue plastic barrels which will give us protection and hiding places if we can get inside. It will be noisy, but we'll be safe from the wind. Hopefully we're not too late. The building could be already locked up tight."

"Can we all get in there?" ST asked.

Fat Cat eyes glared at nothing in particular. He answered harshly, "I'm going to check to see if we can get inside. Go find Sarge and tell him to spread the word around. Everyone needs to get to higher ground."

Sarge was Fat Cat's most loyal friend after ST.

Fat Cat glanced back at Dog Ear, sitting alone on the sidewalk still forlorn about his missing brother, Oscar. It appeared that he was watching the water rise up the retaining wall but Fat Cat knew that he was hoping for Oscar's reappearance.

As an afterthought Fat Cat added, "Hey ST. It wouldn't hurt to ask Sarge if he's seen Oscar."

Fat Cat watched ST, still a very young adult cat, leap across the hot pavement of the parking lot. "It's going to be ugly, I fear," Fat Cat thought. "Cats are able to swim for a short time. They can easily drown in a very short amount of time."

CHAPTER 27: ROAD BLOCKS

No one suspected anything unusual about the white pick-up truck when it pulled out of the stone gravel parking lot of Pine Log Forest State Park. It was a hurricane evacuation, after all. From all appearances it was only someone who had stopped to take care of personal business.

"Dang, this is crap," Vince spit the words out as if he had just bit into a bitter pill. He sneered at Ricky with playful, sinister eyes and curled his upper lip. "This is gonna take forever! Look at all them cars, bumper to bumper. We're crawling along the highway like a bunch of ants!"

To Ricky, Vince's eyes had a wild look of hate mixed with happiness. Ricky tried hard to find words to say, but the sparks he imagined flashed like small fireworks out of the brown crescent of Vince's eye. The spot distracted Ricky's mind from concentrating properly.

Interstate ten was nearly thirty five more miles to the north. As slow as they were moving it would take a long time to get there. At least they would be able to choose which direction to go once they got to the interstate. Would it be better to go east, or better to drive west? All cars were heading north now. Hurricane evacuees were going to a big city destination like Atlanta, Birmingham, or Chattanooga. Normally any one of those cities was a one day drive. At the pace they were driving now it might take two or three days. The thought of going home, finding a hotel room, or staying with family or friends was a comforting thought. Something as simple as a roof and a dry floor was all they needed.

The truth unknown to Vince, Ricky and all other evacuees was that they would most likely end up spending the night in their vehicles parked somewhere along the side of the road. They would not sleep. They would be huddled together, eyes wide open or clenched shut, with fear.

For a long time Vince didn't speak again. He was not the kind of person to mumble out loud when his mind was focused on serious matters. The money recovered from the fishing trip rightfully belonged to Vince. Any extra amount was justified for his trouble to get it back. He wondered how much was in the roll of bills. Once again both hands gripped the top of the steering wheel so tight that his knuckles protruded.

Ricky stared straight ahead in silence. The vacant look in his eyes did not reflect what was going on in his heart. He felt troubled by what had happened at the Pine Log State Forest parking lot. He knew better than to let his feelings show, move a muscle, or say anything. If Vince wanted him to talk, Vince would let him know.

Ricky looked at the waterproof watch on his left wrist. It was something he'd had for many years and always wore. It kept him on time for work and anywhere he wanted to be. It was a good watch to wear on a fishing trip. He saw it was past one o'clock. Now, he decided, might be a safe time to speak to Vince.

"Dang! This traffic is crap. You were sure right about that!" Ricky said with a forced enthusiasm. He turned his head to look at Vince.

Vince didn't look at Ricky. He cussed a few more words about the speed of his travel. Occasionally he slammed on the brakes to slow down.

"Wanna count the money?" Vince suddenly asked Ricky in a deep, secretive voice. Without waiting for Ricky to answer he reached into his pants pocket with his right hand. The knuckles on his left turned whiter as he held tighter onto the steering wheel. Vince had to stretch and straighten his right leg to get to the money. It was hard to control the gas pedal. The truck jerked forward at the same time the roll of bills appeared in his right hand. It was folded in half and at least four inches thick.

"Count it!" Vince said in an excited high-pitched voice. He shoved his arm into Ricky's chest and dropped the wad of money on Ricky's lap.

Ricky's jaw opened wide. His eyebrows lifted and his eyes widened. He looked down at the loose green bills lying on his lap.

It was too much to comprehend. He was stunned by the number of bills. His emotions did somersaults. Only minutes earlier he'd felt uncomfortable about what happened in the parking lot at the Pine Log State Forest. Now he was staring at more money than he had ever held in his hands in his life. It could change his life. Was it good to feel happy?

"Whew! Baaabeeey!" Ricky blew out the words through his skinny lips. He grabbed up the wad and opened it flat.

Lying on the top were several fifty dollar bills, then twenty dollar bills, then a few hundred dollar bills co-mingled with fives, tens and ones.

Vince's eyes cut to Ricky's lap. "Count it! Count it!" Vince hollered.

It took Ricky more than a few minutes to carefully, slowly count the money. He held some of the bills down on his leg with his left elbow so none would blow away on the floorboard or out the open window.

"How much? How MUCH?!" Vince impatiently demanded when he saw that Ricky was finished counting. He knew it was going to be a lot of money.

"Eight hundred and seventy eight dollars," Ricky replied, holding the bundle in a tight fist.

Vince hollered "Yee haw," and nodded his head up and down. A tight lipped grin spread across his face, ear to ear.

"What's our plan now, Vince?" Ricky cautiously asked. "Are we gonna go somewhere and spend the money? Can we split the money?"

"You remember how I never got to live with my momma Ricky?"

"Yaaahh," Ricky drawled the slangy word. He started to fidget. He wasn't sure if the answer he was about to hear was going in a good direction if Vince was thinking about the mamma who'd left him. It might be an answer with a bad ending.

"You know, I believe that she must be a complicated person, Ricky. A VERY complicated woman. Daddy always told me that she never got along with anybody in the family. He said that's why he moved away from Opp after they married. Daddy would say she always had something to complain about. But, ya know what?"

Ricky knew that he didn't have to answer Vince's question. Ricky waited for Vince to continue.

Vince rambled on. "I have to believe that she was also a simple person. Maybe she wasn't very educated, but I don't know if I'd call her stupid. What she did was wrong when we were all kids. Being simple meant she had to be smart and shrewd. She had to survive. She lived her life exactly the way she wanted to. No one bossed her around."

Strangely to Ricky, talking about his mother seemed to relax Vince. He rested his left arm on the armrest of the door, casually slung his right hand over the steering wheel and slowed down to keep at least a distance of one car length in front of him. Ricky couldn't relax. He was nervous about where the one-sided conversation would lead. The money mattered to him, too.

"She must've known that money made all the difference in a person's life and having it made life a lot easier. I think I inherited that from her. Yes, I did. She taught me that. Yes she did!" Vince's voice cracked slightly with emotion. "And, I think if she were here today, sitting there right next to me now, my momma would be proud of me! This money don't have a stink on it."

Ricky sighed with relief after hearing these words. These words reflected a sentimental side of Vince. A small bit of his heart was soft. He didn't show the softness very often.

Ricky remembered the disharmonious relationship, if it could be called a relationship, Vince had with his father, whom he rarely saw and who only spoke the worst of Vince's mother. Vince never knew his mother. Ricky thought he understood the point Vince was trying to make. Vince may have just killed a man but it was more important to Vince to believe what his momma thought of him. Getting his money back, plus more, was better than just getting even to right a wrong. Maybe, just maybe, Vince was hoping in his heart to see his mother again one day. Thinking of her might bring that reality. However, Ricky knew the real story of how and why

179

Vince's mother left her family.

Pamela Hogge, Vince's mother, had five children. There was one girl and three brothers besides Vince. The father drove an eighteen wheeler truck for weeks at a time hauling canned food goods manufactured by the Continental Canning company located on the Savannah River in Augusta, Georgia. The stink from the canning company smelled like money to Vince's dad and most people who lived in Augusta. The stink reminded Pamela that her husband didn't bring home enough money to satisfy her wants and needs.

Even with five children Pamela was very lonely with her husband gone weeks at a time. Still young at heart when her children were not yet even teenagers, she spent many nights at a downtown dance club finding company and comfort into the wee hours of the morning with various men and with a bottle of something containing alcohol. The children, Vince the youngest and still in diapers, were left on their own to eat cereal out of a box. Cereal was often for breakfast, for lunch and sometimes dinner. If she stayed gone through a Sunday night the children had to walk to school without lunch or lunch money on Monday morning. Mostly they just stayed at home and did not bother with school on Monday.

By the time Pamela, also known as Miss Sissy by all of the neighbors, came home and flopped down on her own bed after being out all night she no longer cared where the children were or what they did. All she cared about was that they were quiet, stayed out of sight and out of trouble.

Early one hot mid-summer morning when the gray daylight streaked through the humid air and the slats of the open venetian blinds, Vince's father pulled his truck into the driveway in front of the three bedroom, wood shingled house with one bathroom. He walked to the front door and stood on a concrete porch the size of a kitchen table. He slowly opened the screened door. The warped wood front door with flaking paint was already open. Vince's father walked heavy footed across the pine wood floor, sank into the threadbare cushioned sofa and waited with his arms folded across his chest. He didn't 'peek into any bedroom to say a word to any of his children. The children waited too, in their beds, awake from the noise the truck made when it rumbled and rolled into the driveway. All were afraid to come out and greet their father with any hugs and kisses. He was not that type of father who did that with his children. They knew Miss Sissy was not home. They never heard her come into the house. They only heard a few shouts and a single gunshot.

After Miss Sissy got out of jail, she took off to another Georgia city to live with a deputy she met while serving her time in prison for attempted murder.

After Vince's father recovered from the gunshot wound he moved his family back to his hometown of Opp. He continued to drive his eighteen wheeler truck hauling commercial goods back and forth across the country. Vince's father sent the children to live with friends and relatives who could afford to take them in.

Neither parent reunited with each other, or with their children. Both parents justified their decision on the basis of money. The money, wherever you can make it, or take it, was the most important thing.

Each child grew up living a life separate and away from the family they had known.

Vince quit school as soon as he was old enough and found work doing manual labor.

Ricky, a quiet and scared child, remained a loyal, long-time friend to Vince. Since Vince thought quitting school was a good idea Ricky did it too. Even though Vince bossed him and cursed him, Ricky never forgot how Vince had always protected and stood up for him when he was bullied at school. Ricky always felt loved by Vince. Only now, for the first time he could remember, Ricky felt confused. He wasn't sure how he felt about Vince. And, for the first time, scared of what Vince might do next.

"I really don't know what momma looked like, but I know how important having money was to her," Vince kept talking about the mother he never knew. "It doesn't grow on trees. Daddy told me he'd tell her that after she'd say 'How come everyone one else seems to have it and we don't?' Look how easy it is. It just fell into my lap today," Vince said with pride in his voice.

Hearing Vince talk about Miss Sissy reminded Ricky of the whispering gossipers back in Opp. None of the mothers wanted their children to associate with the children of Miss Sissy's after they found out about the shooting, jail time and deputy boyfriend. Jokes were exchanged on the telephone lines, street-side mail boxes, across back yard fences and front door porches. 'That Miss Sissy sure can get a lot of bang for the buck, or is it buck for the bang? She definitely knows how to chase the buck!' Ricky didn't fully understand the meaning of the words, but did understand the tittering laughs. Ricky knew, also, that Vince blamed his father's drinking for the family split-up, but Ricky heard from the gossipers that Miss Sissy's drinking was the root of everything bad that happened to the family.

"I am so tired of this," Vince suddenly screamed out.

Ricky jumped off his seat. "Traffic is bad, Vince." Ricky mumbled. Although Vince's mood swings were not particularly surprising to Ricky, today was different.

Vince took no notice of Ricky's words. He beat both palms of his hands against the steering wheel. The old truck's front wheels swerved off the side of the road. Vince quickly grabbed the steering wheel with both hands to correct the direction of the moving vehicle.

"Highway 20 is just up the way here a bit, I think," Ricky said a little louder. "Maybe we can turn off and head west on it to get out of this line. There must be a road from highway 20 that will connect us to the interstate. I'm pretty sure there must be."

Vince grunted,"OK. That might work."

Less than five minutes passed and Ricky shouted, "I see it Vince!"

Not far ahead was a flashing red light signal for the intersection of highways 79 and 20. When they reached the intersection Vince swerved the truck into the southbound lane. A long, loud horn blast from a car surprised both men.

"What?!" Vince shouted.

The southbound lane of highway 79, a designated hurricane evacuation route, had just been opened at one o'clock to northbound traffic only. Vince did not check his side or rear view mirrors to notice the traffic merging into two lanes behind him, or the cars in front of him begin to merge into the two northbound lanes up ahead past the signal where a Florida Highway Patrol vehicle was stationed to direct cars.

"Aw shut up," Vince laughed at his ability to anger other people. He turned the steering wheel so sharply that the wheels of the truck squealed as they glided into west bound lane of highway 20.

No cars followed him to go west on highway 20.

Vince laughed sarcastically, "We just left the huge city of Ebro!"

"The highway patrolman didn't even see that trick you pulled," Ricky praised Vince. He hoped it would lighten Vince's tension.

"No line of cars here," Vince said triumphantly.

The two men fell back into silence. Their ride soon took them across the half mile long bridge over the Choctawhatchee River. The muddy waters were swirling fast with white foam touching the low-lying limbs of age-old trees. The water was only a few feet below the bridge.

Vince pressed his foot down more heavily on the truck gas pedal and accelerated to a speed he was more accustomed to. Once over the bridge, and with no other cars ahead, it was easy to maintain the faster speed. Fifteen miles later they reached the town of Bruce. A small blue road sign displayed a white iridescent number ten circled in red. Beneath the number ten was a white iridescent arrow pointing right, the direction to Interstate ten. Fifty feet beyond the sign the road curved north. Both men saw the sign.

"Gonna stay on this road. We can make up some time," Vince announced, and ignored the sign. He sped through the short intersection and past a white wooden building. The Bruce Café on the right was closed. The one pump gas station on the left, across the street from the Bruce Café, was also closed. The parking lots were empty.

"We got enough gas, right Vince?" Ricky anxiously asked. He wondered if they could make it to Biloxi on highway 20 if the gas stations were closed.

Vince's quickly lowered his eyes to the needle on the gas gauge. The needle pointed near the half tank line on the gas gauge.

"I got money and I got gas. I ain't gonna mess this ride up. No

182

way."

"When we get to Biloxi, Vince, do you think we'll have any trouble finding a place to stay?"

"Oh, man!" Vince said, genuinely excited now that they were speeding along down the road. His face became animated, twitching and grinning. He stuck out his tongue and licked his lips. "I can't wait to get to Biloxi and have some fun in those casinos. I bet we'll win big money!"

Vince's mood was lighter. Ricky wondered, "Was it because Vince had been thinking about his mother?"

Ricky thought about his own mother, Debra. She still lived in Opp in the same house where he grew up. He sure as heck knew better than to go visit her. It had been a long time since he had been to visit her. He knew she was still mad at Ricky for quitting school. Even now she'd give him a good tongue lashing for letting himself get in a bad way. She'd remind him 'it's all because you're hanging out with that no good kid Vince!' He could hear her voice, clear as daylight, in his head. That one sentence, repeated many times over when he was growing up, 'How can you let that Vince be your best friend?' The memory of her words silenced his.

As the two men rode neither one noticed, or commented on, the surroundings flying past them. The scenery was monotonous. Trees, bushes, and tall grass bending in the blowing wind. Both stared straight ahead at the black road and painted white lines in front of them listening to the rumble of the truck engine and their different thoughts.

Ricky's mind was churning and spinning. He had a nervous feeling that things were right, and then not right. Should he be afraid of Vince? He'd always trusted Vince...before now. What about what happened to that boat captain when they stopped at Pine Log Forest State Park? Was he alive? Should he be happy about taking all his money and going to Biloxi to gamble? They'd taken other risks in their short time of adulthood, but gambling in a casino was not one they'd done before. They had no experience at gambling in a casino. How long was it going to take to drive to Biloxi? What about the weather? What if the weather turned worse as they got closer to Biloxi? Were they heading in the right direction? Vince seemed different. Maybe it was just the weather. Or was it the money?

Vince was happy after recovering his own money and feeling the spirit of his mother. He had more money than he'd ever had in his lifetime. He would have even more chances ahead in Biloxi. Sometimes dreamers and cheaters prosper, he kept thinking.

Another memory of Vince's unfolded. It was how he felt after riding the merry-go-round at the fair. The operator told all the children in line to pick the best horse and they would win a prize if they caught the brass ring. Vince remembered picking the best horse to ride and spinning around and around until he got the chance to grab the brass ring. He missed it. When the ride was over he got off empty handed with a dizzy head and a huge pit of sadness in his heart because he missed the prize. He was told by the ride operator, who felt bad for the young boy near tears, to leave the spinning world behind and set his sights on the angels in the clouds. That advice meant nothing to a child who didn't know what an angel was. He lived in a world where no one talked about angels. This time, Vince thought, he didn't miss the brass ring.

Vince's stomach was the first to growl. Neither man had eaten a decent meal since they arrived in Panama City Beach. Ricky heard it but said nothing. His stomach growled next.

They were used to living on junk food but there wasn't even any junk food lying around in the cab of the truck. Trash from the junk food already eaten was strewn around the floor of the truck.

They listened to their growling stomachs for another twenty minutes and then the town of Portland appeared.

"Never heard of any place called Portland before," Vince mumbled.

"What's in Portland?" Ricky wondered out loud. He wondered if there would be a place to stop for food.

"Never heard of it," Vince repeated louder.

Vince suddenly slammed on the brakes, throwing the truck into a skidding sideways slide.

The sudden motion jerked Ricky's body forward. He automatically, defensively, put his arms up and forward to prevent his body from slamming into the dashboard. "Yikes!" Ricky shouted.

"Sometimes these little towns have stuff you'd never dream of...like maybe even a gas station." Vince spoke calmly, in contrast to his violent actions handling the truck.

Vince eased his foot off from the gas pedal to slow down the truck. The eyes of both men fixed on the first building of Portland. The wood church, brightly painted white with a rusty tin roof and simple steeple pointing high toward the heavens, shone bright in the landscape despite the rain. Next they saw the remains of a rusted out automobile sitting like a skeleton in the front yard of a house barely held up by a rotten wood frame. Less than a half mile down the road a small red brick post office appeared. It was not much larger than the house they just passed. That was the last building in Portland.

Vince slowed down the truck and rolled into the empty parking lot of the Portland post office. Then just as suddenly as he had slowed down, he pulled the steering wheel to a hard right turn and pushed the gas pedal to the floorboard. The truck's rubber tires squealed and smoked. Vince righted it back to the pavement of highway 20. While Vince held tight to the steering wheel Ricky bounced and bumped on the seat.

"Vince, STOP! Slow down!!! FAST! Look up there," Ricky screamed at Vince. Ricky pointed with one hand while the other hand held on to the handle of the passenger door.

Forty foot tall pine trees flanked both sides of the straight, flat, empty road. It felt like they were riding through a long tunnel, but the framing of the road by the pine trees made it easier to see objects at a further distance. Clearly, up ahead, Vince and Ricky saw cars in the middle of the road.

"Cops. I'd bet on it," Vince hissed and slammed the brakes again. Luckily for Ricky he was prepared this time.

"Damn road block," Vince swore.

"Turn around. Do a U-E," Ricky gulped air. His chest heaved in and out. "I saw another road off the side just a short ways back there."

Vince didn't ask where or why. His foot slammed on the gas pedal. He spun the steering wheel in a full circle to the left, bouncing the truck across the road and quickly had the truck in the opposite lane to go back in the direction they just came from.

He drove slowly, heading back east on highway 20.

"There," Ricky pointed to the right side of the road.

Vince saw a small dirt road, which looked more like a trail for horses, and turned onto it. For a brief moment Vince thought to ask Ricky how he noticed the road on such a monotonous ride, but didn't. His plan to drive to Biloxi was suddenly, rudely, interrupted.

Vince drove the truck onto a bumpy, soft white sandy path flanked by more pine trees, scrubby weeds and scratchy Florida palmetto bushes. It was slower than the drive on highway 79. The road ended after a short distance of a half mile. When they reached the end of the path Vince and Ricky found they were looking at four to six foot white capped waves about thirty feet from the end of the path. Tall buildings, that appeared small in the distance, were in open view across a wide expanse of water.

Vince gulped now. "I don't know what to do next."

Ricky heard fear in Vince's words. Both men sensed danger in the situation.

They were looking at the Choctawhatchee Bay, a rich body of water stretching across two Florida counties from Panama City Beach to Fort Walton Beach. The bay was already showing effects of the strength of hurricane Louise. Only two bridges, each one over four miles long, crossed over the bay. The road block meant that the bridges were closed.

The white caps, white lines on rebellious angry waters, produced fear in Vince. The white lines were a reminder of the scars on his legs, a memory he hated.

The scars were put there by Preacher Wood during one of the whippings he gave Vince for doing something stupid To Vince the whippings had always been about bad timing, being in the wrong place at the wrong time. Vince never did something intentionally stupid. Now he was again in the wrong place at the wrong time.

Vince lived with Preacher Wood's family after the gun Miss Sissy shot wounded his entire family. Preacher Wood had four children, and Vince made five. There was plenty of food to go around in the country shack they lived in on the small farm in a low lying swampy area at the end of a pig trail in the Alabama woods. Preacher Wood wasn't really a preacher. He never mentioned the word angels in heaven to his children. He earned the nickname preacher because he proclaimed 'I'm a gonna whip the devil outta you yet' before he took his children, including Vince, and tied them naked to a tall pine tree before flogging them with rope. Preacher Wood wanted everyone living in his home, if it could be called that, to do whatever he said and he did not like to repeat himself. Everything had to be done exactly the way Preacher Wood wanted it to be done and when he wanted it done. 'Pick up that stick lying in the yard over there.' 'Finish that piece of potato lying on your plate.' 'Put your shoes on now.' 'Comb your hair.' Any number of small things that were important to Preacher Wood at the moment set him into a rage if the children didn't ask 'how high?' when he told them to jump to it. Such strict discipline made Vince care less. Preacher Wood wasn't his real father anyway.

"Whaddya thinking, Vince?" Ricky finally asked timidly. He'd watched Vince mumbling inaudible words for several minutes. Ricky fidgeted. His feet were planted firmly on the floorboard but his knees were knocking back and forth again. He was beside himself trying to understand Vince's behavior in this scary situation. It was not normal right now. It had not been normal since they left the marina.

"I miss my dad," Vince's voice cracked. "He wasn't like Preacher Wood. Whenever I'd get to see him he'd holler at me now and then, but then he'd always have a little laugh after the holler."

"I know, Vince. I know you liked your dad, a lot." Ricky found himself trying to sooth Vince while trying to remember a time when Vince ever spoke well of his dad. He'd never heard anything good about Preacher Wood. None of the kids in school knew too much about Vince's real dad. They all knew about Preacher Wood and about Vince's mom, Miss Sissy. The other parents made sure they spread this word around.

Ricky had enough sense to say, "All us kids liked your dad. We all liked him. Do you think you ought to cut the engine off if we're gonna stay here awhile? Maybe conserve the gas we got?"

Ricky was aware that Vince's moment of happiness thinking of the spirit of his momma was replaced with fear. A fear only a father could rescue him from. It was a fear that Ricky knew well. A fear like the times he was bullied on the playground at school. There was nothing that could be done except wait for a rescue.

It was Ricky's time to be strong and confident.

"You know, truth is, your momma loved you, too, Vince." Ricky knew this was a lie, but wanted to reassure Vince. His longtime friend sat uncharacteristically motionless and afraid. Truth was, Ricky never heard that Vince's mom did anything for her children but leave them. Miss Sissy never came to the rescue. "She'd want you to have that money. She'd want you to have a good time with it. We didn't get to go fishing. But, we're still gonna have fun with it. She'd want that for you. We just gotta ride out this storm that's a comin'. It won't be but overnight. I bet. No betting here. I'm sure. Can we listen to the radio for a little bit? Maybe turn the engine off and not run the battery down too much. We should probably try to listen to some news on the radio."

Vince snapped out of his trance. He was not one to let anything beat him.

He methodically reached down to turn the keys in the truck's ignition to the off position and turned his face toward Ricky. The brown crescent in his eye didn't flash, as if the power had been turned off. It unsettled Ricky to see his friend in this state of mind.

The rumble of the engine was replaced with a new, disquieting noise. It was the sound of crashing waves and whining winds. The men's eyes exchanged a brief look. They knew the predicament they were in was going to be scary, but one they'd have to share.

Finally Vince spoke, but the tone in his voice was dull and flat. "You're a real good friend, Ricky." He reached over to turn the keys in the ignition to power on the battery to listen to the radio, as Ricky had suggested. He turned the dial to tune into a station. In a few seconds the speakers caught the voice of a woman.

"The Emergency Operation centers in Bay and Walton counties are asking people to make their evacuation plans before 5 p.m. All vehicles traveling on Highway 20 in Bay County will be routed east to highways 231. All vehicles traveling on Highway 20 in Walton County will be routed east and allowed to travel north on highway 79 or continue east to highway 231. No south bound lanes on highways 79 and 231 are open from interstate 10. Again, if you are planning to go anywhere, you should be on the road by now and have all evacuation plans in place before 5 p.m. People who wish to stay in shelters should check to be sure that the shelter they plan to go to is still open and accepting people. Keep in mind, too, that pets are not accepted at most shelters. If you are not on the roads by 5 p.m. you are advised to stay home and make preparations for Hurricane Louise, a very, very dangerous storm."

"Dang, Vince," Ricky slapped his knee.

"Yeah, it's really too late to get started out of town now," a man's voice spoke next on the radio. "The roads are really congested right now."

The next words were the woman's voice again. "Even with two lanes open to go north on Highway 79 and all four lanes of Highway 231 open we are getting calls from people on their cell phones that traffic is just moving at a crawl."

The sound of the woman's voice renewed Vince's anger. "Yeah, and don't we already know that!" he shouted, making Ricky jump again.

Vince formed a fist with his hand and angrily punched the radio button to turn it off. The sound of Vince's breathing competed with the noises of nature outside. The breaths, short and heavy, flared Vince's nostrils.

Ricky turned his head to look the other way, out the passenger window. He was trying to avoid Vince's anger. The scenery out the window was worse and just as alarming. Forty foot pine trees were rhythmically swaying side to side, bending and touching each other, caught up in the beating of the sixty mile per hour winds. Ricky had a strange vision that he was watching a southern church congregational choir. He felt the spirit of song in their souls. The long skinny green pine needles shook and shivered at the end of bending branches as if they were musical instruments accompanying the trees with a harmonious mixture of high notes and low notes in the song that moved the trees. Keeping his eyes locked on the swinging and swaying helped Ricky calm down.

"I can hear the waves out there Ricky," Vince said with a hint of fear in his voice. "Do you hear 'em?"

"Yeah, I hear them," Ricky said hypnotically. He felt peace come into his heart. He didn't understand what was happening or why he felt it. It was as if angels had descended down from the sky and into the choir, making a joyful noise through the swinging and swaying.

"I feel the wind blowing in the truck, too. It's blowing strong."

"I feel it too, Vince."

"Ricky, look at me. I think we're gonna have to stay here all night. I mean, if I go back out on the road we're just gonna be stuck in that line of traffic again and end up pulling off to the side of the road in the middle of somewhere. We'll be around a bunch of other people sitting out a hurricane in their cars."

Ricky snapped his head away from the window, focused his eyeballs with a series of fast blinks and smiled at Vince. "I know, Vince. You're right. This is as good a place as any for now." Ricky felt like a guardian angel had entered the truck and was sitting on the seat next to him.

Vince hesitated, somewhat puzzled by Ricky's demeanor. "At least we will have some privacy here, maybe."

"I agree, Vince. We'll sit out this thing until morning and then everyone will be moving again."

Vince was trying to convince himself of something he didn't want to do, but he had no other choice. He did not notice that Ricky began to hum to himself.

Vince continued, "We can just have us our own little hurricane party right here. Near the water, even. I think it's safe. Them waves we see here ain't near as high as ones you'd see in the Gulf of Mexico."

"Right, Vince. It's gonna be just fine here. We still got stuff in the tool case in the back of the truck, don't we? Something to drink at least?" Ricky's words flowed like a melody.

Vince felt something was different about Ricky. Ricky wasn't acting nervous about the situation they were in. He was thinking about something else. Something like eating and drinking!

"Yeah, I think so. I'm pretty sure there are some crackers. We had a loaf of bread and some peanut butter too, remember? I don't know about drinks. Why don't you go out there, Ricky, and check it out. But be sure to watch out for snakes in these here woods." Vince chuckled, but he was giving Ricky serious advice. He knew Ricky was scared of snakes.

Ricky looked at Vince with a face of gratitude.

Ricky opened the door and cautiously hung his right foot out the opening. The strong winds slapped his calf against the door frame.

"Ouch!" Ricky shrieked.

"What?" Vince reacted with concern.

"Just got bit," Ricky laughed. "No, Vince. Seriously, the wind blew and slammed my leg against the door."

Vince laughed too.

Ricky dragged his left leg over to hang out the door alongside his right one. Then he planted both feet firmly on the ground. He held on to the car door and let his eyes scan the white sandy ground covered with brown pine needles and weeds. He took a couple of cautionary steps before walking around to the back of the truck. Ricky opened the tail gate and climbed up onto the bed of the truck. He crouched down to open the tool case, peeking up once more to check his surroundings. "Lots of palmetto bushes and weeds around here," he thought.

"Vince, I found the bread and peanut butter," he shouted. "Hey, there's two co-colas here too." Ricky was excited to find something as precious as a soda. He suddenly realized how dry his mouth was.

Vince flung open his door and jumped out of the truck. "That's great, Ricky! I'm gonna go have my own quick private party over here for a minute."

Vince was unzipping his pants while he walked, taking big steps, a few feet away from the front of the truck. He stopped at a large Florida palmetto and started to release the pressure in his bladder. Before he could finish he heard a noise different than the wind and waves. It wasn't loud, but he heard it and recognized it. It was similar to the sound of small beads in a plastic baby toy when it's shaken.

Vince never saw the snake before the head latched quickly, like a flash of lightning, above his ankle.

"Oh MOMMA it hurts!" Vince screamed. He fell to the ground, moaning and rolling side to side, holding his leg upward and beating his fists on the ground.

Ricky froze in place on the bed of the truck. He turned his head to see Vince writhing in the sand and then an eight foot rattlesnake slithering away quickly, side-winding its way across the ground toward another clump of Florida palmetto.

"Oh my God, Vince. Oh MY GOD!" Ricky screamed the three words over and over. The blustery winds carried the anguished sound of his voice through the shivering pine needles on the swaying pine trees, drowning out the sounds of the congregational choir.

CHAPTER 28: PROPERTY TO PROTECT

The sound of metal crashing against metal traveled with the blowing winds across the water and bounced off the metal walls of the Treasure Island boat storage building.

"Awwww....crap!" Casey said with disgust. His nose wrinkled as if there was a bad smell in the air.

"I think you're right!" Sharkey said with equal emphasis.

"Two cars find each other as easy as two hearts of young kids looking for love," Casey said after hearing the accident.

Sharkey's eyes rolled upward, as if looking for a sign. It surprised him to hear these words coming from Casey. "Lovers?" Sharkey asked in disbelief. "You gotta go check on them, I suppose?"

"Yeah, lovers," Casey said sarcastically then added bitterly, "I'd better go and see if they need my help. I want to go see how they're bonding now."

"I'll be here for a while," Sharkey said. "When you're ready to bring the boat over for storage I'll find some time to get you a slot."

Casey grunted. "Oh, sure. That's all I got now. Lots of time!"

Casey shrugged his bulky shoulders, cocked his head, swung his body around on the tips of his toes, and turned his back to Sharkey. He walked in long, heavy strides. The steel toe oversized work boots on his large feet made a clomping noise on the concrete paved parking lot.

"Listen man," Sharkey called after him as he stood in the doorway of the metal building. "Check back with me, OK?"

Casey stopped and turned his head over his shoulder back toward Sharkey. "I'll do that. Appreciate it," he said in a stiff voice that matched his body language.

He pulled out onto Thomas Drive into a long line of vehicles waiting to pass over the bridge. He drove along the side of the road and heard the sirens of law enforcement. Once he reached the crest of the bridge he could see ahead down the road, past the traffic light at Thomas Drive and the Captain Anderson marina, the flashing blue lights of a patrol car. A serious accident between a minivan and black sports car was already being attended to. The two vehicles, sitting in the middle of the road where they collided, were causing a major traffic back up.

He slowly inched down the base of the bridge. Casey saw, to his amazement, another accident. This one appeared to be a fender bender.

"People are driving too slow and not paying attention," Casey thought. "People always try to see what the accident is all about."

Since the police were already stretched thin Casey decided to help out with the fender bender. He pulled up alongside the two vehicles and put his truck into park.

An elderly white haired man and woman stood in front of a large four door sedan. It was an older model automobile designed for a comfortable, smooth, quiet, cushioned ride. They were alternately moving their heads to look at the damage to the front bumper of their car and the rear bumper of a small compact car.

A young man with long brown hair sat on the front hood of the compact car. Clumps of stringy hair stuck to the back of his neck. His knees, held together by a round circle of two skinny arms gripped together by ten fingers, propped up his chin. His sweaty pale face exuded carefree disgust. He was ignoring the elderly couple's frequent glances at him.

Casey's first thought was, "This is not going to take but a little time to resolve. It will be piece of cake."

In the state of Florida the driver who rear ends another vehicle is always at fault for the accident. Following another vehicle too closely, no matter what the car in front may have done to cause a collision, is considered *your fault*.

Casey's instinct told him the elderly couple who rear-ended the small car would have insurance and most likely the young man would not.

"Write up a quick ticket for the elderly couple," Casey thought. As an officer for public safety he had authority to do this act of public service.

"Both of these parties will want to be quickly on their way," he assured himself. "Better wait to see what's going on and to assess the damage involved. The Florida Highway Patrol are so darn busy. They already have the serious accident two hundred yards up the road. It could take a long time for them to get here. It will take a long time to get someone here from the Beach Police or Sheriff's office for a fender bender. Those guys will appreciate me helping out. The faster I can clear the roadway the sooner everyone can move on. I can get on to my personal business too. Better see what these folks are like and what they have to say."

Casey walked up to the elderly couple and asked with genuine interest, "Everyone okay here? No one hurt?"

"Yes, sir," the elderly man responded timidly but respectfully.

Casey looked at the woman. It was obvious that she had been crying. She averted her eyes away from Casey.

Casey looked over at the younger driver, still sitting on the hood of his car. The young man turned toward Casey, nodded his head upward to acknowledge him and said, "I'm okay."

"If everyone is okay, can you drive your cars? We need to move these vehicles off the road and out of the way."

Both men, younger and elder, said "Yes."

"I think right over there, on the right into that turn lane, will be

192

the safest." Casey pointed to the turn off lane leading into Captain Anderson's Marina. "First thing I'll need to get is your driver's license before you go."

Casey looked at a long line of vehicles backed up behind the two cars, all burning noxious fumes. Casey still had the 'Lucky Two' on his mind, more than the people he was trying to help. The boat was his most important responsibility at the moment. He would be just a little closer to it once he got these two wrecked bumpers off the road.

The young man slipped down from the front hood of his car and hopped to the driver's side to open the door.

"He seems jumpy," Casey thought suspiciously. "Accidents and hurricanes will do that to someone."

Casey turned to face the elderly man who was still standing beside his car. "I'll put a call in to see if I can get a Florida Highway Patrol here to write up the accident information on your vehicles, but I know they're really busy. I don't know how long the wait would be. I can write up the ticket if they give me the say so."

"Sir," the elderly man started slowly. "I know it's a very, very busy day for you and for everyone working in law enforcement. We're all anxious here," he said with caution and extreme politeness. "I know that I am in the wrong. A rear-end accident. It's always the fault of the driver who does the rear ending."

"Yes, sir." Casey nodded, returning the politeness.

"Then, if you agree, can we, the young man and I, work this out together if he is willing?" The elderly man's hands were shaking. Tears were welling in his eyes.

Casey was surprised the old man would ask such a question. He struggled with the dilemma of handling this legally or letting this slip under the rug. However his priority was to get to the 'Lucky Two'.

"I'd have to ask the boy first," Casey said.

Surprised that Casey agreed the elderly man said in appreciation, "Thank you, Sir!"

Casey walked away from the elderly man and stood between the two cars. He called to the young man, "Son? Would you mind coming over here for a minute?"

The young man was sitting with both of his legs dangling out the open driver's door. He jumped out in a hurry and stood up to face Casey. "Yes Sir?" he asked.

"Was there anything you did, anything, to cause this accident?"

The young man's face expressed a mixture of confusion and concern. "OH NO, Sir. I don't think I did anything to cause the accident." The young man used a respectful tone of voice. He fumbled his hands inside his pockets. His knees were shaking.

"This gentleman has asked me if he could talk to you. He would like to talk with you to see if you are willing to resolve this matter privately without involving any legal documents. Are you willing to do that?"

193

Casey's six-foot-four inch frame and massive shoulders stood less than a foot away from the young man. Casey's posture was rigid and his face, an easy ten inches above the young man's, had a look of seriousness. Anyone with common sense would clearly realize that this was not only a man of authority but maybe a man running out of patience.

"Well," the young man started slowly. "Yes, I guess so. I don't think it's a problem. I mean I don't have a problem talking with that good man over there." The young man was confused by the man in uniform and didn't want to disagree.

"He wants to talk to you in private about that dent in your bumper on your car. I assume it's your car. I don't really want to have to call this in to the beach police or Florida Highway Patrol being that we have a lot of serious situations to deal with on the roads today. There is a hurricane coming soon, you know."

Casey's eyes cut a glance toward the young man's vehicle. The body was already dented in several places. It was rusty. It was old. His eyes rested back to the boy, who had been watching Casey's eyes. A silent truth was exchanged between both men's eyes. This person-to-person, one-on-one offer, was a good deal and should not to be refused.

Casey motioned with his hand to the young man to follow him. They both walked back to the waiting elderly couple.

"Okay. Now this young fella has agreed to talk with you, Sir," Casey spoke directly to the elderly man. "You both work this out and don't be staying too long here on the side of the road. There's a bigger situation you guys got to deal with coming real soon. Sorry about this problem. Are there any questions or last words before I go and leave you good people?"

In unison both men responded with a friendly, "No Sir!"

Casey Howard turned his back on the three people. He was relieved he could turn his mind back on the 'Lucky Two'.

His truck engine turned over with a loud rumble. He stomped a little too heavily on the gas pedal before shifting the car into the drive gear. Casey chuckled when he saw the look on the faces of the three accidental friends as they watched him pull out into the traffic.

He passed around the slightly wrecked vehicles and drove into the Captain Anderson's marina parking lot. There were only a few vehicles, mostly boat owners doing last minute preparations, left at the marina.

The scene gave Casey a strange feeling. The parking lot was normally not very full this time of year but its near complete emptiness was troubling

A sickening, queasy feeling overcame over him. In the distance, across the span of black pavement with painted white lines, he saw a familiar person standing at the docks. It was Darryl Kay. It was unmistakable. But Darryl was with a woman. It looked like a younger woman. Darryl's old small white pick-up truck was parked directly in front of the 'Lucky Two'. Darryl and the woman were standing beside the 'Lucky Two'.

Casey lifted his right hand off the steering wheel and laid it over the ring of keys lying next to him on the truck seat. The ring of keys Captain Earl Keith had handed over to him hours earlier in the day. He wrapped his fingers around the keys and tightened his hand into a balled trying to strengthen his connection with the 'Lucky Two'.

The sight of Darryl stirred up anger in Casey. Darryl was the reason he was out late, parked for hours in the dark by the bridge last night. The long hours of an early and confusing morning were beginning to wear down Casey's nerves. He was tired and stressed from too many details. Usually he was good with details. His job of counting fish and recording the information on boats docked at the marina was detail work. But his mind was not good with complicated situations that required decisions. His jawbone muscles tightened and he ground his teeth together. The last person he wanted to face right now was Darryl. But, who was the girl? What was she doing with Darryl?

"C'mon Casey. It's your boat now." He reassured himself, trying not to worry. He slowly drove the truck toward the couple standing at the dock.

Darryl and Eleanore both turned their heads toward Casey's truck when they heard the rumbling of the vehicle engine. They watched as it crossed the parking lot, stopped and parked next to Darryl's truck.

"Been a busy day already, hasn't it Sgt. Howard?" Darryl grinned at Casey after he stepped out of the truck and faced the couple.

"Sure has," Casey answered in the friendliest voice he could force. He looked at Eleanore and gave a nod of greeting to acknowledge she was standing there. "Just had an accident over there," he said pointing his arm in the direction he just left. "Who's this with you here?" He asked Darryl, nodding again towards Eleanore.

"Oh, gosh," Darryl tried to sound embarrassed. "My apologies for not introducing you first," he said politely trying to keep the tone of his sarcasm at a low level.

Eleanore did not recognize the official uniform of this man, however she thought it was important to show respect.

Darryl felt the mistrust in Casey's eyes. Despite their agreement of disbelief during, and over, the strange occurrence of the morning, he was not letting go of his guard. Darryl's instinct told him Casey operated under a different kind of power. Darryl's common sense told him to be careful with Casey.

"Eleanore, this is Sgt. Casey Howard. Sgt. Howard, this is Eleanore." Darryl looked at each person as he introduced them in a formal manner. "I met Eleanore here after I got myself set up, you know, registered I mean, at the hurricane shelter."

"You let yourself get picked up by strangers at shelters very often?!" Casey's tall muscular body stood close to the petite woman.

Eleanore was immediately intimidated by the large man with the sharp, unfriendly voice. "Well, n..n..no," she stuttered, surprised at his question She shifted her balance on her legs to try to regain control of herself.

Darryl jumped into the conversation. "Actually she and I met at the gas station up there on Highway 231 and state road 390. She was there to get gas and I was planning to top off my gas tank. She asked me for directions on how to get to the marina."

Darryl hoped the half-truth wouldn't hurt his reputation with Eleanore. He noticed the effect Casey was having on her and wanted to defend her.

"Both of you are heading in the wrong direction coming down here to the marina, wouldn't you say?" Casey asked in an authoritative voice He was tired and he didn't want any foolishness at this point in the day.

"Ya know, Casey, that's very true. But," Darryl said with more sarcasm in his voice than he wanted, "Eleanore has a friend who owns a boat at this marina."

Darryl felt his pulse begin to beat faster and the blood rushed to his face. "She wanted me to show her how to get to the marina so she could hopefully find her friend!" Darryl grinned big and wide as he watched the look of authority on Casey's face change to shock and surprise. He could hardly suppress laughing out loud.

Casey's mouth opened involuntarily. His eyes popped open, ready to jump out of their sockets.

Painful knots formed in Casey's stomach. Casey was speechless. He knew Darryl for being a talker. Now was the time to let him talk. Normally Casey would not give Darryl the time of day for more than two sentences. Now he needed to listen to the rest of the story, every word of it with all of the annoying details. Casey's had a sickening feeling that his future in possessing a fishing boat was going to float away, right out of his hands. He could feel it coming. The worry over trying to protect the boat from the damage caused by Hurricane Louise was replaced by the feeling he was about to lose the boat under other circumstances.

Darryl didn't say another word. It was uncharacteristic for him to be quiet for very long and it made Casey uneasy. Casey waited until he could no longer wait any more.

Casey nearly choked, the words stuck in the back of his throat, when he finally asked the question he dreaded asking. "Is the friend, the owner of the boat, related to you?"

Darryl locked his legs and let his arms hang stiff and rigid straight down by his sides. He took two steps and moved his body in between Casey and Eleanore. His mouth let loose words like the tap on a water faucet that had been turned on. He repeated his own name several times. He explained that he, Darryl Kay, thought that it would be much better if only one person drove a car rather than two cars on roads already congested with traffic. He, Darryl Kay, was going one last time down to the marina anyway to check on his boat. When he, Darryl Kay, learned that Eleanore was just a concerned friend looking for a friend at the marina he thought it was best to help her out. Darryl shared only a few of the details of the conversation he and Eleanore had during the ride over to the marina, being sure to leave out the incident of tears. He hoped Casey would be careful where he took his next step.

During the one-sided explanation Eleanore mainly watched Casey listen to Darryl. She detected by the look on his face that his mood was changing from active authority to controlled anger. Occasionally she glanced away. She didn't like the way Casey looked at Darryl, or her for that matter. She forced herself to keep her eyes on Casey. She felt like she could trust Darryl more than this man who wore a uniform! It was a strange feeling not to trust a man wearing an official uniform.

"No sir, he's not," Eleanore answered Casey's question when Darryl finally stopped speaking. Her voice was confident.

Darryl noticed a crooked smile returning to Casey's face.

"Well, that really doesn't explain a whole lot. Why are you here looking for him then if he isn't kin to you?" Casey asked Eleanore directly. The softened tone did not match the crooked smile.

"He called me last night at one in the morning. I got worried about him and decided to check on him," she said looking directly at Casey.

Casey said, "Called you, did he?"

"Yes. He wasn't making a whole lot of sense to me," she replied with strong determination.

Darryl was impressed with the return of her composure and at the same time curious, too. He had avoided asking Eleanore any questions about her friend when they rode together to the marina. She had asked Darryl if she knew Earl and Darryl had given her an honest answer.

"Well, what did he say to you?" both men simultaneously asked, eager to know more about the conversation.

"I can't remember all. I was dead asleep when the phone rang. He didn't say much at all really. Just that he missed me. And that he was tired of working down here. He wanted to come back home. He needed me, I guess. And I just hung up on him. I was a little angry about everything." Eleanore turned to look first at Darryl and then back to Casey.

"Nothing else?" Casey asked. He wondered, with hope, if she would reveal anything about the 'Lucky Two'.

"Well he did complain a lot about the deep sea fishing business and there was a hurricane coming to make matters worse for him. I just thought that I should come down here and check on him since I couldn't call him back. He was calling from a pay telephone and I laid awake all night worrying about him after I hung up on him. I thought I could find him if I could find his boat. I think that's his boat over there."

Eleanore lifted her arm to the level of her face and pointed directly at the 'Lucky Two'. Both men's eyes were glued on Eleanore's finger and face. They already knew exactly which boat without looking at it.

"Before he left to move here he asked me to go with him. He told me what he was going to name his boat when he got it. It was going to be the 'Lucky Two' because of us. We were sweethearts."

When Eleanore finished her story a heavy silence bore down on the three people. No one knew what to say next. A strong gust of wind suddenly blew in pounding, stinging pellets of rain.

"Let's run over there!" Darryl shouted.

The three raced down the sidewalk toward the fish cleaning house. Large drops of water bounced up off the concrete all around their feet. Once underneath the covered walkway Eleanore found herself standing closer to the 'Lucky Two', which was swaying in the slip it was tied to. The rope stretched tight with each movement. She looked up at Darryl and shouted, "We're still getting pretty wet standing here under this cover!" The rain was pounding hard, driven sideways by a whistling wind.

"That's okay, honey," Darryl laughed good-naturedly. "Getting wet won't melt you." To Casey he said, "Listen, maybe we should just get out of here now since apparently her friend Earl is not around Didn't we see him leave earlier this morning?"

Eleanore didn't notice that Darryl had called her honey. She was taken aback by Darryl's mention of Earl's name.

"You SAW him?" she asked Darryl in shocked disbelief. "You know his name?! You know who he is?!"

"Well, yeah," Darryl cleared his throat attempting to redeem any damage to his reputation. "We don't always know each other's name around here. Some of us even go by nicknames only," he chuckled. "One thing we all do know is the names of the boats here at the docks."

"Oh," Eleanore said in a small voice. Her face flushed pink. "So that's how you know you saw Earl. Because he was on his boat."

Casey's eyes squinted with jealousy and distrust at Darryl. He didn't know for what specific reason before, but now he had one. Darryl was definitely gaining Eleanore's trust. The next thing that could happen would be Darryl taking over responsibility for the boat.

Casey said, "Maybe Earl's heading to a shelter, just like you Darryl." It was everything he could do to keep his face calm and the anger out of his voice.

"Well, Sgt. Howard, as you can see, his rigs aren't put away and his boat doesn't look all that secured with just the ropes he's got tied up there to the pilings," Darryl responded.

Both men were shaken and unnerved by the revelation of the

namesake of the 'Lucky Two'.

"I can see that Captain Kay," Casey said, wondering what to say next. Then Casey blurted out, "Earl's boat should not be my problem."

"No. I think not. But, it looks like a lot of boats have been moved doesn't it? Some of us try to do as much as we can to protect our property. All I can do is tie mine to secure it. Other captains can take their boats out of the marina to a safer place if they have someone to help them ride out the storm on the water. Dry storage is too expensive for me."

"I just checked at the Treasure Island Marina to see how they were doing." Casey nodded his head in the direction of the massive dry storage boat house across the lagoon. "Sharkey told me that his storage area is full." Casey told the little lie with ease. He didn't need Darryl to know that Sharkey was willing to let him bring the 'Lucky Two' over and store it for free. He felt a strange sensation, however, that he wanted to trust Darryl for the very first time ever. They were discussing something important to both of them, even if for different reasons.

"Guess we could try to tie down the 'Lucky Two' a little more securely," Darryl suggested. "I could try if you're willing to help me."

Casey responded, "I don't know how much that'll work for this boat. It's in good shape, but not in a good place to hold its own for its size. It's smaller than your boat. It won't stand up to what we've got coming with this hurricane Louise."

All three humans stood with their backs flattened against the wall of the fish cleaning building. Suddenly the burst of sharp pounding rain pellets stopped as quickly as they started.

They stepped away from the building and Casey and Darryl began discussing options on how to keep the 'Lucky Two' in one piece. Casey really wanted to take the 'Lucky Two' to Sharkey, but it was too late for him to back out of his lie and go back to plan one.

While they talked, Eleanore let her mind drift back to the last time she had been in this same parking lot looking for Earl. That was the day she had lost her precious cat, Princess. Her emotions were so mixed up right now. She quickly dismissed her feelings to fatigue. It had been such a long day already, and it was not about to end any time soon. The coming hours would be seriously scary. She would need to be strong. She had to make a good decision to focus on the here and now.

"Why am I worrying?" She thought to herself. "I'm putting myself in harm's way, once again, for Earl! And, Earl's not even here!"

Her eyes wandered, like her thoughts. In the corner of her eye she saw something move. She turned her head and gazed down the wall of the fish cleaning building. She spotted a small crack in a wooden panel of the wall and something furry.

"Oh, Gawd," she shrieked and jumped away from the wall.

"What?!" Casey responded first to the terror in Eleanore's voice.

"I hope it's not a rat. I think I saw a rat. It was something down there!" She pointed a shaking finger in the direction of the wall not far from her feet.

Darryl and Casey both laughed.

"Could be a rat or could be a kitten. We got lots of cats hanging out here at the docks. Between the mice, rats, the garbage cans and us fishermen they are well fed," Darryl laughed.

"Well, that's some good news," Eleanore said, calming down. "I still don't like the rats."

"Hey, the rain is letting up," Casey said impatiently. "It's gonna come again, this rain, and go much quicker with the storm getting closer. These gusts and bands of wind will bring even heavier rains. We don't have much time to get ready for the hurricane and leave. You know the owner of the boat, Earl, really well I take it?" Casey looked at Eleanore.

Eleanore locked her eyes on Casey's eyes and nodded a strong yes. The small scare jolted her back to the task at hand. She wanted to regain her composure if she had to deal with Casey.

"You drove all the way down here to find out how he was doing even knowing that there was a hurricane. So I take it he's really important to you, right?" Casey plowed on into Eleanore's spinning senses.

"Yes, even with a hurricane coming!" she said emphatically. "It's nice of ya'll to be concerned about Earl's boat."

Darryl and Casey smiled and nodded at her.

Casey said, "So, he's gone now. You think he'd care, or do you care, if we try to help him by securing this boat? Try to protect it from any damage? I'm thinking that the best thing to do is move this boat away from the dock and marina."

"Can you do that? Don't you need a key to start up the engine?" Eleanore quizzed Casey. This solution seemed a little out of the ordinary.

"I don't know if I should say this, but right now might be the best time and," Casey paused to take a deep breath, "maybe it's the only time to admit this to you. YOUR friend Earl handed me the keys to his boat before he drove away from the marina earlier this morning."

Eleanore's mouth dropped open, but no words came out. She leaned back up against the wall and placed her hands behind her back to support herself. Her knees got weak and wobbly.

Darryl also leaned against the wall, closed his eyes and clenched his jaw.

Casey continued, "Earl told me he wanted someone to have a back-up set of keys in case something happened to him during the storm. Said he had no one else down here. I gave him my business card and told him to get in touch with me after the storm. I told him it might take a couple of days to get through on the phone."

Eleanore turned her head to look at Darryl, who still had his eyes closed but was nodding his head up and down in agreement with Casey's explanation. "Yep," Darryl said.

A long pause of silence passed before someone spoke again.

"I didn't plan to drive down here," Eleanore spoke first. "I decided to drive down here later, after the phone call. I didn't know what to expect. This is so much information to take in right now."

"What 'cha think Captain Howard?" Darryl popped the question half respectfully. After listening to Casey tell Eleanore the story about getting the keys to the 'Lucky Two' he decided Casey was not lying, even if only telling her half the truth. Maybe Casey was moving in a good direction.

"I think this boat should be moved!" Casey said.

Darryl asked, "Where to?"

"Take it up to the intracoastal," Casey said. "Others have done that with their boats in hurricanes."

Darryl agreed. "True," he said. "I've heard of it being done. This boat should be able to handle that okay. Problem is getting it out of here soon and quickly up there. The waters in the bays are probably still easy enough to navigate but it won't last much longer." Darryl began to understand what Casey had in mind. A little encouragement would help his plan.

"Could you really do that?" Eleanore asked. She forgot that she had just met Casey, and she barely knew Darryl. Her gut told her to trust these two men. They discussed Earl's boat like they really cared about it.

Darryl laid out his point of view. "Sometimes the hardest thing we have to do in life is to live with a mistake we've made. In this situation, the way this boat sits now, it would be a big mistake to leave it here. It'll be torn up. Sgt. Howard would know what to do to keep the boat safe."

"If you take that boat, I want to go with you," Eleanore suddenly blurted out in a voice that surprised both men not only for what she said but how she said it.

Eleanore surprised herself. She made a decision without giving it a second thought and couldn't find the nerve to back down from it.

After hearing Eleanore's shocking proclamation Darryl nervously spoke up first. "That would be a little rough for you out there. Especially for someone like you with no experience at all on a deep sea fishing boat. Rough waters, even if it is in the bay." He added protectively, "You can go to the shelter with me. I know I can figure out a way to get you inside."

Eleanore paused. "It's important to me to protect Earl's property. So when I see him again he knows it's there for him. And I...."

"Actually I could use help, a second hand," Casey interrupted.

Darryl was stunned. He'd lost control of the situation in a blink of an eye. He set her up to trust Casey by convincing her that the safest plan was to take the boat out of the marina to the intracoastal.

"Well, let me go with you too then," Darryl raised his arms and slapped them back down against his sides.

"Crowded for three people, don't you think?" Casey snapped.

"You already have a place to stay at the shelter, right?" Eleanore added, trying to be helpful.

Looking directly at Eleanore Casey said, "All I got to do is check my radio log. If you want to stay here, or come with me, it's entirely up to you."

Casey saw Eleanore's eyes shift to Darryl then quickly back at him.

"I'm going with you," she said. Then she said to Darryl, "Which one is your boat? I can meet you again when we get back. I'll need you to help me go to get my car afterward."

Darryl felt something he had not felt in a very long time. It felt like she was reaching out to him with her two arms wrapped around him. The young woman was pure hope wrapped up into a body. His emotions tore at his heart. He couldn't breathe. His mouth was dry. He felt his fingers twitching so he thrust both hands forcefully into his pants pockets. He squared his jaw.

Darryl looked at Casey but talked to Eleanore.

"My boat is right there." Darryl jerked his right hand out of his pocket and thrust his arm out in front of his body. His forefinger slightly trembled when he pointed in the direction of the 'Star Chaser'. The boat, a few slips away, was rocking and bouncing in the water but was obviously far more secured than the 'Lucky Two'.

"Well, that's a nice boat," Eleanore complimented Darryl. "Why are you leaving your boat here?"

Darryl slipped his hand back into the pocket. "I can't take it out alone. It's a bigger boat and far more than I can handle in the rough water without someone to help."

Eleanore noticed the tremble in Darryl's finger when he pointed to the 'Star Chaser'. Her voice changed. She said, "I suppose it would be better if I went to the shelter with you. Maybe I would be safer. I appreciate your concern. I just think I need to do this. It would be different under any other circumstances, whatever those may be, but when I last talked to Earl he sounded so distraught. I can't help but feel that there's something I should do, need to do, to help him, if I can." Her voice got softer. "I don't know what it is, but maybe doing this, watching over his boat, will bring us back together. Earl named this boat for us. 'Lucky Two'. I didn't have faith in him." Eleanore was embarrassed and dropped her head down.

Darryl looked away from Casey and Eleanore and up at the sky.

"Well, let's get started." Casey said purposefully. He turned to walk to his truck. "You can come with me now or stay here and wait. I'll only be a few minutes. I've got to move my truck somewhere out of sight."

Darryl murmured. "Go find yourself a brick wall to hit."

"What?" Eleanore asked.

Darryl was dismayed. He tried not to let it show. "Oh, nothing. Look, I know you're doing what you think is right but is it something that you have to do? It's not too late to change your mind."

Eleanore's soft brown eyes began to gloss with tears. She was light headed, not in control of her emotions. Her eyes locked on Darryl's eyes.

Darryl finally broke down and said, "If you're not going to go with me to the shelter, YOU keep your eyes on Casey at all times. He's a man in uniform and all that but he can be a little different. That's all I got to say."

"I've sensed that," she replied, trying hard not to sound scared.

Darryl back pedaled his warning. "He's a good man to be with in a boat. He knows what he's doing when it comes to that."

Darryl had no idea what Casey's skills were when it came to operating a boat. Casey had to know something to be taking the boat out on the water right before a hurricane. He wouldn't be crazy enough to take a risk like that unless he knew what to do.

"Just be careful and keep your eyes and ears open. Be cautious. Observe everything he does, all of his actions. He won't want advice making decisions. If something happens that he doesn't like he may get angry about it. I don't know any of this for a fact. It's just an impression I get from seeing him around here after all of these years. Just do what he says and stay quiet. Hey, if he protects the boat, and you find Earl, everything will come out good. Just remember a hurricane is a very nasty and unpleasant experience for anyone. It happens and then it ends. You'll survive it and life will go on."

Darryl's words made Eleanore feel a little more at ease. "Well, thanks for such good advice."

Darryl's distaste for Casey at this moment made him feel worse than he'd felt in a long time. He was normally able to let angry feelings pass quickly. He recognized his anger was about Casey taking Eleanore. He would hate Casey if anything happened to Eleanore. He remembered what someone once told him about hate. Hate is temporary and love is essential. This feeling of hate, he realized, would not last forever. It would end. His hope was in finding love. He hoped Eleanore would come back to him. He wanted to fall in love with her and for her to fall in love with him. He didn't even want to consider Earl in the formula.

After what seemed like only a few short minutes Casey was running across the parking lot.

"Ready?" Casey barked out to Eleanore just before he reached her. "Looks like it might rain again soon."

"I'm ready," Eleanore said. She took in a deep breath. She glanced at the small wooden cabin door on the 'Lucky Two' and wondered what it would look like inside. Her decision was final. If she didn't go with Casey and found out later that something happened to Earl, or his boat, she would have regrets that she couldn't stand to live with later in her life. To find Earl was the reason she came here. The money Earl's grandmother had given him went into this boat. The boat was important, but what mattered more than the money or the boat, was the love that went into a lifestyle Earl had hoped to share with Eleanore. It was in Earl's heart all along. It all became clear to her. Earl had been ready to leave the small town talk, to work at doing something he loved, and to share it with the person he loved. She was ready, more ready than ever before in her life, to protect and recover the love represented in the physical presence of this boat, the 'Lucky Two'.

Darryl's feet were stuck to the sidewalk. He watched Eleanore follow Casey and step into the boat. He thought of asking if there was anything, just anything, he could do to have one more moment with her. He knew there wasn't a thing he could do but watch her go.

"Ya'll stay safe now, ya hear!?" he hollered at the two people getting situated on the boat.

Only Eleanore turned her head around to look back at Darryl. He thought her eyes looked sad, but she smiled at Darryl, lifted her hand and gave him a short wave good bye.

Darryl pointed his finger straight at Eleanore and shouted in a firm voice, "I WILL meet you back here after this hurricane business is over. I WILL get you back to your car!"

Darryl helplessly watched Casey, Eleanore, and the 'Lucky Two' pull away from the dock. His thoughts ran amok and roared in his brain.

"The love of money is a dangerous way to live life. Chasing the buck, that's all Casey is in this for. Eleanore, I know is another story. She's putting herself in danger for the love of someone. Now that's a love worth living for. And where, oh where, might Earl be right now? His mind was messed up when he left. I don't know if it was about her or money. She said he called her. What am I thinking? She's here to find Earl who seemed crazy about his money, but maybe not. He must've been crazy to leave her for a boat. Leaving the boat keys with Casey was definitely crazy!"

Darryl slowly walked back to his truck. He waited ten minutes before cranking up the engine. He closed his eyes and listened to the sounds of the wind, the rain, and the rumbling thunder. He prayed.

"God, you are good. Right now I fear you. Dear God, I thank you for all the beauty, pleasures and wonderful things you've given me, us. Thank you for this short life here on earth. Please protect the innocent. Give us strength, courage and hope during this hurricane, which will surely test our endurance. I pray for forgiveness of all past and future sins and your acceptance of my soul in heaven. Amen."

He put the truck into gear and slowly drove across the parking lot, frequently glancing in the rear view mirror in the hope he might see Eleanore one more time. "Not a chance. Not today." he thought.

For the second time in one day Darryl headed to the hurricane shelter.

CHAPTER 29: NIGHT OF TERROR BEGINS

Despite the intensely humid warm air Fluff shook. She was inside the rubber boot lying in the corner of the boat, hiding again, overwhelmed with fear. This situation was far worse than the time she escaped from the car.

"Fraidy Cat" ran through her mind while she listened to the voices of humans talking nearby.

"I must not be afraid!"

A woman's voice, softer than the man's, almost sounded almost familiar. It was impossible to relax in the position Fluff was in, but the woman's voice had a calming effect.

"I must not waste time thinking about that voice! I must think how to keep them from finding me!" Flufff thought nervously.

Her normally bright green eyeballs looked like luminescent black holes painted against the white fur on her face. Her claws, sharp and ready to attack, gripped firmly like glue to the inside of the black rubber boot. Her muscles tensed while she crouched, stuffed like a sausage, inside the boot. Her muscles ached. Even her eyeballs hurt from staring out of the black world she was stuck in. She was ready to leap out and attack anyone if they came near her.

She was on the outside. King was on the inside. He was the lucky cat now. Earlier she felt lucky because she was on the outside. How quickly the tide changed.

The man and woman, were not talking any more.

Fluff heard the sound of metal keys jingling.

Casey pulled Earl's key ring out of his pocket and slipped a key into the metal coin slot shaped hole next to the boat throttle.

Eleanore felt sick to her stomach. She wondered if it was the mix of odors on the boat that made her feel nauseous. There was no chance to change her decision to go with Casey and there was no turning back now. The power of fear gripped her stomach, killing the nausea.

King was wide awake now. His senses were on high alert after hearing the three muffled voices outside the cabin. He waited, still snuggled in the corner underneath the table. He thought maybe he recognized the man's voice, but the woman's voice was totally unfamiliar. "Lots of people walk around these docks every day, talking, laughing and they all sound the same to me. Why are there two people on this boat now?" he wondered.

He hoped it was Earl's voice that he heard. With the best of luck Earl would very soon open up the cabin door. King would get his chance to take a running leap out of the door, between or around

Earl's legs, and jump off the boat. The voice did not sound like Captain Keith's.

King was exhausted. He was hungry, thirsty and tired. He needed energy to escape but, he didn't know where to find it. He wanted out of the cabin so bad, especially if people were on the boat. He did not want to be on the boat with any people. He was never fond, or trusting, of humans since his first owner had mistreated him. They were okay if they fed him, but otherwise he had no affection or need for them. He got along very well on his own and with his cat companions.

Fluff, he remembered, once lived with a human. "Hmmm, Fluff," he thought. "I wonder how she is doing. She is probably out there and scared. She won't know what to do. I can't talk with her now with humans being so close. They will surely discover her and try to scat her away, off the boat."

King felt the boat move when Casey and Eleanore boarded the boat.

"I'll get this cranked up here in a few minutes," Casey said to Eleanore.

Casey reached up to his epaulet where the radio rested and turned the volume off. He did not want any radio signals from headquarters to interrupt this mission. Soon they would try to contact him. He knew turning off the radio would get him in trouble. But, Casey wasn't thinking beyond keeping the 'Lucky Two' from being destroyed by a hurricane.

"If you're wondering what to do I'll open the cabin in a minute and you can check it out. Maybe see what kind of provisions we have in there. We'll need to have some things to at least get us through the night." Casey was taking charge.

Eleanore decided not to talk too much to Casey. It was better for her to observe, as Darryl had advised, and do what Casey told her. The less interaction she had with Casey the better. She was not looking forward to spending time with him even if would only be one night. Eleanore planted her two feet firmly on the deck of the boat, and tried to get her sea legs ready. She wanted badly to separate her feelings of blaming Earl for this situation she found herself in. It was her own stupidity, or stubbornness, that put her in this situation.

She kept a watchful eye on Casey while he fumbled around on the rocking boat. He was checking the engines, peeking into the storage containers beneath the seats, flipping buttons on the console, and testing the gears on the throttle.

"Kinda messy around here, but it's not in too bad of shape overall for what we got to do today," he mumbled.

Eleanore was relieved he didn't sound worried or concerned about the boat's condition.

"He is taking a calculated risk doing something he knows more about than I do. Hopefully his choice will be successful. Everything in life that's calculated is not always successful. Chance and circumstance can find a way to interfere," she thought.

"We'll be okay going out in this boat?" she finally asked Casey.

"Oh, yes!" he answered eagerly. Casey stepped back to the wheel, grabbed the key stuck in the ignition and turned it. The engine started with a loud noise. A cloud of grey smoke, stinking of diesel fumes, billowed out of the stern near Eleanore. "You might want to step away from there and sit down over here on the bench," Casey hollered at her over the noise.

Eleanore did as Casey suggested. When she moved closer to Casey she could see the keys hanging out of the ignition. She felt a tug rip through her heart. She recognized a small metal grey anchor hanging on the ring. It was the keyring she bought for Earl on one of their trips together to the beach years ago. She looked away from the keys and clenched her teeth. She was more determined to see the boat to a safer location now.

The nasty engine smoke quickly blew away.

"You got it going good now!" Eleanore hollered at Casey.

Casey walked away from the steering wheel and stepped over the side of the boat onto the dock. He carefully untied the two ends of rope holding the boat to the dock slip pilings and threw them onto the deck. He unplugged the power line from the power outlet on the closest piling, hopped back on the stern, and dropped the orange power line on the deck.

Eleanore noticed that he did all of this like an expert.

"Now we're set to move," he yelled. Casey pushed down on the throttle with one hand and held the wheel with the other. The engine noise suddenly grew louder and the boat shook. Eleanore felt the vibrations come up through the bench where she sat.

Casey started to talk loudly over the engine roar. "Once we get moving, I'll open up that cabin door and let you inside to check out what we got in there. We'll only need enough to get us through the night. Basic stuff is what you need to look for. Maybe see if there is any canned food to eat. We're definitely going to need water. Plenty to drink so we can stay hydrated. It will get hot again after the storm passes. Maybe there's a microwave or small stove that we can heat up food. If not I'll get some MRE's. You know? Meals Ready to Eat. I'm going to go across the lagoon and stop for gas at the Treasure Island Marina over there, across the way. Hopefully they have enough gas and supplies left. I can't imagine that everyone else has scooped up all of their supplies. People don't usually go out on their boats in this kinda weather and most people don't think to stop at a marina store for hurricane supplies. But, you never know. Some people are wise enough to know that these boating supply places stock up good stuff to carry them through a hurricane."

He slowly guided the 'Lucky Two' across the choppy water of the lagoon. The ride was bumpy and salty water sprayed across her face. Her bottom was already sore from the long ride in the car and she wished the boat cushion seat was a little softer. It wasn't long before she forgot the seat and became awestruck with riding on a boat this size.

The world looked so different in the middle of the water.

"I don't know how much I'll feel like eating out here!" she finally shouted loudly at Casey.

Casey looked back at her and chuckled. "This stop won't take that long," he shouted. "I know I'll need something to eat. It's going to get a whole lot rougher than this out there in the bay."

"How long will it take to get where we're going?" she shouted back. The constant shouting added to the long rope of tight knots in her stomach.

"Oh, I'm not too sure in these conditions. I'd like to say at least an hour, maybe more. It just depends on how well this boat will take the chop of the waves to find out how fast we can move."

"That doesn't sound too bad," she thought to herself.

Eleanore found herself staring at the pile of loose rope lines lying on the floor. She thought to toss them out of the way. She didn't want to trip on them later, but there was no place to put them.

She wanted to find something to do to get her mind off her fear and nausea. She looked past the choppy waves and found the shoreline, the stable ground that she already missed. She tried gulping fresh air.

It was going to be a long, long night with this strange man. She reassured herself that it was for a good cause and it would be only one night. The 'Lucky Two' would stay under her watchful eyes. She would be a witness to everything Casey did. She fought the uneasy feeling that there was something wrong about the connection between Casey, the 'Lucky Two' and Earl. It was the pride she heard in Casey's voice.

She found a quiet voice inside her head telling her to stay focused, be strong and pay attention.

Her eyes randomly searched the rest of the deck of the boat. She noticed a black rubber boot lying on its side in the corner beneath the steering wheel where Casey was standing. A small white patch of something that looked like fur lining stuck to the edge of the top of the boot. Eleanore wondered what the heck the boot was doing on the floor and why would it have white fur lining. Maybe it was just a piece of fabric, old rag, or feathers used on fishing lures. Who knew?

"Why would Earl keep a single boot?" she wondered. "That's really not like Earl to keep something useless lying around."

"Are you doing alright back there?" Casey's shouted without looking back at her.

Surprised, but not startled, she shouted back "Yes." He'd interrupted her thoughts.

Casey asked, "See the sign over there that says 'FUEL'?"

"Yes," she answered.

"I'm pulling in over there to get gas. Hang on and don't move."

He slowed the boat and closed in on the landing at the Treasure Island Marina. Eleanore ached to get off the boat, plant her two feet firmly on the ground and get off the boat to safety. She dismissed the idea. She was thankful she was no longer bouncing, if only for a short time.

Casey slowed the boat to a stop and let the engine idle. He turned, reached down to pick up the rope lying on the floor and said to her, "While I get the gas you check out what's inside the cabin here." Eleanore was relieved that she hadn't touched the rope.

Casey tossed out the rope, like a cowboy with a lasso, and looped it around the wood pole piling. He expertly stepped onto the dock and pulled the rope tighter, then jumped back onto the boat and turned the engine off. He pulled the key ring with the anchor out of the ignition.

"I don't want to be inside the store too long so you be ready to tell me what we got here. It should only take me about four or five minutes to fill up the tank. It looks like about a fifty gallon tank. The fuel gauge is showing pretty low. Don't know if the gauge works right, though. There might be air in the tank and the boat's been rocking a lot. That little rubber ball inside the tank might be stuck on one side. We'll just have to see."

Casey said this all so fast. "Obviously he's in a hurry," Eleanore thought.

Eleanore didn't waste any time. She jumped up to move out of the way to let Casey past her. He turned the handle to the cabin door, pushed on the door until it was slightly open and took a quick peek through the cracked opening. Like an athlete he turned aside and leapt off the boat, causing the boat to pop up out of the water. Casey's long legs swiftly walked to the fuel pump.

Eleanore cautiously stepped forward and, using only her index finger, slowly pushed against the brown slatted cabin door. Her hand shook. She feared what she may see inside.

When the door opened wide enough to let more light inside King scooted backward and pressed his body flat against the sidewall beneath the table. He did not want to be seen before he had a chance to leap past the human. He planned to slip away once the door opened wide enough, but as soon as Eleanore entered the small room she quickly closed the door behind her.

Eleanore's tired eyes surveyed the small cabin room and sniffed at the musty, dank smell. The only thing that looked familiar was the battery operated radio on the shelf next to the table. It looked like the one she gave him as a birthday present a few years ago. It was an ordinary radio that played music. It might be good to listen to music later on.

The long stressful day was a heavy weight on her mind and body. She knew she must put her mind to the task Casey had assigned. She was sure he meant business and would want an answer about the provisions on the boat as soon as he returned.

She took two steps closer inside the cabin and looked past the radio. Another shelf held a couple cans of soup and canned spaghetti. A coffee can was next to the soup and spaghetti. She reached up, took the can off the shelf and pulled off the plastic lid. Inside she found several packets of instant drink mix and packets of sugar. She returned the coffee can to the shelf. Below the shelf was a small cabinet. She tugged on the door handle and found a small storage compartment containing plastic cups and two bottles of unopened water. "Well, that should last two people all of one night," she thought.

She wasn't hungry. She hadn't had time to calm down and get an appetite. If she drank too much water she would have to worry about the problem of using the toilet, which didn't seem so obvious on the boat. She grimaced at the thought of taking care of personal business on the boat.

Eleanore sighed in resignation. She slipped outside and shut the door. She saw Casey still standing at the gasoline pump.

"Two cans of soup and two cans of spaghetti. Two bottles of water," Eleanore shouted to be sure that he heard her.

"That's it? You're kidding me!" Casey barked back. He aggressively shoved the gas pump handle into the holder, making a loud clank.

He returned to the boat and, for the first time, noticed Eleanore's scared pale face. Her sensitive, soft brown eyes looked innocent and tired. He made a mental note: he was a trained professional and should not blame her for Earl's stupidity.

"Not your fault, dear," he said in a more controlled, calmer voice. "I know exactly what we'll need to get us through one night. It won't take me long. I'll go inside to pay for the gas and get some more supplies. You can wait here. Are you comfortable waiting here alone for a few minutes?"

Surprised by the way Casey spoke to her, Eleanore felt a little better. She nodded her head yes but was still wary of this man who commanded authority, still in his work uniform, acting like he was off duty. He was taking her, in Earl's boat, to an undisclosed location, but supposedly safe. She remembered how Darryl reacted to Casey. She absolutely did not feel safe.

As he promised, Casey returned soon. The small supply store carried only the basic, necessary items required by boaters. The large fingers of one hand were wrapped around two one-gallon plastic jugs of water. In the other hand he held a white plastic shopping bag that appeared to be stuffed with cans.

Before stepping back into the boat Casey leaned over and handed the bag of supplies to Eleanore. "Leave the bag on the deck for now," he said to her. He boarded the boat and slid the jugs of water across the deck.

Within minutes Casey had the boat ready to roll again. He turned the keys to crank up the engine and pushed the throttle forward. The boat was steadily gliding straight across the choppy waters.

They soon approached a pole jutting up in the middle of the water. Attached to it was a metal triangle sign with the words *No Wake Zone.*

"What does that mean?" Eleanore shouted above the noise of the engine motor.

"Don't go so fast that you make waves for other boats!" he hollered, turning his head so she could hear him.

They both laughed at the irony of the sign in these conditions.

Eleanore asked, "I suppose that's one of the laws that you enforce?"

"It's for those who have a patrol duty boat. No one will be enforcing it today though. Mostly my job consists of counting fish when the deep sea fishing boats return at the end of the day," he answered.

"Counting fish?" Eleanore was surprised there was a job for that.

"Yup, It sounds interesting, huh? Actually I'm supposed to make sure that the fish being caught are legal size, legal for the season, and legal number allowed by the State of Florida."

"Oh!" Eleanore said politely.

Eleanore could not think of another subject to bring up. Casey looked straight ahead, concentrating on maneuvering the boat over the choppy water. It was too dangerous to distract Casey and tiresome to talk over the noise of the boat's engines.

Eleanore tried to look at the scenery they passed, but couldn't. The high waves splashed and slapped against the sides of the bouncing boat. Salty sea spray stung her skin. Each time the boat slammed a wave, Eleanore's brain pounded inside her skull. The ride made her hurt all over.

She was having second thoughts. "Maybe it would have been better to stay at the shelter with Darryl. The smooth, glassy water on a clear creek or lake in Georgia beats this on any day."

Her shoulders slumped under the weight of worry. It was all about protecting Earl's boat. She began to doubt herself again and thought, "Have I made a bad decision? No! My heart's reason for doing this was hope. I am determined to do the right thing. This is my choice."

She watched Casey again, standing at the throttle. She studied him, noticing the tight bulging muscles in his tanned arms and legs while he stood with his feet firmly planted on the floor. His large hands gripped the wheel of the boat, ready to react. The color of his hair was light, but hard to determine because his head was mostly shaved. The back of his head appeared flat, like a board, except for the ripples of skin folded up against the collar of his shirt.

"He's a great big guy, and not half bad looking, but I don't think I'd want to see him angry." She recalled his slightly erratic behavior earlier at the dock.

Eleanore closed her eyes and imagined his two huge hands in a tight grip around her neck, choking her, with her tongue hanging out of the side of her mouth and her eyes bulging open out of their sockets.

The back of her throat was suddenly dry. She took in several deep breaths and sucked salty air into her lungs. Eleanore licked her lips then bit down hard on her bottom lip. She closed her eyes and shook her head side to side to try and erase the image out of her mind.

She shivered, not knowing if it was her imagination or the wetness of her clothing. "Why am I shivering? It's hot and humid salty air!" she thought. "I need to keep track of the time and where we are going!"

She pulled her shoulders upright and pinched her knees tightly together. She wrapped both arms across her chest in a tight lock. Her fists were clasped in balls. Her long brown hair, weighted by the salty sea spray, stuck to her shoulders like clumps of seaweed.

An hour of silence passed. Homes on the shoreline of the lagoon and bay disappeared. Casey began to guide the boat through an area of open water. Far across the horizon she saw only tall pine trees on banks of shallow inlets of water. The water seemed calmer than the lagoon. Casey was navigating in more shallow, marshy water with tall, thick sawgrass bordering along banks of a desolate sandy white shoreline. Eleanore felt the boat moving a little faster. She hoped they would arrive at a destination soon. It was a tedious, boring ride and she was ever so tired.

A sharp, critical voice, sounding like her mother's voice, suddenly exploded in her head. "What do you plan to do about that car you left up there parked at a gas station on Highway 231? Someone has probably broken into it by now. What about your job? What are you going to do for money? I'm sure the Kountry Kafe has already found someone else to take your job. Without a job and money for gas to put in the car how are you expecting to get back to Pine Mountain? What are you going to do now that you're in this mess? Where are you going to get the money?!"

"Think positive, Eleanore!!!" she challenged herself and tried to organize her thoughts into rational outcomes. "What are the possibilities now? I've got all night to stay awake, at least, to think about this. First of all, I have a good feeling about that man Darryl. I know that if I need him to do it, he'll get me back to my car. He'd probably even give me some gas money too. That is if we don't find Earl."

"Been pretty darn quiet back there," Casey's voice boomed out.

Eleanore, lost in her thoughts, jumped up. She was surprised to see Casey's head turned back. His green eyes were locked on her. Ever since they'd left the marina Casey's eyes had been at work, scanning over the waters. It unnerved her to see his eyes staring at her.

"Not too much to look at around here or talk about, I suppose. You've been pretty busy and I didn't want to interfere with your work," she told him.

"Yeah, it's best that I pay attention to where we go," he flipped his head back around and faced the front of the boat again.

Eleanore was relieved when Casey stopped looking at her. She closed her eyes and lowered her head to fit into the palms of her hands. Her wet hair stuck to her cheeks. Her stomach was still squeezed into knots below her beating heart. She felt more miserable than she could ever remember. More miserable than when Earl left and the night she lost Princess.

Casey didn't ask how she felt. If he did ask, she wouldn't tell him. Closing her eyes was the only light switch available to shut out the misery she felt. The off again, on again, pounding rain against her face; the wind blowing so hard it passed through her body; the noise and gasoline smells coming from the engine propellers; the uncertainty of her future. She couldn't escape any of it.

The time wasn't passing fast enough. Without knowing why, Eleanore spoke. "I know one thing for sure," she said loud enough for Casey to hear. "I can't make up my mind about living in Georgia or staying in Florida."

"What?" Casey turned his head sideways. "Why?"

"Not sure if I want to go back to Georgia again. But, then I don't know about these hurricanes either. So far this one seems to be easy enough to get through!"

He laughed. "You don't know just yet what you're talking about." He turned back to his driving.

Eleanore was surprised by her casual comments to Casey. She didn't really want to call any attention to herself. She lifted her aching head and tried to stretch the stiff muscles in her legs.

"Okay," she thought. "I need to keep my mouth shut and thoughts to myself. Maybe it wouldn't be so bad to stay in Florida. Hurricanes don't come along every day. It's not going to be so easy to show my face back in Pine Mountain. There's really not much for me back there. My job is most likely not going to be offered back, even if I ask nicely and apologize for being late. Johnny said to come back next week, but I don't see how I can get back next week. So, what's there I can do in Florida besides fishing and working in restaurants? Maybe work in a store? When, if, I see Earl again he can help me figure it out.

Suddenly the engine noise softened and the boat slowed down to a near crawl. The boat was gliding into the opening of a small canal.

"Hey, where we at now?' she asked.

"This area is called Dismal Creek. I think we can bank on being safe here," Casey said.

"Oh. Here's where we stay through the night you mean? That's a

214

name that doesn't sound appealing or safe!"

Casey chuckled and looked ahead. He guided the 'Lucky Two' through a narrow passage of water that didn't seem, at least to Eleanore, to be wide enough for any boat. He came alongside a shallow sandy bank and let the boat's engine idle.

"I'm gonna jump out here. When I get on the bank over there next to that tall pine tree you throw this rope over to me," he said pointing down to the same rope lying near his foot. "See that tree there?" He pointed his long arm to the right. "We're gonna tie up to that tree. This is as far as we can get with this size boat."

With his huge thumb and finger Casey turned the key near the throttle. The boat engine died. The rumbling and vibrations stopped. The engine noise was replaced by a high pitched whistle. It came from the speedy winds blowing through the pine needles.

Casey stepped up on top of the bench seat across from Eleanore and deftly jumped over the side of the boat, landing on the sandy bank. The sand was soft and sucked in Casey's right foot. He easily caught the rope, even though her toss was a little short of where he stood. He quickly pulled on the rope, dragging the boat through the water a little closer to the shoreline.

She watched Casey wrap the rope around the tree several times before he tied the loose end into a strong knot. She noticed other large trees, live oaks, with thick dark bark trunks and limbs that touched the sandy banks. She wondered why he didn't use one of those trees.

"Hope we have a little more rope left," he shouted to her, short of breath after pulling and tying up the boat.

Eleanore looked around the deck then shook her head sideways and shouted back, "NO."

"No rope. I suspected there wasn't but I had to ask."

He lifted his right leg high, his knee level with his waist, and placed it over the side of the boat. Then he grabbed the side of the boat and pulled his large frame off the ground and over the side of the 'Lucky Two'.

Casey walked to the front of the boat and found the anchor on the deck. He lifted it up to his chest and with a strong heave threw it into the water. Then he walked back to the stern and said to Eleanore, "Let's go inside for a while. Get out of this blowing wind and wet weather."

Casey walked past her, brushing against her shoulder.

"No telling what we got inside here," he said.

He pushed open the brown cabin door, walked through the entrance and began to clear his throat with a dry, hacking cough. "I'm pretty darn tired after that rough and noisy ride aren't you?"

Eleanore nervously stepped inside the cabin, not knowing what else she could do but follow him inside the cabin. Getting out of the weather sounded appealing, but not going inside the cabin with Casey.

His long muscular arm brushed her shoulder again when he reached behind her to pull shut the cabin door. It felt intentional, but Eleanore didn't have time to think. In a moment's flash of time she found Casey's two large hands placed on each of her shoulders, pulling her toward his large body, bringing his face closer to her face, within an inch of her nose, close to her mouth! His hot breath stank like a garbage disposal in a dirty kitchen sink. Casey's glassy green eyes locked onto Eleanore's frightened soft brown eyes, opened wide with fear.

Casey felt Eleanore's fear. Her legs shook. Her shoulders tightened. Her nose and lips twitched uncontrollably. She held her hands in tight fists with her arms stiff and rigid next to the side of her body.

Neither person said a word for thirty seconds as they stood locked eye to eye. Casey's lips parted and Eleanore opened her mouth.

"Please don't," she barely whispered softly as if the air in her lungs was trapped inside. A silent scream, which no one would hear, was stuck in the back of her throat.

Still holding her by the shoulder, Casey closed his mouth. When he realized and felt her fear he said without passion or emotion, "Sorry."

He cleared his throat, took his hands off of her shoulders, took two steps backward and turned his back to her.

Casey was confused by his actions toward Eleanore

Eleanore took a few steps backward, away from Casey.

It took a few minutes for both of them to shake off their different feelings of insecurity. After an awkward silence Casey turned to face Eleanore and spoke first. "I really want to apologize for that. I am really sorry." He spoke softly, putting emphasis on the word sorry.

Speaking normal he said, "We better get settled in. It's going to be a long night. You might sit over there on that chair at the table and I'll sit on the bunk. In a little bit I'll go outside and check on the ropes."

Eleanore, too frightened, simply nodded her head up and down.

"Listen. We've got a long time to wait this out together tonight. Maybe we could talk and get to know each other a little better. It'll help to pass the time. I don't think that regular radio sitting up there on the shelf is going to work real good, but we have it."

He paused, waiting to see if she would say anything.

"I guess we could talk a little bit about our families. Where we grew up and stuff like that. First of all, you look mighty young. Do you mind if I ask you how old you are? No harm in asking that, is there?"

Eleanore felt composed enough to speak. "Twenty four," she answered, embarrassed to reveal her age.

"No kids, then?" he asked her.

"No. Don't plan on having any kids, or at least any time soon."

Casey laughed and leaned against the wall. "Well, I can understand that. They're a lot to handle these days. Probably could've figured you didn't have any kids, but sometimes women have a child when they're young. Then they take the kid over to their mamma's house to be raised. No offense, but I've seen it."

Casey seemed more casual and relaxed. His mention of family eased Eleanore's fear and worry about what he might do next.

Eleanore let loose of her feelings. "I know what you mean, but that wouldn't be my momma. My momma flat out told me, at the age of seventeen, I was going to be on my own when I left home so I'd better stay out of trouble. She said she was tired of raising kids. I was the youngest of three. I have one sister and one brother but they're living in different cities far away, living their lives apart from me and my mother. I haven't heard from them in years. They were born a year apart. I came along six years later. My parents got married young. She was nineteen. They separated for a couple of years then got back together, but I don't know why. I think my momma couldn't manage on her own with two young kids. I think my dad wanted his kids in his life. My momma was a bitter woman, never happy, never got enough of the things she wanted for herself. She was mostly angry at us kids and my dad. Momma would tell us she could never have anything nice because of us. I know I don't want any kids until I know that I'm ready for them. I want to love them. I want the person who I have kids with to love me and to love my kids too."

While listening to the story Casey's face grew serious. At the end of the story he said with pity, "Whew! That's some heavy stuff coming from a pretty girl like you! Man, that's really sad. I'm sorry." He paused then said, "My ex-wife was kind of selfish like that. She never wanted to have kids."

"Did you want children?"

Casey said solemnly, "I think I did. Maybe I wasn't sure because our relationship wasn't real good."

"Well, my mother didn't either, but in those days she said the kids just came along because you weren't careful. It was not fun growing up in my family. Getting through high school was tough too. She hardly knew how to give me any advice she was so wrapped up in herself. When I got older I decided that you can't choose the family you were born into. You can only choose how to deal with your family."

"Worrying doesn't help either," Casey said. "What happens is not always your fault. It sounds like you have a good heart in spite of the hard knocks. I've learned that love in relationships – family, friends, lovers or whatever—is very elusive. I grew up in a pretty decent family. But now I can't seem to find love and hold on to it."

"That's exactly how I'm feeling too!" she sighed.

At that moment Casey decided he could not make it through a night listening to sad stories. "Let's talk about some of the fun stuff we can remember in our lives. Have us a bite to eat and then talk. It's going to be the only way to get through the night because you can bet that we're not going to get any rest or sleep. It will get worse once it gets dark. There'll be some frightening sounds out there. I'm sure this boat, with a name like the 'Lucky Two' will be the safest place to be for this one night! I know it!"

CHAPTER 30: THE WORST FEAR

When the cabin door of the 'Lucky Two' creaked opened King scrambled to hide. He did not want to be discovered. The rough ride had exhausted him. Without food or water he didn't know how much longer he could last. Fear fueled the little energy left in his body.

The cabin door clicked shut. He ears perked up. He heard a slight cough that sounded like a man clearing his throat and then a woman's soft voice said only two words. King recognized the voice of the man who began to speak. There was no mistaking the voice of Casey Howard. He rarely heard Casey talk when he worked at the docks, but he knew it was Casey.

During the boat ride King nervously tried to keep his attention on sounds. He heard waves slamming against the hull of the boat. He had no way of knowing what was happening outside and what would happen next. The loud rumble of the engines blocked out the human's voices. He wondered if Fluff was still on the boat. He thought it would be impossible for her to hide anywhere. She *must* have jumped off before they left the marina. Somehow it could be possible that she was still with him, here on the boat. The last thing Fluff said to him was that she would stay with him. King remembered telling her it was better to stay on the boat.

After Casey and Eleanore stepped inside the cabin and closed the door Fluff inched her way out of the black boot. She backed out slowly, careful not to make any noise. She hoped that she wouldn't have to scramble back inside soon. Fluff's body ached tremendously from being cramped inside the boot for so long. Her head hurt from the banging and bouncing of the boat slapping on the waves. The rubber boot was no cushion for the beating she took. She needed to stretch and needed fresh air to breath. Her head was dizzy from being crammed inside the toe of the boot for so long.

Once she completely backed out of the boot she turned her nose upward to catch a sniff of the air. She jumped onto the bench seat to take a peek over the side of the boat. When she saw land she leapt, without hesitation, over the side of the boat onto the sandy beach.

Once on the sandy beach she realized she wasn't in a safe place.

Fluff's eyes' welled up with water. The harsh wind was too much to bear. It blew her long white fur, making it stick up in the air like needles on a porcupine. Yet, the fresh air felt good after being tightly trapped in the boot for so long. She was overwhelmed and frightened.

The calculated risk to stay on the boat with King, hoping someone would eventually board the boat and open the cabin door, had turned into a living nightmare. Would King's flying leap to freedom happen on the sandy beach where she found herself now?

Fluff crouched low. She allowed herself to get as close to the ground as possible without touching it. She dug the claws of her four paws deep into the sand. She squinted her eyes and scanned the landscape, trying to avoid getting sand in them from the fiercely blowing wind. It didn't help. Tears flowed from her eyes. Her search soon revealed some low lying trees. With a quick leap she bounded over the tall weeds to take cover under a tree. She crawled behind a clump of Spanish bayonet bushes and quickly discovered if she stayed there she would be cut and whipped by the pointed branches.

Fluff bent her neck and looked up to the heaven and sky. It was getting dark. There was no answer, no sign, telling her what to do, or where to go. All she could see was gray swirling clouds and swaying pine trees.

Something felt familiar. Then she remembered where she was the last time she felt like this. It was the day she jumped out of Eleanore's car in the Captain Anderson's marina parking lot. The long car ride had been nauseating, sickening her stomach, just like the boat ride.

Back then she didn't know about taking precaution before getting herself into a bad situation. Now she found herself in a worse situation. "Why can't I think clearly when I'm anxious and feel sick!" she moaned.

Even though she knew humans can be kind to people, she learned to be afraid of people after the day she found herself lost in the parking lot. The two people who boarded the boat had hardly spoken during the long horrible boat ride. Now they were inside the boat cabin with King.

The voice of the man sounded familiar even though the sound was muffled while she hid, stuffed inside the boot. The woman's voice she was not so sure about. It seemed familiar. She was unsure if she should fear the two humans on the boat.

Fluff thought, "It's that man who wears a uniform. He's the one who always stands on the sidewalk when the boats return to the marina with fish. I know it is! He is not very friendly to us cats."

A new sound distracted her. A pounding noise was approaching, coming closer and closer. She turned her head in the direction of the noise. Not far away large drops of rain splattered down on the sand, sending grains flying high up into the air. A wall of rain was speeding toward her.

"King is on that boat, locked up with that man and a woman, who, oh my gosh, gives me the feeling that everything is going to be all right even with that huge man with her. I just cannot bear the thought of spending any more time inside that boot!!!!"

Fluff faced a dilemma she'd felt before. Doing something that seemed worthwhile at the moment brought only temporary happiness. The consequences of some foolish action, like chasing a

220

mouse onto a boat or jumping out of a car, led her into the predicament she was in. The fact of the matter was her love for King overruled the fear and conflict of her emotions. The longing of the heart, the mysteriously triumphant love for King, fueled her decision to stay with King, who said she'd be safer on the boat with bad weather coming.

The rain reached her and pelted down with such a force that it stung her skin. A sudden blast of wind made a screeching noise, like a wolf howling in the dark in the distant woods.

Without giving another passing thought to what she should, or should not, do Fluff wiggled her hind end and, like an unexpected star shooting across a dark night sky, she sprang from the ground. She flew through the air like a bat, front paws stretched far in front of her and back paws spread out wide behind her. Her front paws barely reached the side of the boat but she managed to hang on. She clawed and clung onto the side of the boat with her two front paws. Her back paws scratched and scrambling below. She feared slipping and falling into the brownish tannic water so close below. With every bit of muscle and energy she pulled her body up until all four paws were securely placed on the thin edge of the side. She stood there, firmly in place while she regained her balance. Then she sprang off the side, landing a little clumsily on the fiberglass deck

"OUCHEEEEE...." Fluff could not help it. A deep gutteral meow sailed with the breezes.

Fluff was worried and relieved all at the same time.

"Did you hear something?" Eleanore asked Casey when she heard the unusual noise outside the cabin.

"Yeah, I think I heard something too." Casey's eyebrows lifted up and pulled together.

Casey was sitting on the small bench seat, legs stretched out in front of him, across from the table where Eleanore sat. Eleanore sat hunched over with her arms folded across the top of the table. Her chin rested on her folded arms. The upsetting encounter was still fresh in their minds but they found common ground by agreeing to talk like kindred spirits to help themselves get through the night they had to spend together.

"Sounded almost like an animal. Maybe like a cat," Eleanore said with interest in the possibility of a cat keeping them company.

"That's not possible. I think we're going to be hearing a lot of strange noises tonight. Better get used to it," Casey responded.

Fluff was scared after the close call falling in the water. She regained control of her nerves and softly padded her way to the cabin door. She sat down next to the cabin door. After shaking and quivering for a few seconds, she summoned up courage.

"Meow. MEEOOW!" she started meowing as loudly as possible.

"Oh my God!" Eleanore jumped up, forgetting that the floor was moving surface, rocking with the waves of water beneath it. "Oh my God!" she repeated as she stumbled to open the cabin door.

"Wait a minute!" Casey called after her, knowing he already lost his authority to control the situation when Eleanore flew up from her seat.

"Oh, oh, oh!" Eleanore's screeched out when she opened the cabin door and saw the dirty white cat sitting on the deck. "It's a cat!"

"Wow! That's a surprise!" Casey stammered. He was stunned too. The sight of a cat sitting in front of him was incomprehensible. "That cat has been on this boat ride all the way here with us. Wow. It must have gotten on board right before we left the docks."

"Oh my gosh!" Eleanore sucked in her breath and shook her head in disbelief. In a soft, soothing voice she said, "It reminds me of the cat I used to have. Her name was Princess. She was all white and the eyes, they look like the same color too. Just like my Princess. As a matter of fact, I lost her on my last trip down here to visit Earl."

"This one here looks calm and tame considering the ride it's been on. The ones that usually hang around at the docks are skittish and don't take to people. They don't like us." Casey stopped to take a hard look down at Fluff, joining Eleanore to stare at the cat that had unexpectedly appeared. "I'm not too much of a cat person," he said. "I'm not afraid of them like some people are, just not crazy about them. I've thought that cats are mostly sneaky and useless, not as loving and loyal like a dog. However, this cat does look familiar to me. I think I remember seeing it down at the marina once. I thought it was a pretty cat."

Fluff didn't move, but kept meowing gently. When she looked into Eleanore's face, for the first time in a long time, she was positive that it was her. She thought she'd recognized Eleanore's voice earlier. Fluff was relieved now that she knew it was really Eleanore, who she could trust, but was uncertain about going inside the cabin with Casey. Being near Casey, so close to him, scared her.

Eleanore listened to Casey with half of her attention. "She really looks like Princess. She really, really does!" Eleanore repeated herself, getting more and more excited.

Fluff was anxious to know about King. She knew he was inside the cabin but where? Why didn't he come running out the open door. "Maybe he's sick," she thought. "Or, maybe he knows it's not very safe outside. Why haven't I seen him now that the door is finally open?"

Casey cautiously asked, "Do you think she might come to you? I don't want to stay out here with the door open much longer. It'll get wet inside and we'll be miserable enough without sitting in a wet cabin."

Eleanore responded, "I don't know if it's her or not. I can't imagine how it could be."

Eleanore stooped down on one knee to get eye level with Fluff. She placed one hand flat on the wet deck and slowly extended her other hand outward. She reached out closer, trying to touch Fluff.

"Princess, Princess," she cooed.

Fluff didn't move. She stared back at Eleanore.

"Look at her eyes," Eleanore said to Casey without turning her head to look up at him. "It almost looks like she's been crying."

Casey bent his head down a little and laughed. "I think you're right. See if you can grab her and get her inside. We need to shut the door."

Eleanore moved her hand slowly a little closer until she was able to pat the matted white fur on her head. She petted Fluff's head a few times.

"Meow, meow," Fluff responded to the touch mournfully.

"She's talking to me!"

"Animals don't talk," Casey laughed again. The scene unfolding in front of him amused him. It took his mind away from the serious situation. "See if you can pick her up and get her in here. It looks like she's shivering."

Minutes passed and nothing happened. Neither Fluff nor Eleanore moved. Casey had never bonded with an animal in any way like the way Eleanore and Fluff were communicating. He was fascinated.

Casey said patiently, but with urgency, "C'mon now. We got to batten down the hatches here. Seal up the cracks, so they say in the navy. We may need to find some loose rags or clothing to put in front of the door now that we've let the wind blow water inside the cabin. Think of tonight as like being on a roller coaster ride. You're going to be bouncing up and down, tossing and turning, getting whip lashed."

"How would you know?" Eleanore asked indifferently, her mind focused on the unreal possibility of finding the cat she had lost over a year ago. She was trying to make herself believe that it was really Princess, who looked pathetic and so different but seemed to be the same cat.

Casey annoyed by her question controlled himself and replied calmly, "Well, truthfully I've never been through a hurricane while spending the night on a boat. I honestly did spend the night inside a solid concrete building and it was still very scary. I'm just telling you."

"Princess," Eleanore spoke in a soft loving voice, ignoring Casey again. "Princess, come to me."

"Princess," Casey grumbled in a mocking tone of voice.

Fluff's eyes glowed with secrets like the glass ball of a fortune teller. Fluff knew it was impossible to believe that she could be like the Princess she once was.

Fluff knew, though, that she would have to go with the two humans inside the cabin. One she could trust and the other she could not be sure about. Better to be inside the cabin than back inside the boot.

223

"Look at her eyes!" Eleanore exclaimed. "I've never seen her eyes look like that!"

"Scared." Casey said, trying to sound disinterested but curious. "Let's get things moving. We have to move on. With, or without, the cat." He had to admit that he noticed the way the cat stared at Eleanore. It was a little unsettling.

Eleanore slowly lifted her arm again to reach out to Fluff. Her hand was cupped upward in a non-threatening way, and her single forefinger was extended to allow Fluff to complete the point of contact.

Fluff stretched her neck and let her nose touch the pointed finger. She sniffed, and then licked the tip of Eleanore's finger twice.

Eleanore wanted to scream, but said in a controlled voice. "It's her."

She gently dropped down to her other knee. With both knees securely anchored to the deck of the rocking boat she scooted forward and wrapped both of her arms around her former feline companion. She remained nonchalant in spite of the stale, smelly, matted, wet fur.

"Eeeeew, you stink terrible," she cooed to Fluff while she cradled the shaking cat close to her chest and lifted her body up. Holding the precious cat gave Eleanore hope. Everything was going to be okay even though Casey was in charge of the boat.

"I should talk to her," Eleanore said as she stepped around to re-enter the cabin.

Casey couldn't help from smiling. "Careful there with your precious cargo," he said. "Watch your step."

He held the door open to keep it from blowing against Eleanore then quickly shut it once they were all back inside.

Once inside Eleanore stooped close to the floor and released her hold on Fluff. As soon as she was free Fluff ran, scooting around the cabin floor aimlessly until she saw King lying beneath the table. She scurried to be near King. She had not expected the inside of the cabin to be this small.

"Leave her alone for a few minutes. Maybe she'll calm down," Eleanore said, relieved to see her cat finally settle down.

Casey laughed again, "Oh, don't you worry. I don't plan to go near her just as long as she stays away from me. She's a little smelly!"

"Golly, I didn't realize how dirty she was when I first picked her up. I'm pretty darn dirty myself now," Eleanor said.

"Well, it's going to be some time before you'll see the luxury of a hot shower," he scoffed.

"Yeah, I *bet!*" she laughed for the first time and said teasingly, "I think we'll have some new things to talk about tonight."

Casey liked the change he saw in Eleanore. He was relieved to finally see her in this happy mood. He said, "I think you're right. Hey, you hungry at all yet? Are you ready for a canned meal?"

Eleanore couldn't' remember when she last had something to eat. "Oh, my! I forgot that I haven't eaten since this morning. I think?" she said.

She was exhausted from the long day's drive from Georgia and the boat ride over choppy waters. "The last time I ate was in the car driving down here. I haven't been very hungry since I got here, though."

"Yeah, this kind of riding on the rough seas does tend to take away the appetite for most people," Casey agreed. His last meal, a frozen dinner in front of the television watching the weather, was not the best last meal. The thought of eating a can of spaghetti was not appetizing to him either. It was not what he really wanted right now. All he wanted was for the long night to be over, too.

"I'm not so hungry, either." Casey said. "We don't have to eat now. However, I'm pretty sure that we won't want to eat later on either. Seas are going to get rougher when it gets completely dark. We're going to need our strength to get through it. We should probably go ahead and get it over with."

Casey reached over the table, picked up a can of spaghetti and began to open it. "Enough for two people here, don't you think? Think your Princess under the table there might be a little hungry too?" Casey bent his knees to lower himself down near the floor. He twisted his head lower than the table to look for the cat hiding under it.

"Oh. My. Gawd!" he said very loud and slow.

"What?!" Eleanore shrieked with a look of panic on her face.

"I do believe that there is a cat hiding over there in the corner!"

"I know. I saw her run under the table. My Princess."

"Well, she's a white cat and the one I'm looking at is a black one!"

"No way!"

Eleanore hurried to bend down and look beneath the table.

"I see it!" she whispered loudly. "It is black!"

"Yup," Casey said in disbelief. He lifted his stooped body back up to standing. "Doesn't appear that either one of them will be coming out soon. The black one looks like it has blue eyes, but they're glowing red. The body is flat up against the wall. White one, your Princess, is huddled next to it. I don't think you'll be able to coax her out with food."

Eleanore crawled down to the floor and, on hands and knees, stared beneath the table. She was able to reach out to Fluff and give her a pat on the head. King buried his body against the wall.

"This is really going to be some kind of interesting night!" Eleanore proclaimed when she stood up.

"That's for sure," Casey agreed. "I'm going to run the engine for a little while now that it's close to dark. I'll be able to listen to the ship to shore radio and see if I can get an update on weather reports. The engine will let us use the microwave oven to heat up the spaghetti. It can't run for too long. We need to save gas for the trip back to the marina. Once it gets dark and the generator is turned off we'll need to stay calm. There will be a lot of strange noises outside. Talking will help us. Probably will help the animals underneath the table, too, hearing us talk. I'll turn the generator back on every so often, couple hours, to check the radio. Anyway it looks like we've got some entertainment. You got any other good cat stories to catch me up on? It will be tough to beat this story?"

Casey and Eleanore laughed together. Fluff and King cuddled together.

CHAPTER 31:
REDEMPTION IN THE DARK

The constant rain pelting on the roof of the truck made a noise so loud it sounded more like tiny pebbles hitting the metal. The noise compounded the memories of what had happened in the last twenty four hours. Ricky's mind was overwhelmed.

What started out as a plan to have a fun on a first-time deep sea fishing trip that never happened, turned into the jaw-clenching, nerve-wrecking present reality. All Ricky could think about was the robbery and possible murder of the boat captain, his best friend being killed by a rattlesnake and now how to survive a hurricane.

Some people live in the category of good. Some live in the category of evil. Ricky had been living in the category of clueless during the years spent with Vince. Now Ricky, alone, had to sort out his problems.

Ricky acted like a scared, caged animal. He sat on the passenger side of the truck with his knees crunched up and banded by two arms locked with gripped fingers. He was trying to control his shaking skinny legs. He'd been crying off and on in the hours since Vince's death. When he wasn't crying he was chewing off his fingernails and the cuticle skin surrounding his nails. Chewing kept his teeth from chattering. The truck shook and bounced with each strong gust of wind. High above the truck, long thick limbs on tall pine trees swayed and bent, making creaking and groaning sounds.

Ricky's nerves were stretched to the limit. Darkness and sheets of driving rain prevented him from seeing anything through the windows. His imagination went wild. He started to believe the groaning sounds came from large animals on the hunt, whipping away at the devil's agents lurking around the truck. The creaking sounds were the bones of devils with their footsteps shuffling nearer and closer to the door of the truck.

His own bones rattled as he sat in complete darkness. It was impossible to keep his body from shaking and trembling. There was no moon or stars to wish away the situation.

Could he be a survivor, he wondered. If he survived the storm where would he go, what would he do?

"Everyone has hardships in this life," he thought. "It ain't just me. Money. Yeah, I got some money. Okay....so that's a positive thing. Wait, nope, that's a bad thing." The moment of hope was erased by the memory of the ill gotten money. His conscious won. "I'd give the money back, but I'm pretty sure the man is dead. How can I give it back? I'm gonna be punished for it. I just know it."

The teachings from his childhood Sunday school days at church were resurrected. Ricky began to pray.

"God's will be done. Just forgive me of my sins and let me see your Son in heaven so I can thank Him for saving me. All that I've done may not have been for your glory, God, but right now, God, I need You to make it through this night alone. I'm asking You, please help me glorify You in the remaining time I have left on this earth. Whether tonight may be my last night, or tomorrow, or years from now, I'll repent every day for all of my past sins I've done. You know them Lord. I know them Lord. Oh, p-l-e-a-s-e God. Make this night end. Quickly, Quickly!"

"Great Gawd," Ricky screamed, trying to make his voice louder than the noise outside. He needed to hear his thoughts. "I know I've been a sinner, but right now I'm stupid. Momma always used to say to me, *'You think I'm stupid? Or are you being stupid?'* I know I'm stupid but I really want to do the right things. Just help me out of here. Please. I know I'm not supposed to make promises, but I do know that I'm gonna find a better way to live. Change my life. Put You first. Make new friends. Money can buy friends but not the right kind of friends. Wait, money can't buy friends. I know that! I need You to help me find a good friend, someone who will not trick me into doing things for their own selfish interests."

Ricky shouted and screamed. Flashes of lightning and booming thunder crashed louder than his rant. His screams were drowned out by the roaring winds outside. When he couldn't hear himself he began to sob. A steady line of tears rolled down Ricky's cheeks, leaving streaks of dirt. He struggled out of the hold on his knees and slid both legs down to the floorboard. He placed his hands flat against the back of his seat and slowly pushed his body down, off the seat, so he could sit crouched on the floorboard. He might be safer below the windows, where any flying object might break through and hit him in the head.

The air inside the truck was stale and thick. He needed some air to breathe. Ricky decided to crack open a window. The rain would drip inside, but he didn't have a choice. The air pressure and oppressive humidity was making him sweat profusely. Sweating was worse than raindrops.

The money that Vince stole from Earl didn't mean anything to Ricky. It didn't bring him love, friends or peace of mind, which he wanted more than anything. It meant nothing to him while he ached with fear and anxiety about the unknowns he faced in the long hours of the night ahead.

"I feel so lost." The words rushed out. "When I get outta here, IF I get outta here, when this night is over and the sun comes up...." Ricky's voice trailed off and stopped.

A loud rumbling roar, like the sound of jet engines, stilled Ricky's wandering thoughts of redemption. From the distance the new noise, scarier than the thunder and lightning, came closer and louder, like a train rumbling down the railroad track. Ricky tried to remember if he'd seen a train. His body shook, twitched and trembled uncontrollably in his uncomfortable position on the floorboard. His lips quivered. His teeth chattered.

Suddenly his feet were pulled away and his body was violently flung upward. His head crashed hard against the ceiling of the truck. Excruciating pain tore throughout his head. His eyes roll backward, he felt pounding in his ears and his mouth hurt. He saw flashes of lights that looked like twinkling stars on a lit sparkler.

When the tornado passed directly over the truck, Ricky's body floated and his arms grabbed aimlessly in the air when the truck was lifted up off the ground. He lost all sense of time and space while the truck spun around, rolled over, bounced and finally slammed hard on the ground.

Ricky managed to grab onto the steering wheel and fall back down onto the seat when the truck came to a standstill. Then he sensed a warm fluid filling up inside of his mouth and quickly realized it was his own blood. He tried to move his tongue. It dangled inside his mouth. He coughed and a large piece of his tongue dropped onto his lap.

"LORD," his thoughts screamed. He closed his eyes and nearly passed out. Confused, he asked himself, "Am I still alive?" He rubbed his head and tried to focus his eyes in the dark. Hearing was the only sense he could rely on. The noisy roar, moving away, sounded distant.

"I'm still alive!" he wanted to shriek with gladness and gratefulness.

Ricky smiled inside and gently nodded his head in affirmation. Overcome with exuberant confidence he thought, "I AM alive. If I can hold on and make it through what just happened then I know I can make it through the rest of the night. I know I can! A Tornado! That was a tornado that just picked up the truck! Holy Cow! Dear Jesus! I just lived through a tornado. Thank you, God! Thank you, Jesus! Amen!"

He quickly realized that he had to stop the bleeding in his mouth. It wouldn't stop on its own. The pain in his mouth was more excruciating than the pain in his head. He tried not to gag and choke. With difficulty he forced his head over his shoulder and spit out the blood. He tore off his shirt, yanking and pulling it off his arms. He stuffed the shirt into his mouth. Breathing from his nose was difficult.

His mind raced over the unanswerable questions.

"Am I gonna bleed to death? Am I gonna get out of this alive? How will I stay alive with half my tongue missing? God, I can't take much more.

"I'm not making any deals with you God! Oh, no. From now on, for the rest of my life, I'm gonna thank you each and every day. I'm ready to see the light of the new sun. I'm not likin' to live in this darkness anymore."

Ricky struggled to shift his body upright but gravity worked against him. The truck was lying on its side. He grabbed the steering wheel with both hands and pulled his body into a semi sitting position. It was the first time he'd ever held the steering wheel of Vince's truck and it felt strange.

Ricky closed his eyes and prayed for the salvation of the souls of all his friends and family, living or dead. He felt a hunger not for the lack of food he missed earlier in the day. His soul hungered for the mercy of God.

"I need your love, Lord, God," he gurgled as loud as possible with his damaged tongue. Silently he turned the words in his head to calm himself. "I know you are stronger above all others. I know only You can call the shots. When this here night is over, and this here hurricane Louise is finished with us humans, I'm gonna get back to home, sweet home, Alabama, to work for You. My soul is Yours forever! I forgot to fear You and that is something I ain't never, NEVER, gonna forget again. Not after today. Lord, I will never forget to fear You and remember to always praise You. Praise You, Lord, for Your power, as I seen this here night and for all that are, ever was, and ever will be."

Ricky knew that God was listening whether he whispered or shouted. "Guidance, my dear Lord. That's what I need. My momma tried to teach me the rules and discipline. I never followed her rules. I feel your discipline now, oh Lord. Once You are finished with this here discipline, and I AM praying for your mercy to get me through this situation, please guide me. Show me the way, oh Lord."

Tears bigger than raindrops rolled down his face.

"Yes, Jesus. You are my friend. Maybe this is not the right way to ask, but I need You to help me. Walk with me now, and in the future. I need to find some new, good, friends to walk with on this earth. My best friend Vince is gone and I feel bad about what happened to him. There's no doubt he done some very bad things, but I feel bad anyway."

What a good feeling at last! He felt relief In spite of all the turmoil. He worked on his breathing difficulties with the shirt still stuffed inside his mouth. He sucked air into his nose and filled his lungs. He let the air back out slowly. All Ricky knew now was his life had been saved. As long as he lived his life he would be walking on a new path of repentance and redemption.

Ricky's mind quieted for the remainder of the dark tumultuous night. He was no longer afraid of what might happen to him even though he continued to imagine other possible catastrophes. Another rattlesnake could crawl inside the truck and strike him dead. Another tornado could lift up the truck and carry it out to the bay and drop into the water where frenzied sharks would attack him while he was still sitting inside the sinking truck. The water from the nearby bay would start rising and seep inside the truck. The truck would rise up to the level of the tree branches and he would get stuck in a tree. Whatever happened didn't matter. It would just happen.

Ricky spent the remaining hours of the night drifting in and out of consciousness in a fitful dreamlike sleep. He heard a voice in a dream say, "So now you will have all night to think in darkness about what you will do when the light comes. You've been given another chance to become a new you. Just be patient, now and forever."

CHAPTER 32: HUNKER DOWN TOWNIES

The idea of spending the entire night inside the Mosley High School Gym was an unbearable thought. Darryl was used to the quiet evening skies alone on the Star Chaser. He was not used to being in close quarters with so many people, including children. There was way too much noise. The concrete walls bounced sounds in every direction. His ears suffered. Hurricane force winds outside of the building would have been preferable, but the winds couldn't be heard inside the gym.

"We're going to turn down the lights at 11 p.m." a woman's voice announced through a loud megaphone.

The noise in the room turned to hushed whispers. People hushed their children and anyone else who made noise.

The woman continued. "The center of the storm, we're told, is about sixty miles away. Fortunately we haven't lost power yet but we think it's going to happen here very soon. Let's all think positive. If the storm passes east of us we'll be on the better side, so to speak. If it passes west of us we'll get the worst effects of the winds. We have back-up generators to keep the lights on if, and when, the power goes out. Dimming the lights will be less of a surprise to everyone if we have to switch to generators."

Darryl half listened to the woman. He knew the drills of a hurricane. He couldn't stop thinking of Eleanore. He wondered what was going on. Could he trust Casey to take good care of Eleanore?

"We have someone watching the radar on our back-up computers. We know that the conditions are very favorable for tornadoes. At least two strong cells appear to be moving toward our area"

After the woman shared this information a collective moan, like a loud groan of pain, filled the room followed soon after by a cacophony of voices talking louder.

"People! People!" The woman tried to get back everyone's attention using a loud and authoritative, but calm, voice. "We're here inside a building built specifically to meet hurricane force winds. It's strong enough to withstand hurricane force winds of 120 miles per hour. However, a tornado is different. It has much stronger winds. If we believe that we are in the direct path of a tornado I will be asking everyone to immediately leave this room and move into the hallways. You will walk through these open doors behind me," she pointed above and behind her shoulder with her free arm. "We will give you enough time to do this in an orderly fashion. We ask that you do not run or rush!"

"Oh great," Darryl mumbled under his breath. He could imagine the next scene unfolding in an already crazy day. "A mob reaction. I don't know which would be worse, a tornado or a mob of angry, scared people ready to trample anyone in the way."

Darryl felt the negative thoughts creeping into his soul.

"STOP that right now. Snap out of it. Think about Eleanore. I wonder what she and the water cop are up to. Spending the night on the boat is not the best place to be. It would have been so much better for her to come with me. Much less miserable if you compare my situation and hers. Yet it was her idea to go with Casey and he didn't say no."

Darryl recounted the events of the day beginning with when he saw Earl leave the marina, Casey tell him that Earl gave him the keys to the 'Lucky Two' and finally when he last saw Eleanore get in the boat.

"Casey Howard wanted those boat keys so bad his hands trembled."

Darryl tried to convince himself that Eleanore would be safe with Casey. Casey, of all people, should know the dangers of the hurricane and how to navigate a boat in rough waters. But Darryl instinctively worried about Casey's darker side. Casey didn't come across as a cold, calculating, mean kind of human being, yet he had displayed anger and greed today. Both were potentially dangerous personality traits.

"Oh I hope she's safe with him!" Darryl couldn't stop his anxiety. It wasn't like him to feel this way. He was normally easy going, but the day had been so different from any other he could remember experiencing.

Darryl got off the cot to take a walk around the room. If he interacted with some of the other people who were sharing their feelings about the predicament they were in it might take his mind off Eleanore.

He winked at the children who looked bored, smiled at jittery young women, and nodded his head at tired worn-out looking adults. Those simple acts made him feel a little better. Normally Darryl would talk to anyone. He could talk a blue streak, non-stop, on any topic if he could get someone to listen. His troubled thoughts kept his voice bottled up inside.

Darryl daydreamed. "Once this long night is over I'm getting back to my boat. I'm going to find my best clothes, get cleaned up and look better when the 'Lucky Two' makes its way back into the marina. She'll be looking into my eyes again."

The nagging in his heart kept the juices in his stomach from turning on the hunger signals in his brain. When his stomach gurgled and growled, it surprised him.

"Well, I can't ignore what my body needs," he chuckled.

Across the gymnasium floor was another set of double doors. Above the doors was a sign painted in green and orange letters. A white arrow pointed to the opening.

"Cafeteria. Ahh, yes." Darryl sighed. His eyes sought the best pathway to move through the crowd of people. It was the first time he noticed other people wandering in and out of the cafeteria doors.

Darryl's nose picked up the scent of coffee. "Perfect," he thought. "Coffee. That will help keep me alert through the next four or five hours of early morning darkness and the next set of wild surprises."

People were settled down to quieter conversations after the woman with the megaphone had made her announcements. Some people with no one to talk with just watched others as they walked around. Darryl made eye contact with many people whose eyes held the look of uncertainty.

Darryl entered the cafeteria and encountered a very different atmosphere. It felt more causal and stress-free. Small groups of people were scattered around the room engaged in quiet conversations. Several rows of eight foot long tables and chairs were set up in the corner of the room. People were playing board games. One table was set up with the coffee pot and another table was set up with simple snack bags of refreshments.

Darryl walked toward the coffee pot.

"Hey there," a middle aged man called out to him. A young teenage boy stood by the man's side.

"Nice to see a friendly face in here," Darryl responded.

"They got bottled water and other snacks on the end of this table," the young boy said with a teenager's enthusiasm.

"Hope it's not too much more exciting than this tonight," Darryl nodded his head to the older man and helped himself to a cup of coffee. He poured a liquid that looked like brown river water from the tap of a large metal pot into a white styrofoam cup.

"Cream and sugar is over here!" Another burst of helpfulness came from the teenager.

"Never touch the stuff!" Darryl grinned at the youthful enthusiasm spurting from the boy. He turned his head and surveyed the other people around the room, holding the cup in his hand, reluctant to take the first sip. "So, tell me. What do you think about the situation?" he asked the elder man, who didn't appear to be much older than Darryl. Lines of experience and hard work in the sunny outdoors were etched on his face.

"Pretty sure it'll be a bad storm for someone. Hopefully not us, but don't wish it on someone else, you know. As if you probably haven't already heard that today!" the elder man chuckled. "People here are acting calm. There's a group of men sitting over there in the corner wishing they had some good music, like a band to entertain them to pass away the next few hours. Maybe it would calm nerves. I guess it depends on the kind of music."

Darryl's attention and energy ignited at the sound of the man's words. His mood swung into a new level of happy.

234

"Now that's the best idea I've heard tonight!" His eyes darted in the direction of a group sitting at a table in the far corner of the cafeteria then back to the man. "You guys would to allow it?"

"Thinking about it, but I don't know. Don't want my boss to hear any bad stories from someone who spent the night here at the shelter. I might get some wrong feedback, you know? Someone might get the wrong idea and report *hurricane party at the high school.* It could turn out good, but then it could also turn out bad. You just never know what some people will think."

"You work here, then?" Darryl asked.

"Yes. Assistant coach for the baseball team and substitute teach PE sometimes. It's only a part time gig for me. My main income is a small lawn care business."

Excited by the prospect of playing music, Darryl introduced himself. "My name's Darryl. My saxophone is out in my car in the trunk. I live on my charter fishing boat, so I didn't want to leave it on the boat during the storm. I didn't want to take a chance losing it, if you know what I mean. It's one of the most valuable, if not the most valuable thing, I own."

"Yeah, I'm living in a single wide up near Southport. It's close to the water but I don't worry too much about flooding where it's parked. Don't have a lot of stuff, but I can't take a chance on it holding up to hurricane winds or a tornado. It wouldn't be very safe there. Basically it's like staying in a tin can. A tornado would blow up the place."

"Oh, boy, you got that right. You got family here?" Darryl asked.

"No, alone," the man hesitated. "For now, I'm alone."

The man's voice had a deep, lyrical, strong musical quality, hitting the perfect notes of his emotions.

"Well, me too. I live alone. I didn't get your name."

"Oh, sorry. I'm Pete. And yours again, sir?"

"Darryl. I'm alone. BUT, today I met someone. It's got me thinking maybe I don't have to be alone!" Darryl couldn't contain sharing his excitement over meeting Eleanore.

Pete chuckled. "Oh? You met a girl today? Is she in here?"

"Oh, no. I didn't meet her in here. It's a rather long and complicated story." Darryl wasn't embarrassed by his outburst.

Pete said, "Most of life is complicated. I've met few people who didn't have a story without a few complications. What I try to do is find time to sing, laugh, play my guitar and try to watch other people smile when I play my music."

"Oh, you play a guitar? Have you ever played music with a saxaphone?" Darryl's eyebrows lifted high and his wide open eyes pleaded for a yes answer.

"Can't say yes, but I can say that I'd be willing to give it a try tonight. Hanging out in this place is killing my nerves."

"Amen!" Darryl said.

Pete shifted the weight on his two legs and turned his body at the waist first left, then right. When he saw no one was nearby to hear he leaned over the coffee table and asked Darryl, "Do you know some good foot tapping music, or are you more interested in bluesy torch songs?'

Darryl guffawed and almost spilled his coffee. He took a short sip to help regain his composure before locking his eyes with Pete's. Both men shared a twinkle-eyed laugh. "Now, man, you caught me off guard." Darryl finally said.

"Good looking girl you met today?" Pete asked, still curious about Darryl's mood and his intentions for the type of music he might play. The content and substance of the music would make a big difference whether he could go along with the idea. People in the gymnasium needed to be soothed, not agitated and uncomfortable.

"Well, it's like this man," Darryl began. "I like to think that I am a pretty darn good judge of people's character. I think I can tell from looking at them and talking to them for a short time whether they are a good egg or a bad egg, if you know what I mean. So I looked deep into her eyes when she talked and it just touched my heart. I believe I touched her heart too."

Pete's tightly closed lips spread into a thin line across his face.

Darryl waited a moment. Then he said, "I'm taking it that you're the quiet, thoughtful type of man."

"Yep, some say that," Pete nodded his head.

"You meet someone for the first time. You just know in your gut that they're going to be someone good to get to know better. A good fit for you. It's corny, but it's that spark that gets lit inside your whole body. It's the eyes, man." Darryl took a deep breath through his nose and continued. "It's that first time you see them look at you, really look into your eyes. It's a first impression man. It's like the first time you came face to face with the school bully in first grade on the playground during recess. You can see it in their eyes. You know that you never want to see that person again and look 'em in the eyes. In this case, you can't wait for the next time to look that person in the eyes again. You've got to see them again."

Darryl stopped, then said as if it was the end of the story, "What else could I say?"

"Oh, I know that feeling," Pete said in a very deep, sincere voice.

"Yeah." Darryl's voice trailed off, trying to feel comfort in this very uncomfortable place.

Darryl reached into his shorts pocket and found a crumbled piece of paper. It was one of his business receipts. Unfolding it he paid no attention to the number for the four men from Hoover who had to already know that their deep sea fishing charter was cancelled. He sat down on the floor, crossed his legs in front of him, straightened his back against the wall and patted the floor motioning to Pete to sit down next to him.

"Oh no, man. If this old man sat down there these old knees would never get me back up."

"Okay. I'll only be a minute."

Darryl absently patted the front of his shirt pocket, then the back of his pants. Nervously, he thrust his hands into the other pocket of his shorts and found nothing.

"A pen. I need a pen," he muttered.

Pete, amused and curious, immediately pulled one out of his pocketed T-shirt and handed it down to Darryl. This man was either some silly nutcase, or he had a really, really good thought in his head that he didn't want to forget.

"Music?" Pete asked cautiously while he hovered over Darryl who crouched over to the side so he could write on the floor. Darryl was writing small words on the scrap piece of paper.

"Maybe," the muffled answer drifted up to Pete's ear.

Finally, after ten minutes, Darryl pushed himself up off the floor and stood before Pete. He proudly smiled and handed him the scrap piece of paper.

Pete quietly read the words printed on the paper.

"Oh soon, oh soon. Can't this night end soon!
My dear, my dear. I want your heart to be here.
A thousand passions are blowing in the wind. That's what I hear.
How far will those winds reach before you are near?
I only want to have your heart with me here, my dear.
I'd rather be anywhere but here alone waiting for the daylight.
Oh let it be soon when I see your face.
It will brighten my heart to see your face again near.
Let the winds bring you to me now.
I want to look into your eyes for years and years.

Darryl shifted from one foot to the other while he waited for Pete to finish reading. When Pete's face lifted up after reading from the paper he held Darryl anxiously asked, "Well?"

Pete began to hum a melody, then stopped, then started humming again with a fast, quick tempo. The notes were deep, low, soothing and warm.

"Man, you really have a good voice. You know just how I feel!" Darryl exclaimed.

"I get the feeling you may want to do some more talking later on tonight," Pete said evenly.

"Maybe I'll need too," Darryl admitted.

Darryl's face changed to a forlorn look.

Pete piped up, "Yeah, well let's see here. I think this is the beginning of a love song. Okay. I can sing and play guitar. I got an acoustic guitar. I like country music. The old-time kind of country music, like the 50's and 60's and 70's. Not too good with the new kind of rockabilly stuff today. I really don't like it that fast. Just give me a good old two step tempo that people can dance and sing to. You know the kind I'm talking about?"

Darryl said, "Torch songs? The kind that light up a fire, rekindle the flame, lover come back, your kids ain't my kids, I hate this work week, I'll see you in heaven...."

Pete was laughing so hard now he couldn't speak. "Hey, now! You'd better be careful! What about that part about looking into your eyes for years and years!"

Both men busted out laughing. Darryl said, "Just trying to figure out how the sound of a saxophone can fit in with the rhythm of a twostep."

Pete laughed, "Take your blues blasting horn and just play four notes when you'd usually play two notes!"

"Heck, I'm heading out to the car now. Meet you back here in ten minutes? I gotta find out if I can get a hall pass to come back inside. I've heard that they won't let you back inside if you leave after it gets dark."

"Funny, no, not funny," Pete said. "I'll get the boss man to let you back in. Be back here in ten minutes. Hey, and that girl you met? What's her name?"

"Eleanore," Darryl started to walk, then turned his head back and flashed a toothy smile back at Pete.

Pete watched Darryl walk through the cafeteria doors to go inside the main gym. He thought it was ironic that people, during times of uncertainty and crisis, will loosen their guarded lives to slip into a coma of love. That song, those words! He wished that it was happening to him, too.

"Yes, wouldn't it be nice. At any rate, I'm glad for that man," Pete thought. "Maybe it's never too late to fall in love. Life can sure be a lonely ride without it. You find it and want it so bad. Trick is to not be looking for it. Love is an enchanting process. Sometimes it's a conscious act, but mostly it happens unconsciously, when you are least expecting it. It's hard to recognize the emotion, yet it's something we value so much. It's not very logical and it cannot be reduced to numbers. It just hits you in the face. Is love an illusion? Is the source of love in the soul? The source of love is in the eyes, the pathway to the soul. That's what Darryl talked about. All our other senses, hearing, touch and smell, are not the primary forces to trigger love. But, oh how we yearn for those senses to experience love. It'll happen for you again one day, ole' Petey boy."

Pete eyes surveyed the cafeteria room, checking out the *guests* in the hurricane shelter. He wondered what happened to the teenager who had been at the table just a few minutes ago, eager to offer information to Darryl. He'd disappeared.

Before Darryl arrived to get a cup of coffee the teenager, with shoulder length red hair, was sitting on the floor near the refreshment table tapping a pair of drumsticks on the floor. He was fidgety and appeared to be alone until a woman, who Pete thought must be his mother, walked across the gymnasium floor clutching an armful of blankets and pillows. As soon as she reached the boy she dropped the bulky load she'd been carrying and snapped at the boy. "You're gonna have to give the drumming a rest tonight," cutting her eyes to the people standing nearby. Pete sensed the woman really didn't mind that the boy was releasing creative energy. She just knew it wasn't the place or time.

Pete's eyes searched the room and finally spotted the boy standing far off in the corner of the gym, as far away from everyone else that he possibly could. The strawberry colored hair flamed against the dull concrete wall. The boy leaned with his shoulders slightly touching the concrete wall and rhythmically bounced his shoulders against the wall, left to right. Each time his buttocks touched the wall, he tapped his fingers behind him to push back off. His lips moved noiselessly.

"People are always talking to themselves when they haven't got anyone else to talk to," Pete thought. Pete stuck his hands inside his pockets and walked over to the teenager. The boy wore loose fitting jeans, a t-shirt with multiple holes, and worn out flip flops with a chunk of rubber missing, like an animal had taken a bite out of it. In spite of his clothing, the boy's shaggy hair and toenails were clean.

The teenage boy didn't smile at Pete when he saw him approach. He stood straight, leaning one shoulder against the cool concrete wall.

"Hey, buddy. You doing all right so far?" Pete's deep voice was caring and sincere.

The teen answered, "Yeah, I guess for what it is." His face was sullen and skeptical. His body stiffened a bit as if expecting a lecture.

Pete stopped a few feet away from the teenager to give him space.

"Not the best place to spend an evening, is it? But, safe, right?"

"Sure, it's safer than home," he agreed, with more trust in his voice.

"Scary night tonight, but it'll be over in a few hours. Tomorrow we'll all get to go outside and face the music, so to speak." Pete continued, "Did I see you a while back there tapping on the floor with a set of drum sticks?"

"You saw me playing with the drumsticks?" the teenager asked surprised to be noticed.

"It didn't bother me a bit. It looked like it really didn't bother your mom too much, although I overheard her tell you to stop. I guess that was your mom who said that to you," Pete said.

"Nah. I mean yeah, that's my mom. She doesn't mind me playing the drums. She likes me having something to do that will keep me home and out of trouble. I'm lucky. I guess maybe she thinks there are other people here who don't like it. Makes 'em nervous, she told me."

The boy's posture loosened up but his fingers started to tap on

239

the concrete wall behind him.

"Yep, people are really on edge tonight. For a good reason, though. Can't really blame them, right?" Pete moved his head in a circular motion to ease the tightness in his neck muscles. "People usually get a little more relaxed around music. What do you think?" he asked the boy.

"Definitely," the teenager showed a little more interest in Pete.

"Still got your sticks?" Pete asked, already knowing the answer.

"Heck yeah," the boy said. Then he asked suspiciously, "Why?"

"My name's Pete. What's your name, son? You don't mind if I ask?"

""No." He hesitated then answered, "My name is Alan."

"Nice name. Be proud of your name. Don't know if you saw me and that man talking at the table back there. The man you helped with his coffee." Pete asked Alan.

"I thought I should leave ya'll alone. Mind my own business."

"Well, that's polite of you," Pete said. "That man told me he plays saxophone. He's gone out to his car to get it. I play guitar. I got it here in the building. He and I want to try to play a little music together. I'll do a little strumming. Don't really know what kind of music goes with a saxophone, but it's worth a try. It's something to do to pass the time. Maybe if I had someone who could play a good beat I could strum a little better with a sax."

Alan rubbed his chin with two fingers and said, "Very interesting!"

"He should be back in a few minutes. What grade are you in?"

"Eleventh." Alan answered.

"Here?" Pete asked.

"Nah....hey, is that him?" Alan pointed to Darryl coming across the cafeteria carrying a black rectangular suitcase.

Darryl arrived and Pete introduced him to Alan. The three men simultaneously smiled, anticipating a bit of fun, and forgot the hazard of the approaching hurricane Louise.

The trio moved to a corner of the hallway, outside the cafeteria walls, and attracted a small group of fans when the sound of their instruments started to float into the ears of people. What they hoped would be a few hours of jamming together lasted only thirty minutes.

The hallway turned dark. The dim back-up lights flickered on. The sound of noisy generators kicked on and drowned out the sound of music.

"Well, it was fun while it lasted," Darryl mumbled glumly. "Killing time with you guys. Take your seats because I have a feeling that the time waiting here inside will be killing us soon."

The three, one young teenage man and two older men, all young at heart shook hands before separating to wait in solitude.

Alan asked before they parted, "After tonight can we get together again? We can call ourselves the 'PADs'."

240

"That's a kind of weird name but I think I like it," Pete said, amused. "How'd you come up with that?"

"Cuz we'll be sitting down on our behinds all night and wishing we had a better pad," Darryl snorted.

Alan laughed too and said, "Nooo...it's for our names! Pete, Alan and Darryl!"

CHAPTER 33: SAFE DUMPSTER

Complete darkness became an increasing frightening reality for both humans and cats waiting for hurricane Louise to arrive. Closed eyes pretended to rest in sleep while brains mustered up bravery against the unknown calamities happening outside. The night seemed endless.

Fat Cat's plan to find a shelter in the Lighthouse Marina boat storage didn't work out. The building was locked up and boarded in places that normally would have been entry points for cats. The only alternative for shelter he could think of was inside the metal dumpster near Smith's restaurant.

Fat Cat had no trouble convincing Dog Ear to follow him inside the dumpster. Dog Ear, more often than not, did what he was commanded.

It took howling, hissing and growling to convince ST to jump inside the dumpster. Fat Cat said to ST, "You can be a fool and get blown away by the wind across the parking lot and into the swirling waves of the brown water over there. How good are you at swimming? Do you think drowning might be more fun than sitting inside the dumpster?"

Fat Cat understood why ST was being stubborn given the history of his accident. He finally pleaded in frustration. "It's death or survival ST."

In spite of his fears, ST followed his instinct to be safe. Once he jumped up to the opening, he cautiously looked inside the cave of the dumpster. He saw that it was mostly empty except for a few cardboard boxes. The dumpster didn't look so dangerous. He didn't see any bulging black plastic bags with unknown articles of broken glass.

"Wonder if you'll get to chase any lizards in here tonight," Fat Cat joked when ST firmly landed on four paws on the bottom of the dumpster.

"NOT funny," ST scowled at Fat Cat, twitching his mangled lip to show more of his fang.

Fat Cat quickly changed the subject. "Wonder how old King and Fluff are doing? Think they're together out on that boat, riding high on the waves?" He wanted to turn attention to something, anything, that would take their mind off being cooped up inside the dumpster. The raging winds outside made the walls of the metal dumpster creak and the foul odor of rotting garbage assaulted his nose.

"Doesn't sound like fun to me," Dog Ear quipped and vigorously shook his head, as if to remove the very bad idea of being on a boat.

ST sneezed the stink out of his pink nose and asked, "Hey, what about Oscar? I wonder what's happened to him?"

"He probably crawled up inside the engine of Captain Keith's truck. I heard that's how he and the whole family of kittens ended up wandering around the docks," Fat Cat sneered. "They were riding shotgun on the struts of a truck. He'll be okay. He's experienced."

Dog Ear giggled at Fat Cat's joke. He knew better. Oscar was his brother, born and raised at the docks.

"I'm sure he's having a good, safe ride in the truck," ST snorted. "Dog Ear, you seem to be in a pretty good mood considering the situation we're in. You're not sure where your brother is, we're in a garbage dumpster instead of a lock tight building, and you're giggling."

"Hey, control yourself ST." Fat Cat hissed at ST through his bared front fangs. Fat Cat's fangs commanded more respect than ST's one bared hanging fang. "Take it easy on Dear. We've got a long night out here in the darkness and we need to support each other. From the sounds I'm hearing inside this dumpster it's not any better outside. You're right, ST. We should be concerned about Oscar. Inside a truck is not necessarily a better place. It may not be any better than what we got here."

ST lowered his eyes and head down to the stare at a dirty puddle of water nearby on the floor and sulked. He didn't like it when Fat Cat chastised him. Fat Cat should be the one taking criticism for not herding the gang of cats to a safer location. All of the cats in the gang were forced to go their separate ways, on their own, in all different directions. ST struggled with the idea that he may not see his friends again. He also did not like being inside the garbage dumpster. If an accident had happened to him inside the dumpster once before, an accident could happen again.

No cat at the docks ever tried to challenge Fat Cat to try to prove they were smarter or more powerful. Every cat knew that Fat Cat demanded respect. Fat Cat barged in front of you when you were taking a walk. Fat Cat made demands to get things done. He tried to control when and how things were done. Things like who was allowed to sneak out of the bushes and steal a fish away from the eyes of Casey Howard as the fish was being tossed off a boat onto the side walk. If he had his way all the time, Fat Cat would try to tell the gang of cats what time to go eat or sleep. "What, when and where is Fat Cat's motto," ST thought to himself and felt satisfied that he had settled the personal grievance Fat Cat's criticism inflicted. ST was loyal to Fat Cat, though, for the reason that Fat Cat was the only cat who tried to be responsible for the gang's safety and welfare. Fat Cat wasn't only out to get things for himself. ST began to purr.

"And why are you purring at a time like this?" Fat Cat growled.

"It calms my nerves," ST answered and promptly stopped purring even though he needed to so something to calm his nerves.

"Great!" ST said to himself. "Now I'm being told when I can purr and when not to purr!" Fat Cat's criticism added another grievance.

The worst possibilities of what could happen while spending the night inside the dark garbage dumpster screamed inside his mind. Would he be forced to race in circles around the trash container to release his nervous energy? The thought of the sound of his nails scraping against metal was hideous. Pacing around the four corners of the metal container would definitely irritate Fat Cat. ST crouched down on his paws as low as possible without allowing his belly to touch the nasty, dirty, wet floor. He swished his tail, jerking it wildly up and down, back and forth.

After a long silence Fat Cat spoke again. "Trouble with you guys is you are all followers. None of you are a leader like me." Fat Cat's fur puffed out. "I know how to make decisions!" he growled with authority.

ST and Dog Ear noticed the fur on Fat Cat's tail puffed out to twice its normal size.

"We know, Fat Cat. We know Fat Cat." Dog Ear mewed respectfully, like a kitten. He hoped to placate Fat Cat's increasing agitation. Fat Cat was making Dog Ear feel uncomfortable. Dog Ear was already a nervous wreck, too. He had just repeated himself. He didn't want to start the other nervous habit he had of pacing. Pacing wouldn't be easy inside the nasty garbage container and it would annoy Fat Cat even more.

After Fat Cat's egotistical outburst, ST thought about King. "King could outdo Fat Cat any day on the leadership scale," ST thought. "He has the respect of the other cats. Now that's powerful! Look at what he did last night, jumping on the boat to chase the mouse, without being told to do it by Fat Cat."

ST asked himself a question and answered it afterward. "What makes a good leader? Naturally a good leader will have a strong inner fortitude that's necessary to persevere in times of challenges. Good leaders live by example of their inner beliefs and live by a good moral code. A good leader must show by example. A good leader must learn what will motivate others and execute motivation in others. A good leader works for the common good of all. A good leader motivates not through fear of punishment. A good leader rewards good behavior. A good leader is slow to anger. A good leader....yeah, you're not all of that Fat Cat."

ST thought over all the reasons why Fat Cat didn't fit into the definition of being a great leader. "All the cats at the dock follow Fat Cat. He's the one who wants to be the boss and take charge in situations when no one else does. They go along with all of Fat Cat's decisions thinking his judgment is quite solid and sound. On the other hand, Fat Cat's bossy nature leaves many of us fearful and resentful of him taking over our daily lives. I've seen a cat achieve a prize fish, or lizard, or mouse, or avoid being run over by a car in the parking lot, or scare an unwitting tourist walking down the sidewalk

244

and Fat Cat always finds a way to take credit for the accomplishment. He's always giving advice and bragging about his skills. He's always finding a way to make himself a part of another cat's success story."

ST wondered why Fat Cat always brought up King. "King, on the other hand," ST thought, "is different. He's the one with real power. He makes decisions for himself and does not let Fat Cat interfere with his coming and going. He's a cheerful, brave, spirited cat who is friendly and kind to all. I think the gang of cats respect King. He is a good example of how a cat should behave. King doesn't need Fat Cat to direct him. I hope King makes it out of this hurricane. I'd like to hang out with him after this is all over."

Dog Ear interrupted ST's thoughts. "A little mousy to eat would be good to find right now."

ST had worked himself into a small frenzy thinking about Fat Cat, but he didn't want to upset Fat Cat or Dog Ear. He said, "I'm too nervous to eat at a time like this, Dear."

"Wonder if King shared his mouse with Fluff," Fat Cat mused, ignoring ST's comment.

"That's if he caught it!" Dog Ear said. The thought of King and Fluff sharing a mouse together made him feel better.

ST thought, "I think Fat Cat is threatened by King. Or, maybe it's just the thought of not knowing where Fluff is."

Suddenly a strong gust of wind blew outside, shaking the dumpster and moving it a few feet. All three cats jumped and shrieked. The noise made by the metal scraping against the asphalt parking lot was almost worse than the jolting ride.

The three cats remained silent, waiting for the next noise or surprise to happen. Talking to each other didn't help their nerves. It wasn't long before the tide rose over the concrete wall, filling up the parking lot. Soon the water seeped inside the dumpster.

Throughout the night the cats sat on their haunches, backs butted up to each other for stability and comfort. Their eyes blinked against the ferocious wind blowing outside that found its way inside the walls of the metal container. Sitting in the extra inches of seawater on the floor of the metal container left the cats' fur wet and stinky. The raunchy, undesirable odors of rotten garbage mixed with seawater made them gag.

Fat Cat had the last words of the night, "Who's in charge of this party?" He hissed and growled after another strong gust of wind slammed against the wall of the dumpster. "I'm prepared to lose one of my nine lives! I'm going to get through this. Afterwards I'll be having my own party. I'll have another birthday party," he nervously chuckled.

ST and Dog Ear exchanged looks of terror. Their eyes, black and glassy, tried to focus in the dark. They knew exactly how Fat Cat felt right now. Each already had their own personal experience of nearly losing their life. They both knew what Fat Cat meant when he exclaimed he wanted to celebrate another birthday.

Ferocious winds blew flying objects and sent them crashing against the metal dumpster walls. The winds sprayed sea water over the top. Salty drops of lagoon water constantly dripped on them all night.

The three cats waited, ears twitching and eyes blinking, throughout the miserable night of darkness, each with their fears and thoughts. Daylight would not arrive too soon.

CHAPTER 34:
ADJUSTMENT TIME

Eleanore and Casey stayed awake all night while the boat rocked and rolled. Casey used his body's clock, honed by his frequent sleepless nights alone, to keep track of the time. His body sensed when the first light of dawn appeared. Eleanore, exhausted from two sleepless nights in a row, struggled to hold up her head and keep her eyes open.

Earlier in the morning, when it was still dark and the winds died down, Casey suggested, "Let's go outside and check things out. I think it might be safe now for a little bit." They both needed fresh air.

She was surprised by the calm brought by the eyewall of the hurricane. Eleanore welcomed the stillness with heartfelt gratitude. Standing outside on the boat deck she said, "I'm thankful that this night is going to be over soon. The stars are magnificent, aren't they?"

If Hurricane Louise's eye wall, a round cylindrical core of sky, had appeared during the daylight it would be impossible to believe that a sky of ferocious wind-blown rain could turn so cloudless and clear blue in such a short time. It would seem unnatural.

"Don't be thankful yet," Casey said, knowing that he had to be realistic. He warned her. "It's not over yet. More than likely it is going to get worse now," he said and lightly touched her arm knowing she would be disappointed to hear this news.

Silent tears welled up in Eleanore's eyes and rolled down her face in multiple streaks, like raindrops on a window pane. This news was another blow to her bruised soul and body. Her arms and legs were sore from trying to brace herself against the table and wall during the violent rocking of the boat. It was worse than being on a roller coaster ride without a seat belt.

"Let me turn on the ship to shore radio again to see if we can hear any weather update." Casey stepped up to the wheel, slipped the keys out of his pocket and into the ignition to crank the boat engine. Even though he wanted to ration gasoline for the ride back to the marina, he didn't want to see Eleanore cry.

Eleanore blinked her eyes, bent her head down to her lap and wiped her streaked face using the bottom of her dirty t-shirt. When she lifted up her head she gave Casey the best smile she could muster.

A woman openly crying was something he learned to ignore. Casey did not, could not, properly respond to it. Seeing a woman cry made him feel a little angry. He felt that somehow he might be

247

responsible for the tears. There were those times when the tears he saw had been his mother's or ex-wife. He could not figure out how to comfort them because they never seemed to communicate a good reason for crying. This situation felt different than those other times in the past. He felt emotionally connected to Eleanore. Maybe it was Earl's boat, 'The Lucky Two', and how she was so strong willed in wanting to protect Earl's property that he thought would be his. This woman silently crying and not looking at him like he was at fault for her tears was a totally new experience for him. She was so different.

"I know you are trying hard to keep us safe. I want you to know that I appreciate it." Eleanore said to Casey.

"Thanks, I'm going to keep giving it my best," he said and opened the cabin door. He stepped back inside the cabin after Eleanore. A swift gust of wind helped slam the wooden door closed.

Eleanore saw Casey in a new light. He was not like the pig headed, puffed up, law enforcement officer she'd met earlier. He seemed more professional and conscientious now.

Eleanore bent her knees and stooped down to look beneath the table. Fluff and King were curled up with their bodies snuggled tight together, in the farthest corner. Neither cat, Eleanore sensed, wanted to be touched. Their noses were tucked underneath their armpits. Eleanore could see the slits of their eyeballs peeking out, keeping an eye on any movement. Their hind paws and forepaws were safely tucked beneath their bodies, ready to pounce if necessary. Their tails were wrapped and curled around their body like a rope. Eleanore stared back at the coal black eyes, flaming and glowing in the darkness of the corner, and blinked at them. Both cat's eyes blinked back at her.

Hurricane Louise marched over land in the middle of the night, in the dark. It was viewed on radar at the emergency operations centers, but humans and animals could only wait in the dark. No one knew for certain if the shelter they had selected would truly protect them from harm.

Darryl lay on his cot, but never slept. All night long he kept his eyes open, staring at the dark ceiling of the smelly gymnasium where the air was stuffy and thick. He blinked his eyes occasionally as any normal human being would do, but he didn't want to close his eyes to even try to go to sleep. He could hear the soft movements of other people tossing and turning on their make shift beds, trying to sleep. Children, who had cried and complained earlier, were snoring away in dreamland, too tired to deal with the circumstances any longer. They were not in control.

Darryl's life, past and future, raced through his brain. He imagined these thoughts to be like a small fish swimming and darting around from one turn to another, taking a deep dive and then surfacing, to find food or escape from harm. Darryl knew where he was in the present moment and he was able to make the best of it. He'd found himself many time practicing the ritual of making good out of a bad experience. He reminded himself that everyone was in the gymnasium because it was a safer place to be. He reminded himself that the situation was only temporary and it would get better. Reality, though, was there was a very good chance that the situation might get worse.

The word bioluminescence popped up his mind. He tried to imagine himself as a creature in the ocean, using the property of bioluminescence in the dark deep water, to escape harm, obstacles and delays. Like the jelly fish, he could use his energy to emit light. He was excited. "Hey, I can't be a jelly fish. They sting. I think I could be a lightening bug when I leave this place. I have so much energy. I could get Eleanore to follow me anywhere!" The thought made him laugh out loud.

His ability to joke and laugh at himself lifted his spirits. His brain searched for another nautical word.

The word leviathan jumped out and shattered the brief moment of lightness. His mood shifted back to a dark place. He forced the image of an evil sea monster away.

He thought, "My boat, so aptly named the 'Star Chaser' is only steered by celestial powers! I can escape from your grips!" he grinned and lifted his crossed his arms from behind his head and let them rest on his belly. "We talked about blue dolphins and pink dolphins. What else? Getting maybe a little tired, here," he thought and rubbed his eyes with the palms of his hands. "Let's see, what else is there to think about?" He thought about the new band he'd formed only hours ago. "The PALs," he said out loud. "That's not a bad crew to have on the boat."

"HUH?" the woman lying on cot near him was also awake.

"Oh, sorry!" Darryl whispered back. "I'm just mumbling out loud to myself."

"Hey, I know how you feel. We're all mumbling zombies right now. I sure enjoyed listening to the music you guys played. It broke up the slow night and it was better than the usual stuff you get around here. It was a little different and kind of interesting. I think it took the edge off everyone's nerves. Thanks for playing."

"Thanks for the compliment. It helped us musicians too. It was okay, I guess, since no one complained. Better than doing the quiet games, reading stuff or staring at the boring grey walls which might drive people crazy. Maybe more crazy than three guys playing some crazy music," Darryl laughed. "I was just thinking about my new band myself. I need to make sure I go find those other two guys before we get out of here."

Darryl stood up, stretched both arms straight above his head as far as he could reach and clasped his hands tightly, folding his fingers into a locked position and sucked in a deep breath. His legs and arms trembled while he held that position. When he let his arms drop, they swooped down to the floor to pick up his mat, pillow and instrument case

With his belongings wrapped in both arms he began to walk toward the table where last night's coffee had been served. The coffee pot was already percolating a new morning brew.

"Any idea on the latest that's happening out there? Like when should we be able to break free?" Darryl addressed the question to Pete. Darryl's eyes cut upward to the big round clock high up on the wall of the gymnasium. It was 6:40 in the morning.

"We're staying in touch with the Emergency Operations Center," Pete answered. His face was lined with tired wrinkles and no emotion.

"Awwww, c'mon," Darryl tried hard to be chummy but his voice sounded impatient and frustrated. It was not what he intended. "Can't you tell all of us any more than that?" he asked in a softer, pleading voice.

"Wish I could tell you more, Darryl." Pete said sincerely.

Darryl reacted apologetically. "Sorry. I know everyone in here is ready to find out, and see, what happened last night."

"Or, maybe not," Pete answered flatly. "First reports we've gotten is that we dodged a bullet, but they still think there's quite a bit of damage. We've probably got flooding of roads, trees knocked down, that kind of damage. We're told many roads may have to be closed. Until we know, we can't tell people which routes will be the safest way to get back to their homes and back into their neighborhoods. People will need to know which roads are safe. Hang loose, or at least try. It could take two, three or four hours minimum to get some reports back. We're gonna turn on TV's for everyone. We hope to make some announcements for everyone around 7:00 a.m. You'll need some coffee and some food first anyway before you head out. You can see everyone here is starting to stir." The lengthy answer was his final words. Pete had no choice but let his eyes look past Darryl's face at the wall across the room.

Darryl knew Pete was trying to make a half-hearted attempt to be calm, but the circles beneath his eyes, drawn-in cheeks and tightened jaws expressed the seriousness of the situation.

"Do you think maybe another hour?" Darryl asked feebly.

Pete's eyes cut back to Darryl again. "We're still running on generators here. I know for a fact that the power outage is widespread," he looked squarely into Darryl's eyes. "I hope you have a full tank of gas," he said. His eyes popped wide, in a scary way, signaling Darryl that he should leave and find someone else to talk to.

"Well, we sort of had a little fun last night, didn't we?" Darryl asked.

"Sure we did," Pete replied and added, "Good luck with the girl."

Darryl said nothing, turned away from Pete and slowly strolled back to his corner where he'd spent the night. He set down his stuff that he'd carried and left it unattended to go find Alan.

"This is going to take a whole lot of patience," he said to Alan

250

when he found him only a few minutes later.

"Oh, I know," Alan said. His red hair accentuated his youthfulness, but even he looked tired.

"Let's go hang and chat with Pete while we wait to get out of here. His heart needs cheering up," Darryl said.

Alan's face perked up. "Really?! That's a great idea!" The happiness Alan felt playing music with two adult men who showed some interest in him was still a treasured memory.

The two walked to the table where Pete was sitting. Pete couldn't contain a big laugh when he saw Alan and Darryl together again. "So it's my partners coming back, or I guess I should call you guys my pals! Come sit down and let's visit while we can."

Even as the three musicians made light conversation, Darryl's patience was being tested. His desire to see Eleanore again was overwhelming. She was the person he'd been waiting to meet all of his life. He already knew it. She was the one person he could spend the rest of his life with. It would make him the happiest person walking on the earth. It was not at all surprising to Darryl, who was normally in touch with reality, that he had these feelings about someone he just met and known only a few hours. He'd never felt this way about any other person before.

Darryl could not stop thinking about her. He wondered how Eleanore was surviving after spending the night with Casey. Did they talk all night? Did they share family secrets? Did they talk about their hobbies? Did they cling to each other in fear while being swept away in a tidal surge on a sinking boat? Did Eleanore and Casey drown? Was Eleanore safe? Did she get hurt?

All of these questions troubled Darryl. He shook his head and tried to shake out the negative thoughts.

He remembered the conversation he shared with Eleanore about blue and pink dolphins. He smiled and said to himself with hope and optimism, "Now I know this is only the beginning of many more stories to share with her! There will be so many good days for us together. After a night like last night I know she will be ready to see me again."

Darryl didn't think about Earl Keith, who so abruptly abandoned the 'Lucky Two'.

CHAPTER 35: SHARKEY'S DISCOVERY

Sharkey spent the night alone in his pink cinderblock house not far from the Treasure Island Marina boat storage facility he managed. The house was older and among the first homes built on the island when development started in the early 1950's. It was a typical concrete block house with jalousie paned windows, two bedrooms, one bathroom, a combined living room, kitchen and dining room floor plan with terrazzo floors, a single car driveway, a small porch at the front door, and a back door leading to a back yard full of sand spurs.

Sharkey knew this house had survived many hurricanes, some very bad ones at that, long before Hurricane Louise. He bought the house nearly twenty years ago knowing at the time of his purchase that the construction and materials used in these first homes was much better than the newer, pastel colored stucco homes built on pilings and wood frame. Therefore the only logical choice for him was to opt out of waiting in his car, in a long line of cars, and breathing gas fumes for a few hours before going to some smelly shelter for a long night of waiting with a crowd of people. Riding out the storm at his house, alone, was tolerable. He had some first-hand, and second-hand, knowledge of the behaviors of this kind of weather. He believed he knew what to expect, was as prepared as anyone could possibly prepare, and decided it was the best place for him to stay. The worst of the storm would last four or five hours. He wasn't worried about storm water surge. The house was five blocks away from the Gulf of Mexico. The water surge would be a big problem for property on the lagoon or Gulf of Mexico.

Earlier in the day a Bay County Sheriff's Office cruise patrol car rolled past his house while Sharkey still worked at the marina securing property in the boat storage facility as best as he could. The officer in the Sheriff's car drove up and down streets announcing through a loud speaker that there was a mandatory evacuation of the island and everyone was to leave by four p.m. All bridges and roads leading off the island would be closed after that time. He had heard the loudspeaker announcement repeated over and over as the cruiser went up and down each street.

Sharkey finished his work at the marina and left his car parked near the office, next to the only solid concrete wall at the facility. He walked home, carrying batteries and the radio weather scanner from the marina store. The walk took about thirty minutes. Driving in the car would have taken longer. He didn't mind the wind and rain too much. It was better than working inside the hot and humid cavernous storage building. He kept an eye at the sky watching for lightning inside the low black clouds that were heavy with rain and rumbling with thunder.

Most of the neighbors' cars were missing from the driveways. He figured some had left their second car and evacuated in one. He knew most people were not staying on the island.

Once inside his house, he shut the door and took several deep breaths to slow down his heart after the walk from the marina. His clothes were soaked and his shirt clung to his heaving chest.

"Guess I'd better get out of this stuff I'm wearing and into something a little more comfortable, even though I'll probably start sweating and get my clothes wet all over again," Sharkey thought.

Sharkey didn't' bother to change out of his wet clothes. He got started on the necessary tasks to prepare for the hurricane. First he filled up his bathtub with water. He emptied all the ice out of his freezer and dumped it into a small cooler. He refilled all the ice trays and hoped the power would stay on long enough to freeze another batch of ice. He filled up empty jugs and pots with water. Then he went outside to bring inside his barbeque grill and lawn chair, items that could fly in the air and potentially fly through one of his windows. He took sheets of plywood he kept stored in the second bedroom closet and nailed them across all windows, hammering the nails into shutters attached to the concrete block. Next, he dragged out all the extra towels from his linen closet and placed them near the front and back doors. Last he searched for candles.

"Yeah, candles. I've never been a candle guy," he said to himself. "However they come in handy when the electricity is gone. At least I know I have extra batteries for my flashlight and radio weather scanner." He shuffled through drawers and found two half burnt candles and a box of matches. "Better put these in some zip lock plastic."

It took a little over an hour for Sharkey to complete his preparations,

Sharkey sat down on his sofa and tried to think of any other things he should do. He thought about the unprepared, uninitiated people who stay at home and have a hurricane party with friends.

"Drinking and hurricanes really don't mix together," Sharkey thought, "but, I might need to have one drink after I finish with all these details. It has been a long time since I felt like I needed a beer to take the edge off my nerves. This will be a long night. Times like this make me think it would be nice to have a cat around."

After his short rest, Sharkey headed into the bathroom to take a long, good hot shower. He let the hot water run down his back, grateful for its soothing power to relax him.

"If I lose power it might be days before I get a shower like this again," he muttered while he showered, still thinking about the different ways people react to a hurricane.

"Yeah, there was that time someone got so drunk and thought it would be a good idea to take a walk out on the pier to see the action. Next thing, a nine foot wave takes out the pier and two people float out in the gulf and drown. Another thing is people and their boats. Like that kid today leaving his boat at the marina and asking Casey to look after it. What kind of fool takes off without securing his property? And what about old Casey? Wasn't he something else today? First he shows up wanting to store it. Then he never comes back. A little while later I see him show up at the gas pumps with the boat and a woman in it! Buys a few supplies from the marina store and takes the boat out into the lagoon. I think he's gone over the cliff. Who was the woman? What stressful times do to people when the stress gets inside their heads!"

While the lights still worked Sharkey sat down to read a book he found at a garage sale about the history of France. Sometimes he felt weird to admit to the fishermen and people he worked with at the marina that he enjoyed reading history. There was something about any kind of history, especially the stories of people who changed history, which appealed to him. The book focused on the era of   . Napoleon and had beautiful glossy color pictures in it. The pictures made the reading all the more enjoyable as he tried to pass the time with the hurricane raging outside.

After the power stopped, Sharkey reclined on his sofa and listened to the battery operated radio to help him stay awake. He'd had a long tiring day but the noise outside wouldn't let him sleep. He waited in the dark trying to imagine the scenes happening outside his four walls.

Sharkey never drank the beer that he thought he needed. This didn't feel like the right time for drinking a beer.

Sharkey was not prepared for the things he saw when he ventured outside his house and to the front porch the next morning. He gasped and choked when his eyes took in the vision before him. The thick salty air stuck in his throat.

"This is just a small microcosm of the world. Thank you Lord for keeping me safe!" he muttered turning his eyes up and seeing a blue sky mostly clear of clouds. His home was spared. He was alive.

The blazing orange sun shone bright in the blue sky. It heated up everything, intensifying the smelly odors that seeped, like the smoldering ashes of a fire, out of the salt sprayed garbage lying everywhere. The gentle breeze that cooled the sweat on his body also spread the smells and sounds of disaster, gas powered engines in the distance. Cleaning up was the only choice for the people who had stayed. The debris and garbage was everywhere. It was on the streets, washed up on the beach, floating in the waterways, hanging in the broken branches of trees and stuck in every crevice or hole.

Sharkey lowered his head and slowly turned his body around in a full circle. His eyes took in all of the familiar and unfamiliar scenery in the neighborhood. Trees of all sizes were destroyed. Some were splintered to the size of toothpicks. Some lay on the road, pulled out of the ground and laid down with the roots facing toward the sky. Some were stripped of every leaf. A tree with leaves left on it looked like it came from another planet. Saltwater spray had turned all of the leaves to a translucent gray. A slight breeze rippled the leaves, as if asking for a final dance before dropping them to their death on the ground.

Sharkey lived on one of the few paved roads in the residential area of the island. The road was now a muddy, rusty red, dirt road like the nearby clay roads. Clay covered many yards too. Stuck in the mud were objects, anything one could imagine, from multiple neighbors' yards. A bathroom sink lay upside down in the yard directly across from his.

"I cannot imagine where a sink would come from, but thankfully it stopped in a yard and didn't fly through one of my windows!"

Sharkey walked back into the house and left the front door open. He proceeded to the back door with a hope that he wouldn't be more surprised by what he saw. "I need a little cross breeze coming through here. The humidity is oppressive after being shut up inside all night!"

Next he removed the plywood from the windows to help get some air circulating in the house. Afterwards he spent a few minutes digesting what he'd seen. He wasn't sure how to prepare for what he might face when he returned to the boat facility at the marina. The water and food he stored would be enough to get him through a couple of days. He turned off the radio hours ago when he heard that Hurricane Louise made landfall. He wanted to conserve his batteries. He turned the radio back on now to get an update on road closures, power outages, damaged property and other important announcements. He heard the familiar voices of the radio personalities.

"......and the news is good for us Jennifer..." the trailing end of a sentence of a man's voice on the radio came through the speakers.

"Right, John, but the folks and friends east of us will certainly need help," the woman's voice came on next.

"Jennifer and John!" Sharkey muttered. He'd been listening to their ongoing reports since yesterday. "What a surprise! They've had quite a long night too. Surprised someone else doesn't come in to give them a break."

"Once again," the voices on the radio continued, "we're going to keep everyone updated on new road openings as soon as they become available to us. Right now we've been advised that the Bay County Sheriff's office has been out on Highway 231 and Highway 79, our two major evacuation routes. They are assessing the damage and notifying the county clean-up crews where they should begin to clear fallen trees. These roads are not opened now but they are expected to be opened later today for those people who evacuated and need to return to their homes. It is expected that all four lanes of Highways 231 will be opened soon and Highway 79 will be opened first only for southbound traffic."

The male announcer, John, continued, "We've haven't received any reports of injury, but we have been informed by the Bay County Sheriff's office that they found the body of a man in a black pick-up truck parked in the area of Pine Log Forest State Park on Highway 79. No identification was found on the man, who appears to be in his mid-twenties, Caucasian, medium build, with blonde hair. The pick-up truck has a Georgia license plate, but we are not releasing the name of the person to whom the truck is registered until the owner can be identified. The Sheriff's office believes, or hopes, it may be someone who is related to the dead man. If anyone in our listening area is aware of a stolen vehicle or missing family member from the area of Harris county Georgia, they are asked to contact the Bay County Sheriff's office at this number......."

Sharkey's skin prickled as he listened to the radio announcer. Something about the story seemed impossible, but plausible, and made him feel uneasy. Yesterday Casey had asked him to store a boat belonging to another man. Could this dead man be connected to the man who left the boat at the marina for Casey to watch over?

"No. That's too weird." Sharkey shook his head as if to wake himself up. He took a deep breath. But then the idea of finding a man alone in his truck in the parking lot of state park on the side of the road during a hurricane evacuation seemed implausible too.

"I think I need to go for a walk on the beach. I want to go see the waves and the surf and whatever else has washed up on the beach. All kinds of surprises, I bet," Sharkey thought. "Perhaps this will put a spark into a dreary morning and some fresh breezes from the Gulf will temporarily blow away my worry."

Walking to the beach put Sharkey in an even darker mood. In the five block walk to the beach he only saw house after house with the same garbage that was strewn in his yard. Some homes had structural damage.

Once he arrived at the beach the normally aqua blue-green waters were churning up dark brown foamy waves. The sugar white sands were littered with anything that could wash out of a hotel room or beach cottage.

"So this must be where the sink came from," Sharkey said. "Anything is possible."

CHAPTER 36: THE DESTINY BOAT RIDE

Daylight arrived. Eleanore and Casey were listening to the radio, she'd given Earl for his birthday. The voices on the radio were a welcome relief from the mysterious noises during the long hours of the dark night. The routine repetitive announcements about winds, tides, and currents now included power outages and road conditions.

Suddenly the subject changed. Eleanore's optimism began to fade while she listened closely to the news.

"....and the Bay County Sheriff's office has reported a dead man was discovered in a black pick-up truck with a Georgia license plate tag registered in Harris County....."

Eleanore didn't hear the rest of the report. She sat up straight and mumbled softly, but loud enough for Casey to hear. "It's Earl. Pine Mountain is in Harris County, Georgia."

He avoided looking at her. She was crying again.

"You okay?" he timidly asked, surprised by the softness in his own voice. It made him feel better that he was able to handle the woman's tears, but realized the situation he might be facing could be worse than all of last night.

Casey thought of reaching over and touching Eleanore's shoulder in an act to comfort her, but remembered yesterday's encounter when he tried to kiss her. He thought it better not to touch her right now. He didn't want to relive his own feelings when he made her shake with fear. It had made him feel like an evil monster.

Tears puddled in her soft brown eyes and rolled down her smooth cheeks. The tears traveled in streaks down her face until they landed on her heaving chest.

"My life is such a mess," she stammered, choking on sobs. "I think it's just going to get worse."

"Oh, honey," Casey said. He wanted to calm and reassure her, but wasn't sure what to do. "You don't know that it's Earl for sure."

Before Casey could say anything more Eleanore continued to speak through her sobs and snivels. Between words she lifted her right forearm to wipe away the tears from her eyes and the snot from her nose.

"Oh, yes!" she cried emphatically. "This past night is just the beginning of a big problem for me. Even though I survived it, I believe my life is only going to get worse, much worse. My hole is very deep. I don't know where to start on digging out of this hole. I have hardly eaten and I don't know where my next meal will be coming from. I probably don't have a job anymore. I know that for sure! And, and…I don't have any money! And, and ….I AM sure I don't have Earl!" Eleanore sobbed and snorted, trying to catch her breath between sobs.

In spite of her outburst, Casey was remarkably calm. He looked in awe at this girl's honest and raw emotions. He never before, in his entire life, felt so trusted by a woman.

"Hang on here," he said evenly. "This is only a temporary situation, honey. We've got good people here in this area and I know they will try their best to help you, whatever you need. It's not the best of times for anyone right now, but I guarantee that I will help you." He was talking in a soothing, gentle voice. "You're going to get to a better place in your life. I will do what I can to help and I know other people who will help. Let's just be patient. Hang on and stay on track until we get back to the marina, okay?"

Casey turned and suddenly yanked open the cabin door, surprising and startling Eleanore.

"What are you going to do now?" she sobbed.

"I gotta get a move on things to get us out of here," he said.

Casey stepped outside and kicked aside the black rubber boot that was lying now in the middle of the deck after being knocked around by the waves bobbing beneath the boat all night.

"Maybe you want to save this rubber boot for a souvenir?" he hollered back at her inside the cabin.

"What for? Why?" she hollered back at him.

"Seeing as how that's where you told me last night where you thought you first saw something white sticking out of the boot while we were riding out to Dismal Creek. Remember, you told me that's where your Princess must have been hiding all along? And, then she turns up at the door meowing like all get out!" he hollered again.

The reminder of her discovery the day before, finding her cat, made Eleanore smile. She suddenly stopped crying.

"Yes, I think that might be a good thing," she agreed.

After taking a few deep breaths Eleanore stepped outside of the cabin and closed the cabin door to be sure the two cats, still snuggled and clinging tight to each other in a far corner, didn't get any idea to escape. The outside air was still humid, but the fresh air was a big relief from the stuffy cabin. The light breeze and clearing sky lifted her spirits. It felt like a load was being lifted off her shoulders. The longer she stood outside, in the open, the clearer her thoughts became. She began to focus on what needed to be done next.

Eleanore watched Casey's long legs spring over the side of the 'Lucky Two' and onto the bank. His large feet sank into the sand. His large hands began to untie the ropes from the tall pine tree that kept the boat from drifting out into the bay. It occurred to her that the strong winds could have easily dropped one of the trees on top of the rocking boat during the night. She felt reason to give thanks.

"Things could get worse," she thought, "but it always feels good to be thankful for something. At least Casey knew what to do to try and keep us safe and secure."

She sat on the bench seat and watched Casey's skilled hands at work, taking care of the business of getting the boat prepared for the journey back to the marina. She remembered what Casey did when they first arrived at Dismal Creek. She began to doubt the uneasy feelings she'd had.

"Maybe I've misjudged this man," she thought. "He frightened me so bad last night and yesterday but now he appears to respect my feelings. He didn't get angry at me when I started to cry. He seems to want to help."

Casey called out to her, "Hey, Eleanore. I'm going to throw these ropes onto the boat now. You don't have to catch them. Just watch out that they don't hit you when they land."

The ropes landed not far from the black rubber boot. Then Casey stepped into the shallow water and pulled his body back over the side of the boat and onto the deck. He pulled up the anchor and waited before starting the boat's engines.

Casey's suspicions had grown. The report of a dead man found in a truck that matched the description of Earl's truck, and Eleanore's reaction upon hearing the report, were strong facts.

Up to now Casey had avoided thinking about reporting back to work. He had formulated no real explanation for his disappearance or plan for returning to the marina with the 'Lucky Two'. He decided that now was the time to turn the sound back on to his radio still attached to the epaulet on his shoulder.

"It may just be coincidental, but I do think we should check it out if we can," Casey said to Eleanore. "I believe I might be able to get us near to that area they were talking about on the radio. The Pine Log State Forest area, you know?" Casey continued to talk before she had a chance to respond. "There are lots and lots of creeks that flow into North Bay from Pine Log State Forest I'm pretty familiar with the area from fishing up here in my small boat. The weight on this boat probably isn't so much that I can't get us close to a creek. The water level is going to be pretty high after the hurricane surge.

"If I can get close enough I may be able to get someone on my radio and ask them to arrange for someone to pick us up in a department vehicle, or a four wheel drive. They could meet the boat at the creek and drive through the woods to the park. Driving to the park in my truck after getting this boat back to the marina would be impossible. It'll take us at least forty five minutes to an hour to get out of the Intracoastal Waterway and through the bay. We would be late getting to the marina. Do you think you can handle it if I can make it happen? I know you're pretty darn worn out."

Eleanore felt a small amount of her composure slip away. She solemnly stiffened her upper lip. "No more crying," she said to Casey and commanded herself. "Maybe the story was about another man, not Earl," she said with no conviction in her voice. "But we need to find out."

Eleanore didn't let her sadness overcome her determination. It had been a long time since she last saw Earl. She wasn't even sure if she would recognize him now, even if it had been only two years. He sounded so different on the phone. She felt defeated about the past, still uncertain about her future, but hopeful because she had been so lucky to meet people who helped her to survive Hurricane Louise.

Casey said, "I think we're doing the right thing to check on it. We can get the boat back to the marina later. I'm not in a big hurry to get it there anyway. The marina's most likely going to be a mess. There may not be a place to dock it."

Casey and Eleanore looked into each other's eyes and nodded their heads, silently agreeing with the plan.

"You might want to look inside for something to clean up with, a towel or something," Casey suggested. "We both look like a mess. It'll make you feel a whole lot better."

They both smiled. Eleanore imagined how bad she looked with her greasy hair and her dirty face after all that crying.

"I suppose if I'm going to talk to some officials I'd better look more presentable," she said.

Casey turned the key in the ignition to start the engine.

"We'll be there in no time. It's going to go a lot faster than it seems," Casey announced as if talking to a crew. He pushed forward on the throttle and gently eased the boat back out of the cove. "It's really not too far from here. I'm hoping I can get close to the park at Crooked Creek," he spoke loud enough to be heard over the drone of the engine. "There's a trail along the creek. A good four wheel can make it to us in the boat. If not, I'll ask them to drive as close as they can get to the old Sawmill Trail. There used to be lots of logging going on around here about a hundred years ago. They took all the long-leaf yellow old growth pine and used them beautiful trees for homes. They'd float those old trees down Crooked Creek. The old Sawmill Trail is not far from Crooked Creek."

"It's good that you know all that information," Eleonore said.

The tired, worn-out Eleanore reached around Casey and grabbed the door handle of the cabin door.

"Don't forget to keep the door shut and keep those kitties inside," Casey reminded her before she stepped inside.

Eleanore looked around at the messy cabin and shook her head in despair. After finding a few paper napkins she returned to the fresh breezes outside and flopped her exhausted body back down on the cushioned seat. She wasn't about to try to talk to Casey over the loud noise of the engines. She braced herself for more bouncing waves and what to expect at the next stop. She barely noticed Casey skillfully maneuvering the watercraft through the choppy waves.

She found herself thinking about Darryl. She wondered if she would see him again. She needed Darryl to get back to her car. He knew where to take her, but what if she didn't find Darryl again? She didn't know where the hurricane shelter, where he said he was staying, was. Would Darryl be able to get back to the marina? Would she be able to find her car without him.

What was she going to do for money? She would need money. Who would help her with getting some money?

Eleanore remembered Darryl had been very kind to her. He had a gentle soothing voice, and the way his blue eyes looked deeply into hers made her want to see him again. She imagined he could provide her with emotional support and perhaps even be willing to lend her money.

Eleanore could do nothing but worry as she watched the passing coastline and wait to see the entrance into Crooked Creek.

"Talk about going up a creek without a paddle!" she thought.

CHAPTER 37: ARRIVAL OF THE PROTECTOR

Ricky was in a state of shock. Ricky moaned like a lost puppy. He felt helpless and hopeless without Vince.

When daylight arrived he struggled to squirm his way out of the truck. He was unable to think what to do, or where to go. He could only think about the nightmare he lived through inside the truck in total darkness. There was also the memory of watching Vince scream on the ground, losing control of his body and succumbing to convulsive jerks and spasms until he died.

Ricky's lifetime friend from grammar school was still lying dead on the ground surrounded by water-logged debris.

After striking at Vince the rattlesnake moved away, sidewinding itself back into the far reaches of the woods, slithering back into another palmetto bush. Nonetheless, Ricky was anxious that the snake still lingered close by. It was the snake's territory, after all. He'd heard at the Rattlesnake festival back in Opp, Alabama, that rattlesnakes always lived in pairs. There was a good chance there was another one just like it.

It took every bit of courage Ricky could summon to crawl out of the cab of the truck. He ran around to the back of the truck and jumped over the tailgate that had been left open. He stood for an hour on the truck that was picked up by the tornado and dropped on its side the night before. Ricky was paralyzed by fear that the snake would return. He didn't have Vince around to tell him what to do or when to do it.

The sun broke through some clouds. Ricky's recalled his proclamation during the night. It was to do whatever God wanted. He had promised to obey God.

"Miss Sissy woulda' never wanted this for her boy," Ricky's lips blubbered with only half a tongue left in his mouth. "Vince. I know that!"

Finally, thinking that it was safe, Ricky jumped down to the ground and slowly walked over to Vince's body. He knelt down beside it. With tears freely rolling down his cheeks and chin he said in a childlike voice, "I ain't never gonna leave you, Vince. There will be a place for you in my heart always."

The snakes didn't worry Ricky when his emotions, his heart, took over. The thinking side of his brain wasn't working.

The sweet spot in Ricky's soul took a strong grip of his heart. More uncontrollable sobs shook his body. If any animal, or human for that matter, had been nearby they would have given Ricky his space to cry.

After another long hour of crying Ricky's breathing slowed to short gasps. He took several deep breaths then relented to touch Vince's cold, gray, stiff body. He placed the palm of his hand flat on Vince's chest, over the heart, with a slim hope he would feel a beat. Then, with both of his hands Ricky caressed Vince's body. He rubbed his hands over the shoulder, across the face, down the arms and finally let his hand grasp each hand. He gripped each one as tight as possible, searching for the warmth and energy of their past friendship. Ricky felt only the cold hard ruggedness of Vince's hands. He felt the cold metal of the ring Vince wore on his right hand. He bent his head down to take a good look at the chunky silver ring Vince always wore for many years and never removed.

Ricky let his fingers slide around and around in circles over the ring. A soft, tender voice in his head said, "I remember this ring. I remember that when you bought it you were so proud to have something this nice to wear!"

A gust of wind snapped a limb off one of the trees. It startled Ricky and broke his concentration. He looked up to the sky and saw wispy while clouds swirling not far above the tree tops. The clouds felt so close to him, like angels. He shut his eyes and covered his ears, wishing he could block the noise of the wind, but the sense of sound doesn't work the same as the sense of sight.

With his eyes closed, though, he could imagine the day he was with Vince at the souvenir shop on the beach. It was a hot, humid, salty summer day. They walked into the air conditioned store to cool the sweat on their sticky skin.

"Let's look over here at this jewelry counter," Vince announced as soon as they were inside the store. It was in a popular location across the street from the county pier. The jewelry case was strategically placed at the front door, where it would be noticed by anyone entering or exiting the store. Peering down into the enclosed glass case Ricky saw chains, rings, and earrings displayed on a black velvet fabric. The kind of stuff girls would wear, he remembered. But, Vince was quick.

"I want that ring," Vince announced in a strange, deep voice with strong emphasis on the word that.

"Which one," Ricky tentatively asked, unsure of the tone in Vince's voice.

"See that big one? The one with the snake head? The snake is wrapped around in a circle, kinda sideways. It looks like a rattlesnake. I like it." Vince said.

It was a big, chunky silver ring. A perfect sized ring for a man's finger. "I wonder if it's my size?" He was excited.

"Don't you want to know what it costs?" Ricky asked.

"Yeah, but I want to know if it fits. I think this ring has powers to protect me. They should have been selling these rings at the Rattlesnake Festival back home in Opp. I would have bought it. I've needed this ring for a long time."

263

As a child who had been a victim, traumatized by the adults who should have been protecting him, Vince believed in the tangible things that could protect him. Vince never talked about the beatings he *earned* from Preacher Wood, but Ricky saw the scars and bruises on his legs.

Vince needed something he could count on.

"Yeah," Vince said as he stared at his hand, hypnotized by the ring once he slid it on his finger. He paid the salesclerk with cash and said, "This is my protector now!"

Ricky remembered seeing the white flash in the crescent of Vince's eye at the moment he called the ring his protector.

Now Ricky gently tugged at the ring on Vince's cold hand. He was surprised that it moved off Vince's finger with very little effort. It was not the best fitting ring on Vince's finger after all, he thought. Holding it in the palm of his hand Ricky was surprised by how large the ring was. Was Vince's hand really that much larger than his own?

Without a lingering look, or pause, Ricky slid the ring onto his middle finger. The fit was snug. Perhaps a little too snug. It wouldn't come off easily, Ricky thought. It sealed the memory of Vince in his own life forever. He was going to always wear the memory of Vince on his hand.

Ricky took a few moments to reflect on the life of Vince while he stared at the ring that was now on his finger. The silver, snake-shaped, chunky ring was not as shiny today. Ricky noticed that it looked a little grey, tarnished and scratched. He didn't notice the tiny spot of blood caked into a brown dot on the eye of the snake.

The ring did not protect Vince and it would not protect Ricky.

CHAPTER 38: FREE AS A BIRD

The Walton County Sheriff Patrol officer driving his green and white patrol car east on highway 20 was giving himself a pep talk to get prepared for the difficult day ahead. Like everyone else, he had spent a very difficult night waiting in darkness for Hurricane Louise to make landfall. He was tired. His personal problems caused by the hurricane would have to wait. He would deal with them when he was off duty, whenever that may be. Now his job was to face the anxious, and often angry, public in a professional manner. He was bracing himself to see anything, and the worst.

The last thing Officer Neil Cooke was expecting to see was a lone man standing at the side of the road in the middle of nowhere. All that was around on the long stretch of highway 20 was woods filled with pine trees. The man was frantically waving his arms in the air.

Cooke took his right hand off the steering wheel and rubbed his eyes with one finger. The human was standing some distance down the road, but he was sure it was a man. As he got closer to the man, he slowed down the cruiser. There was no mistake. A shirtless man in shorts, waving his arms wildly above his head, jumping from one leg to the other leg, was straight ahead.

"This one doesn't look so good," he mumbled. "Let's see what we have here."

Cooke flashed his blue lights to signal the man that he was going to stop. He hoped the man would stop jumping into the road. The last thing he wanted was to hit a human.

Cooke's eyes were trained to be observant and suspicious. He slowed the cruiser to a complete stop. When Ricky ran around to the driver's side of the cruiser Cooke rolled his window down only a few inches.

"How did you get out here, stuck in the middle of the woods?" he asked Ricky. He tried to memorize any details that might be important. The cues he was receiving from this skinny, disheveled man were a mixture of fear, relief, sadness, grief and worry. The blood spattered shorts Ricky wore painted a picture of more problems. The scrawny young man had a look of desperation in his eyes and had yet to say a word.

"So, can you tell me what the problem is here?"

"Whhgg fnd dud," Ricky pointed his finger in the direction of the woods where the truck and Vince's stiff body lie.

"Excuse ME?!?" Cooke was shocked at the man's communication.

"Ah ik ah ungggg," Ricky gurgled and then opened his mouth to reveal the split tongue, now a swollen piece of red flesh.

"OKAY!! Okay!!! I see. Close your mouth!" Cooke shouted back a little too loudly, as if hearing may be Ricky's problem. "Go stand over there off the road. I'm going to pull over and radio in to my headquarters to let them know I've stopped. Wait there. Don't go anywhere. I'm going to help you in a few minutes. Then you can take me to where you're pointing and show me the problem."

Ricky shook his head up and down with vigorous enthusiasm; so much that it caused his remaining piece of tongue to throb worse.

After a few minutes Cooke stepped out of the vehicle and left the engine running. He followed Ricky through the woods, down the sandy trail where Vince had driven the truck the day before. When they came to a clear spot where Vince's body and the truck lay, side by side, both men stopped short of the scene.

"Accident?" Cooke asked Ricky.

Ricky shook his head no and walked up to Vince's body. He bent down on his knees, leaned over and pointed at the leg where the two puncture wounds were still visible. Bright red rings circled around the holes. The fangs were broken off inside the skin, which was now turned to an ashen grey.

"Must have been a big snake, huh?" Cooke said. Ricky shivered when he heard the word snake. The hair on his arms prickled.

Ricky nodded his head up and down more gently. The pain in his mouth had not gone away, but it was more painful to remember watching his friend slip away into death in such an awful way.

"Was it a rattlesnake?"

Gentle nods of yes followed.

"Was it today?"

A shaky, slow, nod no.

"Yesterday?"

One nod yes.

"So, okay, what about the truck? Was this an accident?"

"Nahahah," Ricky tried to say no. His lips formed a circle and he blew air from the back of his throat.

"Tornado?" Cooke quickly guessed.

Ricky nodded yes. His eyes grew big, excited that the patrolman understood him.

"Okay, makes sense to me," Cooke said. He thought he should finalize the visit. The truck and body could be handled later. "You okay beside the tongue?"

Ricky tilted his head and nodded a respectful yes.

"You got any identification for yourself and this man, your friend?" Cooke asked.

"Yaaag." Ricky nervously attempted to say yes.

Cooke said, "Don't try to talk. Just nod your head yes or no."

He resumed his yes or no line of questions. "Do you have any family, or anyone you can call, about your situation?"

Ricky nodded no.

266

"Well, you probably need to go ahead and ride along with me to the next staging point for the responders. You okay with that?"

Ricky, still nervous after being asked to show identification, attempted to say something. "Ugh eww."

"Got anything you want to grab and bring along?" Cooke looked Ricky square in the eyes to get a read on his level of honesty. He searched for something other than distress.

"Yaahhhh!"

Ricky scrambled to the upturned truck. He got down on his hands and knees to crawl inside the cab. On the floor, near where he sat the night before, he found the roll of bills. Ricky didn't want the patrolman to see it, but he didn't know where he could conceal it besides his pants pocket. He had to stand up to do that. He didn't want it to be obvious when he stood up after crawling out of the truck.

"You okay in there?" Cooke said, getting a little impatient after a few minutes had passed. He didn't want to upset Ricky but he wanted him to hurry up.

Ricky grabbed the bloody shirt he used to stuff inside his mouth to stop the bleeding tongue. He slipped the wad of bills inside of it and folded the thin layer of cloth into a small square, hoping the money didn't fall out.

He shimmed his body backward out of the front of the truck cab. When he stood up he was holding the bloody balled up shirt tightly in both of his hands.

"That's it?" Cooke asked in surprised wonder. "That's all you're going to bring? I can probably find a clean shirt for you at the station."

Ricky locked eyes with Cooke and shook his head no.

Cooke was baffled, but didn't think twice about it. "So you're ready now?"

Sadness filled Ricky's eyes. He gave Cooke a trustful nod yes.

"I can't do anything about your buddy right now, but I'll call it in when I get back to the cruiser. Given the circumstances with the hurricane and all, the situation doesn't look real good. It may take a few hours, or maybe even a day, to get someone out here to pick up his body. We can't leave it lying out here for very long, I know. You okay?"

Ricky let his head drop forward then lifted it back up. Cooke noticed the tears that had welled up in Ricky's eyes.

Cooke's eyes met Ricky's. "Let's go son. There's nothing we can do for him now. We'll be back to get him as soon as we can." Cooke lightly touched Ricky's elbow to indicate he could start walking. "I hope you have some information on any family we can contact for him. And maybe we can find someone to help you. First you're going to need some medical attention."

Cooke kept talking as Ricky walked a step in front of him. He was keeping a watchful on Ricky's stability. He also knew that the idle talk may help keep Ricky calm. It was going to take a lot to help Ricky feel comfortable and regain his composure.

Office Neil Cooke had seen a lot of strange situations in his career with the Walton County Sheriff's office. Something about this scenario was very odd, though. How'd these two guys end up here in the middle of nowhere? With the hurricane coming surely anyone with a little bit of common sense might have different traveling plans. How'd they get through road blocks that had been set up? There didn't seem to be anything suspicious about the death of the other man. Shrug it off, he thought. There's plenty of work to be done. There will be a lot more oddities to come, for sure.

"You have to sit in the back seat, but don't let that make you nervous," Cooke said when he opened the door for Ricky to get inside the vehicle.

"Ooohaa," Ricky made an effort to be comfortable once he sat down.

Static buzzes and a constant rattle of voices reporting information sounded over the police scanner.

"You'll probably want to cover your ears and not pay attention to the noise. It can be overwhelming," Cooke said after he shut the door for Ricky.

Cooke climbed into the front seat.

Both men reacted to the raspy voice on the police radio scanner.

"Report of a white male found deceased in a black pickup truck parked near Pine Log State Forest, off highway 79. Suspicious homicide."

Cooke cut his eyes to the rear view mirror to observe Ricky's reaction to another death. He was sure he noticed an expression of surprise in the eyes of the freckle faced young man sitting alone in the back seat. The mouth twitched. The eyes widened and stared back at Neil's eyes in the mirror. No more sadness and despondency were reflected in Ricky's eyes. Office Neil Cooke recognized Ricky's reaction. He saw a pale face reflecting fear.

"You'll need to buckle up your seat belt for this ride. Normally we have someone in hand cuffs and we do the buckling, but your hands are free to do that." Cooke used a casual, controlled voice. He did not want to send Ricky any signal that he noticed the change in his countenance. "I bet you're thirsty and hungry too. It's going to be a problem to get some nourishment into your body right away, but I will do the best I can."

"Eeerrreee," Ricky managed to make a noise.

"Oh, yes, I bet. Me too, but I know I'm not feeling as bad as you're feeling," Cooke said sympathetically. He believed the sound Ricky made was the word for *hungry*.

Ricky instinctively lifted his hand up to cover his mouth after Neil acknowledged his condition and tried to forget the announcement over the radio scanner.

Cooke kept an eye on Ricky in the rear view mirror and noticed the large, rather unusual ring Ricky wore on his middle index finger when Ricky covered his mouth. It seemed much too large for his hand, but he learned a long time ago that people chose strange things to adorn their body. His mind registered the image of a snake's head. The ring presented a creepy coincidental connection to the death of Ricky's friend. It gave him goosebumps thinking about it.

"I noticed that ring you're wearing. Is that a snake?" Cooke asked.

"Ahhhhh," Ricky attempted another word and nodded yes. He squeezed the bloody shirt tight.

"It's an interesting shape and very big. Anyway, I take it that man back there was a pretty good friend of yours?" Cooke's cruiser engine was still running. He wasn't ready to start driving until he had a little more information and laid out some structure for the ride.

Ricky nodded yes.

"Listen, do you know your friend's family very well? If I gave you a piece of paper would you be able to write down the names, addresses and phone number of anyone. I'll need your friend's full name and if you know his date of birth write that down. Could you write this all down for me? Just try to give me as much information about your friend that you can. I need to prepare a victim report for your friend. Any information you can share about your family write down too."

Ricky responded with an affirmative nod, "Ahh, naaa faaaa..." his sad eyes answered as he uttered vowels from the back of his throat. To try and pronounce consonants was very painful, and impossible, with his swollen tongue. "Aaaah...aaah maa."

"You got a mother?"

Ricky gently nodded his head up and down.

"I'll try my best to get you help and then home." Cooke passed a clipboard with a clean sheet of paper and a pen attached to a metal chain behind the seat back to Ricky.

He put the car into gear and accelerated the vehicle into motion. Then Cooke said, looking at Ricky in the rear view mirror, "This may take quite some time. I'm not sure of the condition of the rest of highway 20 in Walton County, but I am pretty sure that road and traffic will be moving by the time we reach Bay County. I'm hoping I can get you to the county line and meet a deputy, or even an emergency vehicle to transport you. There will be paperwork to process for Walton and Bay county Sheriff's department. Just hang on there and try to rest."

Officer Neil Cooke frequently glanced back at Ricky as he drove along the highway at a slower than normal, but steady, rate of speed. He felt uncertain about the emotions reflected in the eyes fitted onto the dirty, ashen, bony face which was turned slightly, enabling Ricky to stare through the passenger window. Ricky's eyes were sunken and tired. That was quite understandable under the circumstances. But, and this was a huge but, there was something else about the man's eyes hypnotically glued to the scenery passing by the window. It was not fear, calm, anger, surprise, or shock. Cooke usually trusted his instincts, but drew a blank on this character. It finally came to him that this looked like a man who was finally free from hurt, pain and humiliation.

Cooke remained quiet, listening to the radio scanner while he drove. When he and Ricky arrived at the heavily barricaded intersection of Highways 79 and 20, Officer Cooke knew there would be a lot of explaining for Ricky, even if he couldn't talk. Nothing added up. The paper on the clipboard was filled in with only a few scribbles. Ricky listed his home as Dothan, Alabama. The last place Ricky wanted to go back to was Opp, Alabama. Ricky wanted to start anew. There were factories with jobs and new people he could meet in the bigger city.

Ricky didn't have a clue what was going to happen to him next, but he didn't think that giving this first small lie would be a step in the direction of the door to the Walton county jail. The identification in his wallet, along with the discovery of the roll of stolen money folded inside the bloody shirt, led to further suspicions. It was too complicated trying to write out any kind of explanation to the stern faced officers in Bay County, who were not nearly as nice as Officer Neil Cooke. As soon as they saw the condition of Ricky they asked Cooke to take Ricky back to Walton County where Ricky could expect to stay for as long as it took to get answers about how he and Vince ended up in the middle of nowhere.

Ricky ended up somewhere where he didn't want to be. It would be for longer than he ever expected. The bloody money, and the blood in the eye of the silver rattlesnake ring, would become the evidence to solve the murder of Earl Keith.

When Ricky found himself locked up in the jail cell on the first night he requested a bible. One was sent immediately. When they closed the door of his prison cell, for the first but not the last time, Ricky was left by himself with only his thoughts. In spite of the trouble he faced, he found a reason to smile.

"It's a great big world. I'm in a very small place. I'm thinking this is another God moment like last night. God I sure do need your help. I didn't do the crime. I know I alone will never be able to prove anything close to the truth to a jury. I can't talk anymore. All I can do is write down my experience. And I'm gonna read Your word while I'm a living in my own small world. I'm living on the inside now, instead of living on the edge on the outside world. I am no longer living by the clock. I'm going to live with my bible and God is my witness."

It was the beginning of a new life for Ricky, living for many more years inside a jail cell.

CHAPTER 39: BROKEN HOMES, HAPPY HEARTS

"I've always preferred convenience to inconvenience, but waiting in this line of cars is getting to be a bit too much of a test of the patience for all of us weary souls," Darryl grumbled while he waited for traffic to move. When everyone was cleared to leave the gymnasium his feelings burst with joy. It didn't take long for his mood to change.

"Any home is better than no home," he clenched his jaws and ground his teeth. "C'mon positive vibes, you can hit me now. My stomach is twisted in knots! Ahhhhh, finally!!"

His right foot lightly touched the gas pedal. The procession of cars leaving Mosley High School's parking lot was beginning to slowly move. A school employee who had worked the overnight shift in the gym was standing in the road attempting to keep a friendly face as he directed traffic out in an orderly flow. Like Darryl, everyone wanted to be first in line and on their way. Being first in line meant an earlier realization of the long wait ahead in more lines of blocked traffic. Everyone was going nowhere fast.

It took Darryl more than three hours driving at a turtle's pace to reach Captain Anderson's marina. Normally it was a thirty minute drive.

To gain entry into the marina parking lot he was required by an officer of the National Guard to show identification that he possessed a boat. In contrast to the busy roadways, the parking lot at Captain Anderson's marina was nearly empty except for a few parked vehicles. Like everywhere else, the parking lot was littered with debris, garbage, and broken pieces of structures not commonly seen in a parking lot. Battered boats lay on the asphalt next to building rooftops.

"Ohhhhh noooo," Darryl shook his head as his eyes surveyed the area. "This looks really bad." The impatient agitation he had felt to get to the marina as quickly as possible was replaced with feelings of sadness and apprehension. His throat swelled up tight.

"Good luck indeed," Darryl repeated the words the National Guardsman said after he checked Darryl's identification and waved him through. He advised Darryl to report back with his personal damage. Then he could be directed to a representative of the Red Cross. The Red Cross would help anyone who needed shelter or assistance.

Darryl parked near Smith's Restaurant, which appeared to be in good condition. He turned off the engine, bowed his head down and sat quietly to pray for a few minutes. He prayed to God to give him strength. He also gave thanks for the new day.

Darryl exited his truck and walked down the sidewalk in front of the fish cleaning house. With an open view of the lagoon he saw a large messy pile of broken boat pieces moving in rhythm with the high tide water. He felt his legs shake. The size of the mess was much larger than anything he'd seen so far on his drive back. Soon his eyes recognized a piece in the heaps of parts. The 'Star Chaser' lay on its side, floating and banging against the concrete seawall. The movement of the waves took lead as the 'Star Chaser's' dance partner. With each bang, the hole in the side grew larger. Small contents from the inside the boat leaked out into the murky water each time the boat rocked.

"Okay boys, let the music begin." Darryl thought about the impromptu band that he played with the evening before. The PALs used the spirit of the music living in their hearts to love the moment in time. "Let's do this song. Maybe I can call it 'Discovery of Love Lost', or maybe better yet 'Love Long, Broken Heart'. We can play it in three quarter time. Slow it down a bit but keep the pace lively."

Darryl rolled his eyes up to the clear sky and walked to the concrete table and bench that remained in the same place. Wind and water had not moved them. He sat down, placed his elbows on the hard concrete table and cupped his chin in his palms. The fingers of his hands reached up to his ears. He tapped the brim of the cap on his head with two fingers from each hand. He stared at the scenery in front of him, moving his tired deep blue eyes left to right. His body ached from the past twenty four hours. His mind ached too. He couldn't think about the battered 'Star Chaser' now. All he could think about was Eleanore. Were they going to make it back today? Would it be soon?

The passage of time is relative to circumstances. Darryl was lost in troubling thoughts for what seemed like forever until his attention was caught by activity picking up around the marina. Other boat captains were arriving to check on the status of their property and assess the damage.

All the conversations covered the same topic: "How'd you do last night? Glad to see you made it through okay! It's going to take some time to clean up this mess, huh!" Some charter boat captains were luckier than others. Everyone nodded heads to each other in greeting. Afterward they shook their heads in shocked disbelief over the losses and the difficult decisions to be made.

After a while Darryl managed to get up. He found the Red Cross tent which had been quickly set up in the parking lot. He politely thanked them for a sandwich, package of cookies, and a few bottles of water. He told the volunteers he didn't know where he was going or what he was going to do, but he would make the decision before he was required to leave the marina at dark. He couldn't spend the night there alone.

He was surprised to see three cats slowly sauntering down the middle of the parking lot near Smith's. He thought that they looked familiar, sure that he'd seen them before. The cats appeared to have suffered a rough night, too. A huge fat cat, with a flattened face and snarly set of eyes led a few steps ahead of the other two. One cat was missing an upper lip and the other cat had a floppy ear that looked like an animal had taken a bite out of it.

"Yes, I know for sure I've seen that cat with the missing lip. Big Joe calls him Snaggle Tooth. I've seen that cat around the docks trying to steal fish. Those cats must be just as dazed and confused as the rest of us," he half chuckled but at the same time felt sympathy for them. "It's just amazing how animals can survive and get through a night like last night. Well, I wonder how Big Joe is doing. Surprised I haven't seen him yet."

When a break in the winds and the first grey light appeared through the cracks in the metal dumpster the cats leapt out of the stinky container through the side opening. They were more than eager to escape the smells and haunting echoes inside the four metal walls where they had spent the night. They were amazed to see that the garbage dumpster, slammed all night by hurricane force winds, was resting up against the concrete wall of Smith's. Broken pieces of wood fence built around the dumpster were lying nearby.

The first order for the quadrupeds had been to find a secure hiding place and commence cleaning their filthy paws and fur.

Now the three cats were stealthily hunting for food. They hurried across the parking lot strewn with debris, using their cat radar to avoid dangerous objects and standing water.

For hours Darryl waited in patient submission.

Finally the familiar sound of a boat engine reached his ears. His eyes peeled to look toward the lagoon pass in the direction of the noise. He wasn't the only person to notice the sound as it came closer. A few other workers glanced up but quickly went back to their work in the few hours of daylight left. Not far away, Darryl's eyes could see the boat coming slowly through the lagoon. It had to be Casey coming back with the 'Lucky Two'! Who else would be traveling on a boat at this time of day in the lagoon under these conditions?

Darryl stood as close to the edge of the boat slip, what remained of it, so he could keep a watch on the boat. He tried to be cautious of his surroundings and the broken wood debris lying all around him, but his excitement was hard to control.

Darryl thought he could see the shape of a woman leaning over the side of the boat, her head resting upon folded arms.

"Good!!" he shouted out loud, unable to control the jubilance he felt when he saw the woman. He needed to stay calm. He didn't want to attract anyone else's attention, or that of the approaching boat's occupants. He wanted to see the reaction on her face when she saw him again. It was a selfish feeling, but it was what he needed most at this moment in time.

When the 'Lucky Two' reached the docks, Darryl made an effort to assist Casey in navigating into a safe place to tie up. The boat slips, broken into pieces, didn't exist. The debris was floating everywhere. Any large piece could damage the hull of the boat.

Casey eased the boat close. He cut back on the engine and slowed down. The expression on his face astonished Darryl. It was different from any other time Darryl has seen him. He looked relieved to see Darryl standing on the concrete sidewalk.

Casey's eyes eagerly pleaded with Darryl's eyes to stay with him. He could only look at Darryl as someone to trust right now. So many things had happened in the last twenty four hours. He put all the memory of sitting in his truck two nights ago plotting against Darryl in the past.

"I got a rope if you think you can find a place to tie me up?" Casey shouted to Darryl over the low throttle of the engine.

"Yes, yes!!" Darryl hopped up and down like a nervous puppy, not giving a second thought to the eyes of the man he usually tried his best to avoid. He stumbled backwards over a yellow piece of nylon cord lying nearby but gave no time to think about embarrassment when Casey yelled with excitement to Darryl, "Catch the rope! Catch the rope! You can tie up to the concrete bench over here. I think that will do."

Casey skillfully guided the boat closer. "I'm going to get as close as possible, then cut the engine off. I'll let you pull the boat in a little more, and then I'll jump off the starboard to help you tie up."

As the men worked in earnest, Eleanore sat motionless on the boat, burying her face in folded arms resting on the side of the 'Lucky Two'.

After quickly securing the boat, Darryl and Casey spent an awkward moment of silence. Eleanore's limp body was still slumped, as if she had not woken up from sleep. Casey and Darryl stared at her for a few minutes and then turned their heads toward each other, waiting for the other one to speak first. Both sets of eyes expressed mutual feelings of exhaustion and helplessness.

"C'mon dear, hop on out." Casey said in a gentle voice of compassion. Darryl could not believe he was seeing the same person. It was the kindest voice he had ever heard any man speak to any woman.

"Is she okay?" Darryl asked Casey, still suspicious and concerned about what might have happened over night.

Casey stuck both hands in the pant pockets of his dirty, wet uniform. He shook his head gently side to side, closed his eyes and formed the word 'no' with his lips

Eleanore didn't move.

"We found out some real bad news," Casey started. Then he turned his body around and began to walk away from the boat. Darryl followed closely behind Casey. They went down the sidewalk a few feet past the fish cleaning house, and away from the 'Lucky

Two'. They turned at the corner and stopped not far from where the plaque for Max Anderson used to be.

"Heard any news on the radio?" Casey asked Darryl.

"Well, sure. Same old stuff." Darryl answered. Then he remembered that he turned off the radio in his truck not long after leaving the hurricane shelter at the high school. Three hours was a long time to listen to Jennifer and John. He had not heard any news since his arrival at the marina hours earlier. "I've heard some news from other boat captains about the reports of damage in other places besides the marina," he said.

Casey shifted his body and looked past Darryl, over his head. His tired eyes reflected deep sadness.

Darryl piped up. "Well, honestly, truth is no. I haven't been listening to the talking heads. I've just been waiting here hoping for you two guys to show up and get back. I know I'll have to spend the night somewhere else, some shelter maybe. Not much I can do right now but wait. Tell me what happened out there last night!!" Darryl demanded.

Casey took a deep breath. In a somber voice he said, "Earl, the owner of the 'Lucky Two', the guy Eleanore came here looking for, was found dead in his truck up on highway 79."

"Ohhhh. Noooo!" Darryl groaned. His head dropped and hung down so far his chin touched his chest. He was unable to find his voice.

A long five minutes of silence passed before either man could talk. Then Casey started the long story of learning about Earl. He began with the weather radio report including the story of a dead man found in a truck over at Pine Log State Forest. Casey told Darryl how Eleanore immediately suspected it was Earl because the tags on the truck were reported to be from Harris County, Georgia. He told Darryl that it seemed a pretty far-fetched stretch but his instincts, after all that had happened yesterday, told him it might be a possibility. Casey explained how he was able to still use the CB radio he wore on his uniform to contact his office and ask them to arrange for someone to drive a four wheeler from Pine Log State Forest down the old Sawmill Trail to the point where Crooked Creek meets the bay. Casey had to quickly explain the connection between the dead man, the 'Lucky Two', Eleanore, and himself to convince them to come.

"When we arrived at the point where Crooked Creek enters the bay a Florida Wildlife Officer and Sheriff's investigator were waiting with a four wheeler to take us to the crime scene," Casey said. "Before we even got there she was convinced that it was Earl. We didn't talk about it much. I think I was convinced too."

Casey continued with the story. He told Darryl how he thought maybe he should go with her. Eleanore insisted that she go alone to see the crime scene. "She told that investigator flat out that she wanted to be the only one to go see the man even though I knew I would be able to identify Earl too. Those guys were skeptical of course, but because I was with her and I gave the nod, they allowed her to ride to the scene. I stayed back and waited with the boat. I mean, realistically someone had to stay with the boat anyway. They were gone for what seemed like hours. I don't know how long really. It gave me a lot of time to think about things."

Casey paused. "When they brought her back she looked at me with puzzled, big, watery eyes. She was also carrying a cat! She silently climbed back into the boat, let the cat loose in the cabin and has not lifted her head or looked at me again the rest of the ride back. The investigator quickly filled me in on a few details then told me to continue as best as I could back to the marina. That's all they needed from Eleanore for now. With everything going on it could take days, or even weeks, before they will ask her to come back for a deposition. It looks like a strong case for murder."

When Casey finished telling the story he waited for Darryl to say something, but Darryl just stared at him in disbelief. "It's all been pretty darn bad," Casey finally added. "Look, Captain Kay. Can I call you Darryl? I don't know about you, but I really want to help this woman, Eleanore."

Darryl felt his head float above his body. He was in shock from the news he heard about Earl, Eleanore, and now Casey Howard asking permission to call him Darryl. It didn't feel normal to be speechless and at a loss for words.

The two men stood face to face cutting their eyes nervously back to the 'Lucky Two' to check on Eleanore. Had she moved?

Casey spoke again. "I know for sure that I will need to report to work. She's gonna need help and a place to stay. Darryl, do you have a place to stay tonight?"

It embarrassed Casey to be asking Darryl, but in the current situation it was necessary.

The question caught Darryl by surprise and he was still not recovered from the shock of Earl's death and Casey's respectful manner. He snapped back, "I thought maybe I'd stay in my car. I have not thought beyond thinking about you guys making it back safe."

In a more serious voice Casey said, "I know this is out of character for me. I realize there's a history between us. A lot has happened to me in the last forty eight hours. I haven't been to my house yet. I need to head over that way and check things out. I'm thinking my house will be in good shape. Then I have to report to work. I'm not sure about what shape I'll be in at work. My boss knows that I've been out all night on the 'Lucky Two', and about Earl, and the girlfriend who came down here to find her boyfriend. It's all tied together in a weird way. I've got a lot of things to explain."

"Very weird, indeed," Darryl finally spoke, agreeing with Casey. He pursed his lips tight. Suspicion entered his mind, again. "Let's cut this short. She hasn't budged. She's been glued to her seat.

Maybe she's in shock."

"And that's why I think she should, or needs, to stay at my house tonight for as long as she needs to stay. I told her that on the ride back, but of course she didn't answer me. I think it would be good to have another person at the house with her, since I won't be there. You've already spent some time with her in your car when you guys drove here together to the marina. She probably trusts you. Would you be willing to stay with her at my house?" Casey rattled out the words so fast that Darryl's felt his head float up higher, spinning in circles. He raised his eyebrows, squinted, and tightly shut his eyes.

"Marowwww.....marowww," the belly-aching guttural sound of a cat drifted out of the cabin of the 'Lucky Two'.

"Oh yeah, we found her cat too," Casey said matter-of-factly.

The casual manner in which Casey announced this news pushed the limits of Darryl's comprehension of the situation. He anticipated so many things when he returned to the marina, but none of the things he'd heard. Darryl forced open his eyes.

Both men turned their heads toward the 'Lucky Two' again.

The noise from the cat stirred Eleanore. She lifted up her head. The light was blindingly bright but she could see the silhouettes of two men standing, staring back at her. She tried to stand, but her legs were shaky. She held on to the side of the boat, then stepped away and stretched her arms out to the side.

Darryl and Casey jogged back to stand near the boat.

"I am so tired I can't think straight." Her voice was weak, but solid and steady. She moved her eyes back and forth to each man for a moment then continued, "I've been listening to you two talk and could hear most of what was said. I do know this. I have nothing else in the world except for my cat that I have found after missing her for more than a year. Everything else is lost. Earl's gone. My job is gone. My mother doesn't care. She told me a long time ago I was on my own. So, yes, I need a night or more to recuperate. And yes, Casey, I would be very grateful and thankful if you would let me stay at your house tonight or a couple of days. And yes, Casey, it would good to have the company of Captain Darryl."

"Very well, little lady," Casey grinned and tried not to appear overly excited. "I am very, VERY happy to help!" Then he looked at Darryl and said, "The offer is still open. You are more than welcome to stay too."

Darryl was overwhelmed with emotion. "Well Officer Howard, it's really nice of you and I think I will take you up on that offer too!" he said with sincere gratitude and added, "Let the past be the past."

Casey seized both acceptances with enthusiasm. He grabbed Darryl's hand and shook it vigorously.

"All right! Now let's not waste any time," Casey spoke with urgency. "Eleanore's got a lot to do and your help is going to be good for her. Do you think you can help?"

Darryl eagerly agreed. "YES, of course!"

"She will have to go back to Pine Mountain, Georgia, most likely." "She's a very strong woman," he added with conviction, remembering the painful events of the last twenty four hours. "Eleanore gave a brie deposition to the Bay County Sheriff's officer, but they have so many things going on right now with the hurricane. This case will get worked, eventually. Eleanore agreed to let them take Earl back to his home in Georgia, to be his final resting place. She said he didn't have much family left but it would give peace to them that's there." Casey glanced at Eleanore when he mentioned Earl's name. It was difficult to read her emotions. He thought he saw both sadness and anger in her eyes.

"MAROUWWWW!"

"I believe that's my cat," Eleanore said stiffly. All three reacted to the interruption in their conversation and jumped at the sound. "We have cats in the cabin. They need to be set free. I suspect my cat is probably just as happy hanging around the docks with all the other cats around here, if there's any left after the hurricane."

"I already saw a few," Darryl assured her and quickly added, "Did you say cats? I like cats!"

Eleanore forced a genuine smile, directing it at Darryl. She turned her back to the two men and stepped toward the cabin door. She opened the door and called out, "Princess! Black Cat! Come on out!"

King flew out first. His tail was straight and stiff. Four claws scratched across the fiberglass deck. Fluff followed quickly after him. Both cats took a high leap off the bow of the 'Lucky Two', landed onto the concrete sidewalk and skidded past the two standing men.

A third cat, a reluctant, piebald calico ran out last. It was Oscar, scurrying and racing to keep up with Fluff and King.

Fat Cat had been right about Oscar hitching a ride on Earl's truck. The spunky cat dug his claws deep into the windshield wiper fluid container all the way to Pine Log State Forest. He was too afraid to jump out during the brief stop at the One Stop convenience store. It didn't feel like the right place to get off the truck. It was, after all, just another parking lot. But he decided to leave the truck in search of something to eat when it remained parked for hours on the gravel parking lot at Pine Log Forest State Park. Oscar survived the hurricane huddled beneath a Spanish bayonet, suffering cuts and bruises as the winds whipped the dagger like leaves of the bush against his body. He kept his face buried in the dirt most of the night, lifting it only when he needed to take a breath.

"I don't know anything about the first cat and the last cat, but the one in the middle, the white one is mine. Those two were adjusted to the boat ride. I have to tell you that whole story sometime, Darryl. The third cat was found lying beneath Earl's truck. It was all bloodied and a nose filled with dirt. It was so eager to be rescued and wasn't even scared when I called him over to me. It came right up to me when I arrived at the crime scene. I held it in my arms and never let it go. I carried it on the ride on the ATV back to the boat. Then when it got inside the cabin it snuggled up right alongside the other two cats during the ride back here to the marina. It's a nervous wreck, but seems to be okay."

"Well, then." Casey chuckled. "There they go. Eleanore, you'll have to come back and feed them from the boat you're standing on. I suspect they're used to being fed from a boat, right Darryl? Haven't you been doing that for years from the wrecked boat over there? Remind us of the name!"

"It's called the 'Star Chaser'!" Darryl moaned. "I've always believed in following the celestial path. When you're a fisherman you never know what you're going to catch. It's all about hope, and believing. When you are looking up at the great big sky in the nighttime darkness it's impossible not to believe. And, I think I remember you telling me on our ride to the marina your cat's name was Princess."

"Well that's right," a surprised Eleanore said. Both men cocked heads to listen. "I'm impressed that you remembered my cat's name. I am lucky to find her. More importantly I can tell you both today I feel so very lucky to be alive! Thank you, Casey. And, thank you, too Darryl. What did you tell me your last name was?"

Slightly embarrassed Darryl said his name. "It's Kay."

Eleanore blurted out, "Yes, that's right. Darryl Kay!"

She'd had time to think about many things during the boat ride back to the marina. She hoped she didn't forget any of the words she had carefully chosen to say when she made it back to the marina.

"I've heard people say that they are waiting for their ship to come in. You know, waiting for their luck to change. Right now, I know that my boat is here and I am ready to walk on board. We all have a time in our life that we have to make a difficult decision. A decision made with good intentions will never fail our hearts. In other words, we'll have no regrets. Life is a gamble. The luck of the draw, so they say, whoever *they* may be."

The two men watched her in awe. Both men attentively, eagerly, waited to hear what she would say next.

"So, I have decided to stay here. I am not going to let this ship, the 'Lucky Two' be here without me. I am going to plant some roots here. There's nothing, no one, for me to go back to in Pine Mountain. Anyway, all that I had there was get up, go to work, go home, go to sleep, every day, day after day. On the ride back on the ATV, while I was holding that cat, trying to make it feel safe and secure, after identifying Earl," her voice cracked when she said Earl's name, "I saw a rainbow on the eastern horizon of the sky. Nothing else has made me feel more hopeful than that moment.

"The 'Lucky Two' was a dream Earl had for both of us. It was not my dream. I was too scared to live it with him. I thought that he loved the boat more than me. I thought he loved the promise of living an easy life, maybe getting rich doing something he loved, more than me. He loved fishing. He was good at it!

"We have choices to make. Sometimes we don't realize how lucky we are to be given a choice. We're offered the colors yellow and green, but we really want to pick between blue and red. We get confused and upset because we're not given choices that we want. Then we don't make the right choice. When I saw that rainbow I thought about Earl making a choice to call me. He wanted to come back to me. He doesn't have a choice now, but I do have a choice.

"After a terrifying night spent in darkness and wondering if I'd survive the dangers of hurricane Louise, I've been given the light of a new day. I hope that light shines in my life forever. My future begins today, right now, and each new day will begin with me giving thanks.

"Like I just said about having a choice, some people spend their entire lives waiting for their ship to arrive. I say my ship is here now and I have the choice. I have never been so ready to board it!"

Eleanore's eyes locked onto Darryl's eyes and his were on hers. Both were reading into the soul of the other.

Casey's eyes did not miss the transaction.

She continued, "I know that for me to carry out a decision I've made I'm going to need the help of the two new friends that I've made."

"We will help you," both men said together, nodding their heads in agreement, not even knowing what she was about to say.

"I know now, as never before at any time in my life, I am not in control of each day and what it might bring. I might think I might know what happens tomorrow, but I don't. Even if I make a choice to do something that is good, or maybe not good, my circumstances may change with the strike of a match, or a bolt of lightning. The choices may not be to my liking. BUT, I do know one thing. I am in control of my decisions with the choices I have been given. Here's what I'd like to propose. I can see that this boat is likely to become my responsibility. I hardly think that anyone back in Pine Mountain will come after me, or this boat once they learn what happened to Earl. They won't be interested in all the trouble it would be to fix it up, take care of it, or tow it back to Georgia. They would be just as happy to know that I am down here taking care of those matters. Since his grandmother died no one paid attention to the life of Earl. Everyone was mad about him getting all that money from her. They thought his money was spent on junk, wasted away, when he told them he was going to become a deep sea fishing boat captain. No one believed he could be successful at it. Even I didn't."

Eleanore turned her attention to Darryl and said, "Mr. Kay, I believe that you might be a successful boat captain, but now you don't have a boat, right?"

Darryl answered, embarrassed, "Yeah, that's true."

"Do you think you would like to take over the 'Lucky Two'?"

Casey and Darryl were dumbfounded by Eleanore's bold offer.

"Wait a minute," Casey stepped up beside Darryl. "I think he's probably got some insurance on his boat, don't you Darryl?"

"Yes, I do. I don't have much though," Darryl wondered why Casey asked. "I'm sure I don't have enough to replace it."

Casey responded, "So maybe you could use some of your insurance money to buy this boat. That would help Eleanore get back on her feet!"

Both men waited for a reaction from Eleanore.

"I'm not sure how long it's going to take for me to get back on my feet. I'll need work. I worked at a small restaurant back in Pine Mountain. Maybe I can find work in a restaurant here. I can cook, clean and serve food," she said.

Darryl didn't want a dark cloud to form over Eleanore's enthusiasm but had to say, "I'm sure there's paperwork somewhere with Earl's name on it for the boat."

"Well, the insurance money and the paperwork to transfer the boat to your name will take some time, don't you think?" Eleanore asked. "Until then maybe you could fish from the 'Lucky Two' until things work out."

"And, what about Casey?" Darryl asked cautiously.

Casey answered Darryl's question in a gruff voice. "I can take care of things for myself. I may be in some trouble at work, but they're not going to fire me. At least I don't expect they will once the complete story is told."

"Hey, you guys! Glad to see you all made it!" The big booming voice of Big Joe carried across the parking lot as he walked toward them.

With happiness in their voices both men yelled in unison, "Big Joe! It's good to see you too."

"I had to come down here and see what happened. Looks like your boat took a beating, Darryl," Big Joe said solemnly. "Hey, the 'Lucky Two' made it though. Where's the boat captain? Earl Keith?"

"You knew Earl?" Eleanore blurted out. An untimely, loud gurgle erupted from her stomach when she asked Big Joe the question.

Big Joe couldn't curtail a big laugh. "Somebody is hungry. Yes, I bought fish from Earl."

Before Darryl could get in the first word Casey began to talk fast. "Before we go on any further, let me just say there's a lot of explaining to do. I need to report to work. This girl is Earl's former girlfriend and she needs a job. I know she'd make a good waitress at Smith's. If you have the time, Darryl can do all the talking and explain everything that's gone on in the past twenty four hours if you'll feed her."

Big Joe looked over the young girl. He saw a range of emotions and fatigue. He was skeptical if he should get involved, but he had a big heart for people who were hungry and suffering. Under the circumstances, he didn't mind having Darryl hanging out with him at Smith's either.

"There doesn't look like there will be many customers around here for quite a while. I've got to get in my kitchen at Smith's. I'll see if I kind find something to cook. Maybe I can feed you both and hear a good story from Captain Kay while I work. I know he can talk. Give me about thirty minutes then come on over. The back door to Smith's will be open."

"Well, I'm feeling too lucky. Everything is happening so fast!" Eleanore inhaled deeply through her mouth. "Let's join hands."

The three joined hands and formed a circle in front of the 'Lucky Two'. They barely contained the happiness they were feeling while holding hands. Smiles on their faces erupted into loud laughter.

"Now, wait," she said turning serious. "There's a lot to be done, but my first order of business is to rename the boat."

Casey broke in, "You know it used to be called 'My Girl'?"

Darryl vigorously nodded his head, agreeing with Casey.

Both men looked at Eleanore with grins as big as a crescent moon.

Eleanore didn't pause when she heard this bit of news. "My first order of business," she repeated a little louder, "is to rename the boat. As we stand here, the three of us holding hands, I believe in God and ask for His blessing on the renaming of this boat to be 'Two Lucky'!

Eleanore cut her eyes toward the western sky and then turned her body half way around to embrace the complete landscape. She still held hands with Casey and Darryl as she said with a joyful voice, "Look over there. Look at that beautiful sunset and the rainbow in the clouds!"

Behind the trio of humans two cats sat side by side, huddled beneath a pile of broken wood lying against the fish cleaning house.

"Did you hear everything that Eleanore just said?" Fluff asked King in a breathless voice. They'd been listening from the inside of what was left of the shed that King called his castle.

King looked directly into Fluff's glowing green eyeballs. He felt his own happiness mirrored in her eyes.

"Yes!" he answered energetically, forgetting the ordeal of the last two days. "Yes, I DID. And I heard her call you Princess when she discovered you on the boat. From now on I am going to call you my Princess. We'll have to spread the good news to all the other cats!"

"Absolutely," she said. "Aren't we two lucky cats?!"

King and Princess purred with contentment.

A ball of gray fur with a long, skinny hairless tail leapt off the bow of the 'Lucky Two'. The rat, the object of the cat gang's attention two nights ago, scurried past them to find a safe new hiding place. It was a reminder to King that his reputation might be different now.

"That rat was no fool. Fat Cat wasn't created for the chase. He set me up to chase the rat. I think I could trick him into kissing a blue dolphin. I've heard a story about a cat that kissed one," King mused. "All I'd have to do is find a way for Fat Cat to take a ride in Darryl's truck."

Princess laughed hard and said, "Fat Cat will have to do more than ride in a truck and kiss a dolphin to take away Oscar's bragging rights!"

EPILOGUE

The severity of the damage inflicted by nature, be it a hurricane, tornado, earthquake or fire, is often measured in the financial costs. The severity of the damage to a living soul can only be measured by the time it takes to repair a heartbreak, which may take a lifetime.

Fortunately no humans drowned or died from damage caused by the winds of hurricane Louise. Animal death tolls were not counted.

The new day began like all others with opaque light breaking through dark shadows. Living animals opened their eyes to light. Hopes began to replace fears.

Surprising soft sounds of nature returned. Doves cooed. Seagulls cheered. Cicadas chirped in rhythmic harmony. Pelicans perched. Birds warbled. Bees hummed and buzzed.

Men and women greeted each other and tried to be civilized, sympathetic, and helpful. Children cheered the sunshine.

Soon the sun's rays cast full daylight and the joyous feelings of surviving the dangerous night were replaced by a frantic new desperation, not so different than the day before.

Where are the loved ones I need to find? What will I find when I return home? When can I go home? Will I find food and water? Where is my shelter? How am I going to take care of all this mess? Who will help me if I need help?

When will I know the answers to these questions?

Where do I start?

It is better to not be alone to when searching for answers.

It is written in Ecclesiastes 4:9-10:

"Two are better than one, because they have a good return for their work: if one falls down, his friend can help him up. But pity the man who falls and has no one to help him up!"